Rites of the Starling

Devney Perry is a *Wall Street Journal* and *USA Today* bestselling author. Born and raised in Montana, she loves writing books set in her treasured home state. After working in the technology industry for nearly a decade, she abandoned conference calls and project schedules to enjoy a slower pace at home with her family. Writing one book, let alone many, was not something she ever expected to do. But now that she's discovered her true passion for writing romance, she has no plans to ever stop.

Rites of the Starling

DEVNEY PERRY

RED TOWER
BOOKS™

PENGUIN MICHAEL JOSEPH

UK | USA | Canada | Ireland | Australia
India | New Zealand | South Africa

Penguin Michael Joseph is part of the Penguin Random House group of companies
whose addresses can be found at global.penguinrandomhouse.com

Penguin Random House UK,
One Embassy Gardens, 8 Viaduct Gardens, London SW11 7BW

penguin.co.uk

Published by Penguin Michael Joseph, part of the Penguin Random House
group of companies, in association with Red Tower Books,
part of Entangled Publishing LLC 2026

002

Copyright © Devney Perry LLC, 2026

The moral right of the author has been asserted

The Red Tower Books name and logo are trademarks of Entangled
Publishing LLC and are used here under licence

Penguin Random House values and supports copyright.
Copyright fuels creativity, encourages diverse voices, promotes freedom
of expression and supports a vibrant culture. Thank you for purchasing
an authorized edition of this book and for respecting intellectual property
laws by not reproducing, scanning or distributing any part of it by any
means without permission. You are supporting authors and enabling
Penguin Random House to continue to publish books for everyone.
No part of this book may be used or reproduced in any manner for the
purpose of training artificial intelligence technologies or systems. In accordance
with Article 4(3) of the DSM Directive 2019/790, Penguin Random House
expressly reserves this work from the text and data mining exception

Cover design by LJ Anderson
Interior map original art by Elizabeth Turner Stokes
Interior map frame images by MassyCG/Shutterstock, DestinaDesign/Shutterstock

Set in 13.5/16pt Garamond MT Std
Six Red Marbles UK, Thetford, Norfolk
Printed and bound in Great Britain by Clays Ltd, Elcograf S.p.A.

The authorized representative in the EEA is Penguin Random House Ireland,
Morrison Chambers, 32 Nassau Street, Dublin D02 YH68

A CIP catalogue record for this book is available from the British Library

HARDBACK ISBN: 978–1–911–75018–5
TRADE PAPERBACK ISBN: 978–1–911–75019–2

Penguin Random House is committed to a sustainable future
for our business, our readers and our planet. This book is made from
Forest Stewardship Council® certified paper.

ALSO BY DEVNEY PERRY

SHIELD OF SPARROWS SERIES
Shield of Sparrows
Rites of the Starling

THE EDENS SERIES
Indigo Ridge
Juniper Hill
Garnet Flats
Jasper Vale
Crimson River
Sable Peak

TREASURE STATE WILDCATS SERIES
Coach
Blitz
Rally
Merit

CLIFTON FORGE SERIES
Steel King
Riven Knight
Stone Princess
Noble Prince
Fallen Jester
Tin Queen

CALAMITY MONTANA SERIES
The Bribe
The Bluff
The Brazen
The Bully
The Brawl
The Brood

HAVEN RIVER RANCH SERIES
Crossroads
Sunlight

LOST LEGENDS SERIES
Bluebird Gold

JAMISON VALLEY SERIES
The Coppersmith Farmhouse
The Clover Chapel
The Lucky Heart
The Outpost
The Bitterroot Inn
The Candle Palace

MAYSEN JAR SERIES
The Birthday List
Letters to Molly
The Dandelion Diary

LARK COVE SERIES
Tattered
Timid
Tragic
Tinsel
Timeless

RUNAWAY SERIES
Runaway Road
Wild Highway
Quarter Miles
Forsaken Trail
Dotted Lines

STANDALONES
Clarence Manor
Rifts and Refrains
A Little Too Wild

Author's Note

Dear Reader,

Writing in the romantasy genre has been a dream of mine for years, and the love for *Shield of Sparrows* continues to fill my heart each and every day. Thank you for going on this adventure with me.

From the very beginning of Odessa's story, I had an idea of where I wanted to take this second book. It's one of those ideas that has been in the back of my mind for a long, long time, just waiting to be told.

You're going to meet some new characters in this book. I hope they steal your heart the way they've stolen mine. And I hope that a few of the twists and turns in this story are as unexpected for you as they were for me. The unexpected journeys are usually those I love most.

Again, thank you for reading. I am beyond grateful for your trust in telling this tale. Now I invite you to turn the page and return to Calandra for *Rites of the Starling*.

Devney

Rites of the Starling is an epic romantasy set in a world of monsters and mysteries. As such, the story includes elements that might not be suitable for all readers, including combat, violence, blood, gore, death of humans and animals, injury, dismemberment, illness, hospitalization, arson, alcohol use, poisoning, trafficking, threat and mention of rape, graphic language, and sexual activity. Readers who may be sensitive to these elements, please take note.

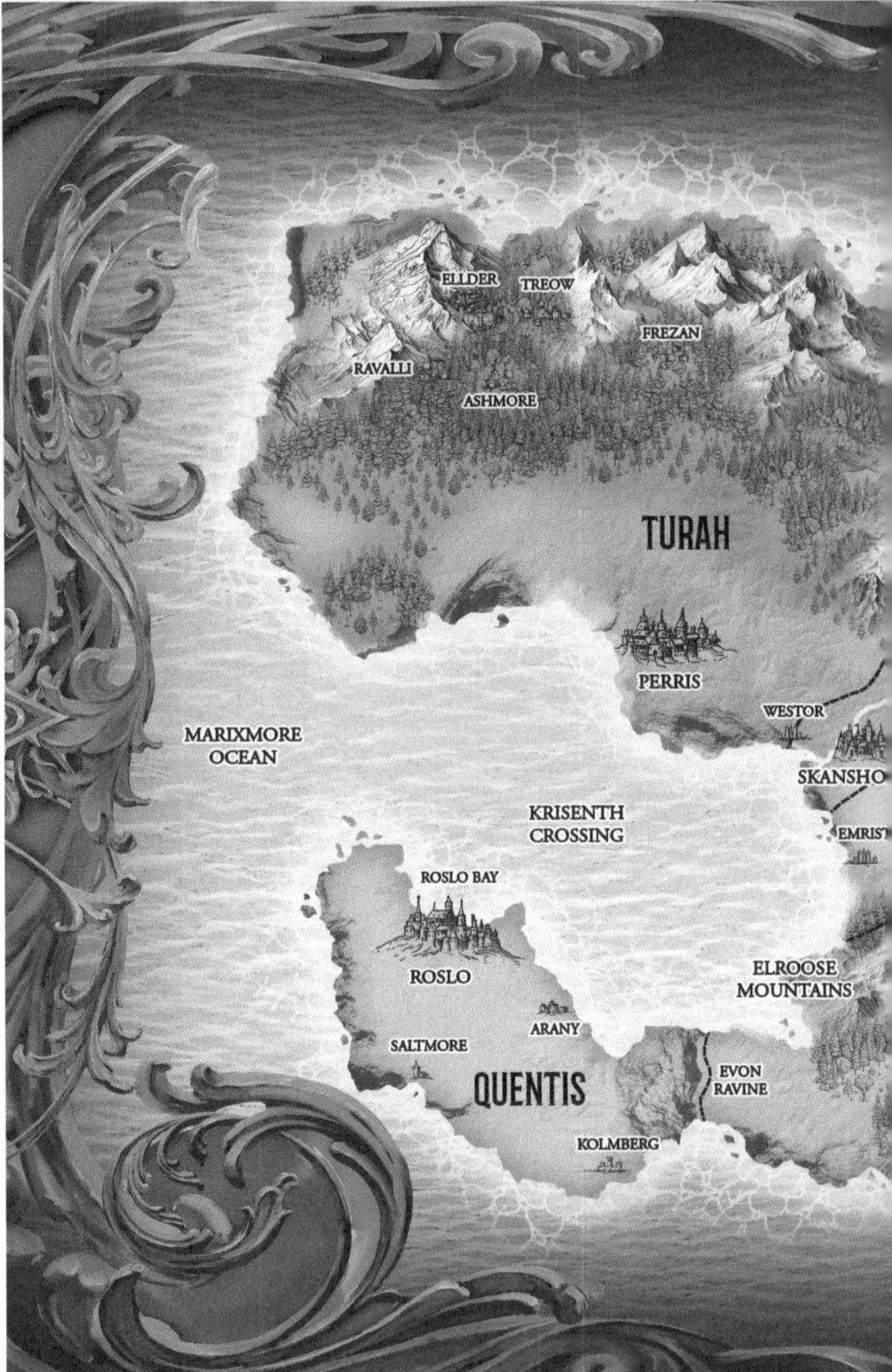

Prologue

Sparrow Wolfe's fate rested in the hands of five men.

The five kings of Calandra.

They stood around an oval table, their focus on the treaty splayed across the grooved wooden surface. The ink on the parchment was still wet. The cleric who'd penned the document hurried to collect his belongings, then scurried out of the room now that his task was complete.

The underground cellar was cloaked in shadow. The scents of dank rock and acrid smoke filled the air. One of the lamps was sputtering out, the oil in its reservoir nearly gone after hours and hours of negotiations.

Sparrow stood against the stone wall as a silent observer of the discussion. A fire crackled in the hearth, but its heat could not chase away the cold that had crept into her bones. She clenched her teeth to keep them from chattering.

A numbness was taking hold of her body, creeping into her fingertips and toes. With the Goddess Daria's luck, that numbness would soon dull the ache in her heart.

Not one of the five kings paid her any attention, not even her father. They were too busy debating who she would marry.

The Voster High Priest hovered behind the men. His bare feet hadn't touched the floor since he floated into the cellar. The dim light leached any hint of color from his pale white skin.

His eyes, those solid, dark pools, stayed locked on the treaty. The moment the kings came to an agreement, he'd seal their oaths in blood.

The priest's hands were clasped in front of him, and the

thick, dark-green nails protruding from his fingers were so long they curled into his robes, the burgundy fabric as dark as the storm cloud over her heart.

The kings were dressed in bold fabrics, reds and greens and blues and teals, each proudly representing their respective kingdoms in color and the emblems stitched into their clothes.

Sparrow was dressed in gray, a shade as empty as she was of hope.

This treaty was a necessity. She'd told herself that countless times. It would end the wars that had plagued their continent for generations. It would bind the five kingdoms of Calandra together forever.

Either they would find a way to live together. Or they'd die trying.

The logical princess her father had raised, the fledgling politician, knew this was essential for survival. But the young woman with dreams of finding love had begun to wither the moment marriage stipulations had entered the conversation.

There was a reason Sparrow was in this cellar, something she hadn't realized until it was too late. She was not here as her father's heir. She was not here to observe and learn.

She was a token to be traded in the name of peace.

These kings of men were worried that exchanging goods alone was not enough to maintain the accords. What better way to tie kingdoms together than to bind them by blood? By future generations. By the children she would someday bear. Children tied to two kingdoms.

A silence settled around the table, making the hairs on the back of Sparrow's neck stand on end. She stood taller as the kings nodded.

"Do we have agreement?" the High Priest asked, his voice as silky as her chestnut hair.

Every king, including her father, murmured, "Yes."

The moment this treaty was signed, each king and their

future heirs would be expected to maintain its stipulations. To break their oaths would mean death.

It went against her nature as a Turan to give up her free will. Her father likely felt the same. Yet Turah had no choice but to participate. Their kingdom was strong but not strong enough to stand against the rest of Calandra. Especially while they were trying to recover from the crux migration.

Her father couldn't stop this treaty, but that fact didn't make her fate any easier to accept.

One by one, each king drew a dagger or knife from a sheath. They sliced open their palms, dipped their quills, and scrawled their names in blood.

Her father went last. With his pen poised over the treaty, its tip glistening in red, he cast her a long look. The pity and apology in his steely gray eyes made it hard for her to breathe. The green starbursts in his irises flared for a brief moment before he dropped his gaze to the parchment. The harsh scratch that came with his signature was quick, like an arrow through her heart.

Sparrow dropped her chin so the kings would not see the tears in her eyes.

Done. It was done.

Calandra was in ruins from the crux migration. Now the kingdoms would rebuild together. Trade together. Live together.

Breed together.

Tonight, Sparrow had become a brood mare like her favorite horse, Helena.

Would she ever see Helena again? Would she ever return to Turah? Or would she be taken directly from this miserable cellar in Ozarth to a city in Genesis, where she'd be paraded as their new queen?

Would the people of Genesis hate her the way their king, Tanis Oak, hated her father?

The idea of spending the rest of her life tied to a man

who loathed her family, her people, made her stomach drop. Would Tanis take his anger out on her? Would she be made to suffer for a rivalry that went back far beyond her years?

The treaty forbade him from killing her, but there were fates worse than death.

Tanis, at least ten years her senior, was the only unwed king in this room. And she was the only princess in Calandra of age to bear children. Maybe after she birthed him a son he'd forget about her. If the gods were merciful, she'd be left alone.

Sparrow squeezed her eyes shut as dread and sorrow threatened more tears. No doubt Tanis would not take kindly to a simpering wife. And she was a Turan.

She would not cry.

The gods were to blame for this. *Bastards.* The Six had cursed Calandra with their monsters. With the crux. She'd survived this past migration only to trade one nightmare for another. The gods could rot in their shades. And so could the Voster, with their oaths and magic used to manipulate men.

With her teeth gritted so hard they cracked, she steeled her spine and lifted her chin.

The High Priest's gaze was waiting.

She loathed him more than anyone else in this room. He would trap her in this treaty without remorse. She could taste the hate for his magic on her tongue, like the coppery tang of blood.

With a slight incline of his head, he summoned her to the table. "Your name?"

"Sparrow Wolfe." Her voice was steady and calm, not betraying her racing heart.

He stared at her for a long moment. "This treaty shall be known as the Shield of Sparrows."

Another princess might have appreciated having a treaty named in her honor.

Sparrow swallowed a scream.

"Do you, Sparrow Wolfe, princess of Turah, vow to uphold the Shield of Sparrows with your union to Tanis Oak, king of Genesis?" the High Priest asked.

Every king in the room seemed to hold their breath, waiting for her reply.

Tears filled her father's eyes as he gave her a nod.

"I, Sparrow Wolfe, make this vow," she whispered.

Without meeting her gaze, her father passed her his knife.

She opened a palm, refusing to wince as the blade cut through her flesh. Signing her name in blood was done with a quick flick of her wrist.

Then Tanis's name was beside hers, his own vow spoken aloud. His voice was smooth and deep. Emotionless and cold.

A shiver raced down Sparrow's spine.

The High Priest placed both of his hands on the treaty, closing his eyes.

There was no sensation. No visible hint of his fluid magic. But when he opened his eyes and lifted his hands, there was no doubt in her mind that she was now bound to this treaty.

The Shield of Sparrows.

"It is done." The High Priest's declaration stole the air from her lungs.

Tanis marched out of the cellar.

The other kings swept out after him, climbing the stairs that would take them away from this secret chamber beneath Ozarth's capital city.

The High Priest pressed both of his hands over his heart and gave her a slight bow.

She bit her tongue to keep quiet.

Then he rolled up the treaty into a neat column. The ink, her blood, had barely dried as he left.

Her father deflated once they were alone. A breath rushed

from his lungs as his shoulders curled inward, his broad, towering frame shrinking before her eyes.

It cleaved her spirit in two.

None of this would have happened if there were no crux. If there were no more migrations.

"Why have the Six cursed us with these monsters? Why do they hate us?"

"Because they are petty gods," he said. "Because only humans have the power to make the gods insignificant."

Sparrow stared at her father, taking in his strong profile. "I will never worship them again. And I will never trust the Voster."

"Neither will I." He gave her a sad smile, opening his arms. "I am sorry, my daughter."

She collapsed into his chest, into the strong embrace that had held her since she was a baby. "What do I do?"

He kissed her hair. "Be bold, my Sparrow. Be brave."

PART I

DIVISION

I

RANSOM

Treow was a tomb.

The commons were deserted. No guards were posted in the watchtowers. A breath of wind caught the rungs of a rope ladder, swaying it back and forth with a creak. The treehouse above was as empty as the rest of the encampment.

Where was Odessa? She should be here.

The panic coursing through my veins was making me dizzy. I lifted my fingers to my lips and whistled. The shrill call ricocheted off trees before it was swallowed by the forest.

And as it faded, there was nothing but silence.

A chill skated down my spine.

Something was wrong. She might have gotten lost in the dark after leaving Ellder, but she would have found her way at daybreak.

The thunder of hooves echoed from afar. I held my breath, hoping it was Odessa and Evie, except the rider sat alone and her hair was stark, sleek white, not wild red curls.

Cathlin slowed her dappled mare to a stop and swung to the ground. She tied the horse to the same tree trunk where I'd tethered Aurinda.

My stallion's black coat was still damp with sweat from the punishing ride from the fortress to the encampment.

"You should have stayed in Ellder," I told Cathlin.

She stood at my side, a tendril of her white hair lifting in the breeze. "You were angry. I was worried that…"

"That I'd harm my own wife?" My nostrils flared.

Yes, I was angry. Scared. Frantic. Confused. But I'd sooner drive a knife through my own heart than hurt Odessa.

"No." She pressed both hands to her flushed cheeks. "I was just worried. I don't know what to think, Ransom."

"Neither do I."

The image of the crux, a woman, was burned into my mind. How was it possible? What kind of magic was this? Or was my mind playing a trick on me?

I'd walked out of the fortress certain I was trapped in a nightmare. Even after I found Aurinda and saddled him for the ride to Treow, it had felt like moving in a fog. Going through the motions until I woke from the dream.

"Her hair," Cathlin whispered.

The crux had shifted from beast to beauty. To a woman who shared enough features with Odessa, from her hair to her nose to her delicate chin, that I couldn't unsee the resemblance.

And her blood...

"Do you think Odessa knows?"

"No." I refused to believe she'd keep that kind of a secret from me.

Reaching into my vest, I pulled out a lock of the shapeshifter's shorn hair. I twisted the silky curl around my finger, letting the orange and strawberry and copper colors catch the light. Then I released the strands into the wind.

"Did they burn the corpse?" I asked.

"Yes."

"Good."

"Where is everyone?" Cathlin asked, searching the trees. "The watchtowers were empty as I rode past."

"Gone. Treow is deserted."

Where are you, Cross? Where the hell are you?

I'd already lapped the encampment twice. I'd shouted for Odessa and Evie until my voice had cracked and my throat had gone raw.

If my father had taken them, if he hurt them, I didn't care what blood oaths I'd sworn, I would rip every limb from his body. And if a different kind of monster had found them in the night, I prayed Odessa had a safe place to hide.

"Odessa and Evie should be here," I said. "I sent them to the dungeons and told them I'd meet them here."

The color drained from Cathlin's cheeks.

"Where the fuck is she?" I dragged a hand over my face. "I never should have let her leave."

Cathlin put her hand on my shoulder. "We'll find them."

I would find them. Here, or in the shades.

"I saw these in the street on my way to the paddock." Cathlin moved to her saddlebags and took out two knives.

Odessa's knives.

Blood stained both blades.

Fuck. I hated that she didn't have them. That she was out there somewhere without protection. Without me.

The crack of a branch had both Cathlin and me whirling in the direction of the commons. My heart stopped, then sank when Mariette came walking through the trees.

"Guardian." The caretaker bowed. "Cathlin."

"Where is everyone, Mariette?" Cathlin asked.

"Gone." Her hair hung limp over her shoulders, the graying strands having escaped a severe knot. Her dark-brown eyes were weary and bloodshot. She wore a thick, gray cloak and carried a bag, stuffed full, on her shoulders. "I was the last to leave. I was past the final watchtower when I heard a whistle and came back. The king and his soldiers rode through before dawn and warned us of the crux scout. We're following his caravan to Allesaria."

"Were Odessa and Evie with him?" I asked.

She shook her head. "I didn't see them. The king didn't arrive with many. Only twenty or so soldiers. They gathered supplies but didn't stay long."

"Fuck." I clenched my jaw. "You should go. Catch up to the traveling party."

Get the hell out of Treow while she had a chance to escape.

Mariette hesitated a moment, her gaze lifting to the treehouse above my head. Odessa's treehouse. She stared at it for a moment like she was uncomfortable abandoning Treow. Like she wouldn't see it again. But the hesitation faded, and as quickly as she'd appeared, she hurried off, weaving past thick tree trunks until she was gone.

"If she's not with your father, then where?" Cathlin asked, turning in a slow circle.

Where? Where the fuck was my wife?

A terror unlike any I'd ever known settled deep in my bones. It chilled my blood. "How many people know of the crux?"

"Not many. Few survived the night."

"Go back to Ellder. Pay the guards for their silence about the crux, the woman. Anyone else if necessary." I walked to Aurinda and fastened Odessa's knives to my saddle with a spare length of leather. "Stay with Zavier. Watch over him. If he wakes, send word. If he doesn't…bury him beside my mother."

Tears filled Cathlin's eyes. "And where exactly should I send word?"

I swung onto the saddle, turning away from the path where Mariette had disappeared. Turning away from the road that would eventually take me to Allesaria.

There was a chance Odessa would use the etchings on my cuff and go in search of the capital city. But I had a feeling she'd take Evie somewhere else. A place where she could hide my sister from our father. A place where she felt safe.

"Quentis."

2

ODESSA

What if I ran away?

Sitting on the shore of a lake with no name, I stared across water as still and smooth as glass, willing myself not to break. Not to give in to the heartache and fear. Not to crumble into a thousand tiny pieces like the round pebbles beneath my seat.

The lake was a mirror of snowcapped mountains, lofty evergreens, and a pastel sky. A flawless reflection of a realm turned upside down.

This meadow was the picture of serenity. A haven for the weary soul. A cell without bars or locks.

What if I ran away?

I wouldn't get far. *We* wouldn't get far. Besides that, I was lost. Entirely lost.

Evie was curled in my lap, fast asleep. She'd finally stopped shivering from the bath I'd forced her to take in the frigid water. Her clothes were filthy and covered in dried blood, but at least it was out of her hair and off her skin.

Despite rinsing off in the lake, we still reeked of smoke, of death. It had been five days since Ellder, and I was beginning to fear the smell would haunt me forever.

I pressed a kiss to Evie's wet hair as a hawk swooped overhead and loosed a sharp caw. My entire body flinched.

Evie whimpered, curling deeper into my arms.

I kissed her hair again, rocking her gently back and forth until she relaxed.

Faze purred as he nuzzled against my leg.

Water lapped at the shoreline.

My stomach growled.

Small noises to break the silence, but noises too quiet to chase away the screams. The beat of massive wings, the piercing screams of the crux, still rang in my ears.

I opened my hand and traced the pink scar on my palm with a fingertip. A scar with a mirror on Ransom's palm. Twins cut into our flesh on the day we signed the Shield of Sparrows treaty in blood and vowed to be husband and wife.

Maybe if I touched my scar enough, he'd find his way to my side. Maybe I'd feel the echo of his pulse and know he was still alive.

"Praise Ama. Beloved Mother," I whispered, "let him live. Let us find our way to each—" My prayer was cut short by the prickle of Voster magic at my nape.

Brother Dime walked through the grasses that surrounded this lake, his burgundy robes swishing against the golden green stalks. He reached for a yellow wildflower, skimming its blossom with a thick, grooved fingernail.

The early-morning sun cast the meadow in soft, creamy light. It was the only time of day that the priest's pale skin seemed to hold a hint of peach color.

He came to a stop where the grass ended and the rocks along the shoreline began. Far enough from where I was sitting that the sting of his magic wasn't unbearable, yet close enough to hear each other speak. With his hands clasped behind his back, he bowed. "Have you rested?"

"No." My voice didn't sound like my own. It was too flat, too lifeless.

Too numb.

There were too many horrors to face at the moment. Learning of Jocelyn's betrayal. Killing General Banner. Watching Brielle's death. Hearing Evie scream as Zavier bled out on the street.

Later. Those nightmares weren't going anywhere. I'd deal with them when I wasn't traipsing through the wilderness with a Voster who may or may not be trying to save my life.

"We cannot linger," he said.

We'd been riding for five days, stopping only long enough to keep from hobbling Freya. Evie and I were both on the verge of collapse, and these short reprieves were barely long enough for us to catch our breath, let alone rest.

I needed a lifetime to recover from that night at the fortress, not five days and a few stolen moments beside a godsdamn lake, even if it was breathtaking. "We cannot keep going at this pace."

"You must, child."

I ground my teeth together to keep quiet.

As hard as we'd pushed, he never seemed to tire or sleep.

Brother Dime had walked these past five days while Evie and I rode Freya. Not once had his energy waned as he led us farther away from Ellder. From Treow.

From Ransom.

"Where are you taking us?" I asked for the hundredth time, and for the hundredth time, he did not answer.

"I will fetch your horse." He turned and retreated to the meadow where Freya was grazing.

When we stopped before sunrise today, I took off her saddle, using it to lean against, but I left her halter on so she'd be easier to catch. Not that Brother Dime ever had trouble catching my horse.

As he approached, she swished her black tail and walked to his outstretched hand, letting him stroke her gray cheek.

Maybe the reason I hadn't fought harder to escape Dime was because I feared Freya wouldn't leave his side. Or because I was scared to return to Ellder and witness the aftermath of what we'd left behind.

I was terrified I'd return and learn there was a reason for this aching hole in my heart.

He's alive.

Ransom was alive. He wouldn't die, not when we had so much left to experience together.

He was probably in Treow, furious I wasn't. When he found us, I'd gladly suffer his best glower and an epic ass-chewing. As long as he was alive.

If going back to Ellder meant learning any other truth, meant losing him to the shades, then maybe I'd stay in the Turan wilds forever.

On a sigh, I stroked Evie's cheek. "Time to wake up, little star."

It took a moment for her gray eyes to flutter open. Her cerulean-blue starbursts flared bright, then faded with every blink until they were nearly engulfed by the gray.

I gave her a smile she didn't return.

She simply stared up at me, hopeless, like she was waiting for me to rewind time. To take her back to a life where Zavier was alive. A life where her father's blood wasn't crusted on her shirt.

He'd given his life to save ours. Mine.

It wasn't fair that she'd lost so much. A father. And her mother.

What would Luella say to Evie? How would she help her daughter move past this pain?

Help me. I sent the silent prayer to the shades, then swallowed the burn in my throat, refusing to give in to the tears. I couldn't break, not yet. Not while she needed me to stay strong.

"Are you hungry?" I asked.

Evie shook her head.

She wasn't eating enough. Neither was I.

Not only had the long, endless days sapped my strength, but the constant bombardment from Brother Dime's magic had dwindled my appetite.

He worked to keep a distance, always careful not to touch

my skin with his. He held the long ends of Freya's reins as he led us through the forest, but those reins were only so long. And he had yet to let us out of his sight.

What if I ran away? Would he stop us?

I feared his magic enough not to try.

He hadn't treated us like captives, but I wasn't fool enough to believe we were free.

The night we rode away from the dungeons in Ellder, I asked Dime to take us to Treow.

Ransom had told me to follow the moon, Aurinda, and it would lead me to the encampment. I'd been so relieved that we'd have an escort, even if it was magical. When we turned the wrong way, away from the twin moons, I told Dime we had to turn back.

He'd taken Freya's reins from my grip and continued on into the dark.

I'd learned over the past five days that the Voster delivered most of his orders without a word.

"Up we go." I brushed Evie's hair away from her face, then helped her stand before getting to my feet.

Faze stretched out his front legs, his claws digging into the pebbles as he flicked his tail in the air. Then he pounced forward, jaw snapping at a bug. His ribs were more pronounced than they'd been in Ellder.

I'd been feeding him bits of the dried meat that Brother Dime gave to Evie and me, but Faze was used to drinking milk, too. And he was as sick of riding as we were. It had been too many days tucked in his carrier. The constant jostling and his own lack of freedom meant he was grumpy.

When I fished him out earlier, he'd bared his fangs and hissed. I'd flicked him on the nose.

Evie trudged to the shoreline, her arms limp at her sides.

My hand came to my heart, rubbing at the ache. How did I do this? How did I help her? I had no idea how to tell her about Luella's death or help her cope with losing

Zavier. She was too young to have seen so much blood and violence.

"Ease the burden on her heart, Goddess Carine." I signed the Eight, circling my hand around my face and around my heart. "Give her peace."

If the prayers for myself went unanswered, I would survive. But I hoped, for Evie's sake, there was a god or Eight listening.

Faze bounded forward, winding around Evie's legs. There were times when I was sure he felt her pain. Despite the growls and snarls he sent my way, he'd rarely left her side these past five days. He was always close, always patient. When she'd pull him into her arms and bury her face in his pink fur, he didn't so much as squirm.

I turned away from the lake, mentally summoning the strength to lift Freya's saddle, when movement at the trees beyond Brother Dime made me go still. A rider on a black horse trotted into the meadow.

For a single heartbeat, I thought it was Ransom. I thought he'd found us and could lead us somewhere safe. But then my eyes caught up with my hopeful heart and I realized the horse wasn't black but another blue roan. And the person in its saddle was another priest.

In one gnarled hand, he held the roan's leads. In the other was a rope haltered to a brown horse trotting close behind.

Brother Dime led Freya to me, careful, as always, not to touch my hand as he transferred the reins.

Did Dime know why I could feel Voster magic when others couldn't? I'd been too dazed since leaving Ellder to pester the priest for information, but if we were going to be traveling together, maybe I could get some answers.

"Who is that?" Evie appeared at my side, staring up at Brother Dime.

He dropped to a crouch, but he was so tall that even on bended knee she had to lift her chin to keep his gaze.

"Brother Skore. He will be accompanying us as we ride to Ozarth."

"O-ozarth?" I blinked. "Wait. We're going to Ozarth? Why?"

He ignored me.

Maybe I needed to have Evie ask the questions from now on. She had better luck getting answers.

Brother Dime lifted a hand, drawing the water from her hair and spinning it into a crown.

It seemed like a lifetime ago he'd done the same for me outside an art gallery in a castle in Quentis. A stinging sensation crawled up my skin, but I held back a cringe, not wanting to take a moment of magic away from Evie.

Except she didn't stare up at the shimmering crown in wonder. No smile lit up her face. Instead, her gaze fell to the dirt. She stepped out from beneath the ring of water, moving closer to my side so her arm could hook around my leg.

Brother Dime sent the water away with a flick of his wrist.

It wasn't easy to read his expressions, but the line of his colorless lips softened in what had to be pity. He stood and backed away a few paces, far enough that the bite of his magic lessened.

The other priest rode to Brother Dime's side, coming to a stop and dismounting his horse. He wore pale blue robes that draped around his bony frame. His nose was the same hawkish shape as Dime's.

Brother Skore let the animals free to graze as he came to Dime's side. Both priests pressed their hands over their hearts and bowed.

Their combined magic rocked me on my heels.

"Go wait with Faze," I told Evie, watching as she walked to join the tarkin at the water.

If Dime thought he could keep up this breakneck pace, the priest was dreaming.

Evie needed a place to sleep that wasn't in my lap. She

needed a meal and a real bath and a safe space to cry. And Freya needed longer breaks than she'd been given.

"We must leave," he said.

"No." I raised my chin, hoping I looked braver than I felt. "Not until you tell me why we're going to Ozarth."

"It is the path you must take."

"That's not an answer to my question."

"It is the only answer I can give."

I scoffed. "Then we're leaving. We're going to Treow to find Ransom."

The priests shared a look that made my heart drop. A look that said I wouldn't find him there.

"What? Is he…" I couldn't finish the question. My head began spinning too fast, and the ground beneath my boots seemed to tilt sideways.

He's alive.

Ransom was alive. I wouldn't let myself consider any other outcome. If anyone could survive the crux, it was the Guardian. I gripped the leather cuff on my forearm, the cuff Ransom had given to me, letting this piece of him steady me.

"I do not know his fate, child." Brother Dime spoke gently, like he knew I was moments from collapsing to my knees. "But this is where your paths divide. He is loyal to the High Priest."

"Aren't you?" I certainly didn't trust the High Priest, or Dime for that matter, but weren't they all a part of the same brotherhood?

"This is a journey you must take alone. It is the only way to discover your dynasty."

"My dynasty? I don't have a dynasty." I pointed behind me. "I have a terrified little girl who saw her father get murdered. So answer my question. Why Ozarth?"

Brother Dime nodded to my saddle on the ground by my feet. "Turah is not safe for you. And I promised your father I'd keep you safe."

"Then take me to him."

Ransom had told me that if something happened to him, to Zavier, to get Evie out of Turah. To take her to Quentis. To put the entire continent of Calandra between her and King Ramsey.

If he didn't find us in Treow, Ransom would look for us in Quentis, so that's where we were going. My father would protect us, and we could shelter with my family during the migration.

"We don't need to cross the border to Ozarth," I said. "There's no reason to travel east. We should ride south to the coast, then sail the Krisenth."

"We will not be sailing to Quentis."

I tossed up a hand. "Why not? It's the fastest route."

The priests shared another look.

"What aren't you telling me? Why do you need to go to Ozarth? Unless you're planning on riding the entire length of this continent, then there's no point in…" *Oh, gods.* The realm tipped sideways as realization dawned. "No. It's too dangerous. It's too far. What about monsters? What about the migration? It will take weeks."

From Turah to Ozarth, then Laine and Genesis. I couldn't even fathom the idea of making that journey.

I shook my head, heart pounding. "We're not going with you."

"You are." Brother Dime moved closer, the sting of his magic intensifying.

"Do I have a choice?"

"No."

I glanced over my shoulder to Evie. Why hadn't I left the Voster days ago? He wouldn't have been able to catch us on foot. But now that this new priest was here with two horses, we'd never get away.

Unless I fought them. My gaze shifted to the sword beside my saddle.

"Should the girl ride with me instead?" Brother Dime asked.

"No." I stepped sideways, blocking his path to Evie. "She stays with me."

"Then saddle your horse."

This bastard was going to use her to manipulate me, and until I came up with a plan to escape, I was stuck. "Fine."

"This will not be an easy journey," he warned. "But you must find the strength to endure. For all of Calandra."

"And if I can't?"

"You must." With that, Dime walked away.

Brother Skore cocked his head to the side, studying me for a long moment. Then he raised a hand and snapped his fingers.

A gust of wind came rushing from behind, nearly blowing me over. I lurched forward to catch myself, tripping over Freya's saddle.

Damn these Voster.

I really should have run away.

3

CASPIA

A man with silver eyes drives his sword through Emery's heart. Feathers turn to flesh. Wings collapse to arms. Talons transform to toes.
  She falls from the stars with the silver-eyed warrior.
  My sister plummets to the earth.
  Until there is nothing but blood and dust.

...

I woke from the vision with a jolt. My hair was stuck to the sweat on my brow, and every bone in my body felt as if it had been crushed, like I'd been the one to fall from the starry sky. There was a punishing ache in my chest, like the sword had gone through my heart, not Emery's.

"Not again." My hands gripped the bedsheets as I closed my eyes, giving my heart a chance to sink back down my throat. Then I kicked the blankets from my legs and stood, shuffling across the stone floor to the open windows of my room.

The salt breeze kissed my cheeks. The cool air filled my lungs. The scents of spice and sweet smoke floated to my nose.

The vision of Emery's death would haunt me for hours, and as the weight of her loss settled on my shoulders, I sagged against the open sill, staring down at the sleeping city sprawled beyond the palace's feet.

Moonbeams bathed Showe in gray and white. The streets were empty. The city was quiet, though that silence wouldn't last long.

Soon, the sun would rise from the ocean's depths to kiss the sky good morning. By dawn, the coastline would be dotted with fishermen steering boats with colorful sails. Wagons would stream toward the countryside fields to collect a harvest. Herdsmen would ride their steeds beyond the city's walls to tend to their flocks. And miners would pile into carts bound for the elfalter mines, where they'd reap the precious metal from Nelfinex's rock.

The noise and chaos from Showe's streets would filter through every open window in the palace, making it impossible to sleep. Not that I'd have time. Not with my chores and strict training regimen.

I'd be smart to crawl back in bed and rest until dawn, but I knew the moment I closed my eyes, I'd see Emery and the silver-eyed warrior.

Who was he?

Where was she?

I shifted to a seat in the wide windowsill, hugging my knees to my chest. In my heart, I knew she'd left for a good reason. But if my vision was true, if Emery had been murdered by that man and called to the afterlife by the Divine, we'd never know why she'd met that horrible fate.

I'd never have the chance to say goodbye.

"Emery," I whispered to the wind, hoping the vision was wrong. Hoping the sun would come when she'd whisper back.

It wasn't my first sleepless moon spent in the window, soaking in the light from the stars. By the time golden rays shone on the horizon, my back was stiff and my eyelids heavy. My body would be sluggish during training, and I could already hear the lecture from my tutors.

Footsteps sounded in the hallway beyond my bedroom. A moment later, knuckles tapped on the door and the knob turned. Xandra never waited for an answer or invitation.

"Caspia, are you awake? If not, wake up." My cousin walked into my room and clapped twice.

Her long, coppery red-and-orange curls were pulled into a tight knot at her nape. She was in uniform, her ecru pants molding to the lean curves of her hips and thighs. The matching sleeveless vest left her strong arms bare. Wrapped around her biceps and forearms were the elfalter metal bands that indicated her station. *Our* station.

Quiescent.

Xandra and I were both waiting to go through the ritus. Then we would be Starling, and those gleaming armbands would be replaced by rings on each finger.

Rings to represent loyalty to our country. To the Nelfinex people. To our family.

To the Starling.

"I'm awake." I unfolded my knees and swung my legs over the windowsill to hop down.

Xandra took in my unmade bed and flowing white robe. My own fiery-red curls were loose and hanging to my waist. Normally when she barged into my room, I was fast asleep, drooling on a pillow. Those two claps of hers had become my morning call to arms.

Her eyebrows knitted together as I slumped on the edge of my bed. "You had another vision, didn't you?"

"Yes." There was no point denying it. I didn't need a mirror to know my eyes were haunted.

"Was it the same one? About Emery?"

I nodded, picking at my thumbnail.

"Vexx," she cursed.

"Don't let anyone else hear you say that word."

Cursing was strictly forbidden for the Quiescent. We were to be the epitome of stoicism, and cursing was an emotional crutch, according to my aunt.

Xandra frowned. "I know you don't want to tell her about the visions again, but—"

"I don't." I stood and walked away from my cousin—from this conversation—and into my dressing room.

Aunt Oleana didn't want to hear about my visions, especially this one. No matter how many times I told her they were more than dreams, she'd only ever considered them my imagination run wild. She dismissed them as nonsense, as moon terrors that would stop after the ritus.

Even when the visions were true, when I had proof that what I saw had happened, she didn't believe. I'd stopped telling Oleana about them when I was sixteen. For years, I'd acted as her dutiful Quiescent, and if she wondered whether or not I still had *dreams*, she hadn't asked.

But after this vision of Emery had come again and again, I'd decided to break my silence.

She'd dismissed it with a flick of her wrist.

So no, I wasn't going to tell her about it again.

Clothes littered the floor of my dressing room. There was a towel in the doorway to my bathing chamber. The chest of drawers against the wall was nearly empty, its contents strewn in various piles.

I stripped off my robe, tossing it onto the nearest heap that I'd sort through later. Then I rummaged through the mess for the cleanest of my uniforms. All were wrinkled and had been worn at least once.

Instead of sitting in my window, I should have done my washing. But laundry was my least favorite chore and the least of my worries, so I donned my pants and vest, the same as Xandra's, and began braiding my hair in twin rows.

Xandra was making my bed when I emerged from the dressing room.

"You didn't have to do that."

"I don't mind." She shrugged and straightened a pillow. "Where's Hop?"

"Graciella asked if he could sleep in her room."

"If you're not careful, she's going to steal your fenek."

"You're probably right." I laughed, righting a corner of the linen blanket, running a hand over the saffron-colored fabric. Then I sat on the bed's edge to pull on my knee-high leather boots.

Xandra took a seat at my side. "If you tell her, she might believe you this time."

"She won't." Of that, I had no doubt.

"But this is the only vision that has repeated. That must mean something."

"Yes," I murmured as a sinking feeling settled in my belly.

I'd had visions my entire life. They'd come infrequently when I was a child, but as I'd grown from Nestling to Quiescent, as I'd matured into a woman, they'd come more often. Sometimes every four or five suns.

Yet in all that time, the vision of Emery and the silver-eyed warrior was the only one I'd had more than once. Last moon's marked the sixth time.

Nothing good came from the number six.

"You must tell her, Caspia. If not for your own peace of mind, for Graciella. If it's true, she has the right to know her mother isn't coming back. And if Emery has been murdered, there must be retribution."

She was right. We both knew she was right. *Vexx.*

For Graciella's sake, I needed to tell my aunt. And Emery deserved vengeance.

It was the Starling way.

"Fine," I muttered.

"Thank you." Xandra took my hand, holding it tight. With her other, she lifted the elfalter pendant hanging around her neck and brought it to her lips. The red-and-orange metal glimmered in the sunlight. The silver wing inlaid into the circle sparkled like a star. "By the grace of the Divine, she will listen."

I lifted my own necklace, pressing a kiss to the emblem of Nelfinex, of the Starling, as I gave a silent prayer.

By the grace of the Divine, give us the rite.
By the grace of the Divine, turn us true.

"We should go." I stood, tugging at the hem of my vest in the hopes of it working out a few wrinkles.

"To speak to Aunt Oleana?" Xandra asked.

"Yes. Before I lose my nerve."

"Make a vow. Then your courage won't wane."

The Starling honored loyalty. We believed in vengeance and strength and discipline. But above all else, we kept our vows. Or died trying. So I pressed two fingertips to the center of my forehead. "You have my vow."

"Thank you."

I went to the tray on my vanity where I kept my elfalter bands and quickly slid them on my forearms and biceps. Then I followed Xandra out of my room.

She and I took the nearest staircase, jogging up eight flights. When we reached the palace's top floor, we passed a servant coming out of Saskia's suite.

"Princess Caspia. Princess Xandra." His caramel eyes were bright as he passed us for the stairs, carrying a tray with Saskia's half-eaten breakfast.

"Good morning." I returned his warm, kind smile.

Once we were through the ritus, once we were Starling, the servants and attendants would be required to drop to their knees and bow when we met them in the halls. They would treat us as they did the Starling. As they did Aunt Oleana, the queen. For once we completed our ritus, we would be royalty.

But we weren't Starling yet.

I'd miss the easy smiles and casual greetings. I'd miss the informality of being a Quiescent. I'd miss my room on the middle level of the palace, where I was closer to the city. I'd miss visiting the Nestlings each afternoon in the libraries.

At least as Starling, I wouldn't have to do my own laundry.

Xandra and I walked past a row of arched openings that overlooked the city and the Marixmore Ocean beyond. The scents of sage and citrus and salt wafted into the hall, and I drew in a deep breath, holding it in my lungs.

Emery once told me that her senses had sharpened and changed after the ritus. She'd lost her love of crystalized lemon and candied honey. I hoped that when my transformation was complete, I still loved the smell of the sea.

We passed door after door as we walked the length of the palace. Each belonged to a suite occupied by a Starling. Sisters. Cousins. Aunts. Great aunts. Grandmothers.

A giggle echoed from an open room. A girl with wild, bouncing red curls—Starling hair—came racing out and into the hall with a fenek giving chase.

"Graciella." I smiled and bent to a crouch, arms opening wide.

She crashed into my chest, laughing as I swept her up and spun her in circles. "Hi, Aunt Caspia."

"How is my sweetling girl?" I kissed her cheek and tapped her freckled nose before setting her down.

She pushed a stray curl out of her face. "Bored and hungry. We're sneaking into the kitchens for a treat. It was Hop's idea."

"Oh, was it?" I reached to scratch behind Hop's ears. "Hello, my pretty pet."

He nuzzled against my leg and purred. His cinnamon fur was nearly the same shade as the tiled floor, rich and warm and soft. The white tusks that extended below his jaw were as bright as the walls. Hop swished his bushy tail, then nudged Graciella's hand, a silent order for her to follow him into mischief.

"Don't get caught," Xandra warned.

Graciella laughed, her gold eyes dancing as she skipped after my pet. "I never get caught."

Xandra shook her head as we continued down the hallway for the staircase that would take us to the mews. "That girl is too much like her mother."

The ache in my chest was instant. "That she is."

Graciella was only six summers, but even this young, she

was Emery's in every way. They were mirrors of each other in looks and personality.

It surprised no one that Aunt Oleana had taken over care of Graciella after Emery's disappearance. Oleana had done the same when my mother left Nelfinex, leaving three daughters behind. And Emery had always been Oleana's favorite niece.

The niece she now refused to discuss.

Maybe she'd listen this morning. For Graciella's sake, for Emery's honor, I would try.

One last time.

We reached a set of curving stone stairs and climbed to the level above. The sounds of beating wings and chirping notes greeted us when we reached the landing.

The mews were still full this early. Nearly every nest was taken by a swift. As the sun rose higher in the sky, by the time the temperature reached its peak, these nests would all be empty. The massive birds would leave the palace to hunt the large elk and goats that inhabited Nelfinex's rocky mountains. But for now, they were crowded and noisy.

I walked to the closest nest, to a young female with glossy black feathers. "Hello, pretty girl."

She lifted her enormous beak to my outstretched hand, then nuzzled closer so I'd stroke the feathers between her dark eyes.

Most swift lived in the wild, but a select few of the smartest and strongest stayed in the mews.

Xandra wandered to the opposite end of the space to find Bisten, her favorite male and the largest swift who called this palace home. His auburn feathers had a golden sheen in the early-morning light.

"Caspia." My aunt's voice rang through the room, carrying over the other noise.

She stood at the mouth of an open archway, hands clasped

behind her back, staring out over Showe. Her expression was blank and unreadable.

Oleana's hair was bound by thin straps of leather. The plait they formed fell down her spine in a thick line. She was dressed in an amber gown, the light fabric swishing in the breeze above her bare toes.

She'd never had children, choosing instead to raise me and my sisters as her own. Of her three nieces, it was said that I took after her most. That when she'd been my age, we would have been mistaken for twins. We had the same straight nose and bow-shaped lips. The same oval face and delicate chin.

In appearance, we might have been similar. But in spirit, we were as different as the sun and the moons.

Aunt Oleana wasn't a loving woman. She was a leader, a ruler, and a politician. She was bound by duty to her people, to this country, and to our bloodline.

She viewed my tender heart as a weakness. A queen could not afford affection. Not even for the girls who were raised as her daughters.

As I joined her, the female swift I'd been petting stood, stretching her wings as much as the space would allow. She hopped to another archway, and with a single push off her strong legs, she leaped from the ledge, her wings stretching wide. The spikes at their leading edge sliced through the air.

"Beautiful, isn't she?" Aunt Oleana asked as I took the place by her side, both of us watching as the female flew higher and higher.

"Yes."

"If Graciella isn't able to shift after her ritus, I'll pair them as riders." She spoke so quietly it seemed more of a passing thought than a statement she'd meant to share. A dread she hadn't meant to voice.

"Why don't you think she'll be able to shift?"

"A contingency plan." Oleana gave me a small smile, her

eyes dropping to the bands clasped around my arms. That hint of a smile vanished.

At twenty-five summers, I was long overdue for my ritus. Oleana had shifted at fifteen. Emery and Saskia both by sixteen.

My mother left Nelfinex when I was a baby, and since no one in my family spoke of her, I wasn't sure if or when she'd gone through her ritus.

Every Starling felt the calling at her own time, and there was no rushing or forcing the change.

We simply prayed to the Divine that it called.

Xandra's mother, my aunt Ophelia, had never gone through a ritus. Neither had her eldest daughter, Hara. They'd been born with Starling blood, yet they could not shapeshift. They would forever be Quiescents, flying on the backs of the swift rather than wings of their own.

Xandra's biggest fear was that she'd never go through a ritus.

So was mine.

In the Starling's written history, there was no record of the gift ever failing to manifest. To my aunt's knowledge, Ophelia had been the first. Hara the second.

As much as I hated to think there was a chance I'd never be a Starling, it was possible. The gift in our blood might have passed me over. It could happen with Graciella, too.

"Emery shifted at sixteen," I told Aunt Oleana. "Her gift was strong. I'm certain she gave it to Graciella."

The queen stayed quiet.

As always, any mention of Emery was met with silence. Just like the mention of our mother.

The only thing Aunt Oleana had ever said about my mother was that she'd been a dreamer. Part of me wondered if my mother's "dreams" were visions like mine.

A piercing scream carried from above a moment before a huge male swept down from the palace's towers. Then came a shout, free and joyous, as the bird leveled out, wings outstretched. Hara rode on his back, her saddle harnessed around his chest.

My cousin, with a beaming smile, twisted to wave.

Oleana lifted her arm to wave back. If I didn't know better, I would have thought the moisture in her eyes was tears. But I knew better.

She did not cry.

My aunt was not a woman to accept unfortunate fates. Instead, she'd built these mews so that the swift we tamed could be Ophelia's and Hara's wings. So that my daring cousin could fly, even if that meant doing so on the back of her precious bird.

In two or three or four generations' time, maybe the Starling gift would have dwindled to nothing more than a memory. Maybe by that time, whatever it was in our blood that made my lineage special would be so diluted that we'd lose the gift entirely. But this way, we could still fly.

Hara and her male flew beyond the city walls, his horns gleaming beneath the sun as they raced into the distance.

"You must begin to tend to Bisten." Aunt Oleana turned and nodded to where Xandra stood, stroking the swift's feathers.

"Why?" Bisten's temper was legendary, and he snapped at all the keepers except for Xandra. My cousin loved his prickly temperament, but I found it irksome. "He's better suited to Xandra."

"Possibly. But I have chosen him for you."

I nodded, knowing better than to argue. Oleana had a reason for every decision.

Like Bisten could sense we were going to be stuck with each other, he let out a low chuff and set off for an archway window, leaving his nest empty as he flew away from the palace.

Xandra went to the rack of tools to get started on her

chores. For those of us who had not gone through the ritus, our suns started with chores. Xandra and I were assigned to the mews, and when we were finished here, we'd move on to lessons and weapons training.

"If necessary, she can choose a different male," Oleana said. "She gets on well with most."

"I hope it won't be necessary. For either of us."

"So do I."

Our country was vast, the largest on the continent of Kenn. But Oleana was not the only ruler, and the three southern countries were controlled by tyrants.

If they suspected the strength of the Starling was weakening, they wouldn't hesitate to strike. The kings from the south were as hungry for power as they were for land.

We needed to stand strong.

We needed to ensure that anyone who harmed a Starling was dealt a fast death.

"Aunt Oleana, I must tell you something."

She turned to face me, her attention fixed so firmly I nearly shied away. "Your ritus? Do you feel it calling?"

"No." Not yet.

"I see." Disappointment flashed over her face before she schooled her expression to cold indifference. "What must you tell me?"

I steeled my spine. "I had a vision of Emery's death again."

If there was any hint of warmth in Oleana's golden eyes, it vanished. "Emery is not dead."

"I don't want to believe it's true, either. But what if—"

"She's not dead." Her voice was as sharp as a blade. "She left us to go on some ridiculous journey with that man. She abandoned her family, her daughter, when I expressly told her she was not to leave. She defied my order. She has forsaken her duty. But she is not dead. She will return and take her rightful place."

"But the vision—"

"Enough." Oleana sliced a hand through the air.

I hid my fists behind my back. "I've had the same vision of Emery six times, Aunt Oleana. It's more real than anything I've ever felt. There is a man with silver eyes who—"

"I said enough," she shouted, so loud I rocked back on my heels. "You will not speak of this again. I forbid it, Caspia."

It wasn't an order from my aunt. It was a command from my queen.

I ducked my chin, ever the obedient princess. "Yes, Majesty."

She hooked a finger under my chin, tilting up my face until I met her gaze. "They are only dreams, Caspia. That's all they've ever been. Nothing more. Your sister is alive. And by the grace of the Divine, she will return soon."

Dreams. No matter how many had come true, no matter how often I pleaded with her to believe, they'd only ever be dreams. "Yes, Aunt Oleana."

She cupped my cheek. "We must focus on our family. This country. The Beesan king has been pushing against our southern border. If he learns that Starling blood is wilting, he may get reckless ambitions. I will not let a single Nelfinex person suffer the same fate as the Velvi'os-telfer. We will not be driven from our own land and hunted to near extinction. We must stand strong. Together. Do you understand?"

"Yes." I nodded.

"Good. Now, get on with your work." She swept past me and walked to the stairs, lifting the hems of her skirts as she set off for her auditorium, where she'd spend the sun ruling our country.

I waited until she was gone before I let my shoulders sag.

Xandra abandoned her shovel and crossed the room, joining me at the open archway. "I'm sorry. Maybe I shouldn't have pushed you to tell her. I thought… I thought she might listen."

"It's not your fault." It wasn't my aunt's, either.

She didn't want to believe Emery was gone, and my visions were something she simply could not understand. Only two people had ever believed they held merit.

Xandra.

And Emery.

When—*if*—I went through the ritus, would the visions stop? Part of me hoped I'd never dream again.

Turning away from Xandra, I let my gaze wander to the ocean, where waves crashed against the shore. The coastline was as blue as an azure jewel, the sand as bright as our uniforms. The water was endless, darkening as it stretched toward the unknown.

A tingling sensation crept up my arms, raising bumps on my flesh. My blood stirred. Something inside me tugged toward that dark blue, pulling so hard I took an involuntary step forward and gasped.

The ritus.

"Caspia?" Xandra asked. "What is it?"

"Nothing," I lied, not ready to name the sensation quite yet. I lifted my hand to the pendant resting over my heart, and the elfalter metal warmed as I covered it with my palm.

There were answers across the sea. Answers for Emery. Answers for myself.

Oleana had told me the ritus beckoned us in different ways. Some were called to journey into the mountains. Others would trek across the desert.

My future was beyond Nelfinex's shores.

"Oh, I don't like that look," Xandra muttered.

I tore my gaze from the sea, feigning surprise. "What look?"

Her mouth flattened into a thin line. "The look that says you're going to get us into trouble."

4

ODESSA

A tree branch slapped me in the face.

"Ouch." I batted it away, tasting pine needles and sap. I carefully touched the sting on my cheek, and my fingers came away wet.

Just when I thought this night couldn't get worse, now I was bleeding. *Son of a bitch.*

Shades, I *hated* this.

I hated trees. I hated nature. I hated my saddle, and I hated this night.

The faint light from the crescent twin moons, Aurinda and Aurrellia, was barely enough to see my own hand in front of my face, let alone oncoming tree branches. Trying to see in this darkness was giving me a headache. And Brother Dime, riding ahead of me, couldn't be bothered to warn me to duck.

I silently glared into the darkness, hoping he'd feel my irritation the same way I could feel his magic.

If not for the sound of his horse's hooves and the prickle of that magic, I wouldn't have a damn clue that he was in front of me. The same was true of Brother Skore. He trailed behind, probably to make sure I didn't get any ideas about leaving our delightful little parade.

It had been three miserable days since we left the mountain lake, and I ached from head to toe. Not even my first journey across Turah, riding beside Tillia, had been this painful.

Thinking of her beautiful face made my heart ache. Was

Halston alive? Had he survived losing his leg to the crux? Would he get the chance to meet their baby?

What would Tillia do in this situation? Would she continue riding with the Voster? Or would she say to hell with it and try to escape?

Evie wiggled in the saddle, tearing me from my thoughts.

Her body was pressed against mine, her weight in my arms with her head on my shoulder as she slept.

Even if it cost me everything, I would find a way to get this girl to Quentis. To keep her safe. So I stared ahead, catching the occasional glimpse of Brother Dime's shadowed figure as we rode into the night.

With my hands loose around the reins, I traced the scar on my palm.

The hole in my chest felt bigger at night. It was too quiet, too lonely, in the dark.

He's alive.

He was alive. He had to be alive. He wouldn't have waited long in Treow before returning to Ellder to retrace our path. Would he catch up to us soon?

Or did Brother Dime have a way to hide our trail? Maybe they were using wisps of wind to blow dirt over our tracks.

Gods, I hated the Voster. I hated their magic. I hated their vague statements about fate and destiny. I hated their creepy fingernails and eerie eyes.

The hate simmered under my skin, a constant burn in my chest. And stoking this rage made the heartache easier to forget.

Ransom trusted the priests. That had seemed like enough of a reason to follow Brother Dime out of that dungeon in Ellder. But maybe my husband was wrong. Maybe I'd been right all along to be skeptical of the brotherhood.

Doubt and fear were wearing me thin.

We'd stopped more frequently over the past three days to let the horses recover. It should have been enough time for me to rest, but each time I closed my eyes, I'd panic that the Voster would take Evie while I slept.

Our last stop had been at midday. I'd finally managed to sleep for a few hours, until a dream had jolted me awake.

Long after the sun had set, the nightmare of Luella's death still haunted my thoughts. In this darkness, it was hard to block out the memory of her body being cleaved in half by the crux.

Another tree branch swung for my face, but this time, I managed to swat it away.

After we left the lake, Brother Dime had warned me that we'd have to ride through the night. He'd insisted these mountains were crawling with grizzur. Zavier had once told me the monsters don't see well at night, so it was safer to travel after the sun went down.

Were there monsters in these woods? Or was the threat of death by fangs and claws another one of Dime's ploys, because traveling by night was the most effective way to ensure I stayed lost?

We could be in Turah or Ozarth or the Evon Ravine for all I knew.

Brother Skore murmured something from behind me, the low hum loud enough to reach my ears but too quiet for me to understand the words. After three days and nights listening to those quiet words, I'd come to the conclusion that he was praying.

Except he never signed the Eight. He didn't speak to any of the Six. Instead, he kept invoking the Divine. Was that another term the Voster used for Ama and Oda?

As tempting as it was to ask, Brother Skore did not seem overly fond of this princess.

In fact, I'd say he was about as happy to be trekking through the mountains at night as I was. Maybe we could bond in our shared misery.

A blast of wind came from behind, Skore's signal I was going too slow.

Maybe not.

I twisted over my shoulder, pulling free the smelly curls he'd whipped into my face, and gave him my fiercest glare. Could he see in the dark like Ransom? Oh, I hoped so.

"Papa." Evie's body jerked, her leg kicking.

The jolt was enough to stir Faze awake in his carrier. He squirmed, his paws pushing into my ribs so hard I winced.

"Shh." I rocked Evie. "It's okay."

She whimpered and kicked again, her mouth turning down in a frown.

Her nightmares were getting worse, and these long, dark nights weren't helping. Last night she'd fought me so hard I'd nearly dropped her. It was like she was reliving Ellder again. Like she was fighting me as I'd dragged her away from Zavier's body.

"It's okay. You're okay."

She kicked harder, squirming to be free.

"Wake up, Evie." As much as she needed to sleep, my arms were too tired to hold her while she thrashed. "Wake up."

Her eyes popped open, wide and terrified. She blinked up at me, like she was still stuck in the past. Then reality came crashing down.

A reality where her father was gone.

Fat, soul-crushing tears spilled down her cheeks. "I want Papa."

"I know, little star."

Her body shook as she buried her face in my chest, letting free the sobs that had been building for days and days.

I didn't care if it pissed off the Voster. I pulled hard on Freya's reins, forcing her to stop. Then I wrapped both arms around Evie, holding her while she cried.

"I want Papa." Her tears coated my shirt. The sound of her heartbreak filled the night, echoing off trees until it floated above their tops like smoke, destined for the shades.

"I'm sorry, Evangeline," I whispered into her hair. "I'm so sorry."

A gust of magical wind hit my back. I ignored it.

Brother Skore could rot while we took this one godsdamn minute to mourn.

I curled around Evie, stroking her hair as she cried, shielding her from the wind.

He could blow and blow and blow. *The asshole.* I wasn't moving.

Only when the sound of hooves stopped at my side and the prickle of magic intensified did I finally look up.

In the dark, his white skin and pale robes glowed.

"What?" I snapped. "Just give us a few—"

A roar sounded in the distance. A roar that was close enough to stop Evie's sobs in a snap and make her sit up straight.

Oh, hell. I knew that roar. *Grizzur.*

Skore pointed to the trail ahead. If the other gusts of wind he'd sent were subtle hints, the blast that slammed into my shoulders now was an order.

I was already moving, gripping Freya's reins as I kicked her forward. We bolted into the trees, quickly catching Brother Dime as we sped from a walk to a canter. I adjusted my seat, the muscles in my legs screaming as I struggled to find a rhythm at the faster pace with Evie in front of me and Faze in his carrier against my ribs. My satchel full of books and the dagger Ransom had given me bounced where I'd secured it to the saddle. My sword in its sheath smacked me against the spine.

"Hold on," I told Evie. Told myself. "Just hold on."

Another roar sounded, loud enough to hear over my pounding heart and Freya's hooves and Evie's cries. Brother Skore's wind was relentless, pushing us forward as he stayed at my side, his robes flowing off his gangly frame.

We rode hard and fast for what felt like days until finally

we broke through the trees and into a clearing kissed by moonlight.

Brother Dime drew his mount to a halt, waiting as we came to a stop at his side. He panted, and for the first time, it seemed that this grueling pace had finally caught up to the priest.

"We can't keep going like this." My lungs burned, my voice hoarse. Something wet hit my forearm, and it took me a moment to realize it wasn't a raindrop but one of Evie's tears. "Please. We need to stop."

"You masked our scent?" Dime asked Skore, earning a nod.

The wind. It wasn't to push me forward but to hide our trail from the grizzur.

"We're nearly there." Brother Dime urged his horse forward, thankfully at a walk.

I sucked in a deep breath and wrapped my arms around Evie, giving her a hug and a kiss. Then I reached into Faze's carrier, scratching his head as I nudged Freya forward.

We followed Brother Dime through the clearing and into more trees. When we emerged into a rolling field, a light shone in the distance. It grew steadily larger as we rode to a cabin at the edge of another wood.

The house reminded me of the homes in Ravalli, built from rough-hewn logs and sunken into the ground. There were no spikes on its roof. I hoped whoever lived here would add them before the migration.

Beside the house was a barn built level with the earth. A horse with a white stripe down its nose grazed in a fenced corral.

The front door of the house opened, and a man climbed the stairs, a lantern in one hand, a crossbow in the other. He was a colossus with brown skin and black hair braided in rows. His eyes were hard and focused as he raised his weapon. Then his stern expression vanished and he let the crossbow drop to his side. "Brother Dime."

"I am sorry for the intrusion, Damon."

"No apologies. Welcome." He quickly rushed down the stairs to the house, shouting through the door, "Sally. We have visitors. Put on a kettle."

Both priests swung off their horses.

"Are we staying here?" If we were leaving again, there was no way I was getting down. I'd never get back up, not tonight.

Brother Dime nodded.

"Thank the gods." I signed the Eight and got down, then helped Evie out of the saddle.

She hurried to hide behind my legs.

Weeks ago, she might not have been the first to introduce herself, but she wouldn't have cowered. I blamed this newfound wariness on Banner. On the pride and violence of vengeful men.

Banner could rot in Izzac's hell for all I cared, and I wished him constant torment from the God of Death.

Damon walked to Brother Dime, bowing to the priest before taking his horse's reins. "What do you need?"

"Shelter for the Sparrow."

Damon's eyes darted in my direction as he lifted the lamp. He took in my wrinkled, filthy clothes. His gaze lingered a moment too long on Ransom's cuff before he offered the same bow he'd given the Voster. "Of course. It would be an honor."

"Thank you." I shifted, forcing Evie into the light. "This is Evangeline."

Damon gave her a smile. "Hello, dear one."

"And this is Faze." I fished the tarkin from his carrier, bending to set him on the ground. If we were going to be staying in this man's home, he should know we came with a pet.

Faze's steps were wobbly, like he was still shaken up from the harrowing ride. He let out a growl, then sniffed the air.

"Th-that's a..." Damon sputtered.

"Tarkin." I gave him a sweet smile. "Do you have any milk?"

"Another bowl?" Sally asked, stirring the pot of stew with her ladle.

"No, thank you." I dabbed the corner of my mouth. "It was delicious."

The meal was rich with meat and vegetables, and their home smelled of savory spices. But after too many days with too little food, my stomach protested being full.

Evie had barely eaten half of her serving and was nibbling a yeasted roll as she leaned against my side.

Sally gave me a kind smile before going to tidy her kitchen.

It was almost strange to be clean and fed. Strange and wonderful and energizing and draining.

While Damon had stayed outside to help the Voster with our horses, Sally had ushered us inside the house. She'd taken one look at us in the light and immediately shown us to the small bathing chamber attached to their house.

She ran a hand pump that sent a spray through a hose in the ceiling, and though the water was cold, most of the dust and dirt washed down the drain.

As I combed out Evie's hair and my own, Sally found us fresh clothes. I was wearing a pair of her pants, slightly too big, but I'd cinched them with a rope. The tunic I'd borrowed was a simple tan.

Ransom's cuff was hidden beneath my sleeve.

My necklace was tucked under the collar, the metal warm against my skin.

Evie was dressed in a blue shirt that had been Damon's when he was a child. It smelled stale from the cedar chest where it had been for years, but it was clean. There hadn't been any pants in Evie's size, so I'd washed hers in Sally's laundry tub, then hung them to dry.

The door swung open, and Damon ducked inside. He'd gone out to dispose of our dirty wash water and check on the Voster, who were staying in a loft in the barn.

For the first time in days, I didn't feel the crackle of their magic. It was bliss.

Faze was in a corner of the room, licking his paws after his own meal of milk and meat scraps.

Damon crossed the room to Sally, kissing her honey-colored hair, then took the bench seat across from the one that Evie and I shared.

A necklace I hadn't noticed earlier swung free from the collar of his tan tunic.

Evie sat up straight, eyes locked on the black claw tied to a string of leather. "What's that?"

"Oh, it's from a lionwick. My father gave it to me." Damon lifted it to catch the room's light. "The story goes, he found the monster in a trap. As a gift for setting the beast free, the monster gave my father this claw. He wore it like this, around his neck, and never fell sick. He never felt pain. He gave it to me the day he decided to take his place in the shades. Now it keeps me healthy and strong. And someday, I'll give it to my son."

The bench might as well have been pulled out from beneath me.

No. Fucking. Way. I fought to keep my jaw from dropping as Sally slid into the space beside her husband.

Damon's hand splayed across her rounded belly.

"A fanciful story." Sally tapped the claw necklace. "I think they both just like how it looks."

Damon laughed, his dark-brown eyes alight with love. "Maybe you're right."

Or maybe it was magic.

How was it that, not so long ago, I'd sat around a different table and heard this same story? Luella had said it was in the journal with the emblem of my own necklace on the cover. A journal that had led her to create the elixir that played its role in Lyssa.

A journal in my satchel.

Had the person who wrote that story known these people? Had Luella met them before? Maybe tomorrow, I'd pull Damon aside and ask. But right now, I didn't want to mention Luella's name with Evie so close. I wasn't ready to tell her that Luella was dead.

Evangeline yawned, her mouth stretching wide.

"I think I'd better get her to bed." I stood, picking up my bowl.

"Leave that." Sally waved me off. "Get some rest. We'll see you in the morning."

I collected Faze so he wouldn't shred their armchair in the night. Then I whisked Evie to the spare room where we'd be sleeping. Once she was tucked into the cot and asleep, I tiptoed to my satchel and took out the black leather journal.

My fingertips skimmed the embossed wing inlaid in a circle. Then I opened the clasp and cover to pages filled with sentences I couldn't read.

The old language.

I wasn't sure how or when, but even if it took me months, I'd read every page of this journal. If there was a chance it held the clue to a cure for Lyssa, I'd memorize every page.

5

CASPIA

Moonbeams streamed through the windows as I took a final look around my room. The floor was spotless, the bed neatly made. The vanity top was clear save for three letters on its wooden surface.

One for Aunt Oleana. One for Xandra. And one for Graciella.

By the grace of the Divine, I'd see them again and those letters wouldn't be my final farewells. But in case I didn't get that chance, I'd penned them each a note goodbye.

I prayed that I'd return. That soon I'd fly home as a Starling and have summer after summer with my family, soaring over my city. And when—*if*—I returned, I'd happily suffer Oleana's wrath for disobeying her orders. Maybe her anger would be tempered if I completed my ritus and avenged Emery's death.

Since the moon when I'd seen Emery's death for the sixth time, the calling I'd felt standing in the mews had only grown stronger.

My blood was stirring. Something beckoned from across the sea.

In my soul, I knew the vision and my ritus were linked. And it was time to answer the call.

Maybe Aunt Oleana was right, and after I completed my ritus, the visions would stop. Until then, I'd use what the Divine had shown me to bring honor to my sister's death. I'd follow this calling to learn the truth of her fate and kill the silver-eyed man who'd dared take a Starling's life.

The leather pack at my feet was stuffed with a spare change of clothes, a canteen, and a healing salve. The pockets held a bone comb, two books, and one tiny canister of hair oil for my curls. And tucked in every empty space I could find were various teas I'd bought from an apothecary in Showe. A tea for seasickness. A tea for headache. A tea to help me sleep and another to keep me awake.

My kukri was secured across my spine, hidden by my hooded cloak. My sharpest knives were strapped to my forearms and around each of my thighs.

I picked up the pack, slinging the straps over my shoulders. Its weight was as heavy as my heart.

There was a chance that I was wrong and this journey would prove to be a mistake. And even if I was right, if this was my ritus calling, there was a chance I wouldn't be strong enough for the change.

Not every Quiescent survived her first shift. The rite was as dangerous and deadly as it was powerful.

Was that why my mother had left Nelfinex? Maybe she'd been called by her ritus after birthing three daughters, and the change had taken her life. I would always resent Aunt Oleana for not speaking of my mother.

The secrets in our family would be our demise.

My pulse pounded as a tug drew me toward the windows, like a rope tethered to my chest, pulling me away from Nelfinex. A *thrum* vibrated through my body, spreading from my heart to my hands and feet. It was like a chord being strummed on a guitar, the notes in perfect harmony.

Beyond my sleeping city, the ocean stretched to meet the moonlit sky. The waves glittered in the starlight. Every time I looked toward that unknown place on the horizon, I felt that *thrum*.

It was time to go.

Before I lost my nerve, I crossed the room and opened

the door, pausing on the threshold to take one last look over my shoulder.

"Goodbye," I whispered, hoping my farewell would linger long enough for Xandra to hear in the morning.

When she came to wake me, clapping twice, she'd take one look at the tidy room and know immediately that something was wrong. By that point, I'd be a league away, sailing into the dawn.

Divine, guide my path. I closed the door and moved on silent feet to the nearest stairwell.

The ship I'd hired had cost me a fortune, nearly all of my elfalter armbands, but it was fast, and more importantly, the captain, an infamous pirate, hadn't asked questions.

There was a chance Aunt Oleana would fly out over the Marixmore and fetch me. When she shifted into a swift, there wasn't a vessel in Nelfinex that could match her speed. But I hoped that when she read my letter, when she realized this was not simply a quest for vengeance, she'd let me take this journey for my ritus.

My boots whispered on the stone stairs as I hurried to the main level. When I reached the palace's vestibule, I flipped up the hood on my charcoal cloak, hiding my hair from view.

When I became a Starling, I could come and go as I pleased. Saskia's favorite time to fly was at moons' peak. So was Oleana's. But as a Quiescent princess, I was under a strict curfew.

To leave the palace, I was required to keep with a company of guards. It didn't matter that I could best any of them in combat. Until I could shapeshift, until the time came when I could take the form of any animal to defend myself against a threat, I was under the protection of the queen's Royal Blades.

I walked softly on my toes. I kept my hood drawn low.

The sounds of footsteps and male voices drifted from a hallway ahead.

I scurried to the closest wall, tucking myself into an alcove just as a pair of guards rounded a corner and stepped into the vestibule.

Both men were dressed in ecru uniforms and armed with swords, knives, and daggers. The Royal Blades were aptly named.

I held my breath, waiting until they passed, none the wiser to my presence. As their hulking figures rounded another corner, I slipped away from the wall and scurried for the hall that led to the gardens.

The moment I was out the door, a cool breeze kissed my face. The overwhelming urge to cry burned in my nose.

Not once in my life had I spent a moon outside this palace. A small part of me had doubted I'd even make it this far. An even smaller part hoped that I'd be caught. That I'd miss the ship waiting for me at the docks.

I swallowed the lump in my throat, then quickly crossed the garden's stone pathways, weaving past vibrant blooms and drawing in their fragrant scents as I set off for the nearest iron gate. As it came into view, I took a fortifying breath and squared my shoulders, flipping the hood off my hair.

The guards in the gardens were not Royal Blades. Only the best warriors were allowed inside the palace halls.

The men and women stationed outside were simply sentries, tasked primarily with keeping people out, not in. And unlike the Blades who trained with the Quiescents every sun, the sentries were not familiar with my face. In the dark, I was counting on them mistaking me for Saskia.

The ten rings on my fingers should help.

Only the Starling wore elfalter rings, a symbol of status and ability. They were wide, spanning the lower half of each finger. The rings on my hands were Emery's. I'd stolen them from Aunt Oleana's room when I went to visit Graciella—to leave Hop in her care and hug her goodbye.

When my sister left Showe with Max, she'd left her elfalter rings behind. Just like she'd left Graciella.

It was probably intended to be a slap in our aunt's face after their horrible fight about Max. Since Oleana had no daughters, Emery was supposed to be her heir. My aunt had forbidden Emery from taking a Beesan as consort and delivered an ultimatum.

Leave Max or forget becoming queen.

The next morning, Emery was gone. And she'd left her rings—gifts from Oleana upon completing her ritus—at Graciella's bedside table.

I didn't blame Emery for choosing the man she loved. But to leave her daughter? That, I didn't understand.

We'd been abandoned by our mother. Emery knew how it felt. How could she do that to her own child?

Despite her quarrels with Oleana, Emery loved Graciella. I had to believe that my sister wouldn't have left unless she'd planned to return. Maybe Emery had been on her way home when she'd been killed by the silver-eyed man.

I intended to find out.

It felt wrong to wear her rings, but at least they would grant me my freedom.

I hardened my steps so the thwack of my boots would catch the sentry's ear. Then, with my chin lifted, I extended my hand so the rings would gleam in the moonlight.

"Starling." The man bent at the waist, eyes cast downward.

"The gate, sir." It was only by the grace of the Divine that my voice remained steady.

He lifted the rail that barred the gate closed and, with another bow, pushed open the iron bars. The hinges creaked as it swung outward.

If he wondered why I'd leave through a gate rather than fly over the walls, he didn't ask.

Without a word, I marched through the opening and onto the nearby street.

The sentry's gaze was hot on my shoulders as I walked away with measured strides. Not too fast, not too slow, until the street sloped away from the palace, and I ducked behind a building, pressing flat against its rough white stone.

"Vexx." I slapped a hand over my racing heart, and the rings resting against my knuckles clinked together. One by one, I slipped the thick, smooth bands off my fingers and into the pocket of my pants.

This pirate I'd hired would earn my elfalter bands as payment, but I didn't want him to know I had these rings. I didn't trust him not to change the price of this voyage if he knew I had more to offer.

Quiescents had very little wealth individually, despite our family's vast fortune. That would change after I went through the ritus and became a Starling. My inheritance of elfalter, gold, silver, and jewels would make me one of the richest people in Nelfinex.

But I wasn't rich yet.

With the rings safely stowed, I pushed off the wall and hastened through Showe for the docks.

The streets were empty, illuminated by the light of the two moons and the occasional house lamp. The white stone used for every building gave off its own faint shine, allowing me to make out different colors.

Red tile roofs. Mahogany wooden doors. Umber brick roads. And over my shoulder, a palace the color of pale peaches with shining lamps and gleaming elfalter roofs.

The temptation to turn around, to return to my room, was so overpowering I tripped over my own feet. But I caught my balance and kept going, not letting myself look back again for fear the palace would lure me home.

By the time I reached the entrance to the docks, my stomach was in a knot and my head was spinning.

This was my ritus. It had to be. I refused to believe I'd fallen victim to a meaningless dream. Still, my steps slowed as doubts spread like poison through my mind.

Was I wrong?

A short, shrill whistle rang through the dark.

Another moon, I would have been annoyed that a pirate had summoned me like a dog. But right now, I needed that whistle to keep me going.

Cap leaned against a lamppost, chewing on a toothpick. His bulky arms were crossed over his barrel of a chest. He stood with one ankle casually draped over the other. His blond hair was long on top and shaved on the sides. A row of golden hoops decorated the shells of his ears.

He looked like Emery's Max, handsome and roguish with a devilish glint in his cobalt eyes. I could see why my sister had fallen for her own pirate and why she'd let Max take her away from Nelfinex.

"Ready, Starling?" he asked, pushing off the post and tossing his toothpick aside.

"I'm not Starling." Not yet.

"As long as I am paid by your Starling elfalter, I don't care what you call yourself." He held out a meaty hand.

I took the elfalter bands from my cloak's pocket and passed them over. "Your payment, per our agreement."

He inspected the jewelry, tilting each band from side to side so the metal would catch the light. "They're real."

I rolled my eyes. "Of course they're real."

"Can't be too careful." Cap flashed a dazzling smile, then led the way through the maze of wooden walkways, taking me past stalls and huts where fishermen and merchants would trade their goods at dawn.

Our footsteps mingled with the sound of water slapping against the dock's pylons. Once we reached the outermost row, we passed ships and boats of all different sizes until we came to a stop beside a ship with lofty black sails.

Cap swept out an arm for the plank that bridged the gap between the boat and dock. "After you, Princess."

"Thank—"

A piercing scream rent the air.

My gaze whipped to the sky, searching for beating wings. I found her soaring around the castle's tallest spire, circling the mews.

Aunt Oleana.

Even in the dark, even from this distance, I knew her beautiful silhouette as it blotted out the stars.

I pressed two fingertips to the center of my forehead. "I will avenge her, my queen. You have my vow."

Cap cleared his throat. "Your ship, Starling."

I didn't bother correcting him again. With a nod, I crossed the plank and stepped aboard.

The ship rocked beneath my boots.

And before I was ready, we set sail into the black.

6

ODESSA

A scream rips through the night. Brielle stares at me, tears streaming down her face. Blood coats her hands. Two knives glint in the firelight from where they lie in the dirt. Smoke clouds the air.

One moment, Brielle stands in the street. The next, she is gone.

...

I gasped awake, sitting upright so fast the small bedroom began to spin. It took a moment for me to remember that I wasn't on that street in Ellder. That I was safe in this house, far away from the fortress.

Shit. I pressed my fingertips to my temples, rubbing small circles as I gave my heart a few moments to stop pounding.

If Evie's nightmares felt as real as mine, it was no wonder she jerked and kicked and whimpered in her sleep.

She was curled against my hip, her hands clasped beneath her cheek. Her eyelashes were dark crescents above her soft cheeks. A lock of her wispy brown hair had curled beside her temple.

Careful not to wake her, I slipped out from beneath the patchwork quilt and stood from the cot. The floor was cold on my bare feet as I crept to the corner chair where I'd piled my pants and socks. I pulled them on, then took a seat, picking up the stack of books I'd left out last night.

They seemed heavier this morning, like the weight of their words was growing by the hour.

The journal with the emblem from my necklace was unreadable until I learned the old language, so I set it aside.

Then I fanned through Luella's other two books that I'd found hidden in the compartment in the stairs of the migration cellar. Each was full of Luella's handwriting.

One contained the detailed ingredients and instructions for creating the elixir she'd given Ransom and taken herself. It included her notes about where and how she'd harvested supplies. From korakin to cave ginger, it had the recipe to create her elixir and a list of every person who'd had it injected into their body.

The other journal wasn't as organized. It was full of notes and scribbles about how to find a cure for Lyssa. It was her theories and tests. Some were circled. Others were crossed out with angry lines.

I hoped that if I gave these two books to my father's alchemists and healers, they'd be able to take Luella's notes and find a cure. And that with the help of the clerics in the castle's sanctuary, I could decipher the journal with the winged emblem.

Did the Voster know the old language? I loathed the idea of asking Brother Dime for help, but maybe he could teach me on our trek across Calandra.

I put Luella's journals aside and opened the last of the books I'd stuffed into my satchel. My own journal, filled with sketches of monsters and an incomplete map of Turah.

Now that I had Ransom's cuff, I could finish the map and plot the road to Allesaria.

For generations, the Turans had kept the city's location a secret. Most suspected it was hidden deep in the mountains—or a myth altogether. Perris had once been the capital, but after it was decimated during a migration, the king had left the former castle in ruins and moved his stronghold. Turah's wealth, knowledge, and history were now in Allesaria.

I pushed back my tunic's sleeve, studying the cuff beneath. My fingertips skimmed over the lines and etches that Ransom had carved and notched into the brown leather, some grooves soft and faded while others were fresh and bright.

A map. Possibly the only complete map of Turah in existence.

Maps were forbidden in Turah, and to be found with one was punishable by death. Yet Ransom had made this cuff anyway. He'd plotted towns and villages along with notches for the monsters killed with Lyssa as he'd tracked the infection's spread across his kingdom.

And he'd cut a thin line that marked the path to a hidden city.

The road to Allesaria.

A capital guarded by blood oaths and magic. Yet, somehow, Ransom had circumvented the nuances of a blood oath.

Every king in Calandra would kill for this cuff, including my father.

Father had sent me to Turah not only as the Sparrow to fulfill Quentis's obligation to the treaty, but also as his spy. He'd tasked me with finding the way into the Turan capital.

Except I wasn't a spy. I'd failed spectacularly at gleaning information from the Turans. The only reason I knew Allesaria's location was because of Ransom. He trusted me enough to take this cuff and safeguard its meaning.

He trusted me not to betray his people. *Our* people.

I wasn't sure what my father wanted in Allesaria, but until I learned his motives, my map would stay unfinished. After closing the book, I tucked it into my satchel. Then I pulled down the sleeve of my tunic, covering the cuff.

One by one, I put the other books back into my satchel, praying the seams of the bag were strong enough to hold until Quentis.

Faze uncurled himself from the cot where he'd slept on my feet all night, keeping them warm. He jumped down and stretched, then prowled over and hopped into my lap, nuzzling a hand.

"Still spoiled," I whispered, scratching behind his ears.

He gave a quiet *rawr*.

Two new rows of red-and-orange scales were forming along his spine. Four rows were becoming six. His fur was still pink, but it was slowly darkening, and the stripes at his ribs were more pronounced with every passing day.

"What am I going to do with you?" I asked, my voice low so I didn't wake Evie. "We can't keep you forever. Maybe we should leave you here. I don't know if it's a good idea to take you to Quentis."

As if he knew exactly what I was saying, his vibrant, violet eyes locked with mine, and he gave me a pleading look that reminded me so much of Evie it was uncanny.

"Do you two conspire against me when I'm not looking?"

He purred.

"Thought so," I muttered, giving him another scratch before setting him on the floor. I grabbed my boots from beside the folded pile of our dirty clothes, then slipped out of the room.

Sally was in the kitchen, shaping a mound of dough. The room smelled of sage and yeast and sweet smoke.

My stomach growled.

"Good morning." She smiled, her cheeks rosy.

"Morning." I went to the table's bench, pulling on my boots. "Thank you for letting us stay."

"My pleasure. We are originally from Westor, and there was always a family member or friend who'd pop by. We'd have visitors every day. It was rare for Damon and me to share an evening meal alone. But now that we've moved away from the city, we don't get many guests. I'm still learning to cook for only two. It's lovely to have you here."

"And where exactly is here?" I peered out the window, but with the house sunken into the ground, all I could see was grass and dirt.

"We're at the southern end of the Axmar Mountain range. About half a day's ride from the Ozarth border."

Shades, no wonder my entire body ached from day after day of riding. We'd crossed nearly the entire kingdom of Turah in eight days.

The Axmar Mountains acted as the border between Turah and Ozarth. It was the longest and most treacherous range in all of Calandra. And somewhere in those mountains, if I was reading Ransom's cuff correctly, was Allesaria.

"Damon always wanted to live in the countryside," Sally said, smiling as she plopped the roll of dough into a cast-iron dish. She covered it with a lid and carried it to the hearth, sliding it onto a rack so the bread could bake. "It's taken some getting used to. We only go to town every few months for supplies. In the winter, it will be even less. But we both thought it might be safer during the migration if we weren't in a city full of other people. The couple who lived here before us survived two migrations."

She went to the center of the room and tapped a carpet with her foot. "There's a tunnel here that leads to an underground cave. There's fresh water, and we'll stock the cellar with supplies. It's large enough that we'll be comfortable with the baby. By next spring, he'll be old enough to stay underground."

Except the migration wasn't coming next spring. The crux scout in Ellder meant the migration was months—or worse, weeks—away. The crux horde would be here before winter.

"You should prepare now. Don't wait."

Her eyebrows came together. "But it's not even winter."

I opened my mouth to tell her about the crux scout, but before I could warn her, Evie emerged from the bedroom, dressed in the bloody, dirty nightshirt she'd worn before her bath. "Evie, what are you wearing?"

"My shirt." She looked down at the stains, then to Sally. "Can I have my pants?"

Sally nodded, moving to the line where they'd hung all night to dry.

I stood and took them from her, then waved Evie into the bedroom, closing the door before kneeling in front of her with the pants in my lap. "How about we wear the clean shirt you slept in last night?"

"I wanna wear this one."

"It's too dirty." I lifted the hem, but she pushed my hands away and stepped back.

"Evie—"

"This is my shirt."

The shirt marred with Zavier's blood. "You can't wear this, little star."

"Yes, I can." She stomped her foot and crossed her arms.

I closed my eyes, summoning strength for a fight that would hurt. "Take it off, Evangeline."

She shook her head as tears filled her big, gray eyes and she backed away. "No."

"I'm sorry," I whispered, and this time when I reached for the shirt, I didn't let her push me away. "I'm so sorry."

"No!" she wailed as I stripped it off of her and tossed it aside.

She kicked and squirmed, fighting me every moment as I swiped the clean shirt from the floor. Her hands pushed at my jaw, and her head whipped back and forth. But somehow, I managed to get the shirt over her head.

"I'm sorry." I repeated the apology over and over, hoping she could hear me through her screams.

By the time the clean shirt was on, she was a sobbing mess, her whole body shaking and limp as the fight drained from her body. "I want Papa and Luella. I wanna go home."

"I know you do." I hauled her into my arms, rocking her in my lap. "I know."

She crumpled, burying her head in my shoulder.

As long as I lived, I'd never forget the sound of her heartbreak. It went so deep, it etched itself on my bones.

The burn in my throat, the sting in my nose, was unbearable. I bit the inside of my cheek to keep from crying.

Not yet. I'd have my chance to break down, but not yet. Not in front of Evie.

Beyond the bedroom, the door opened and closed, Sally likely leaving to give us some privacy. The sweet smell of baking bread infused the house. A horse whinnied outside. And Evie cried and cried until finally, she slumped in my arms, hiccupping as I dried the last of her tears.

When I helped her stand, she took a long look at the discarded shirt on the floor. For a moment, I expected her to try to put that shirt on again.

I wouldn't have the strength to rip it off her a second time.

But she left it on the floor, her shoulders drooping, and shuffled to where Faze was licking his paws. She hefted him into her arms and carried him to the cot, curling up on the pillow with her back facing me.

I didn't blame her for being mad. I'd be angry with me, too.

Snatching the filthy shirt from the floor, I left her alone and returned to the main room, where Sally's loaf of bread was cooling on the table.

The house was stifling, the air thick with grief and guilt. Gods, I needed air. I marched outside, jogging up the steps and into the field of grass. My body felt too hot, my heart beating too fast, my chest too tight.

What did I do? How did I ease her pain?

If only Ransom were here. She needed him.

I needed him.

The cool Turan air filled my lungs but did nothing to chase away the fire in my throat. Tears pricked at the corners of my eyes, and the sting in my nose was twice as sharp as that from Voster magic.

Don't cry, Odessa. Not yet.

"I lost my parents when I was a child." Sally came to stand beside me, her gaze fixed on the snowcapped mountains in the distance. "It will take time, but eventually, she'll find her way through the sorrow."

"She needs her mother." My voice wobbled. "I'm a poor replacement."

"Oh, I don't know about that." Sally took the shirt from my hands, holding it up to the morning sunlight. "You know, we might be able to salvage this. Damon gets horrible stains when he's working with cattle. I've got a soak that works wonders on dirt stains."

"It's not dirt. It's her father's blood from the night he died."

Sally didn't so much as blink. "Well, let's see what I can do."

If she managed to get those stains out, if she could save Evie's shirt so my little star had a piece of home, I'd be eternally grateful. "She has a stuffed rabbit. Its name is Merry. Would you mind trying to clean it, too?"

With a nod, she left me in the field and returned to the house.

No sooner had her footsteps faded than a tingle crawled up my neck and the hairs on my forearms stood on end.

I groaned, knowing what I'd find when I turned. One night without Voster magic wasn't enough of a break. I scratched at my forearms, rubbing at the crawling sensation. On a sigh, I turned my back to the breathtaking view and found Brother Dime walking my way.

His hands were clasped in front of him, his burgundy robes swishing in the grass and over his bare feet. He came to a stop a few paces away, bowing at the waist. "You will stay today to rest. Then you will continue on. Brother Skore will accompany you and keep you safe. I will be leaving now. The High Priest is expecting me, and I've delayed long enough."

"You're leaving?" I resisted the urge to clap.

With Brother Dime gone, maybe we could slip away from Skore. Escaping one priest had to be easier than two. And now that I had a better idea of where we were, Evie and I could make our way to Perris and hire a ship to take us to Quentis.

"Do not test Brother Skore's patience. Stay with him," he warned, like he could read my thoughts.

I nodded. "Of course." *Not.*

He studied me long enough that I started to squirm, but then he bowed again to leave.

"Wait." I held up a hand, but it was shaking so badly I dropped it to my side. "You said Ransom was loyal to the High Priest and made it seem like a fault. But you're going to meet him?"

"We all have our role to play."

Shades, these vague answers were about to make me rage. "What role are you playing? Be specific. Is Ransom in danger?"

"This is not the time for questions."

"Then when? You're leaving. This is my last chance. What do you want from me? Why couldn't we sail to Quentis?"

He turned and started walking away.

"Why did the High Priest ask about my mother? Why can I feel your magic?" I called both to his back, knowing he'd ignore them.

He did.

"I need to learn the old language."

That seemed to get his attention. He stopped and glanced over his shoulder, holding my gaze for three pounding heartbeats. "Brother Skore will teach you."

"How? Can he even talk?" Or was he going to teach me a nearly dead language by blowing wind gusts in my face?

"He speaks when necessary."

That didn't make me feel better. "He's terrifying."

"Yes." Brother Dime smiled. Well, the Voster equivalent to a smile. He looked marginally less creepy and frightening. "We will meet again, child."

"Can't wait," I deadpanned as he walked to the barn, where Damon emerged, leading his horse.

I tilted my face to the blue sky, watching a puff of white clouds limned by yellow sunlight float by as the sound of a horse galloping away filled my ears. As it faded to nothing, I closed my eyes and traced the scar on my palm.

I miss you, Ransom.

Another shiver ran down my spine, like I was being watched. I turned to find Brother Skore behind me.

With a gasp, I took one step, then another, putting some distance between us. He'd snuck up on me without a sound. Not a hint of his robes brushing the grass or his feet on the dirt. Could he levitate like the High Priest?

The sleeves of his robes were so long they covered his fingertips, the hems fluttering in the slight breeze. He didn't blink as he stared down at me. He didn't so much as move.

"Um, Brother Dime said you'd be taking us to Quentis."

Skore said nothing.

"And he said you could teach me the old language."

Still no reply.

Well, if he could speak, I guess this wasn't one of those *necessary* moments.

But creepy. Definitely creepy.

"I, um…" I backed away another step, hooking my thumb over my shoulder. "I'd better go check on Evie."

It took until I was in the house, sitting beside Evie at the table as she inhaled a piece of bread, to realize that the reason Brother Skore had snuck up on me was because I hadn't felt his magic.

Not a tingle. Not a prickle. Nothing.

If he was weaker than other Voster, maybe there was a

chance we could actually escape. We'd ride from the Axmar Mountains to the coast. If we could get to Perris, then I could find a ship to sail the Krisenth. And maybe, just maybe, find my husband.

Ransom had promised to find me, here or in the shades.

Well, not if I found him first.

7

CASPIA

The sea breeze tangled my hair into knots and flipped an errant curl into my eyes. My hands gripped the ship's wall, my nails digging crescents into the wood as I fought the temptation to turn away from the bow and look over my shoulder to Showe.

Dawn's chill was fading as the sun lifted higher and higher above the Marixmore.

My stomach was as knotted as my hair, my insides churning, not from the constant rocking of the ship on gentle waves but from the great unknown stretched across the sea. There was nothing but endless waters and clear skies.

But something was out there beyond all that blue. Something calling me closer.

The tug in my chest felt stronger. Steadier. Like every beat of my heart was a reminder that I was traveling in the right direction. It was exactly how Emery and Saskia had described the lure of the ritus.

Divine, give me strength to endure the journey ahead.

I might not be seasick, but I was already homesick. By now, Xandra would have already barged into my room, clapping twice to rouse me from bed. Had she alerted Aunt Oleana that I was gone? Had she delivered my letters? Had she read her own?

Were we still in view of the city? If I turned, could I still see Nelfinex? My nails dug in deeper, to the point of pain, refusing to let me turn.

We'd sailed through the moon, and I'd stayed rooted to this very spot, staring into the darkness. Even when Cap had offered to show me my quarters belowdecks, I hadn't wanted to move.

He'd promised my room had a lovely view out of the back of the ship. But I didn't want to watch my home disappear, so I'd stayed here instead, eyes aimed forward.

"Cap!" a man shouted. "Got a problem."

A commotion stirred behind me, bootsteps thudding on the wooden boards as the sound of a struggle came from the main deck.

The sound of the woman's yelp made me stand taller.

I was supposed to be the only woman on this ship. Before I'd hired Cap for this voyage, he'd made it a point to inform me that his crew was entirely male.

It hadn't been a warning, simply a statement. He'd assured me I would be safe, that these men would be respectful. I'd caught enough wary glances when I walked onto the ship that I was certain this crew had a healthy fear of the Starling.

Even a Quiescent.

"Let me go," the woman ordered.

No. My heart stopped. She wouldn't dare.

Except she would. I knew that voice as well as I knew my own.

I released the ship's wall and turned toward the scuffle.

Two men dragged Xandra across the deck.

She was dressed in black pants and a matching vest belted at the waist. A dark cloak hung loose over her arms and shoulders.

Apparently, we'd both donned the same attire to sneak out of the palace.

"What's this?" Cap asked, coming down from the quarterdeck, where he'd been at the helm.

"A stowaway, Cap." One of the men gripping Xandra's arm sneered.

She could break out of that hold and have him on his back before he could blink, but she was playing nicely.

Cap's eyes narrowed as he came to a stop in front of my cousin. He crossed his arms over his bare chest, biceps flexing.

Most of the men on the ship had stripped off their shirts this morning, though none were as brawny and built as Cap. He stood at least three inches above the rest, his body honed from the physical exertion it took to run this ship.

"Stowaways are thrown overboard," he told her. "Unless they can pay for passage."

Xandra's gaze swept up and down his body, and the sly smile that stretched across her mouth made me huff a dry laugh.

Cap had every right to toss her into the ocean depths. He looked like he might be tempted, too. But was she frightened? No. Not Xandra. She looked at him and saw her next lover.

"Then I guess I'll have to pay." She gave both of the men still caging her between them a pointed stare.

After a nod from Cap, they released their holds.

She flipped back the fabric of her cloak, revealing the elfalter bands wrapped around her biceps. "How many?"

Cap grinned. "All of them."

"Half," she countered.

He took a step closer, bending until his nose nearly brushed hers. "All. Quiescent."

"Say please." She snapped her teeth like she was about to bite his mouth.

Cap laughed, his blue eyes locked on hers. "I say we throw her overboard."

The men clustered around them gave grunts of agreement.

Xandra's smile only widened as she stripped off her bands, placing them one by one into his wide palms. "All of them it is."

"Welcome aboard the *Cirrina*. Your name?"

"Do you really need it?"

"No." He winked at her, then jerked his chin for the men to get back to work while he returned to the wheel.

Xandra stared at Cap's retreating form, her gaze locked on his muscled ass, before she smiled and sauntered my way.

I pitied the man already.

By the time we reached wherever it was we were going, she'd have crawled under his skin and into his bed. She'd probably leave here with all of her elfalter bands and his heart in her pocket.

"I should order him to turn this ship around." I crossed my arms as she ascended the stairs. "You could at least have the decency to appear guilty."

She walked straight into my space and wrapped me in a hug. "Guilty for what?"

"You're impossible." I sighed and hugged her closer.

When we finally let each other go, we went to the bow, turning our backs to the crew to talk quietly. My fingertips skimmed the wooden wall, finding the crescent grooves I'd gouged with my nails.

"You should not be here, Xandra."

"Neither should you, Caspia."

"This is my ritus."

"What if it's my time, too?"

I stared out at the ocean ahead, feeling that tug in my chest. For her sake, I hoped she felt the same call. "Is it?"

"No," she whispered. "Not yet. Maybe not ever."

"I'm sorry."

She shrugged. "I've made peace with it. If the gift has not graced my blood, then at least I'll take this journey with you to wherever you must go. This is more than your ritus, isn't it? You're going because of the vision. To seek vengeance for Emery."

"Yes." I was too exhausted from a sleepless moon to pretend otherwise.

"Then this silver-eyed man will face us both." She took my hand, clasping it between hers.

The ritus was a journey each Starling took alone. Having her along wasn't at all customary. Aunt Oleana would insist that Xandra return to Nelfinex.

But maybe our customs needed to be broken. Maybe the Divine knew we'd be stronger together.

"Do you know where we're going?" she asked.

"No, but I feel it."

"So that pirate will just sail at your command?" She twisted to look over her shoulder and grinned. "I wouldn't mind giving him a few orders myself. He is…wow. Do you want me to stay out of his bed?"

I laughed, something I hadn't thought possible this morning. "Better you sleep in his bed than crowd me in mine."

Xandra leaned in and kissed my cheek. "This is why you're my favorite cousin."

I closed my eyes, resting my head against her shoulder. "I'm glad you're here."

"Me, too."

Our quiet moment together was interrupted by a shout from one of the crewmen.

"Marroweels. Starboard side. Two of them."

The crew burst into action, unhooking harpoons and spears from where they'd been mounted on the walls.

Xandra and I shared an eye roll before she walked to the starboard side of the ship to lean over the wall, her arm extended toward the water.

I went to the port side, taking up a similar stance.

Waves beat against the ship's hull. The spray tickled my palm. And then sapphire scales tipped in turquoise broke from the water's surface.

The marroweel rolled along the ship, its spine dipping in

and out of the water. An iridescent white fin glimmered as it caught the morning sunlight.

The creature swirled, diving deep before it surged up from the depths, crashing through the surface with the bone that extended from its skull. It was a female, sleek and refined compared to her male companion. She touched my outstretched hand with her nose before diving back into the water. Then she surfaced again, once more seeking the stroke of my palm.

My cousin's laugh sounded across the deck as the male marroweel on the other side of the ship came up for a playful nudge against Xandra's hand.

"Starling," one of the men whispered from over my shoulder.

Not Starling. Not yet. But Starling blood filled our veins. And after the ritus, that blood would let us take on the shape of any creature in the world, including this beautiful ocean beast.

The sailors were smart to fear the marroweels and their five rows of razor-sharp teeth. But their weapons wouldn't be necessary, not with Xandra and me aboard this ship.

The Divine had bonded our bloodline to the creatures of this world. I'd never once feared an animal, no matter how dangerous they might be.

The marroweel returned again, her scales rippling as she rolled them against my hand.

"Swim free, beauty," I murmured as she dropped below the waves, not to surface again. Then I turned from the wall, shaking the water from my hand, the droplets landing on the deck.

The crew, all armed and ready for battle, stared at Xandra and me with slackened jaws and stunned expressions.

Cap stood behind them, his gaze locked on Xandra. A coy smile played on his lips.

They were going to be insufferable, weren't they? Divine willing, my quarters did not share a wall with his.

He let out a short whistle. "Back to work."

The men obeyed, and as they stowed their weapons, I returned to the bow, closing my eyes and letting the sun warm my face.

"Do you think Emery turned into a marroweel to swim alongside Max's ship?" Xandra asked.

"No." I smiled. "She loves to fly too much."

"I hate flying," Xandra said on a dry laugh. "I can't believe I said that out loud, but it's true. I hate it. Hara took me once. She laughed the entire time, and all I could think about was how badly I wanted the ground beneath my feet. If I ever go through the ritus, I want to change into something with a little more bite."

"A marroweel?" I asked.

"Depends on how things go with your pirate." She gave me a mischievous grin.

"Oh, I think he's your pirate now."

"Was it intentional, choosing Max's brother?"

I scrunched up my nose. "I didn't think you'd notice."

"Please." She huffed. "Give me some credit. They look exactly alike. Are you hoping Max might have told Cap where he and Emery went?"

"Yes," I admitted. "That, and Cap agreed to do this without many questions."

"Do you think he's searching for Max while you're looking for Emery?"

"It's possible."

Xandra tapped her fingers on the ship's wall. "Let's say your vision is wrong. That Emery wasn't killed by the silver-eyed warrior. And let's say that we find her and Max."

I didn't like the seriousness in her voice. Or where she was going with this hypothetical scenario.

"What if she doesn't want to leave him? What if she refuses to come home?"

"I pray to the Divine my vision is wrong," I told her. "But

if it's not, and if she won't return with us, then I don't know. I hope, for Graciella's sake, she does."

I hoped, for Graciella's sake, that Aunt Oleana was wrong about Max's influence over Emery.

Oleana believed Max had corrupted Emery's fidelity to the Starling. That he'd poisoned her mind against our family and traditions.

Maybe my aunt was right.

Max was not Graciella's father, nor was he Nelfinex. He was from Beesa, and though he'd left his homeland as a child when his parents deserted their country, they were our sworn rivals.

I had faith that Emery would not be deceived by a handsome face. She was five summers older than me and had always shared Oleana's pragmatism. She was realistic and logical in almost every way, usually agreeing with our aunt on most topics.

The only exception was my visions.

When I was five, I dreamed of a theft in the palace. A man disguised as a Royal Blade had stolen one of the bejeweled elfalter eggs on display in the queen's auditorium. The robbery had been such a shock that the entire castle had been abuzz. I'd told Emery of my vision and described the man. He had a long, jagged scar that cut from his ear across his cheek. When my aunt's Blades caught the thief, he had that scar.

When I was twelve, Saskia was called to her ritus. Two lunes after she left, she still hadn't returned. We'd all begun to fear that the rite had taken her life. Then I'd had a vision of my sister in the desert, flying over the western sands. She returned two suns later.

Other visions had come and gone, some I could prove and others I could not. But Emery had always believed I had a special gift to see glimpses of the past. She believed my visions were more than mere dreams.

It was the only thing I'd ever seen her argue with Aunt Oleana about. Then Max came into her life. And the arguments became a constant.

I didn't blame Emery for needing an escape. But I wished Graciella had not lost a mother. I wished I still had my older sister.

"Do you think she went to find the swift's mating grounds?" Xandra asked. "She was always curious where they went. Maybe that's where she met the silver-eyed warrior."

"It is forbidden."

"All the more reason that she might have gone there. Simply to spite Oleana."

Every generation, the swift left Nelfinex to breed. They flew across the Marixmore and returned to lay their eggs.

The swift were only born once every thirty summers. The mystery of where they went to breed was one never solved. Maybe they simply flew to the edge of our world and back. The few times a Starling had attempted to follow the flock, the shifters had never returned.

In my lifetime, it had always been forbidden.

"But Emery didn't leave during their migration," I said. "She wouldn't know which direction to fly."

"Unless Max had an idea."

The Starling weren't the only ones curious where the swift migrated. If they'd found a place unknown beyond the horizon, it might be an opportunity for the Beesan king to expand his tyranny to a foreign land.

"I don't know what to think about Emery. All I know is that I mourn for her. And in my heart, it feels as if she's gone."

"Then our quest remains unchanged. Vengeance."

I nodded. "Vengeance."

The silver-eyed warrior's suns were numbered.

A yawn stretched my mouth as a fresh wave of exhaustion crashed against me like water against the ship.

Xandra put her hand on my shoulder. "You should get some rest."

"What about you?"

"I also need some rest." She batted her eyelashes, then turned to scan the deck. "I guess that means I'll have to talk to that pretty pirate about my sleeping arrangements."

8

ODESSA

"'A man with golden hair stands on a...'" I studied the next word in the book, trying to translate it from the old language. "Clelvi'if-selfayd."

Brother Skore urged his horse closer, peering at the page. The sting of his magic was worth his help in translating this journal. "Cliffside."

"Cliffside," I repeated. "Got it."

With a grunt, the priest moved away.

Skore had begrudgingly agreed to teach me the old language, and for the past three days, if he wasn't instructing or correcting me, he was his normal, silent self.

We'd started deciphering this journal the day Brother Dime left Damon and Sally's house. The lessons were short—not only was there a limit to how long I could stand being around his magic, but Brother Skore seemed equally bothered by my company.

Though not bothered enough to leave us alone so we could escape.

Since we'd left the cabin, the only time he gave Evie and me space was so we could relieve ourselves in the trees—he made sure to always keep Freya in those moments.

So while I bided my time and waited for an opening to bolt, I was learning the old language.

Thankfully, it wasn't all that complicated. It was more of a dialect that Calandrans had shortened and simplified over time.

We'd made it nearly halfway through this journal, and I stumbled over words less and less frequently. There was a music to the old language, a cadence I'd started to hear when I read it aloud or whispered phrases to myself.

Mostly, I struggled with the handwriting in the journal. Some pages were clear and crisp, the elegant, swirling scrawl a work of art. But on others, the writing was sloppy and smudged. The pages were wrinkled, too, like Luella had spent more time studying some than others.

"'A man with golden hair stands on a cliffside,'" I continued. "'A ship is anchored in an ocean bay, the waves rocking it back and forth. Seven circles of women sit huddled together on the deck, their heads bent in quiet prayer. But one woman with unbound red hair stands apart from the others. She keeps post at the stern, watching as the last rowboat of her sisters pushes away from a sandy beach beneath the cliffs. Only when those women are aboard, nestled in their own prayer circle, does the woman look to the golden-haired man. The call to raise the anchor rings out, mingling with the caw of seabirds. Tears stream down her face. The man stands on the cliffside until the sun sets, crying for his beloved as she sails into the unknown.'"

Like most of the tales in this book, the story was short. But reading it took forever as I paused to interpret the sentences and squint at the illegible sections of script.

Cathlin had said the book read almost like a person's dreams. Like *Sonnet's Ninety*.

I wished my friend was here to talk about it with me. To help me understand how Luella had taken inspiration from these tales to create an elixir that contributed to the most deadly and dangerous infection our continent had ever known.

Was Cathlin alive? Had she survived the night of the crux in Ellder? Gods, I hoped so. I signed the Eight, praying that one day, we'd meet again.

"Do you think she ever came back to the man with golden hair?" Evie asked, staring at the journal in my hands.

"I think so."

Evie thought about it for a moment. "Me too."

In truth, I had no idea if they had ever seen each other again. But right now, I needed to believe in lovers reunited. That the man had found his beloved before they went to the shades.

"I'm hungry," Evie muttered, looking to Brother Skore. "Can we stop?"

He didn't reply.

That meant no.

"That means no," Evie mumbled, making me laugh.

Day by day, she was clawing her way back to herself. We still had plenty of tears and sad moments, but my brave, sassy girl was breaking through her sorrow.

"When we get to Quentis, you'll get to meet Arthalayus," I said, hoping to distract Evie from her hunger.

"Who's that?"

"My brother. We call him Arthy. He's about your age, and I bet you'll be friends."

It was a small hope for us both. We were clinging to small hopes at the moment. Anything to look forward to. Anything to keep us going until we reached Quentis.

I closed the journal and tucked it into my satchel. I'd learned the hard way that reading too much while riding meant a miserable headache and dizzy spells. "How about another story? One I read about in a book of myths and legends? Did Cathlin ever tell you the tale of Sora?"

"No. Who's Sora?"

"Sora was a woman who sailed across the realm. She was gone for one hundred years, and when she returned, she brought with her creatures we'd never seen before."

"What kind of creatures?" Evie twisted to look up at me. "Animals? Or monsters?"

"Monsters," I whispered. "In Sora's story, they were created by a powerful god. A god we don't know. And she brought them to Calandra."

Evie gave me a sideways stare. "Luella told me that monsters were created by the Six."

"They were."

"But who is this other god? What's his name?"

"I'm not sure. I only know of the Eight. Maybe his name was Harry. Or Hank. Or Herman."

"Herman?" Evie dissolved into a fit of giggles that filled my heart.

"Okay, maybe not Herman."

Sora's legend was just a story, likely a farfetched children's tale. But if it earned me a laugh, then I'd spend hours listing silly names for a make-believe god.

"I bet Luella would know. She knows lots." Evie faced forward and hummed. "I miss Luella."

"I miss her, too."

Keeping Luella's death a secret felt more and more like a lie, but I couldn't bear to add more to Evie's grief, not yet.

Evie didn't even know she'd lost her mother. To her, Luella had always been a caregiver and a teacher. When the time came to tell her the whole truth, I wanted it to come from Ransom.

There were secrets upon secrets wrapped in this girl's identity.

She had no idea that Ransom was her brother. That she was the daughter of the king and queen of Turah. And she didn't know that Zavier was not her real father.

Hell, Zavier wasn't even his name.

It was Dray.

Dray was Ransom's cousin, and because of their resemblance, he'd been the prince's royal double for over a decade. Yet I couldn't seem to make myself think of him by any other name than Zavier. The name might have been given to Ransom, but it belonged to his cousin.

Zavier was the man I'd thought I'd married. Zavier had introduced himself to my father as the crown prince. Zavier was Ransom's most loyal ranger.

But he was not a prince, nor was he Evie's father.

That was King Ramsey, a man I loathed with every fiber of my being.

Someday, Evie would need to know the truth. But I was in no hurry for that day to come. Not when it meant she'd lose her papa all over again.

"Do you think we'll ever see Damon and Sally again?" she asked, tearing me from my thoughts.

"I hope so."

And I hoped someday, we could pay them back for their kindness and hospitality.

Sally had made sure our bellies were full, and she'd managed to get most of the bloodstains out of Evie's shirt—only a hint of discoloration remained. Even Merry, the fuzzy rabbit with floppy ears, looked as good as new.

Damon had spoiled Freya, giving her grain and a bath. He'd found a set of saddlebags so that I didn't have to carry everything in my satchel. And when it was time for us to go, they'd sent us on our way with spare clothes, food, and canteens for water.

Without gold or coin, the only way I'd been able to repay them for their generosity was with a warning. As I bid Damon farewell, I'd told him about the crux scout and urged him to prepare for the migration sooner rather than later.

The day we left their cabin, we rode around the southernmost tip of the Axmar Mountains. That night was the last I'd slept beneath the Turan sky.

We'd crossed into Ozarth today and had since been traveling along the other side of the Axmars. The landscape was much the same as it had been, an evergreen forest at the base of towering, jagged mountains. But it wasn't Turah, and all day, I'd had this nagging feeling that we were going the wrong way.

We were too far from home.

And to get to Quentis, we had a long, long way to go.

Evie tipped sideways, holding on to the saddle's horn as she craned her neck to stare up at the trees. She scrunched up her nose.

"What?" I asked at the same time I caught an acrid scent. "Brother Skore, is that smoke?"

He lifted a finger to his thin lips, then veered off our current path, riding through the trees.

The scent grew stronger as we followed. Past trunks and limbs, a slight haze rose in the distance.

Skore was leading us straight toward it.

"Is that a good idea?" I whisper-yelled.

He kept riding.

I frowned, gritting my teeth as we followed him toward the smoke. It got thicker and thicker, enough to singe my nostrils and make Evie cough. Then, with a gust of magical wind, it was gone, floating up past treetops and into the azure sky.

With the smoke cleared, a fire came into view, orange flames bright against the brown-and-green landscape. A loud *pop* boomed off the trees, followed by a constant crackle.

A woman with stringy gray hair tossed a heaping pile of pine needles on a blaze built as tall as Brother Skore. She wore a dingy tan dress that might have once been white. The sleeves were gone, cut off at the shoulders to reveal thin arms and pink, wrinkled skin.

She stared at the fire as a cloud of gray smoke billowed, oblivious to us riding up behind her. Another *pop* snapped her out of her trance, and she hurried to a nearby blanket, swaying as she walked. She dropped to a seat beside a wicker basket, a pail of water, and a knife.

Brother Skore held up a hand for me to stop as we drew

close enough to feel the heat from the fire. He dismounted his horse, tossing me the reins as he walked toward her.

The woman finally noticed him. The corners of her mouth turned down as she looked at the Voster and extended an arm.

There was blood on her wrist, two dark streams trickling from twin puncture wounds.

Brother Skore took a step closer, but she waved him away and twisted to remove the lid on the wicker basket.

With her uninjured arm, she lifted out a rope.

No, not a rope.

A snake.

Evie tensed in front of me, her body leaning deeper into mine.

The reptile didn't coil or slither or worm to get away, because, as I saw when she finished lifting it from the basket, it was missing its head.

"Where there is poison, there is a cure." The woman set the snake's body in her lap and faced the fire. "It's not hot enough."

My stomach dropped.

Not because of her wound or the dead snake, but because I knew this. I knew what happened next.

It was a tale I'd translated from Luella's book the first night after my first lesson in the old language from Skore.

Once the woman deemed the fire hot enough, she'd throw the snake's body at the edge of the blaze. And after it was charred and black, she'd take the blistered, charred skin and apply it to the bite.

Where there is poison, there is a cure.

"Gods," I murmured, unable to tear my attention away from the woman as she waited until the pine needles were ash and the flames grew so hot Freya shied away.

My eyes watered from the shock and smoke.

Just as I'd read about in that journal, the woman forced herself to her feet, staggering as she walked to the fire. The heat from the flames blew back her hair, singeing the fragile ends. With both hands, she tossed the snake's body into the base of the fire.

Her legs tangled in the skirt of her dress as she backed away, but somehow, she managed not to fall. Without taking her eyes from the burning snake, she went to the blanket and retrieved the knife and pail of water. She waited one breath before rushing toward the fire, so quickly I feared she'd fall into the flames.

Brother Skore must have thought the same. He reached for her, but she was already on her knees, slicing away the snake's crispy skin.

"Close your eyes." I reached to cover Evie's eyes, but her hands were already there.

She twisted, burying her face in my chest as I cupped my hands over her ears.

I pressed hard, hoping to block out the old woman's agonizing scream as she laid the snake's skin on her arm, her flesh sizzling from its heat.

She sank down on the dirt, sobbing as she endured the pain. Then, when she'd had enough, she plunged her arm into the pail. The noise from the fire was too loud for me to hear the hiss of steam, but I saw the brief puff of white before it evaporated.

In the story from the journal, the woman lived on for years, surviving a bite that should have killed her. She taught her granddaughter about poisons and cures. She wore the wrinkled, mottled scar on her forearm with pride.

But the story told nothing of how Brother Skore hauled her away from the fire, laying her on the blanket. How he soothed the burn by summoning water from a nearby tree and encasing her injury in ice.

The only Voster I'd seen conjure ice was the High Priest.

Who exactly was this traveling companion of mine? Where did he rank in power with the brotherhood?

I'd thought he was weaker than Dime when I hadn't been able to feel his magic, but maybe I was wrong. Maybe he had a stronger leash on his powers.

He left the woman, asleep on the blanket, as the flames began to subside, the fire already collapsing in on itself. As he walked to his horse, he didn't spare her a backward glance.

If not for that journal, I would have refused to leave her side.

But she would live. I knew it down to my bones.

Without a word, I followed Skore as he turned his horse around, retreating from the fire and back into the forest.

By the time my head stopped spinning, I could no longer smell the smoke except for the scent that lingered in my hair and clothes.

"Brother Skore, I read—"

He silenced me with a raised hand and tapped the pointed shell of his ear. It was as colorless as his skin and shaped closely to his head.

I closed my mouth, straining to hear whatever had caught his attention.

Click. Click. Click.

Terror, cold and paralyzing, ran through my veins. My heart stopped. *No.*

Freya tensed. Faze squirmed in his carrier like he knew exactly what those clicks meant.

Bariwolves.

"No." I tightened my grip on both Evie and Freya's reins.

Brother Skore's lip curled. "They're hunting us."

"Dess?" Evie whimpered.

"Oh, gods. What do we do?"

"Ride. Hard." He pointed forward. "Go. Now."

"Hold tight," I told Evie, then with a tap of my heels to Freya's flank, I gave my horse her head.

She took off running, picking up speed as we weaved through trees, my heart pounding as loudly as her hooves.

I risked a quick glance over my shoulder to see Skore following behind, his light-blue robes whipping around him.

It was all too familiar and all too unwelcome. We were exposed, and this time, it wasn't a grizzur chasing us but a pack of wolves.

"Dess!" Evie cried as a streak of black came out of nowhere, the wolf emerging from the trees, teeth bared.

Shades, it was huge. The top of its back was as high as the bottom of my saddle. No matter how many times I saw the monsters, their size, their teeth, and their claws always took me by surprise.

The front half of the beast was covered in black fur molded over powerful muscle. Its rear half was covered in scales, each with a protruding, razor-sharp spine.

These were monsters designed by the Six for one purpose and one purpose only.

Death.

I clicked my tongue and urged Freya faster, using every bit of strength to keep Evie and myself in the saddle with Faze squeezed in between.

The bariwolf changed course, running alongside us. With every stride, its spines contracted and flexed, and I knew that if we got too close, they'd slice into Freya's flesh.

I steered her away, hoping it was enough distance.

And only then did I realize the monster was playing with its food.

It was herding us.

It took me a moment too long to realize the bariwolf was pushing me toward another member of its pack. The other monster came racing for us on our other side, trapping us in the middle.

"No," I cried, searching for any way to break us free. My hands were full. There was no way for me to reach for my sword, not without dropping the reins, Evie, or both. All I could do was hold tight and ride.

A blast of wind so powerful it nearly flung me forward whipped past my shoulder, slamming into the oncoming bariwolf.

The beast lost its footing and rolled three times, slamming into a tree trunk. Its fur and scales were covered in dirt and needles, but it scrambled to its feet, its black eyes still locked on us as we sprinted ahead and into the forest.

Brother Skore sent another blast of wind to the bariwolf still giving chase, but it only faltered a step before it kept coming.

I rode as hard as I could, my eyes watering from the wind and tears. A gap in the trees ahead gave me hope that we might have a chance to break away.

Except three more monsters appeared, coming from the exact place we were racing.

A pack of five.

We were dead.

Freya came to a skidding stop, rearing up so quickly we nearly toppled out of the saddle.

It was only Evie's hold on the horn and my hold on her that managed to keep us seated until Freya was back on all fours.

The bariwolf on our heels growled and lunged, but the moment its feet were no longer on the ground, Skore sent another blast of wind that knocked the beast off its trajectory and sent it flying to the side.

I yanked on the reins, steering Freya away from the oncoming wolves and kicking her back to a run.

When bariwolves had attacked in Ellder, the High Priest had killed them with spears of ice. We needed spears. We needed anything, because this wind of Skore's was not working.

We raced through the trees, and I didn't dare look back for fear the monsters would be right behind us. I kept riding, faster and harder, until the forest seemed to disappear ahead, opening to nothing but sky. Dirt and earth turned to rock, and I managed to pull Freya to a stop before she took us careening over a sheer ledge.

The drop wasn't all that far. It would be like jumping from a house's roof. But I knew we'd never stay on Freya, and if we fell, the wolves would pounce.

Brother Skore stopped at my side, staring over the ledge. He must have come to the same conclusion because we turned our horses around at the same time.

Five snarling bariwolves prowled our way, their ears pinned and teeth bared.

If we'd been trapped before, we were fucked now.

"Save us, Oda," I prayed, a tear sliding down my cheek.

Even if I drew my sword and dagger, there was no way I'd be able to fight five monsters.

Gods, I hated that this would be our end. That Evie would feel pain. That I wouldn't see Ransom's face one last time.

"I love you, little star." I dropped the reins and wound my arms around her, holding her close. "I'm sorry."

"I love you, Dess," she cried, her shoulders shaking as she clung to me.

"Praise Ama. Beloved Mother," I prayed, "bring us to your shores of starlight. Grant us quick deaths, Izzac, and let us know peace, dear Carine. Give our love to those we leave behind, Arabella, and take us quietly into your shade."

I held tighter to Evie and Faze, closing my eyes as I waited for the strike.

But it never came. And a heartbeat later, the growling stopped.

I sat straighter, opening my eyes to see Brother Skore's arms stretched wide.

He splayed his fingers, and something changed with the wolves.

They seemed to withdraw. Or try to withdraw. They were frozen in place, like statues pinned to the earth.

Brother Skore murmured something I couldn't understand, and then a wounded howl came from the pack.

One of the wolves collapsed, its legs curling as it writhed on the ground. Two more dropped, then the fourth and fifth.

Their whimpers and screams were born of pure, undiluted pain as thin streams began to trickle from their eyes and nostrils and mouths.

Blood.

It didn't pool on the ground or seep from their bodies. It formed a web in the air, veins that floated and twined as they flowed toward a single source. Brother Skore.

"By the mother." I held Evie's face to my chest, keeping her eyes hidden as I watched, unable to look away.

The Voster leeched the monsters' blood, drawing it from every opening in their bodies.

Thin, viscous rivers flowed past his outstretched hands and over his head, the horror disappearing somewhere over the ledge.

The bariwolves kicked and twitched as their bodies were sucked wholly dry.

Skore didn't stop until the monsters lay lifeless on the ground, eyes empty and sunken. Five husks.

Only then did the blood stop flowing.

The last drops floated overhead. The last green drops.

Those monsters were infected with Lyssa. It had spread to Ozarth.

After everything Ransom's rangers had done to keep the infection from moving past Turah's borders, it hadn't worked. And if Lyssa had made it this far, it was only a matter of time before the infection stretched across Calandra.

His worst fears were about to come true.

When the crux came, it was inevitable that they'd be bitten. They were vicious without Lyssa. With it?

It could mark the end of our realm.

Even if we found a cure, it might be too late.

The notion was as terrifying as the Voster at my side.

I stared at Skore, unable to speak. A shiver rolled down my spine, and the shock of what I'd just witnessed dulled some of the sting of his magic.

"Do all Voster have that power?"

Brother Skore dropped his arms, not answering. His shoulders slumped as he heaved a breath. But whatever exhaustion he felt was short-lived. He held my gaze for only a moment before he sat tall and urged his horse forward, riding past the monsters left to decay.

My stomach lurched.

"Who are you?" I whispered.

A gust of wind hit my back.

It was answer enough.

9

CASPIA

My fingertips traced the crescent grooves in the ship's wall. They were deeper now from so many moons spent at the bow, staring out over the water. And their once rough edges had been smoothed by my constant touch.

Hopefully, when this voyage was over, Cap wouldn't be too angry that I'd marked the *Cirrina*.

The two moons hung low in the sky, their light dimming as dawn neared. It had been suns and suns since we'd left Nelfinex, and we had yet to see land. Yet still, the ritus called, as steady a beat as my heart.

The harsh clip of boots on the deck behind me was my only warning before Cap appeared at my side. His jaw was still clenched, and he looked as angry this morning as he'd been last moon.

The linen fabric of his shirt pulled tight over his wide shoulders and muscled arms. It had grown colder the farther we'd sailed, and the suns of the crew going shirtless were gone.

"Good morning." Maybe some cheer would defuse his anger.

"We're turning back," he barked, crossing his arms over his chest.

So much for cheer.

On a sigh, I turned away from the sea and squared my shoulders for a repeat argument with the pirate. "Not yet."

"There is nothing out here, Princess." He stretched an

arm over the ship's wall, shaking a pointed finger at the endless expanse of waves and water. "This is the farthest I have ever sailed from Kenn, and there is nothing."

"There is. I can feel it." The pull of the ritus was getting stronger and stronger each passing sun.

"I don't give a damn what you can feel. We've been sailing according to your feelings for too long. We're past the halfway point on our rations. If we don't turn back now, you'll condemn us all to death."

"One more sun."

"No. We turn back now."

I shook my head. "One more sun."

"You've said that three suns in a row."

"Yes, I have. Please, just give me one more. Tomorrow, I won't argue." I pressed my fingertips to my forehead. "You have my vow."

He frowned. "Your vow will mean very little when we die of thirst."

"You may have my water rations for your crew."

"It won't be enough."

"It might. And it could rain."

"By the grace of the Divine," he muttered, running a hand over the beard he'd grown during our time at sea.

Surrounded by water and yet we were running short.

Cap wouldn't place the blame on Xandra, not after all the time they'd spent together, sharing his bed. The man was entirely infatuated with my pretty cousin. But she was another person on this ship who needed food and water. A person who they had not planned on having for this journey.

The food shortage had been an easy enough problem to solve. The men fished to replenish the stores. But fresh water was not as easy to come by without rain, and the barrels stored belowdecks were beginning to wane.

We needed a storm. Or we needed to reach land.

Was this the direction Emery had gone with Max? Cap

didn't know where his brother had taken my sister. But there had to be something out here. We couldn't turn back, not yet.

"Please. One more sun?"

He growled. "One. Tomorrow, I will not ask."

I sighed. "Thank you."

Cap muttered something under his breath before he marched away, barking orders at a crew as grumpy as their leader.

We were all more than ready to get off this ship.

I covered a yawn as Xandra joined me at the bow, taking Cap's space. She leaned her elbows on the wall and stared at the horizon.

We were dressed the same, in charcoal pants and vests. It was cool enough this morning that she'd donned one of Cap's jackets.

"Did you sleep?" she asked.

"No."

Sleep had become a luxury as of late. Visions plagued me the moment I closed my eyes, nearly every moon. The people and places I saw were unfamiliar, and the visions came so frequently that the details were beginning to blend together.

All I wanted was for them to stop.

"What did you see?" Xandra asked.

"There was a boy sitting on a floor. He had silky black hair and eyes so dark they shone blue. All around him were books. He picked one up and tossed it into the air. But the book didn't fall. It floated higher and higher."

"Floating books?" Xandra raised her eyebrows.

I nodded. "Floating books. Maybe that one was just a dream and my imagination running wild."

"Did it feel like a dream?"

"No." There was a realism to the visions that made them sharp and clear. Dreams had fuzzy edges, and the moment I woke, they began to fade. The visions lingered like memories.

"Then I had a vision of a young man in a forest. He was

hunting with a bow and arrow. His cloak was as green as the trees. He came across a golden cat snared in a trap. The trap's teeth had pinned the beast's leg and severed its toe. No matter how hard the cat struggled, it couldn't get free. The man approached the cat, and the beast whipped its barbed tail, warning him away. It hissed, flashing sharp, black teeth. But the beast had been trapped for suns, and its strength was fading."

I'd never seen an animal like the cat from my vision. There were rumors of golden cats that lived in the southern countries in Kenn, but beasts like the one in my vision didn't roam the Nelfinex wilds. Its coat was leathery and sleek, the color as pure and vivid as the yellow light of sunset.

"It collapsed," I continued. "And when the man approached, it did not struggle or try to fight. He pried open the trap and backed away with his hands lifted in surrender and peace. The cat did not attack him, but before it wandered off, it nudged its own severed toe toward him. Then it disappeared into the forest. The man took the black claw and wore it around his neck."

I'd seen him return home from that hunt to his lovely young wife. I'd watched as he became a father to an adorable boy with brown eyes and curly black hair. The man spent his life smiling until he eventually grew old, his black braids speckled with gray.

"He wore the claw for the entirety of his life. He was never sick or feeble. He was never in pain. Then one sun, he gave the claw necklace to his grown son. The father then left his home to explore a nearby forest. He sat down beside a tree to rest and died."

"So this golden cat's claw prolonged the man's life?" Xandra asked.

"Possibly. Or maybe it kept him strong. Or maybe it was just a claw he wore around his neck as an ornament. I don't know. I don't know what any of these visions mean."

A crease formed between her eyebrows. "It is the ritus. It has to be."

"Or too many suns aboard this ship have addled my mind." I pinched the bridge of my nose. "Tomorrow, Cap is turning us back."

"I'm impressed. You talked him into another sun?"

"More like begged. We're close. I can feel it."

Xandra exhaled, looping her arm with mine. "I can feel it, too."

My face whipped to hers. "You feel it? The ritus?"

A shy smile spread across her mouth. "I feel it. Finally. It's strange. I can feel the very blood moving through my body. It's urging me forward. And there's a different beat in my chest, like another heart."

"A thrum."

She nodded. "Yes. It feels like a reward for going in the right direction. Even the idea of turning around…"

"Hurts." That gentle, soothing strum vanished, and in its place was a sharp twist. An ache so uncomfortable it would be impossible to ignore.

The ritus called, and we were driven to answer. "I made Cap a vow. This sun is the last. Then we must turn back. He's worried about the crew."

"*You* made a vow. I did not." Her smile widened. "If we need more time, we'll see how persuasive I can be."

"My biggest regret is not packing cotton for my ears."

She laughed, her cheeks turning pink as she glanced behind us to where Cap stood at the stern. "He is incredible. Did I tell you that his cock is pierced along the shaft? Divine, it feels good."

"Stop. Now. I beg you," I groaned. "It's bad enough sharing a wall with his quarters."

She laughed again, louder and carefree. It had been a long time since I'd heard her laugh without restraint. Either Cap and this relationship of theirs was more than a way to entertain themselves on this journey, or it was the relief that the ritus had finally called. Probably both.

"You and Cap. It's more than a tryst, isn't it?"

She shrugged.

Yes, it was more.

I leaned my head on her shoulder, another yawn pulling at my mouth.

"You should try to sleep," she said.

"Okay." Maybe I was finally so exhausted that I'd crash.

I let go of Xandra's arm and made my way to my quarters. The room was cramped with a small bed and chest where I stashed my few belongings. After pulling off my boots, I settled on top of my thin quilt, closing my eyes as I relaxed into the pillow.

Sleep came easy.

So did the vision.

...

A man with brown hair and a broad frame sits astride a bay stallion. In front of him in the saddle is a young girl with gray eyes. She smiles up at him and beckons him closer. Once she has his ear, she whispers something that makes them both laugh.

Still smiling, he urges the horse forward with a tap of his heels. The pair rides away, trotting through swaying grasses, weaving a path toward indigo mountains capped in white.

...

The sound of the girl's laugh echoed in my ears as I stirred awake. The final frame of the vision lingered like a portrait painted on the wooden ceiling.

I'd never seen mountains so blue or tall. They towered into the sky with jagged peaks. What was the white on their tips? Sand? Or rock?

The landscape of this vision was familiar from others. But the man and the girl were entirely new.

He was handsome, with a chiseled jaw and straight nose. The girl was one of the most beautiful I'd ever seen.

Something about her reminded me of Graciella. Maybe it was that they looked to be about the same age, six or seven summers. Maybe the familiarity was the girl's infectious laugh.

Graciella's laugh never ceased to make me smile.

I pressed a hand over my heart as it ached for my niece. For my home. Even for my aunt.

Was Oleana angry at us? Was she worried? Already, we'd been gone far longer than was normal for a ritus. Had she dismissed us like she had Emery? Or was she still holding out hope that we would return as Starling?

The *thrum* in my veins surged so strong it pulled me up to a seat. It swelled higher and higher until my chest felt so full, I could barely breathe.

Thrum. Thrum. Thrum.

I lifted off the bed, like invisible wings pulled me to my feet. To my toes. My arms floated up at my sides, weightless. My fingertips tingled.

My gasp filled the room. And the thrum went quiet.

I sank to my heels, frozen as I waited for it to return, but it was gone.

My gaze shot to the ceiling as a shout came from above. A single word that explained why the pull was gone. "Land."

10

ODESSA

Brother Skore added another branch to our campfire, sending orange sparks into the night. They vanished beneath the bright glow of the twin moons.

He sat cross-legged on the other side of the flames, his robes spread out around and beneath him. He placed his wrists on his knees and opened his palms to the starry sky as he closed his eyes.

Was that how the Voster slept?

Tonight was the first time he'd stayed close after dark, and though the sting of his magic made it impossible for me to sleep, I was grateful for his protection.

Evie was asleep, draped over my side, while Faze had claimed the other.

After the bariwolf attack today, the ride to our camping site had been a blur. It had taken hours for my hands to stop trembling and for Evie to stop shaking. When the fright finally started to fade, a bone-deep exhaustion had taken its place.

When Brother Skore stopped riding, informing us we'd camp here for the night, I'd practically slid off Freya's back.

Shades, I was tired. Sore. Cranky. Scared.

Was it my fault the monsters had hunted us? Were they drawn to us in the forest because of whatever was wrong with me, the thing that made my eyes gold and allowed me to feel Voster magic?

If I asked Brother Skore, he might give me an honest answer for a change. An answer I wasn't quite ready to hear.

Now what? As much as I wanted to escape Skore, his display of magic today was something I couldn't ignore. If he could leech the blood from those monsters, what was stopping him from doing that to Freya? To Faze?

To Evie?

Just the thought made my stomach roil. So much for making an escape. But I couldn't risk them. And if not for Skore, we'd all be bariwolf food.

I closed my eyes, tracing the scar on my palm.

Where was Ransom tonight? Was he on his way to Quentis? Had he already reached the coast and hired a ship to sail the Krisenth? Gods, I only hoped that he wasn't hurt, trapped in the infirmary in Ellder and fighting for his life.

The not knowing was beginning to fester like a putrid wound, growing and sucking away hope with every passing day.

He's alive.

Every time I began to doubt he was alive, I'd say it over and over again in my mind.

He's alive.

"By the grace…" Brother Skore's murmur made me open my eyes. His words were so low I couldn't make out the rest of his prayer. His lips and tapered chin moved, but otherwise, his body was entirely motionless. His chest didn't even seem to rise and fall as he breathed.

It felt like an intrusion, watching as he prayed, so I stared into the fire as a yawn tugged at my mouth.

"You should sleep." Skore's dark-green eyes were waiting when I glanced up.

"Who do you pray to?"

"The Divine."

"Oda?" There were some who considered the Father the greatest of all the gods, though I preferred to speak to Ama, the Mother.

"No. The Divine."

"Is that a god?"

"There is only one god, girl."

A chill raked down my spine, and I fought the urge to sign the Eight.

Was this god of his the deity who'd granted him such extraordinary powers? That allowed him to manipulate wind and water and blood? To suck the life out of a monster by his own sheer will?

Another shiver trickled over my shoulders, and I pulled Faze closer for his warmth.

"There is a story in that journal written in the old language about a woman and a snake. It's told exactly how it happened today. How is it possible that I read a story before witnessing it with my own eyes?"

Skore held up a finger, twirling it in a small spiral. The smoke from the fire mimicked the motion, swirling above.

"Magic?" I guessed.

"No. By the grace of the Divine."

"I don't know what that means." I sighed, too tired to be angry or annoyed. "You and Brother Dime share the same talent for answering questions without actually giving answers."

He sent a puff of smoke into my face.

I batted it away and glared across the fire. "Where are we going?"

"Orson Canyon," he said.

It felt precious, asking a question and getting an answer. Like a gift.

Too bad I didn't have a godsdamn clue where Orson Canyon was.

It took four days to reach Orson Canyon.

The endless hours of riding through the forest meant

those four days blended together with nothing to set them apart, and I was so tired of staring at trees, I could scream.

The rocky canyon would have been a welcome change of scenery except for the fact that it was creepy as hell.

We rode through a narrow channel bordered by sheer rock walls that towered above us. It was as if Oda had struck the earth with all his might, cleaving it in two. There were stretches of the gorge where we had to ride single file and the tips of my boots skimmed along the cliffs.

The light was dim but not dark. Was the Evon Ravine like this? I'd never traveled to the gulch that separated Quentis from Genesis, but it was said to be terrifying and as black as death at the bottom.

Brother Skore rode ahead of us, his body swaying with the movement of his horse.

In such a tight space, his magic should have been punishing. I should have been able to feel it zinging off these rock walls.

But from the moment we entered the canyon, the stinging had stopped. It should have been refreshing, except I couldn't stop worrying about *why* I couldn't feel his magic. Was he channeling it somehow? Stockpiling it up to use later?

Could the Voster even do that?

I nudged Freya to get closer, hoping it would encourage Skore to pick up the pace. But he seemed entirely unbothered by the fact that we were trapped.

We could be attacked by monsters and have nowhere to run. Though I guess he wouldn't be afraid, not when he could suck the blood from every living creature in his presence, myself included.

"I don't like this place," Evie said, struggling to sit still.

"I don't, either." I shivered, gritting my teeth against the sensation that the walls were closing in on us. "How much longer?"

Skore ignored me.

"Are you sure you're going the right way?" Shouldn't we be leaving the mountains for the Ozarth plains that would take us south to the Harrow River?

I glanced over my shoulder as the hairs on the back of my neck stood on end.

There was no one and nothing behind us. Above was only gray rock. But I couldn't shake the feeling of being watched.

"Brother Skore, where are we going?"

The sting of his magic hit me at the same time as a gust of wind.

I grimaced, rubbing at my arms. "You could have just answered my question."

"I did." His voice echoed off the walls.

Bastard.

Evie stuck out her tongue at his back.

Desperate for a distraction, I pulled the journal out of a saddlebag, flipping it open to an entry I hadn't read yet. After the incident with the gray-haired woman, I'd been more reluctant to plow through the journal, almost afraid of what I might learn. But I forced myself to read at least one story every day, only sharing them with Evie once I'd deemed them safe.

...

A man with three raw gashes on his face skins a beast hanging from an iron hook. The animal's hide is a shade of lime green, almost as bright as the sun in some places. The scutes fit together in raised, hard squares.

Blood drips from the beast's severed neck. Its head has been separated from its body, lying on the ground. Its open maw is full of jagged white teeth. The creature's long tail is draped over the hook and falls the length of its body. Even then, it's still long enough to curl in a circle on the ground. Its four legs are short, its feet tipped in gray claws.

Three claws, like the three cuts on the man's face.

The knife the man uses to flay the creature is sharp, but the hide is so thick and hard, he has to constantly stop and sharpen the blade. He starts at the tail and makes his way to the head. He slices and cuts, taking to the carcass the way the creature took to his face. Without mercy.

Only when the skin is hung on a line, the blood washed away, and the leather left to dry does the man finally set down his knife.

The hide becomes fabric. The man sews an overcoat and cobbles a pair of boots. He creates a mask to cover his scars and conceal the empty socket of his lost eye. And the next time he encounters a lime-green beast, it does not attack. For in his disguise, the creatures cannot see the path he walks.

...

An alligask. That must be the monster described in this entry. I closed the book, deciding to keep this story to myself.

Evie sighed and squirmed. "How much longer?"

I opened my mouth to wager a guess, but Brother Skore beat me to it.

"We're nearly there. Listen," he said.

A faint rush of noise tunneled down the canyon's base. The sound was like wind rustling through leaves, except there were no trees.

"What is that?" Evie asked.

"Water." Waves but without a pulse. The steady flow was either a roaring river or a waterfall.

The trail's incline steepened, shifting me back in the saddle. The rock walls became shorter as we climbed, opening up to the sky above and letting in more light. And with every step, the sound of the water grew louder until it was so fierce that Evie cupped her hands over her ears.

I held my breath as we reached the mouth of the canyon, passing between the rock columns onto a platform.

Across a hole so deep I couldn't see the bottom was a waterfall that towered to the sky. The water fell from another sheer cliff on the opposite side of the hole. It formed a curtain of white that vanished into an abyss.

Freya shied away from the edge, following my tug on her reins.

The air was damp, the spray cool on my face. It smelled of wet stone and moss.

The noise wasn't as loud now that we were out of the canyon, but as Brother Skore's mouth moved, I couldn't make out his words.

He continued on, riding a narrow path on the outer rim of the hole, seemingly unbothered by the fact that a single misstep would have us falling to our deaths.

"Shit," I hissed, urging Freya to follow Skore's mount. *Don't slip, girl. Please, don't slip.*

As we approached the waterfall's cliff, Evie held out her hand, fingertips dragging along the rock as she leaned away from the hole and open air.

Every time Freya lifted her leg, I held my breath and tensed.

Skore was as relaxed as if he were riding through a flat meadow of wildflowers.

My grip on the reins tightened as we drew toward the waterfall, the path narrowing until we were all but hugging the rock. The closer we got to the water, the faster my pulse raced. An ache bloomed behind my eyes, and each drop of water that hit my face felt like it cut, like they were ice crystals biting into my skin.

In a blink, Brother Skore disappeared in the spray, swallowed by a cloud of mist.

"Dess?" Evie clung to my wrists.

"Damn it." I pulled back on Freya, making her stop. There wasn't enough room to turn around, and a quick glance over the edge made my head spin.

We had no choice but to go forward, so I relaxed my hold on Freya and let her follow the priest.

Drops poured down my face, falling into my eyes, blurring my vision. Water soaked through the fabric of Faze's carrier, making him wiggle. I held tight to Evie, bending over her in an effort to save her from the onslaught of water as we rode behind the falls.

One moment, we were being soaked in a torrential rainstorm. The next, the water stopped, the light dimmed, and I wiped my eyes dry to see a rounded cave.

"What are we doing here?" I shouted over the noise.

Skore swung off his horse and pointed to a tunnel I hadn't noticed at the back of the cave.

The darkness and the noise only seemed to make the pounding in my head louder, and I was in no mood for his silent orders.

"Answer the question. What are we doing here?"

He waved for me to get off Freya.

I shook my head.

His lip curled.

My nostrils flared.

"There is something in this cave I need to retrieve," he said, shouting over the roaring water.

"Great. We'll be here when you're done."

"You're coming with me."

"Why?"

"Because I cannot find it. And I need your help."

I brushed water droplets from my forehead. Now it made sense why we were going the wrong way. Was he ever going to take us to Quentis? "Why didn't you tell me this before?"

"I'm telling you now."

I gripped the reins to keep from giving him an obscene gesture. "After I help you find whatever it is that you're looking for, we are going to Quentis. No more unexplained detours. Understood?"

It was the first time I'd had any leverage in this relationship. If he wanted my help, then he was going to make me a promise.

"Agreed." He pointed to the tunnel. "Come."

"Take Faze," I told Evie, pulling him out of his carrier.

A drop fell from the ceiling and landed on his nose. He

growled and jumped to the ground before she could take hold.

"Faze, no." Her voice echoed in the cave.

"He's okay." My legs felt weak and stiff as I dismounted, my head spinning faster. My boot slipped on the wet rock, and before I could catch myself, I crashed. Hard. Pain exploded along my hip as I hissed.

"Dess," Evie cried.

"I'm okay." I took a breath, letting the ache dull. Then I slowly got to my feet.

Skore's magic felt different in here. It didn't sting on the surface, crawling up my skin. Instead, it seemed to drive straight to my bones, making me dizzy and sick.

"It's slippery," I told Evie. "Be careful."

She nodded and held tight to my shoulders as I lifted her out of the saddle. Once she was on her feet, she hurried to Faze as he lapped water from a puddle.

After a fortifying breath, I held out my hand for Evie. "Okay. Let's go."

"Evangeline stays with the horses," Brother Skore said.

"What? No. I'm not leaving her alone."

"This is no place for a child."

"Then you should have thought about that before bringing us here," I snapped.

"Please." It was the first time he'd used that word, and it surprised me enough to listen.

What the hell was down that tunnel?

"Will she be safe here?"

He nodded.

Fuck. I sighed and dropped to a crouch as Evie came to my side.

"No." Her eyes were blown wide as she shook her head. "I don't wanna stay by myself."

"We'll be fast. I promise." I pushed a lock of wet hair off

her forehead. "Can you be my brave girl and watch Faze and Freya for me? Make sure they don't wander off?"

She shook her head, clutching my hand with both of hers. "No."

"You can do this." I kissed her head, then wiggled my hand free. "We'll be right back."

The corners of her mouth turned down as tears filled her eyes.

"We'll be right back." I stood and stepped closer to Skore, leveling him with a glare. "If anything happens to her, no amount of magic in this realm will save you from my wrath. I'll rip your fucking heart out."

He dipped his chin. "No harm will come to the girl."

"Good. Let's go."

With a swish of his robes, he set off through the tunnel's opening.

I followed, and before we were out of sight, I glanced back to Evie.

Tears spilled down her cheeks as she clutched Faze to her chest.

Watch over her, Ama. Keep her safe.

It didn't take long for the tunnel to narrow. The ceilings lowered enough that Brother Skore had to crouch as he walked. The sensation of his magic was so strong, so draining, that I swayed, pressing a hand against the wall.

"What do you feel?" he asked.

"Your magic." I gritted my teeth, breathing through my nose. The light from the cave was all but gone, and I couldn't see a thing but the faint outline of his bald, white head. "Do you have a torch?"

"We won't need one."

"Can you see in the dark? Because I sure as hell can't."

A growl came from the priest, sounding so much like Faze it was uncanny. "Keep walking."

I obeyed, skimming one hand on the wall as I tested each step before planting my foot.

It took ten paces before a strange glow came from ahead, and after another ten, I understood why we didn't need a torch.

Veins of iridescent aqua blue threaded through the rock, illuminating the space.

"What is this?" I pulled my hand away from the wall, seeing the blue on my fingertips. It was almost like paint.

"I do not know. In all my years and travels, I have never found anything like it. But it will light our path."

"If you've been here before, why do you need me?"

He waved me forward, taking me to a place where the tunnel split in three.

"Which one?" I asked.

"That is for you to decide."

Now it was my turn to growl. "Speak plainly."

I was drenched and cold. The throbbing in my head seemed to get worse with every passing moment. If he wanted this miserable adventure to continue, he was going to have to be specific.

"Follow the pain," he said.

"What?"

"If you can feel my magic, you can feel the magic in this tunnel. Follow it."

This was why he'd wanted me. Because I could feel magic. "What is this place?"

"Ancient," he answered.

A chill snaked down my spine.

"The longer you fight me, the longer that girl is alone."

"You're a manipulative bastard," I hissed, but the warning worked. I marched past him and down a tunnel.

It wasn't until the ache behind my temples began to ease and the pressure in my chest lessened that I realized I was alone. That the only sound was my ragged breath and pounding heart.

Follow the pain.

There was no pain, not down this tunnel. So I retreated to the entrance where I found Skore waiting.

I took the second tunnel, walking alone until the pain eased. "Damn. A little help, Daria?"

If there was ever a time I could use help from the Goddess of Luck, it was today.

The air felt different as I made my way down the third tunnel. It was hot and thick. Every inhale felt shallow, like my body was protesting the path.

Guess I was on the right track.

"It's this way," I called back to Brother Skore.

He appeared moments later, his body still hunched to not scrape his head on the tunnel's roof.

"Now what?" I asked.

"Keep going."

We walked deeper and deeper, winding around corners and stepping over puddles. The eerie blue light began to hurt my eyes, and the headache became so unbearable I bent forward and retched.

"Ugh." I wiped spittle from my mouth and sagged against the wall. My groan was swallowed by the caves. I summoned my strength, and when the tunnel split again, I took the path to my left. When the pain didn't stop, I trudged forward.

Another divide. Then another and another. Each time, I'd test the path, and if the pain stopped, I'd retreat.

It was a maze designed to make me lose my mind. There was no way these tunnels were created by the water. Someone must have carved them into the cliffside, using the waterfall to hide the entrance.

What was this place? I saved that question for when I wasn't coming apart, my insides twisting and every fiber of my being screaming to *leave, leave, leave.*

This place was wrong.

My toe caught on a rock, and I toppled forward, landing with a *crack* on my knees. Tears sprang to my eyes. "Fuck."

"You must keep going."

"Going where?" I shouted, using the surge of fury to stand. "What the hell is down here? We'll be lucky if we don't get lost."

Silence.

I let out a frustrated scream that I hoped hurt his ears as much as it did mine. Then, only because I knew he wouldn't let me leave and there was a girl waiting on me, I kept going.

We walked and walked, so far I was sure we'd step through to the other side of the mountain. The tunnels were like worm trails, winding in all directions.

My legs were so heavy that each step felt like ten. Until I turned a corner and stopped.

The end.

The tunnel came to a close with a wall of solid rock. There was nothing but blue lines and nowhere else to go.

"There's nothing here." Brother Skore's disappointment filled the chamber. "You took a wrong turn."

"No, I didn't." I rubbed my temples. "I did exactly what you asked. Now take me back to Evie."

He lifted his hands, frantically feeling over the wall like he was searching for something.

"Please," I begged, and when my plea went unanswered, I sank to the floor, leaning against the rock as the Voster examined the tunnel.

There was a small pool beside me, about the length of my arm. Its surface was black and smooth like so many others we'd leaped over or stepped aside. I reached for the water, skimming my fingertips over the glass.

Piercing agony ripped through my hand, shooting up my arm like a slash from the sharpest blade.

I screamed, scrambling away from the water as I clutched my wrist against my heart and sobbed.

Brother Skore was in front of me in an instant. "What did you touch?"

"Please," I begged, tears leaking free. "Please let me go."

Brother Skore glanced to the puddle, then back at me. "Well done, girl."

Before I could shy away, he touched my hand.

And the realm went black.

11

CASPIA

Cap was the last man to board the *Cirrina*. He climbed a rope ladder as the rowboat that had ferried us all to this land was hoisted to the deck.

Once both were aboard, he walked to the stern and looked to the shore.

To Xandra.

She pressed one hand to her heart and stretched the other out at her side, her arm extended straight with her palm facing forward. Then she bent at the waist in a bow.

A Nelfinex farewell to a loved one.

Cap mirrored the gesture. Then he touched the center of his forehead with two fingertips.

Xandra did the same. "I vowed I'd fly across the ocean and find him when my ritus was done."

"What did he vow?" I asked.

"To listen for the beat of my wings." Her chin quivered as he turned away and strode across the deck for the helm.

I took her hand, holding it tight as we stood together, side by side on a narrow stretch of sand. With waves lapping at our boots, we watched as the crew raised the ship's anchor. Tears dripped down her cheeks as the *Cirrina*'s black sails caught with wind.

Xandra sniffled, wiping her cheeks. "I cannot believe I'm crying over a pirate."

"You'll see him again." I put my arm around her shoulders, pulling her close.

"I hope so," she whispered.

Cap had offered to stay, but Xandra had insisted he return to Kenn with his crew. He would only be a distraction for her ritus. And if by some chance it took her life, she did not want him trapped across the Marixmore, far from his home.

We reached this foreign land two suns ago. The shore had been nothing but towering, rocky cliffs. It had taken hours of sailing along the coast to find this stretch of sand. By then, it had been too late to ferry over, so we'd spent a restless moon on the *Cirrina,* each person aboard anxious for dawn.

The crew had rowed to shore at sunup, the men armed with spears, knives, and harpoons, ready to defend against any attack. But all they'd found past the beach were lush green hills and a fresh stream to replenish their drinking barrels.

Once the crew had deemed it safe, Xandra and I had rowed over with Cap to explore.

I'd been ready to say farewell to the pirate and his crew, but Xandra had asked for one last moon. So while she and Cap slipped away to his quarters, I'd stood at the ship's bulwark, staring at this strange place.

Was this where Emery had come with Max? Was this land home to the silver-eyed warrior? Was this where my sister had died?

Soon, we'd find out.

The *Cirrina* was well on its way to the horizon when I turned away from the sea. The blades strapped to my arms and legs felt heavy as I trudged up the beach. But there was a comfort in wearing them again, knowing they would keep me safe until the rite was complete. The pack on my shoulders was stuffed as full as it had been when I left Nelfinex.

I walked in no hurry, enjoying the softness of boot sinking into sand, knowing Xandra needed a few more moments alone. By the time I reached the line of grass and started up a hill, following the stream, she was jogging to catch up.

The grasses beyond the beach were thick. Their green was

so vivid it almost hurt my eyes, and stomping through the knee-high stalks was like wading through water.

"What is this place?" Xandra skimmed the stalks with her fingers. "It smells like nothing I've ever known before."

I inhaled, holding the air in my nose. There were apothecaries in Showe with countless herbs and teas and oils and perfumes. But not once had I experienced a smell like this, cool and fresh and clean. Earthy, yet sweet. It lacked the spice and salt of Nelfinex.

"Do you think that since neither of us can feel the thrum any longer, now we're supposed to follow our noses?"

"Maybe." Xandra laughed, nudging my shoulder with hers.

"Are you nervous?"

"Yes."

"So am I."

Xandra took a step and tipped sideways, her shoulder crashing into mine before she caught her balance. "Vexx. Sorry. I am not used to walking on ground that isn't swaying beneath my feet."

"I feel unsteady, too." My knees felt wobbly and my legs weak. The sensation was strange enough that I stopped walking, giving myself a moment to adjust. "We should find a shelter before the moons rise."

"Where?" She shielded her eyes from the sun as she turned in a slow circle, taking in our surroundings.

The rolling hills of green were endless, stretching before us like another ocean.

"Where do you think we are?" I asked.

Xandra shook her head. "I don't know. I've never read about a continent other than Azzon or Eliam."

They were the two continents south of Kenn, both within a lune's sail. Except we'd sailed north.

"This must be where the swift migrate."

"If it is, Aunt Oleana is going to be livid when we get back."

Starling did not do the forbidden without extreme consequence. But that was a worry for another sun. We were trapped here until we went through the shift. Our only escape was to change and fly home.

A shiver rolled down my spine as the hairs on my arms stood on end. A sense of dread I couldn't explain made my stomach churn.

"Do we stay by the ocean? Or continue inland?" Xandra asked.

"Let's follow this stream and see where it leads us."

She nodded, then together, we set off through the grass.

We were dressed in matching pants and vests with our dark cloaks fastened around our shoulders. Xandra had left her curls loose while mine were fastened in a tight knot.

By the time the sun was directly over our heads, she'd pulled up her hair and we'd both shed our cloaks. The noise of waves crashing against cliffs had vanished, replaced by the swish of grass and the steady thump of our boots.

"My ears feel empty without the sound from the ocean."

"Mine, too." Xandra slowed to a stop and shook her head. "I can't seem to catch my balance."

"Neither can I." I dropped my hands to my knees, closing my eyes. The unsteadiness of my feet only seemed to get worse the farther we walked. But I'd never spent time aboard a ship. It would probably just take a few suns for my body to adjust to being back on land.

Xandra let her pack swing off one shoulder, taking out a canteen of water for a drink. "Divine, I'm dizzy."

"So am I." My head was beginning to ache. "Do you think it's the beginning of the ritus?"

"Maybe. If it is the start, do you think it will take long?"

"I hope not." My hands trembled as I took out my own canteen.

Each ritus was different, an experience unique to every Starling.

Emery told me once that she'd never been more scared than the sun she left for her ritus. But that was the point of this rite. We left alone so that we could give in to the fear and anxiety.

The ritus called so that it could eventually break us down.

We were stripped of our comforts and finery, drawn into the unknown, where we learned to embrace the fear. We let it transform our bodies into something powerful. Something fierce and bold.

The Starling could shapeshift into any beast of their choosing, though most chose the swift. Not only were they beloved and beautiful, but there was no creature in the world with as much might. The massive birds were gentle, affectionate, intelligent beings. And the Divine had gifted them with bodies of size and strength unmatched by any other.

But transforming into such a large animal came at a cost. Before we could take on the shape of a swift, we must endure agony.

Saskia warned me that the pain of the first shift was excruciating and slow. She said it felt as if her entire body was being turned inside out. Thankfully, it got easier after the first time, and after a few shifts, the pain became nothing but a brief pinch.

Xandra and I were no strangers to pain. Quiescents were pushed, both mentally and physically, with their training regimens so that our bodies were strong enough for the shift, our minds sharp enough to control the beasts we'd become.

"I'm scared of how much it will hurt." I was scared that I wouldn't survive it.

She put her hand on my shoulder. "By the grace of the Divine, give us the rite."

"By the grace of the Divine, turn us true." I finished the Quiescent prayer, then spun in an easy circle, gaze sweeping the surroundings.

Far in the distance, the green came to a stop, the hills

giving way to a line of tan cliffs. But there wasn't a sign of other people. Of a city or township. "It's so...empty."

"Where are all the people?" Xandra shielded her eyes with a hand, scanning the hills.

Showe was the largest city in Nelfinex. Every ten or fifteen summers, the wall was expanded to make more room for homes and buildings. Beyond the wall, towns dotted the countryside. On any road, in any direction, a person could walk from one town to another in less than a sun.

This place seemed entirely void of people.

"Let's head toward the cliffs and see if we can find a place to make camp," I said.

We filled our canteens in the stream, then set off for the cliffs. As they drew closer, the foliage became thicker, forcing us to weave past bushes and trees.

My pack got snagged on a branch, and as I tugged it free, another branch smacked me in the face.

"Gah." I drew my kukri and hacked it to the ground.

Xandra was short of breath, sweat dripping down her temples as she leaned on a tree trunk. "Thank the Divine we're almost there. My head aches."

"Just a little farther." I pushed on, taking the lead. Every step felt like my body was betraying me, expecting the motion of waves instead of unmoving dirt and grass.

A clap of thunder rolled from the rain clouds gathering, covering the sky in a haze of gray.

"We need to find shelter before it rains." The words were no sooner out of my mouth than the clouds burst, drenching our clothes, plastering the fabric to our bodies.

"Vexx," my cousin and I said in unison.

Water dripped from my hair and down my face, getting in my eyes and mouth, as we pressed on. The drops pelted my head and shoulders, and the next boom of thunder was so loud I flinched.

"Caspia," Xandra shouted over the noise. She pushed her

soaked curls out of her face and pointed to the cliffs. "Is that a cave?"

I followed her finger, squinting as I searched. A dark arch marred the otherwise light-colored rock.

Please, be a cave. We shared a nod, then changed direction, hurrying through the trees. The closer we got, the larger the opening loomed. Definitely a cave. It sat above a crumbling heap of boulders and fallen rock.

They shifted and slid as we climbed, the rain making solid footing nearly impossible. But finally, I made it to the top, reaching back to help Xandra crawl inside.

"Divine," I whispered, taking the satchel from my shoulders and letting it drop to my feet as I stared up at the towering ceiling.

The stone was a yellowish brown, like the cliffs outside. The cave was as wide and tall as the palace's grand vestibule. The scent of dank rock filled my nose as I took in the odd statues around us. It was as if the stone had liquefied, melting into piles, like candlewax before it hardened.

From the ceiling, cones and columns narrowed to tapered points, each dribbling water. The same cones covered the cave's floor, pointing upward.

"Teeth," I said. "It's like this cave has teeth."

And each tooth had a mirror. Each column on the ceiling dropped water onto its counterpart on the floor.

Where the columns met against the cave's walls, they formed a lattice maze, almost like twining roots and branches.

"What is this place?" Xandra asked, her voice echoing in the dark space.

"I don't know." I touched a fingertip to a column, testing its slick, smooth surface. "But I think we should stay in here until the rain stops."

Outside, it continued to pour in a thick sheet.

"We won't be able to light a fire," Xandra said. "It's too wet in here and out there. I doubt our clothes will dry, either."

"Probably not." I sighed, stripping off my cloak. I scrunched it into a ball to wring out the water. "Emery once told me that her ritus was misery and anguish."

Xandra laughed. "Well, then I guess we're doing it right."

"I guess so."

Let the ritus begin.

12

ODESSA

"Do the orange ones next." A sweet, musical voice pulled me from a dreamless sleep.

My eyes were slow to open, my lids heavy. Above me was a cerulean sky and treetops with green and yellow leaves.

The last thing I remembered was an iridescent tunnel and a black pool. Where the hell—

"Evie," I gasped, sitting up too fast. Blinding pain shot through my neck, turning my vision white. I winced and rubbed at the ache. "Ouch."

"Dess!" A small body crashed into mine, sending me flat onto my back again. "You're awake."

My arms wrapped around her as the pain faded and the spots cleared from my vision.

"You're okay?" I felt up and down her shoulders and back, her head and arms, making sure she was whole. "You're okay."

She climbed off of me, grabbing my elbow as she hauled me up to a seat. "You've been asleep forever."

There was a log behind me, a backrest to my bedroll. I sagged against it, blinking away the last of the fog as I took in Evangeline.

She looked...fine. Perfectly dry and alive and unscathed. She plopped down on my lap, her knees on either side of my legs. "I got kind of scared, but Brother Skore promised you'd wake up."

"I'm sorry." I tucked a lock of hair behind her ear, then took in our surroundings.

We were camped in a grove of pretty trees with white trunks and spade-shaped leaves. The grass around us was spotted with wildflowers. The horses were drinking from a stream that cut through the grove, and our saddles were hitched over the log at my back.

Seated on a log of his own, across a smoldering pile of ash and coals from last night's campfire, was Brother Skore.

"What happened? Where are we? And how long was I asleep?"

"Two days." Evie climbed off my lap and went to Skore, plucking a bundle of white flowers from his hand. Their stems were braided together.

Beside Skore on his log was a pile of orange blooms she must have picked from the field.

The apprehension she'd shown before the waterfall was gone. She seemed as comfortable around Skore now as she was around me. Still, I didn't want her anywhere near the Voster, not after what had happened in the tunnels.

"Evie. Come sit with me." I waved her back, breath held until she was at my side.

She handed me the white flowers as she knelt on my blanket. "These are for you."

"Thank you. They're beautiful." The relief that she was unharmed, that there was even a smile on her face, was as welcome as it was exhausting. Part of me wanted to curl up and go back to sleep. "Where's Faze?"

"Hmm." She tapped her chin as she scanned the grass, eyes narrowed. Then she cupped her hands around her mouth and let out a cooing noise, not quite a whistle, more like a birdsong.

A few moments later, Faze bounded over the log.

"Where did you learn to do that?" I asked, scratching Faze's ears.

"Brother Skore taught me. We've been practicing. Faze gets a treat when he comes."

She leaped up, and before I could grab her, she went to the priest, Faze following close behind. She took a piece of dried meat from Brother Skore's hand and gave it to the tarkin.

The entire time, the Voster's endless gaze stayed locked with mine.

"Why don't you get me another bouquet of flowers while I talk to Odessa?" he said.

She frowned but obeyed, trudging through the grass with Faze on her heels.

"What happened in the tunnels?" I asked once Evie was far enough away she couldn't hear. "What was wrong with that water?"

"The way you phrase your questions always interests me." Brother Skore stood, shaking out his robes.

"What. Happened?" I shoved to my feet but swayed, the blood draining from my head so fast I had to sit on the log so I wouldn't fall over.

"Rest a while longer. This is a safe place." He walked away and toward the horses, taking the rope around his mount's neck.

I stood again, slower this time, as he brought the horse over to his saddle. "Where are you going?"

"Follow this stream. It will take you south to Norcrest. If you leave soon, you'll be there by nightfall."

"Wait. You're leaving us?"

"Yes," he said. "I must go. I've already delayed too long."

It seemed too good to be true. I'd been dreaming of a way to escape. Now, we were free.

Lost.

But free.

"Wait." I rushed for his saddle to stop him from lifting it off the ground, but with a sharp sting of his magic, a gust of wind rocked me on my heels. "Where do we go after Norcrest?"

"South, across the Harrow. When you reach the bogs, you will find people who know the way to Quentis." He saddled his horse as he spoke, not sparing me a glance. "Do not delay."

We'd be gone as soon as I could load Freya. But if this was the last time I saw Skore, I wasn't losing my chance to ask about the tunnel.

Not caring how much his magic hurt, I marched to his horse and ripped the lead rope from the priest's grip. "What was in that tunnel?"

"Liberty."

A frustrated growl rumbled in my throat. "That's not an answer."

"Tell no one of the waterfall. Your father's life depends on your secrecy."

"What does the waterfall have to do with my father?"

He pulled the rope so hard I had no choice but to let go so it didn't rub my palms raw. We stood close enough his magic should have been uncomfortable at the very least, but other than that single moment, it was gone.

"Why can't I feel your magic right now?"

He raised a hand, bony fingers opening wide. One breath, I felt nothing. The next, it was as if a thousand spiders were crawling up my arms and legs.

I scrambled backward three steps, jaw dropping. "You can stop your magic. H-how?"

Brother Skore went back to saddling his horse. "There is a warrior in Calandra. A warrior who will save this realm. Find her."

It was almost comical that he was leaving me to traverse the continent alone yet still delivering orders. "Sure. Do you have a message you need me to deliver to this all-powerful warrior? Does she have a name?"

Surprise to no one, he ignored me.

Gods, my headache from the tunnel was coming back.

"I am not your enemy, girl."

I scoffed. "You touched me, and I was unconscious for two days."

"I'm letting you go, just as you asked. I ended your pain in that tunnel and brought you here."

"Where exactly is *here*?"

"We are half a day's ride from the waterfall. I brought you and Evangeline down from the mountain to rest."

Did he expect a thank-you? Well, he wasn't getting one.

"We will meet again," he said. "It is my destiny."

"When?" Not that I was looking forward to that reunion.

"After you fulfill yours."

It had been a while since my destiny and fate had entered the conversation. I hadn't missed it. The only thing I cared about for my future was that Evie survived and I found Ransom.

"Are you returning to the High Priest like Brother Dime?"

"Heed this warning." He looked down his hooked nose to make sure I was listening. "Stay away from the High Priest."

"But Ransom trusts him."

"You cannot."

I swallowed hard. "He asked about my mother. Why? Could she feel Voster magic, too?"

"Very few in the brotherhood knew your mother before she died."

"Did Brother Dime?"

"Follow the stream. Find the warrior." The sting of his magic returned, pricking my skin like needles and sending me back another step as he swung into the saddle. He kicked his bare heels into his horse's flanks. And then he rode past me, forcing me out of the way. Skore galloped through the grasses where Evie stood with two hands full of orange wildflowers.

Then, he was gone.

It should have been a relief. It should have loosened the knot in my stomach. Except now we were alone and vulnerable. The only person who could save Evie from a monster was me.

So we were not sticking around.

I hurried to the log and my blanket spread out over the ground, then quickly balled it up. "Evie, come on. We have to go. Get Faze."

She dropped the flowers and ran for the tarkin, scooping him up and bringing him over.

"Put everything in the saddlebags," I said, stuffing in the blanket. While she collected her things, I hurried to catch Freya and get her saddled, then I stomped out the last of the fire.

"Where are we going?" she asked as I lifted her onto Freya's back.

I turned away from the trees and toward the stream. "What happened in the tunnel? When Brother Skore came out?"

"He was carrying you," she said. "He put you on his horse and said he had to tie you up so you wouldn't fall. Then he made me ride Freya and carry Faze while he walked."

"Did you go back through the canyon?"

She nodded. "It was really scary at night."

"I bet it was." I gave her a sad smile, wishing I hadn't blacked out for so long. "Then what happened?"

"We came here, and he said we'd camp until you woke up."

"Other than me, did you see him bring anything else out of the tunnel?"

"No."

Damn.

"But he did take something out of his bag and sneak away to the trees last night. He thought I was asleep."

Pride swelled in my chest. Gods, this girl. My tiny little spy. "What was it?"

"Something round and shiny. Kind of clear, too. It was this big." She showed me with her hands, making a shape about the size of a melon.

An object that size could have easily been in the bottom of that pool in the tunnels. But if he'd had it with him, shouldn't I have felt it today? Unless he'd taken it into the forest and my body had finally recovered enough to wake once it was gone.

Was it a source of magic? Did it bolster his own powers? My stomach knotted at the realization I'd helped him find it in that cave.

"Okay. Let's get out of here." I climbed into the saddle behind her, settling in for another day's ride.

"Where are we going?"

"South," I told her.

"Where's south?"

I barked a dry laugh and urged Freya forward to follow the stream. "Your guess is as good as mine, little star."

13

CASPIA

Xandra clung to my hand as we staggered through a forest. Her palm was clammy, her face pale gray.

I stumbled a step, my ankle rolling, but her grip kept me from falling. My head was spinning so fast the world looked like a streak of green and brown and blue sky. My breaths were coming in shallow pants, and the sweat soaking my body did nothing to cool the fire raging in my veins.

For three suns we'd been trekking across this strange land, waiting for the ritus to change us. Xandra and I had worried the dank, moldy air from the cave had made us both ill, but maybe we should have stayed. With every passing sun, we'd both gotten sicker and sicker.

I'd hoped we'd find a shelter where we could rest until the illness passed. But the only thing we'd found were trees and more trees.

"I need to stop," I murmured.

Xandra released my hand, and like it had been the only thing keeping her on her feet, she dropped to the mossy forest floor. Her arms wrapped around her middle as she rocked back and forth, curling on her side. Tears welled in her eyes and cascaded down her cheeks.

My knees buckled, slamming into the ground as I collapsed. And just like Xandra, I curled into a ball on the wet, green earth.

It rained constantly, from thundering downpours to gentle drizzles. I couldn't remember what it felt like to wear dry clothing. We were soaked to the bone, but the water was a minor inconvenience compared to the pain.

Divine, it hurt. My insides were being shredded by invisible claws. My head was throbbing, every pulse of my heart was a hammer cracking against my skull.

Neither of us had been able to eat since that first moon in that strange cave. The dried fish we'd packed from the ship was untouched, though probably not so dry anymore. That moon, we slept against the slippery rock walls, and in the morning, we both woke to stomach cramps.

The first sun, we'd managed to gain quite a bit of distance, both of us pushing through the discomfort as we traversed past the cliffs and into this dense forest, hoping to find a town or village to rest and ask about a silver-eyed warrior. As we walked, I marveled at the intensity of the green, so bright and vivid it was unlike any forest in Nelfinex.

Now, the color was an assault to my eyes. It was as blinding as the noontime sun, and all I wanted was to find another cave where the darkness could block out this nauseating green.

Even when I squeezed my eyes shut, all I could see was green. All I could feel was pain. The cramping in my stomach was ten times worse than it had been in the cave. My skin was hot to the touch and every muscle sore. Breathing ached.

"I don't think this is the ritus, Xandra," I murmured. "What if something is wrong?"

"I don't know," Xandra whimpered.

"I'm sorry." A sob escaped my lips, but it hurt too much to cry so I swallowed the next. "I never should have brought us here."

We should be in Showe, in our palace, with our family.

"It is not your fault." Xandra reached to take my hands in hers. "The ritus called to us both."

"What if this is not the ritus?"

"It is. It has to be. We must endure it." Her eyes fluttered closed, the tears still streaking down her face as she began to cry. "Caspia?"

"Yes?"

Her breath hitched. "I don't want to die here."

"Neither do I." The pain was nearly unbearable as I wrapped my arms around her, holding her close as we both cried.

There was a reason it was forbidden to follow the swift to their migration lands. There was a reason no Starling came this far for the rite.

We were going to die here.

Never again would I return to my beloved homeland. Never again would I hear Graciella's laugh. Never again would I cuddle with Hop and pet his fluffy tail.

And Xandra would not have the chance to find Cap on the Marixmore.

We would die in this green forest.

We would be lost to the Starling.

"At least we are together."

"By the grace of the Divine." Xandra opened her eyes and gave me a sad smile as she cupped my cheek with her palm.

"By the grace of the Divine."

There was something wrong with her eyes. The gold hue was dull, and her irises had a milky-white sheen, like the flame within her was sputtering out. Like the life force in her blood was waning.

My fault.

If I'd never come on this journey, Xandra would be safe at home. She'd be in the mews this morning, stroking the soft feathers of the swift we were supposed to become.

Except there would be no shift. There would be no flying, not for us.

My tears blurred my vision. "I'm sorry."

Xandra's thumb stroked my cheek. "I'm not."

I rested my forehead against hers, and together, we cried

for the life we would not lead. Until blackness stole away the pain.

And erased the cursed green.

Xandra's claps woke me from sleep.

My eyes fluttered open, and for a brief moment, I was home. Warm in my bed with the spicy scents of Showe drifting through the castle's arched windows.

Except as I pushed up off the mossy earth and stared into the surrounding forest, the harsh reality came crashing back.

Home was across the world.

The noise came again, not Xandra's claps, but a string of sharp and crisp notes, like the click of a tongue. The clicks were so loud that they bounced off the trees and sent a chill down my spine.

"Xandra," I whispered, shaking her shoulder. "Wake up."

She groaned, curling forward around her stomach.

"Xandra, hurry." With the little strength I had, I stood, swaying on my feet. Then I bent to take her arm, jostling her until her eyes cracked open. I was too weak to haul her off the ground, but I managed a strong tug.

"W-what?" Her eyes fluttered open. They were milky white.

"Get up. Now."

She glared at me, like she'd been lost to a dream of her own. Like I'd stolen her away from Cap's bed on the *Cirrina*. But then the clicks came again, and she jolted fully awake. "What is that?"

"I don't know. But we can't stay here." With a grip on her hand, I helped her to stand.

Neither of us had bothered to take off our packs when we collapsed earlier, so with her hand in mine, we set off through the forest, weaving around rocks and stepping over branches, as those clicks seemed to follow us on our path, getting closer and closer.

The air was sticky and damp. The thick moisture made every breath a chore, and sweat dripped down my brow and into my eyes. "We should hide."

"Where?" Xandra panted. "There is nothing. Where are all the people?"

We were surrounded by trees, but their branches and trunks were too slippery to climb, not that either of us had the strength. Rocks and boulders were sprinkled through the trees, large enough to make stepping over them difficult. But they wouldn't conceal our forms.

Maybe we could pry up heaps of moss to cover our bodies. Except as those clicks got louder and louder, I knew that whatever was following us would not be easily fooled.

The sound was so close it rattled my bones.

Xandra trembled, her eyes meeting mine. "Caspia?"

I pulled my kukri from where it was secured across my spine. Xandra took a dagger from a sheath on her thigh.

"Ready?"

She shook her head.

"Run."

We tore off through the forest, stumbling as we ran side by side. Terror chased some of the haze from my mind as we pushed harder and faster.

If the clicks kept coming, they were drowned out by the roaring of my pulse and heavy, labored breaths. This forest was too thick for much speed. At our fastest, if something was chasing us, we would still be too slow.

Then, by the grace of the Divine, a narrow trail of brown interrupted the green. A road with twin wheel tracks cut through the trees.

So glad to see a clear path, I misplaced a step and tripped on a rock. My ankle rolled, my knee bent, and I flew forward, landing on the road, my face and belly sprawled on the dirt.

"Caspia." Xandra rushed to my side, taking my arm.

"I'm okay." Pain shot through my ankle, but I pushed it aside as I let her help me to my feet.

"Come on." Xandra looped her arm through mine. "Maybe this road will take us somewhere safe."

Every step was agony as I limped to hurry along, constantly checking over my shoulder. The clicks seemed to fade away as we clambered down the path, until the only sound was our ragged breaths.

"What do you think that was?" Xandra asked.

"I don't know." I slowed to a walk, pressing a hand to the cramp in my side.

"How is your ankle?"

It throbbed, and putting pressure on it sent a bolt of pain through my leg. "It's fine."

"Don't lie to me."

I sighed. "In the scheme of what hurts at the moment, the ankle is not on the top of my list."

"Fair." She planted her hands on her hips, tilting her face to the sky, looking past treetops and branches. The blue skies from this morning were being overtaken by gray clouds. "It's going to rain again."

"By the grace of the Divine, this road will lead to a town." I wasn't sure what kind of coin the people of this land would accept, but Emery's elfalter rings were in my pocket. Even though I hated the idea of giving them away, if sparing one meant survival, then so be it.

I limped forward, and Xandra fell into step at my side, moaning as she wrapped her arms around her stomach. "I think I'm going to ret—"

Click. Click. Click.

We stopped, turning slowly as the sound came from somewhere in the trees.

"Vexx," I whispered. We were fools to have stopped running. Fools to think we might survive.

Xandra drew a knife as a dark streak shot through the forest.

A four-legged beast leaped onto the road, its curved claws sinking into the earth. It stared at us with eyes as black as its hide.

"What is that?" A shudder ran over my shoulders as it took a step closer.

The creature was similar to the jackals that roamed the Nelfinex wilds, with a long snout and pointed ears. Though this animal was twice as large, nearly the size of a horse. Its fur stopped past its ribs, giving way to scales that rippled as it prowled our way. And each of those scales ended with a pointed quill.

Xandra took a step toward the beast, her hand shaking loose of mine.

"What are you doing?"

Her answer was to take another step forward.

The beast snarled and bared its white fangs, the spines on its back bristling.

She raised her hand, palm out like she was waiting for the creature to come closer so she could scratch behind its ears.

In Nelfinex, I would have been right beside her. The Starling did not fear beasts. But this was unlike any creature that roamed my homeland. It wasn't a fenek or marroweel or swift. And the sinking feeling in my stomach said this was not a wildling that any Starling could tame.

"Xandra," I hissed. "Stop."

"It's beautiful," she murmured, entranced by the strange jackal.

"No." I took a step with my uninjured leg, stretching out a hand to take hold of her elbow. "Something is wrong. They are not like the beasts from home."

As if to confirm I was correct, the animal lifted its head, pointing its nose to the sky. With its throat exposed and bobbing, it let out a series of those clicks.

A snarl came from the trees.

Xandra and I both whirled toward the noise. Another black beast prowled through the foliage, its teeth bared.

Those clicks were to call its pack. To hunt us from all sides.

"Xandra." With a yank on her arm, I pulled her out of her stupor.

She jerked, like she hadn't even realized I'd been touching her.

"Come on." I urged her backward.

There was no way we could outrun these creatures, not with my injured ankle and the weakened state of our bodies. But I wasn't sure we stood a chance in a fight against those claws and fangs.

Xandra's gaze shifted to me and past my shoulder, staring down the road. Her eyes blew wide as she gasped.

I followed her gaze to see a third beast closing in, this one having snuck up behind us, moving with such stealth it could have attacked without any warning.

Dead. We were dead. By an animal of all things.

"Do we run?" I let my pack slip from my shoulders, not wanting the weight of it to slow me down.

Xandra shook her head. "We'll never survive."

"Then we fight." I took my kukri's grip with both hands, finding my center so that when I had to strike, it would be quick. And if I missed...

By the grace of the Divine, make our deaths quick.

A growl, low and menacing, came from the beast still prowling through the forest. The other two crept closer, lowering their heads and shoulders, preparing to pounce.

Xandra shook her head so fiercely her hair whipped into her face. "No."

The scream tore through her throat as she closed her eyes, her hands fisting at her sides. It grew louder and louder, morphing from a woman's shout to an animal's roar.

The ritus.

Tears sprang to my eyes as I brought a hand to my mouth, watching as my cousin dropped to her knees. Finally. If she shifted, she could save us.

The sound she made was so raw and savage that the beasts stopped their pursuit, the two on the road backing away.

Xandra bent forward, dropping to her hands as her back arched. She twisted to stare up at me, her eyes no longer gold or milky white. They were black as ink, the whites entirely erased.

"Run," she ordered between gritted teeth.

"What? Xan—"

"Go. Now." Another roar came from deep in her chest, her mouth stretched wide as she sank back to sit on her heels. She rocked back and forth, hands digging like claws into the ground.

I took a step closer, reaching for her, but instead of taking my outstretched hand, she bared her teeth.

Teeth that were not part of her normal, lovely smile. They lengthened as I stared at her, growing into tapered, razor-sharp fangs.

Was this why we went through the ritus alone? Because we were not safe to be around during the change?

"Xandra?"

The growl that came from her throat was not human.

Her eyes flickered to gold, the black receding for only a moment. "Please. Run."

"But—"

"Go, Caspia." The gold vanished in a blink, and the feral snarl she unleashed made me stagger backward.

Terror took hold, and I whirled for the trees, running as fast as I could, despite the pain in my ankle.

Xandra's scream followed me into the forest.

I lost track of the other beasts as I kept running, heart in my throat. Risking a look over my shoulder, all I could see was green. When I faced forward, I turned too quickly, and my balance faltered. My toe caught on a stick and sent me crashing forward.

My palms slammed into a mossy rock, the impact jarring enough I dropped my kukri. I let out a single cry, snatched my blade, then pushed myself to my feet, checking behind me once more.

The sight of a black beast perched on a rock, its eyes locked on me, made my blood run cold.

"Xandra?" Or was this another one of the creatures? Had I left my cousin on that road to die?

The beast lifted its nose like it was searching for my scent.

I backed away, weapon raised. "Xandra, if that's you, please know me."

Its ears twitched.

Click. Click. Click. The noise from the other creatures filled the air, and the beast's attention shifted to the side.

With its focus elsewhere, I spun around and did as Xandra had ordered. I ran until my lungs were bleeding and my legs were on fire.

The sound of rushing water cut through my terror. The trees opened up, then stopped at the edge of a sheer cliff. The river below raged with rapids. The ravine was too wide for me to jump.

"No." I came to a sliding stop at the edge, peering down the long drop. Then I backed toward the forest to run another way. My curls stuck in my face as I turned.

Three beasts came at me like a wave, crashing from all directions, leaping over fallen logs and rocks.

By the grace of the Divine, turn me true.

The only way I was surviving those beasts was by becoming one of my own.

I ripped a knife from a sheath at my wrist, and with a flick, sent it flying toward the nearest beast.

The knife drove into the jackal's black fur, but the horror

kept running at me with an ear-splitting roar. It opened its jaw and pushed off all four legs, ready to slam into my body.

I raised my weapon over my shoulder, ready to strike down with all my might, but then another beast came charging from the side, slamming into the animal that had been a heartbeat from making me its lunch.

A ball of black fur and scales rolled in front of me, slamming into a tree trunk. Then came the snapping of teeth, followed by the sickening gurgle of a throat slashed.

Xandra. No. My eyes swam with tears as the larger of the two beasts stood over a lifeless body.

Blood seeped from four deep gashes in the dead animal's throat.

Time seemed to slow, to move in languid images, almost like my visions.

The other two beasts backed away, heads lowering like they were cowering before a new leader.

Xandra.

It had to be Xandra. When Starling died, we returned to our human form. The beast bleeding over the forest floor was still an animal.

She growled at the others, then raised her head and let out a series of those clicks.

Was it a warning? An order? They seemed to bow to her, dropping to a crouch, giving her allegiance.

I lowered my blade, my entire body trembling. "Xandra?"

She looked like she was about to come close and nuzzle against my hand.

Until her lips curled up at the sides. Until a low, menacing growl came from her throat.

Until she took one prowling step my way.

"Xandra." I backed away from her and the other two beasts. "It's me. It's Caspia."

For every step I took, she followed, five steps, then ten.

Until she'd pushed me to the edge of the cliff with nowhere to go.

"Xandra." I repeated her name again and again. "Xandra."

She only snarled.

"Xandra." My voice cracked as tears streamed down my face. "Don't do this. Come back. Shift back. Xandra, remember who you are."

The other two beasts lurked behind her, awaiting her command.

"Xandra!" I screamed, hoping it would break through to the woman, my best friend, somewhere beneath the beast.

She lowered her shoulders, eyes locked on mine.

"Xandra." I sobbed, my chest racking as I cried. "Xandra, please."

Except Xandra was gone. She was lost. She was nothing but the beast.

And I would not let my cousin destroy me.

If this was my end, then it would be my own doing.

She leaped, maw opening wide, claws outstretched.

But I was already gone, jumping over the cliff's edge.

Flying, for the first time in my life. Flying, for only a moment.

Until I fell.

14

ODESSA

There was a rock under my bedroll that had grown larger and sharper overnight. It dug into my hip, waking me from a fitful sleep.

"Hey. Woman. Wake up."

Not a rock. A boot.

Someone was kicking me.

I gasped and shot upright, pushing the damp hair out of my face as I peered up at the person standing over me.

An old man with hooded black eyes frowned as he prodded me with his boot again, his gloved hands fisted on his hips. His hair was wrapped in a blue silk scarf that matched the starbursts in his irises. His chin was covered in long, wiry gray whiskers that bounced as he spoke. "Get up."

"W-what?" I squinted against the sunlight streaming through the tree branches overhead.

"Get up. Get yourself on the road before the town patrol finds you here. Norcresters don't take too kindly to outsiders sleeping in their gardens." Warning delivered, he turned on a heel and walked to a horse-drawn cart waiting on the road.

As he drove away, I pushed the blanket off my legs and stood, taking in our surroundings. It had been nearly dark last night when we chose to camp against this tree. I hadn't realized that it marked the entrance to a vegetable garden. Rows and rows of different plants stretched across the fields around us.

"Evie." I bent and gently shook her shoulder, rousing her from sleep. "It's time to wake up."

"No." She frowned, squeezing her eyes closed as she shook her head.

Last night had been too short for both of us.

I left her to wake up slowly as I got Freya saddled and loaded. My back and legs protested the idea of another long day of riding, but the last place I wanted to be was in an Ozarth jail cell.

Just as Brother Skore had promised, the stream Evie and I had followed out of the mountains yesterday had led us to Norcrest. The ride had taken the entire day, and for the last hour, I'd been certain we were lost. But then the town lights had sparkled into view, and I'd nearly cried.

Norcrest was built in a basin encircled by steep, terraced hills. The town square was located in the center of the bowl, with an inn, livery, mercantile, and other businesses. Its homes were all built into the hillsides, their roofs covered in thick grass. Their doors were all wide and sturdy, some arched to follow the curvature of the terrain. It was as if each enclosed a private cave, likely dug deep enough into the land to protect their owners during the migration.

We'd ridden into Norcrest as the sun was setting, and I'd followed the road that spiraled to the basin's bottom.

The town might have been charming if not for its people. They were as welcoming as the wet blanket I'd slept under that night. Not a single person had offered a warm smile. Most only sneered and glared. And without any coin or gold, the innkeeper had slammed his door in my face.

So we'd retreated out of the basin, and when I'd spotted this large tree, I'd decided we could sleep here for the night. No sooner than we'd unsaddled Freya, the skies had opened in a deluge.

The tree had provided us some shelter but not enough. I was tired of being wet and cold. I was tired of sleeping on the ground and wearing these clothes. And mostly, I was tired of hearing Evie's stomach growl.

How were we supposed to keep going? We'd gotten to Norcrest, but now what? We had to continue south and find a way across the Harrow River that divided Ozarth down the center. But from there, I didn't know the best way to Quentis.

Once we made it out of Ozarth, I'd have to ride through Laine and Genesis. If we made it that far, if I managed to keep both of us alive, we'd have to get through the Evon Ravine.

Did I keep riding? Should I try to get to the coast? Maybe if I sold Freya, I could pay for passage to sail the Krisenth.

Except I didn't want to sell my horse. She was nearly as precious to me as Faze. She'd kept us alive, kept going without complaint.

I rubbed the scar on my palm, closing my eyes.

What would Ransom do? *Keep going.* All we could do was keep going.

Shades, I missed him. I missed the strength in his arms. I missed the softness of his lips and sleeping on his bare chest. I missed his arrogant smirk and gravelly voice.

I missed feeling safe simply because he was near.

Evie's groan pulled me out of my thoughts as she stood with a scowl.

"I'm sorry we can't sleep longer," I said, holding out my hand.

She took it and let me pull her into a hug.

"Want to steal some vegetables with me?" I asked.

Her sly smile made me laugh.

After weeks of traveling through the forests and mountains, riding through the Ozarth grasslands was unsettling. We were too exposed in the open. Too vulnerable. But at least we were on a road, and at least we weren't alone.

"What's in this box?" Evie asked Wells, tapping the lid of the crate she was crawling over in the back of his wagon.

He didn't look over his shoulder to answer. "Lard."

"*More* lard? Is that all you have?"

"Yes."

"Why didn't you just say that earlier?"

"You didn't ask."

"Oh." She sighed, drawing in her knees to sit cross-legged.

Wells, the old man who'd woken me up at dawn, was now our travel companion. It hadn't taken long for us to catch up to his cart after we raided the garden, stuffing our pockets and bags with carrots and tomatoes and beans and peas. I'd even dug up a handful of round potatoes.

Wells was on his way to the Harrow River, and when I'd asked if we could ride alongside him, he'd agreed and even offered to let Evie sit in the cart.

It was strange not to have her in front of me. My arms felt empty and too big, but she seemed much happier with room to squirm. And Wells, while a bit gruff, indulged her string of questions.

"What is lard?" she asked him.

"Fat from a pig. It's cooked down and melted, then put in jars."

Evie grimaced. "Sounds gross."

"Gross?" Wells harumphed. "My lard makes the best pie crust in all of Calandra."

"Where are you taking it?" I asked.

"Ripfell. It's about a day's ride once I cross the Harrow. This is my last trip over for a while. Should be back in Norcrest in a few days if I sell quickly. Then I'll stick close to home until next summer."

Until after the migration.

"Do you have a good shelter?"

"Yes. It's already stockpiled and has been for months."

"Good." When the crux came, he'd be ready.

Wells glanced over, taking in my dirty, wrinkled clothes for the tenth time. "Where are you going?"

"Quentis."

He frowned and shook his head, muttering something under his breath.

Evie yawned and lay down on the crates, tucking her hands under her cheek. It didn't take her long to doze off.

"Do you worry about monsters?" I asked Wells.

"I've crossed paths with my fair share of tarkin." He gave the carrier slung across my body a wary look.

I shifted Faze to my other side. "Have you ever been attacked?"

Wells reached over the edge of his bench seat, tapping the crate secured beneath. "She didn't ask me what was in this crate."

"Weapons?" I asked.

"Piglets. Three of them. The minute I see a tarkin, I'll let them loose. They're easy enough prey and make enough noise that the monsters forget about a thin, old man."

Unless the monster had Lyssa. Then I doubted any number of piglets would be enough of a distraction to quell its bloodlust.

We rode through the rest of the morning in comfortable silence, following the two-track road through sweeping fields and over rolling hills. Not long after Evie woke from her nap, she heard a squeal and discovered the piglets. And as the afternoon bled into the evening, she was back in the saddle, riding in front of me as the road widened and merged with other trails.

Another wagon appeared ahead of us as two fell into line behind us. They were all merchants like Wells, hauling goods in carts.

I hoped most had heard news of the crux scout and were fleeing to shelters and cities.

With strangers nearby, Evie's questions stopped, and the

only noise came from the clop of hooves and the crunch of wheels on dirt.

The grasses grew taller and thicker the closer we got to the river. The road was still muddy in certain patches from last night's rain. The smell of smoke greeted us not long before we reached an expanse of tan canvas tents. Clustered along the road and trampled grass, they stretched as far as I could see, forming a makeshift city alongside the Harrow River.

Everyone ignored us as we rode past, busy with their own tasks. People bustled in and out of their tents and tended to horses. Some were busy cooking beside ringed firepits.

It reminded me of the first camp I'd ever seen, a camp made on the Turan plains not long after I'd sailed across the Krisenth to my new kingdom. It was the camp where Ransom had first started training me to fight, all because I'd demanded a sword.

That camp had been a lifetime ago. Before I'd fallen in love with Turah. Before I'd learned the Guardian's true identity. Before I'd fallen in love with Ransom.

My heart twisted, and I stroked the scar on my palm.

A bell rang out, clanging so loud Faze poked his head from the carrier.

"What's that?" I called to Wells.

He snapped his horse's reins. "Last ferry for the day. Hurry."

We kept pace as he raced for the Harrow, trotting toward the river's edge where a flat wooden boat was tied to a sturdy post. Two thick planks connected it to the shore.

Wells dug into his pants pockets, pulling out a coin. He flipped it to the ferryman and drove the cart onto the boat's platform.

I urged Freya to follow, but the ferryman—a broad, hulking figure wearing a leather oilskin coat—stepped into my path, holding up both hands.

"That'll be two darrics. One for each of ya."

My stomach dropped. "I don't have any coin."

The man crossed his arms over his chest. "Then be gone."

"Please," I begged. "We have to get across."

The river cut from one coast of Ozarth to the other. There was no going around.

His gaze drifted over my shoulder to the hilt of my sword. "I'll take that from you."

"No." Not a chance I was giving up my only weapon and a gift from Ransom. Besides, it was worth well more than two darrics.

"Suit yourself." He shrugged. "Back away."

"Here." Wells took two other coins from his pocket. "Let them cross."

The ferryman walked over and took them from Wells. He bit one, making sure it was real, then he waved us onto his ferry.

"Thank you, Wells." I swung off Freya, helping Evie out of the saddle as the ferryman untied the boat. "I will repay you."

"Keep that sword. Keep that girl alive. Payment enough." The old man walked to the edge of the boat, taking a seat on the floorboards as he pulled off his boots and rolled up his pants.

As the ferryman hauled in the planks and pushed away from the shore, Wells dropped his feet into the river.

The Harrow was so wide I could barely see the other shore in the fading light. But the water was calm, lapping against the boat's sides.

We flowed downstream for a bit until the boat caught the current. Then the ferryman steered us with a large oar off the stern.

"How does he get back upstream to the other side?" I asked Wells.

"The ferrymen float from side to side, dropping passengers along the way. He'll pick up others and cross back tomorrow, always working downstream. Usually they go about ten landings. Then they'll dismantle the boat, load it into wagons, and come back to the top. This is the farthest landing from Skanshon."

"Are there boats that go straight to Skanshon?"

"Yes. But they aren't cheap. And there are too many men on this river who'd let you keep that sword to take payment in other ways, if you know what I mean."

"Yes." It wasn't only monsters I had to fear on this journey. Men could be just as cruel.

"Don't stay long in the camps," Wells said, his voice low. "When we get there, whatever way the ferryman walks, you go the opposite."

"Understood." I glanced over my shoulder, finding the ferryman's eyes waiting.

The hungry look in his gaze made me shiver. I pulled Evie closer, keeping a hand around her waist as she skimmed her fingers on the water's surface.

It was nearly dark when we made it to the opposite shore.

Fires burned in barrels, lighting the landing. Like the other side of the river, tan canvas tents were clustered in the grass, most with their own campfire burning, too.

"May Daria grant you luck on your journey." Wells gave me a single nod farewell, then climbed on his cart and drove through the camp.

The ferryman was still busy with his boat, so while he was distracted, I put Evie in the saddle with Faze, leading them as I walked through the tents, keeping my head down as I passed.

Ahead, Wells's cart rolled past a small wooden cabin. He twisted back and pointed to the building, and then he was gone, swallowed up by the tents.

I quickened my steps, walking straight for the house.

The sound of children's laughter erupted as the door blew open and five kids streamed outside. A round woman with olive skin and long, brown hair shooed them away, lingering in the door's frame to smile at the brood.

She was about to turn back inside when she spotted me. Her eyes narrowed as she wiped her hands on a threadbare apron.

"Um, hi." I offered a kind smile, hoping she'd take pity on us tonight. "My name is Odessa. This is Evie. We're just passing through, and I was wondering if you have a safe place where we could sleep tonight. We traveled this way with Wells. From Norcrest."

Shades, I hoped she knew Wells, because I'd forgotten to ask if that was his first or last name.

The woman's gaze was inscrutable as she gave me a once-over, then Evie. Only then did her expression soften. Maybe it was the blue starburst in Evie's eyes that matched the woman's own. Or maybe she simply had a gentle heart for children.

"You can sleep in the lean-to off the side of the house. It's not much, but it'll keep the rain off."

"Thank you." I sighed. "I don't have any coin."

She waved a dismissive hand, then led us to the lean-to.

It wasn't more than a wooden roof and a few piles of straw. But there was a post to tie up Freya and a trough of clear water. An oil lantern hung from a hook on the wall.

"Water pump is around back to wash up before dinner."

"Oh, you don't need—"

"Wash up before dinner," she ordered.

"Of course." I dropped my chin, feeling like I'd just been chided by my stepmother.

If only Margot could see me now. She'd be aghast at the state of my clothes and hair. Who knew what we'd look like by the time we made it to Quentis.

The mental image of her horror-struck face when we walked into her pristine, gleaming castle almost made me laugh.

Evie and I unloaded our things and left Freya to graze while we washed our faces and hands at the water pump. Then we went inside the cabin, where the woman handed us each a loaf of warm bread and a bowl of stew.

I opened my mouth to say thanks and ask her name, but she pointed to the small table.

"Eat." Then she was gone, marching out the door.

So we ate.

As soon as our bowls were empty, I washed them in a tub of soapy water, set them aside to dry, and took Evie back to the lean-to.

We saved the bread for a hungrier day.

Not once in my life had I feared for food. If I was hungry, all I'd ever had to do was ask. A meal was not something I'd take for granted again.

I lit the lantern and hung it to illuminate the space, then spread out our blanket over the straw, tucking Evie beside me as the prattle of the children returning home carried inside.

Shouts and singing drifted from the tents, a few peals of feminine laughter mingling with the voices of men.

The mood was jovial and light. No one seemed panicked or worried about the migration. Maybe word of the scout hadn't reached this part of Ozarth yet?

Tomorrow, I'd mention it to the woman so she could take her children somewhere safe.

Evie yawned as Faze explored the lean-to, sniffing and marking his new territory.

The fangs on his lower jaw were beginning to protrude above his lip. His stripes seemed more pronounced each day. And I'd felt another row of scales growing in along his spine when I pet him earlier.

There were more tarkin in Ozarth than there were in any other of the five kingdoms. Maybe this would be the safest place to let him go. Let him find his way back to being more wild than tame.

But I couldn't imagine leaving him behind. Not just for Evie's sake, but mine, too. Besides, he was too young. It was too dangerous.

"Dess?" Evie said, snuggling into my side. "Will you read me another story?"

"Sure." I reached for my satchel, taking out the journal in the old language. I flipped to one of the entries I'd already translated and knew was safe for her small ears.

It was an entry I'd been pondering ever since Brother Skore's mysterious instructions yesterday.

There is a warrior in Calandra. A warrior who will save this realm. Find her.

"'A woman sits atop a brown horse,'" I read, squinting in the dim light.

...

Her body is covered in gray leather and metal armor, the silver pieces reflecting the afternoon sun. Her braided hair is as pale as the clouds.

Her cheek is inked with a row of four-pointed stars, their thin black points as sharp as needles. They stretch from the side of her nose, beneath her eye, to the largest that covers her temple.

She is surrounded by sand and dunes. Her eyes are lined with kohl and are as bright as flames as she searches the sky. She hears the caw before she sees the falcon, and as the bird soars over her head, she extends her arm, wrapped in leather from wrist to elbow.

The falcon lands on her arm, adjusting his perch as she unfastens a ribbon tied to his leg. She sighs at the message written on a small scroll, then crumples it into her fist and tosses it at her horse's feet.

She strokes the bird's wing, then releases him back into the wind. With a fluid swing, she is off her horse and walking through the sand, shedding her weapons and armor piece by piece. By the time she sheds the last of her uniform, a heavy breastplate laced at her ribs, the other pieces are being swallowed by the sand.

She stops and looks to the sky. She lifts both arms, stretching them wide like wings. And the smile on her face says she's finally free.

...

Evie touched the corner of the page as I finished reading. "Who do you think she is?"

"A warrior." Was she the person Brother Skore intended for me to find?

"Cathlin has white hair."

"She does." I smiled down at Evie.

"I miss Cathlin."

"So do I."

A throat cleared from the dark, making us both jump.

"Sorry." A man in a long overcoat with a hood pulled over his head stepped warily into the light, both hands raised in peace. "I didn't mean to startle you."

"What do you want?" I reached for the sword on the ground at my side.

"Wells is a friend. My name is Sryker. You met my wife." He pointed to the cabin. "Edda."

"Oh." The breath I'd been holding came out in a rush as I set down my sword. "Thank you for letting us stay here tonight."

He nodded, about to turn away, but stopped. Slowly, like he didn't want to scare us, he lifted off his hood. And when he stepped farther into the light, Evie's body went rigid.

So did mine.

Three large scars marred his face. A black patch covered a missing eye. And the coat I hadn't seen clearly until just now was made of a fabric I'd never seen before. A fabric of lime-green scutes.

This was the man from the journal. The man who'd killed an alligask and used its hide for his clothes.

"Wells told me you're going south. To Quentis," Sryker said.

"Yes."

"Then you'll need a guide through the bogs. We'll leave at first light."

"Thank you." A part of me wanted to ask why he was

offering his help. But the other part was simply grateful to accept it. "We'll be ready."

He walked away, toward the house.

"Wait here," I told Evie, hurrying to stand and chase after him. If he was in the journal, maybe he knew this warrior, too. "Excuse me, Sryker?"

"Yes?" He turned.

"I'm searching for a warrior. A woman."

"The only warriors around here are the Mavins. I don't know if there are any women, though."

"Mavins? Who are they?"

"Mercenaries, mostly. For the right price, you won't find a better lot of fighters." He chuckled. "They're almost as famous as the Guardian. Have you heard of him?"

I traced the scar on my palm. "Once or twice."

15

CASPIA

A woman with wild orange, red, copper, and caramel curls sits alone in the dark.

Her hair is the same as mine. As Saskia's.

As Emery's.

Her feet are bare. Her clothes are in tatters. The stone floor beneath her is cold and wet. She rests her head against iron bars as she prays to the Divine.

But she is not alone.

In the cell beside hers is a man with light hair, his clothes as dirty and soiled as her own. He is too thin. They both are.

The man grunts as he points to a dark hall. Someone has cut off his tongue so he cannot speak.

She shakes her head and reaches through the bars, taking his hands in hers. Where there once were five fingers on his right hand, only three remain. Blood still seeps from the stump where the last was severed.

She will not leave him until the Divine has called him home. She cannot shift with a child growing in her womb.

She hasn't decided if she'll tell the man yet. Or if she'll let that secret follow her to Gloree.

And so she sits in the dark, praying for their lives. Praying for death.

Until the enemy drags her off the stone floor for another experiment.

When they strap her to the table, when they slice open her wrist to steal the gifted blood in her veins, she doesn't even bother to fight.

...

I woke to a scream—my own.

Pushing up off my pillow, kicking loose the blanket tangled

around my legs, I wrapped my arms around my knees and closed my eyes, breathing through my nose.

A dream. It was only a dream.

I couldn't bear the thought that it was real. That before Emery had been killed by that silver-eyed warrior, she'd suffered, not only the loss of Max, but of a daughter.

I refused to believe that vision was real.

My throat was on fire, my heart racing. As much as I wanted to curl up in bed and go back to sle—

I gasped.

A bed. I was on a bed.

My eyes flew open, and for a single heartbeat, I was sure that I'd see my room. That I'd be in Showe and everything that I'd experienced since leaving Nelfinex would be no more than an awful dream.

Except I wasn't in my room. And this was not my bed.

The heartbreak was instant. A cry tore from my lips as I closed my eyes again, not wanting to face this new reality.

Xandra. The black beasts. She was one of them now.

And she'd tried to kill me.

I slapped a hand over my mouth to keep another sob from escaping.

The last thing I remembered was falling. Then…nothing.

Was this Gloree? Would I walk out of this room and into the open arms of the Divine, finding him waiting to welcome me to an eternal paradise?

But I wasn't ready to be a part of the afterlife. I hadn't avenged my sister. I hadn't completed my ritus. And now, I had to save Xandra.

As much as I wanted to give in to the anguish and grief, I was on a bed that was not my own, so I forced my eyes open and swung my legs to the floor.

The wooden boards were cold as I eased to my feet, testing my ankle. It was tender, and the moment I gave it my weight, a sharp pain shot through my calf, sending me back to a seat.

"Vexx," I hissed, lifting it up to see my skin mottled with purple and blue.

Blue, like the color of my pants.

I gasped and took in my wardrobe. A blue shirt, much too large, with sleeves that draped past my fingertips. Pants equally as loose and long but cinched at my waist with a cord.

Someone must have found me in the river. They must have brought me here and changed me out of my wet clothes. Who? How long had I been asleep?

A shiver raced down my spine as I pushed myself up again, this time careful to keep off my sore ankle.

Was it Xandra who'd brought me here? Had she shifted back and come to my rescue?

"Xandra?" My voice was hoarse and weak.

The room was practically empty, with only a narrow bed pushed against the wall. There were no windows, only walls made out of beige stones and held together by plaster of the same shade. The yellow hue reminded me of the cave Xandra and I had stayed in our first moon.

I limped to the door, then twisted the knob to ease it open.

The room beyond was bigger than the bedroom, though still small and crowded. There was a round table with two wooden chairs. A kitchen held a washbasin and a few narrow cupboards. A small stack of clay dishes rested on a shelf. In the corner was a leather cushioned chair with a pillow and blanket folded on its seat. The footstool was tucked neatly beside a fireplace.

Whoever lived here must have given me the bed while they slept in that chair.

"Hello?" I stepped deeper into the room, peering out a square window.

The forest outside appeared to be the same one I'd trekked

through with Xandra. The green wasn't as offensive now that my head wasn't spinning and my skin wasn't on fire.

It was almost...lovely. Almost. That vivid, verdant color was tainted from the sickness and Xandra's shift. Now, that color made me heartsick.

Where was my cousin? Was she alive? Had she survived the rite?

There was only one way to find out.

Where were my boots? My clothes? I was about to retreat to the bedroom and make sure I hadn't overlooked something when footsteps outside made me freeze.

My hand went to my hip where I usually carried a blade. Where were my weapons? My eyes stayed locked on the door as my entire body began to shake.

I wanted—*needed*—it to be Xandra. But something in my heart said I was going to be disappointed.

The knob rattled, and the door swung open. A man with sandy hair stepped into the room. He was dressed in brown leather pants, and his shirt was a rich greenish blue. It was the color of the dragonflies that flittered around the palace in Showe.

He was tall enough that he had to duck to clear the threshold. His broad, muscled physique reminded me of Cap, but this man's wavy hair was much shorter.

The moment he spotted me, his tawny eyes went wide and he lifted his hands like he was trying to tame a wild beast. When he spoke, it was in a language I didn't understand. His voice was gentle and soothing, but it did nothing to quell the fear.

I was trapped in a house, alone with a man I did not know, on a continent across the world from my home. And even if I escaped this room, where would I go?

I had nothing, not even my shoes.

The man kept speaking, his voice low and calm, but whatever he was trying to communicate, I hadn't a clue what language he was using.

I shook my head, backing away until my shoulders hit the wall. Tears filled my eyes as I stared at this stranger, his mouth still moving. He kept talking and talking, the words crashing on me like stones, until I couldn't take it any longer.

"Stop."

He blinked, mouth snapping closed. Then he lowered his hands and studied me, eyes narrowing as he cocked his head to the side. "Stelvi'op?"

Stop. Stelvi'op meant stop. It wasn't Nelfinex, not exactly. It was more closely aligned to a dialect from Beesa. But it was familiar.

I'd said stop.

And he'd understood me enough to say it back.

Hope that I might find a way to understand this man soared.

"Who are you?" I asked.

He pondered my words as he ran a hand over the stubble dusting his chiseled jaw. It looked like he was replaying my question in his head, shuffling the words into something he could interpret. Then he gave me a single nod and touched a hand to his heart. "Andreas."

"An-dre-as," I repeated, enunciating each syllable.

He nodded.

I mimicked his gesture and placed a hand on my heart. "Caspia."

"Caspia."

A shiver, involuntary and not at all unpleasant, ran down my back at the sound of my name in his thick accent and rugged voice.

Andreas held up a finger and went to the kitchen, where he bent to open a cupboard. He lifted out a stack of neatly folded clothes and a pair of boots.

My boots. My clothes.

When he brought them over, he stretched his arms long, keeping as much space between us as possible.

The moment I had my things clutched to my chest, he lifted his hands again and backed away, like he knew I was scared.

I dipped my chin in a silent thanks, then hurried into the bedroom, never turning my back on Andreas as I closed myself inside. There wasn't a lock, so I changed with one hand, keeping the other on the door itself as I stripped out of the oversized shirt and pants, swapping them for clothes of my own.

When I went to pull on a boot, there was something inside. I tipped it upside down, letting my necklace and ten elfalter rings drop into my palm. In the other boot were two knives that had survived the river.

With my pack gone, lost on that forest road, these pieces were all I had left. My only remnants of home.

I clutched the necklace in my fist, breathing through another wave of pain. Then I straightened my spine and fastened it around my neck, tucking it beneath my vest. After slipping the rings in a pocket and strapping on my blades, I wrapped my cloak around my shoulders, flipping its hood over my unbound hair.

Without my pack, I felt underdressed and unprepared to leave this home, but I raised my chin and opened the door.

Andreas was in the kitchen, carrying two bowls to the table. He nodded at one chair while he sat in the other, its legs scraping across the floor. He plucked a berry from his bowl and popped it into his mouth, his jaw flexing as he chewed.

My stomach growled so loudly the noise filled the room.

His eyes softened as he pointed to the empty chair.

The food was too tempting to ignore, so I took the seat, unsheathing a knife and setting it on the table as a warning.

He chuckled, the deep vibration like tingles on my skin.

I sat across from him, chair as far away from the table as it would allow, and silently ate berries, nuts, and seeds.

Andreas mostly focused on his own meal, but from time

to time, he'd glance up. An amber starburst mingled with the tawny striations in his eyes. The flecks were so bright a yellow, his eyes seemed to glow.

I'd never seen eyes like that before. They were as striking and mesmerizing as they were unsettling. They were another reminder that I was far, far away from home. A reminder that stole my appetite.

I pushed the bowl aside and dipped my chin in a silent thanks. But when I moved to stand, he held up a hand and gave me a pleading look. I sighed and sank into the seat.

Andreas set his own bowl aside, wiped his hands on his pants, and leaned his elbows on the table. He opened his mouth, then closed it, like he was struggling with what to say.

So was I.

There were so many questions to ask, but I wasn't sure where to even begin.

Which left us both speechless, staring at one another.

He had angular, handsome features. The symmetry of his face, from his square jaw to his full lips to the straight bridge of his nose to the strong line of his brow, made him arguably the most arresting man I'd ever seen. Something about him felt familiar, yet I would have remembered his face from a vision.

Maybe Andreas had visited me in a dream.

"Elvi'old lelvi'ang-gelfwij," he said, breaking the silence. "Old language."

The first two words were spoken in the Beesan dialect I recognized. The second pair must have been his attempt to translate into his own tongue. So I did what he had earlier and repeated them back—or tried. "Old lan-uge."

"Language."

"Lan-guage."

"Yes." The corner of his mouth turned up as he grinned. His eyes crinkled at the sides, and my belly fluttered.

Vexx. This was not the time to be enthralled with a man.

The sooner I left this house, the better, even if I had nowhere to go.

The call of the ritus had faded since the *Cirrina*. I hadn't felt the thrum since we came ashore. I wasn't ready to accept that my rite had failed.

Which left me with only one choice.

To avenge Emery. To find Xandra.

If nothing else, this journey could at least secure justice for my sister's death. And if I found Xandra, at least she could fly me home.

Which meant it was time to find the silver-eyed warrior. For that, I would need to learn the language of this land.

"What is this continent?" I asked Andreas.

It took him a moment to parse my question.

"Calandra."

16

ODESSA

Evie gagged and plugged her nose. "It stinks."

"Yes, it does." I breathed through my mouth, but the odor was so powerful I could taste it on my tongue.

I inhaled. And heaved, slapping a hand over my mouth.

The smell permeated the valley before us, the scent so heavy it thickened the air as we rode toward the bogs.

My friend Samuel Hay had once told me that I'd never enjoy the sweet, spicy candy they made from crystalized cave ginger after smelling a bog. And oh, how he was right.

How were the paperman and his son? Were they still in Ellder? Had they survived the crux attack on the fortress?

After the death of his wife and the fire that had taken his home in Turah, Samuel had endured enough hardship. I hoped he'd found somewhere safe to wait out the migration. I hoped that someday our paths would cross again and I could tell him about this foul trek through a cave ginger bog.

"You'll get used to the smell," Sryker said as he rode beside us, seemingly unbothered by the stench of rotten flesh and rancid milk.

"I'm not so sure about that."

"You sound like Edda." He chuckled. "She hates the bogs. But by nightfall, we'll be through the thick of it."

"Thank you for taking us."

"That's the tenth time you've thanked me this morning. You don't need an eleventh. It's no hardship. And it wouldn't have been right to send you off alone."

Maybe if I had more confidence in my abilities to keep Evie safe, I would have taken offense. But I'd take all the help I could get from people like Sryker and Edda and Wells if that meant getting through Ozarth.

If I focused on crossing one kingdom at a time, traveling the continent didn't seem quite so daunting.

The bogs marked the middle of Ozarth. The swamps stretched through a valley that ran parallel with the Harrow River. This area was the only place in Calandra where cave ginger was grown. It thrived in these bogs that the alligasks called home.

While it certainly would have smelled better, traveling around the bogs was not without risks. Sryker had warned me that the lush riverlands were crawling with tigercats and tarkin. It would have added a week to our journey, and with the migration quickly approaching, a week seemed too precious to waste. Cutting through the bogs was the shortest way across Ozarth and south to Laine.

One day with this stench seemed our best choice.

Edda had bid us farewell this morning after a hearty breakfast of boiled eggs and hard cheese. Their children had clung to Sryker's legs, giggling as he shuffled outside, dragging them along. And his family had stood outside their home, waving as we rode away.

"Do you miss farming?" I asked Sryker.

"Not even a bit." Sryker had once been a cave ginger farmer, but after he was attacked by an alligask, Edda had begged him to find another job. So he'd traded his farm for a small mercantile along the Harrow, where he sold supplies to travelers crossing on the ferries.

"Why do they call it cave ginger?" There was a note in one of Luella's journals she'd made about the plant. *Not a cave in sight.* I smiled at the idea of her riding through these bogs, scribbling details about the bogs and monsters within.

"I've always wondered that myself." Sryker shrugged. "I have no idea. Have you ever tried the candy?"

"It was a favorite." Until now.

"And what about you, lass?" Sryker asked Evie. "Have you tasted it before?"

"My teacher gave me some once." She scrunched up her nose. "It was spicy."

"My kids don't like it, either," he said.

The ginger had a sharp flavor, a taste I hadn't acquired until I was older.

"Dess?" Evie twisted to stare up at me, and the serious look in her eyes made my heart sink. I knew before she asked exactly what her question would be. "Where is Luella? Is she in the shades with Papa?"

As much as I wanted to say no, I couldn't lie. "Yes, my love."

Her eyes filled with tears as she whispered, "And Ranse?"

"No. He's not in the shades." If I had to believe that truth into existence, so be it. "We're going to find him. I promise."

She nodded, falling sideways into my chest.

I'd never heard Evie call Ransom by his nickname before, but it made sense. Zavier had called him Ranse.

She spoke the name low enough for only me to hear, just like she'd been taught. Just like she knew not to acknowledge Zavier as Papa. Like she knew never to tell anyone she was a Turan princess.

This girl was the keeper of too many secrets.

She buried her face in the arms I had wrapped around her middle and clung tight as she softly cried.

Sryker gave me a worried glance.

"It's been a long journey. From Norcrest," I added quickly.

With Evie's blue starbursts, I hoped that people would think we were from Ozarth. If it meant they'd help us get through their kingdom, they could think anything they wanted.

"As we get into the bogs, keep that crossbow close." Sryker pointed to the weapon he'd given me before we left the riverside today. "It won't kill an alligask, but a bolt through an eye will slow it down."

The end was secured to a leather strap that I'd looped around my torso, the crossbow dangling at my hip. But at his warning, I tucked it under my arm, took the pouch of extra bolts from my saddlebag, and handed them to Evie. "Can you be in charge of these?"

"Okay." She wiped her face dry and nodded.

"That's my brave little star." I stroked her hair, then made sure Faze was tucked in his carrier in case we had to ride faster.

He'd been wiggling more than usual today, and twice I'd had to stop him from trying to squirm free.

"We'll go single file through the bogs," Sryker said as we approached a narrow, beaten trail that wound through the valley.

The grass was so thick I feared we'd never see an attack coming.

"Alligasks are not stealthy monsters," he said, likely reading the worry on my face. "You'll hear the grass rustle and see it move. In the water, they're lightning fast. But on land, their legs are too short to give them much speed. The fences slow them down, too. If you see a monster, just keep riding."

"All right." I swallowed the rise of panic as he maneuvered in front of us, adjusting his own crossbow so it was easy to reach.

The smell got worse, but the fear of where we were headed pushed it out of mind as the fences came into view.

The dark, rusted posts were spaced closely together, the gaps as wide as my foot. They were taller than the grass but short enough that we could peer over the top to the bogs.

Countless small ponds filled the valley. They were surrounded by tufts of grass. Some were glassy enough to reflect the blue sky while others were covered in a haze of green algae.

A splash sounded beside us, and I jumped, searching the water for a monster, but all I saw were ripples.

The hair on the back of my neck stood on end from the feeling of being watched. Hunted.

Evie's body trembled.

"How is it harvested?" I asked Sryker, needing something to break the quiet. "The cave ginger?"

"We bring bait to the bogs, usually pigs or sheep." He twisted to speak over his shoulder. "It gives the alligasks something to hunt. Then we use a special rake to skim the ginger berries from the top. I was harvesting one day when an alligask came at the fence. It managed to break through a weak section and attacked. Daria's luck was on my side."

"And now you wear its skin."

"I do. It started as more of a trophy, and a reminder that I'd survived when most would have fallen. I was still farming then, and I noticed if I was in this coat, they didn't pay me much attention."

Exactly like the story in the journal.

There was a cart and horse stopped against a fence ahead. A man was quickly drawing a rake through a gap in the fence posts as a woman scooped the berries into baskets and loaded them into their cart.

Neither paid us any attention as we approached, too focused on their task.

The squeal of a pig rang out from where it was stuck in the mud in the next bog over. The bait.

Evie looked up to me, her eyes wide.

"Don't look," I said.

She twisted the other way just in time to miss the alligask.

The monster surged from the bog, unhinging its jaw to swallow the pig whole.

"By the mother." They were enormous, larger than I'd

expected. Out of the water, their bold hides were as bright as the overhead sun. But as it sank down in the water, giving its thick, long tail a swish, it vanished beneath the surface.

As we rode past, the water was already calming, concealing the monster lurking in its depths.

I tightened my grip on the crossbow.

Faze wriggled so hard he almost worked himself free of the carrier.

"What's wrong?" I let the crossbow hang by its strap and lifted him up, checking his paws and belly to make sure he wasn't hurt.

He bared his fangs and hissed, not at me but toward the water.

Lime green flashed at the corner of my eye an instant before a loud *thwack* and roar filled the air. An alligask slammed into the fence beside us, snarling and thrashing against the bars, trying to get free.

"Ride," Sryker ordered, urging his horse into a gallop.

Freya jumped away from the monster, then took off, chasing after Sryker.

Except my feet weren't set in the stirrups, and I wasn't holding tight enough to the reins. In a blink, I lost the control I'd been clinging to for weeks.

I pitched sideways, sliding to the farthest edge of the saddle as I bounced hard, my head whipping back and forth.

Evie's scream mingled with another roar from the alligask as it banged into the fence again.

Pain exploded through my muscles as I clung to Evie and the saddle horn, dragging myself into the seat.

Our bodies crashed together, jostling to the other side as we barely hung on and, somehow, managed not to fall.

But something had to give.

And that something was Faze.

He flew out of my hold, yelping as he hurtled to the ground.

"Faze!" Evie yelled, reaching for him.

"No," I gasped as she toppled to the side, keeping her with me as I pulled with all my might on Freya's reins.

But my horse didn't want to stop. She kept running, until I pulled her head so hard she had no choice.

"Stryker," I called.

He slowed his horse and turned, his eyes going wide as he looked past me to the trail.

I twisted, following his gaze as I forced Freya around.

She bucked, coming up on her front two feet, just as the alligask broke through three fence posts, making enough room for it to claw free.

It opened its jaws, flashing sharp teeth the size of my fingers.

"Faze!" Evie's shout filled the air as my stomach dropped.

"Gods." I fumbled for the crossbow, lifting it up and firing at the beast. But we were too far away, and my hands were shaking so badly my aim was shit. "Give me a bolt."

Evie kept screaming Faze's name, holding her arms out for him to run to her.

The alligask might have been slower on land than water, but it was still faster than our little tarkin.

"No." I kicked at Freya, forcing her to move toward the monster even though she was shaking. I ripped the bag of bolts from Evie's hands, my fingers trembling as I fished one free. It slipped and fell to the ground. "Damn it."

Panic surged as I took out another, the tip slicing through my flesh. Blood poured, coating my fingers and making it almost impossible to load the bolt. But I managed to get it notched and loaded. Then I forced a steady breath as I lifted the weapon and fired it at the monster.

The bolt sank into the alligask's milky-white eye.

But it didn't stop coming toward Faze. It snarled in my direction, like a promise that I'd be next.

"*Faze!*" Evie's voice cracked as she screamed at the top of her lungs.

I pulled Freya to a stop, not willing to get any closer as I took out another bolt. *Please.* I prayed a god was listening. *Please don't take him from her.*

From me.

I loaded the bolt and lifted the crossbow, holding my breath as I fired. It bounced off the monster's thick hide and into the grass.

Evie fell forward, screaming and hysterical as the monster's tail flicked forward over its head toward Faze. It swiped his body to the side, knocking him off his feet.

I reached for my sword, knowing there was nothing I could do. I wouldn't risk Evie by taking her any closer, but I couldn't just stay here and watch as that monster devoured Faze whole.

Don't even think about it.

Ransom's voice echoed in my mind, like he was sitting beside me, knowing exactly what I was about to do.

"I'm sorry." I shifted sideways, about to swing off the saddle, when a horse and rider blew past me, nearly hitting my shoulder.

A blur of white and silver and steel flew through the air as an ax glinted beneath the sun. Then that ax drove through the alligask's skull, cleaving its open jaw in two.

I blinked, sure I was dreaming.

A woman with hair as pale as snow knelt on the beast's twitching corpse—a warrior dressed in gray leather and metal armor, the steel pieces gleaming beneath the sun.

She looked up and met my gaze. Her light-brown irises and the persimmon starburst from those born on the soil of Genesis made her eyes appear like twin flames.

She was as beautiful as she was intimidating. Younger than I'd imagined from the story in the journal. Older than me, but not by much.

Her hair and kohl-lined eyes might have been enough to

tie her to the journal, but the tattoos on her face were exactly as the book described.

A row of five four-pointed stars was inked across her cheekbone. The largest covered her temple with thin lines that extended from top and bottom points.

Evie's quick inhale meant she recognized the woman from the journal, too.

The thunder of hooves came from behind me a moment before we were surrounded by horses and riders, each clad in the same leather and metal armor as the woman.

One man rode to retrieve her horse while two others went to the broken fence, picking up the fallen bars. Each had a star tattooed on his temple.

The warrior pulled her ax free from the monster's skull, frowning at the blood on its rounded blade.

Putrid, green blood.

Lyssa.

That monster would never have been stopped by a fence. The infection running through its veins, the infection that had turned its blood from red to green, that had clouded its raspberry eyes with a white film, had driven it to kill simply because it could.

Or because it had felt me riding through the bogs.

If not for that woman, Faze would be dead.

"Another one." Her lip curled as she wiped the green blood on a nearby tuft of grass. "Gods, it stinks. That's three with green blood in as many months."

It was spreading, faster and farther. As hard as Ransom had tried to keep the infection from crossing Turah's borders, it was too late. Lyssa was creeping across Calandra, and it was only a matter of time before it stretched from one side of the continent to the other.

She stood tall and stared at me, her eyes narrowing. "Who are you?"

I opened my mouth to answer, but Sryker appeared at my side, his hand going to my shoulder.

"Are you all right?"

I sighed, glancing down to Evie and then to Faze, who'd hurried over to stand beside Freya's feet. "We're okay."

"Your hand." He shook his head at the blood, reaching for his saddlebags to take out a strip of cloth.

"Thanks." I wrapped the wound and was about to get down to collect Faze when a man dressed entirely in black leather walked up from behind us.

He was built like Ransom, tall, broad, and muscular. His dark hair was short and neatly combed. He moved with grace and a confidence that made me take notice. His face was clean-shaven, the lines of his jaw and cheekbones as sharp as blades.

Other than the three stars tattooed on his temple and cheek, he could have passed for a nobleman in a Quentin court.

The man picked Faze up by the scruff of his neck, earning a snarl from both the tarkin and Evie.

"I'll take him." I stretched an arm out for Faze, but the man swung him out of reach. My heart climbed into my throat as he tsked.

"Interesting pet," he drawled, his voice as smoky as his eyes. The magenta starburst of Laine was barely visible in his inky gaze.

"Give him to me. Now." I infused as much authority as I could muster into my voice and snapped my fingers. It was as close to sounding like Margot as I ever had—my stepmother would be proud.

A baby monster, live and relatively tame, would trade for an exorbitant price on the black market.

The corner of the man's mouth twitched as he studied Faze for another heartbeat, then handed him over.

Evie hauled him into her arms, burying her nose in his fur.

"Who are you?" I asked.

His mouth stretched into a smirk.

A smirk that reminded me so much of my husband that my heart ached.

"She doesn't know who we are, Thora," he said to the white-haired woman as she came to stand at his side.

Together, they were terrifying.

The warrior—Thora—didn't spare me a glance. Her focus was on Evie and Faze, her eyes hard like she was debating killing another monster today. When her attention shifted toward me, her expression was blank and assessing.

My pulse boomed in my ears as she stared and stared.

Then she dismissed me with a blink and walked away, as if I was nothing but a trivial inconvenience in her day of monster slaying.

Wow, she was intimidating. The air rushed from my lungs before I could stop it, and the man's smirk widened.

There was only one smirking man in this realm I would tolerate, and it wasn't this one. "What?" I snapped.

"You really haven't heard of us?"

"No."

He took a step away and gave a flourishing bow, another reflection of a nobleman. "We, my lady, are the Mavins."

No sooner had he stood tall than another one of the men walked over. His hair was a rich auburn, shaved at the sides but unruly from the top to his nape. His starbursts were as blue as Evie's. In his meaty grip, he carried a bloody crossbow bolt.

The bolt I'd shot into the alligask's eye.

"Want this, Jodhi?" he asked.

"Thanks, Mathias." Jodhi took it from him and touched the green blood at the pointed tip with his gloved finger. Then extended it to me. "Did you fire this?"

"Yes." I ripped it from his grip.

He chuckled. "Nice try, doll."

17

CASPIA

A woman with brown curls holds a broadsword at a man's throat. Her nostrils flare as she stares down the blade. It is too heavy for her to wield. The strength in her arms wanes, her hands beginning to tremble.

But she holds strong a moment longer, enduring his test as she glares at his hazel eyes.

He bats the sword from her grip, sending it into the air, flipping it end over end. He catches it and turns it on her in a blink. He lifts her chin with the pointed tip of his blade.

His eyes flash emerald green.

She backs away from the sword, walks away from the warrior.

With her back turned, she does not see the color shift in his eyes. Gone is the green.

And all that remains is silver.

...

My eyes popped open as the vision jolted me from sleep.

It was the first time I'd had a vision of the silver-eyed warrior besides the one of Emery's death. Who was the brown-haired woman? Would she lead me to him?

"I told you that book was dull," Andreas said from his seat at the table. The gentle scrape of charcoal on paper filled the room from his sketching.

"And you were right." I was resting in Andreas's chair in the cabin.

When our eyes met, the corner of his mouth turned up before he returned to his sketch.

The book I'd been reading when I drifted off was splayed on my lap. Well, the book I'd been trying to read.

After suns of fumbling through language lessons with Andreas, I'd wanted to try reading, hoping that written words would help bridge the three-part gap between Nelfinex, the Beesan dialect—what Andreas called the old language—and Calandran.

As much as I wanted to learn about Calandra's different sports, even with the challenge of translation, this book was drab enough to bore anyone to sleep. My eyes had started to cross when I reached the second chapter that listed rules of a popular game where a ball was kicked into various sizes of hoops.

This book would be markedly better if the author had included illustrations.

"Sorry I don't have anything else to read," he said.

"That's okay." I stood and stretched my arms over my head, wincing slightly at the tenderness in my shoulders.

When Andreas went outside last evening to chop firewood, I'd decided to help. Too many suns without training had gone by, and my muscles ached from the exertion. The soreness was a reminder that it was time to stop lazing around in this cabin. It was time to do what I'd come to this continent to do.

The sun I awoke in Andreas's bed, dressed in his clothes, I'd insisted on leaving.

So he'd escorted me outside and waved goodbye.

I'd set off into the forest, limping on my sore ankle, following the narrow road that wound away from the cabin.

I'd barely made it an hour before my legs grew weak and my head started to throb. My ankle had given out again, and I'd stopped to catch my breath. The next thing I knew, I was waking in Andreas's bed again, this time dressed in my own clothes.

He'd found me unconscious on the road and carried me back.

The next time I told him I was leaving, two suns later, he'd blocked the door with his towering frame and ordered me to rest.

So I'd rested.

As the strength slowly returned to my body, as the sickness passed, Andreas and I had spent most of our time stumbling through languages and stories, trying to understand each other.

He'd found me washed up along the Coraness River, and after rescuing me from the riverbank, he'd brought me here, to his hunting cabin, to rest.

I'd spent five suns with a fever, delirious and on the brink of death. He'd forced me to drink broth and water. He'd tended to the scrapes and cuts I'd gotten in the forest and river. When he confessed to changing me out of my waterlogged clothes and into something dry, his cheeks had turned a handsome shade of pink.

Without question, Andreas had saved my life. Not just after the river, but by keeping me here so I could recover. And by teaching me about his continent and the language of his land.

I'd learned we were in Genesis, one of five kingdoms in Calandra. The Coraness River where I'd been found was named for the capital city on the other half of this kingdom.

That city seemed as good a place as any to begin my search for the silver-eyed warrior.

I walked to the table, taking the chair opposite his.

He eased his sketchbook away, tilting it up so I couldn't see the page.

"What are you drawing?"

"Nothing." The corner of his mouth turned up as he kept sketching.

I couldn't help but stare. His hair was pushed away from his forehead. His jaw was dusted in stubble. I'd spent hours studying the perfect symmetry of his face. *Vexx*. He was perfect.

My aunt had always said that the Starling were cursed with easy infatuation.

She'd blamed that curse for Emery leaving with Max. Oleana had always refused a consort or lover, not wanting anyone to distract her from ruling Nelfinex. But to me, it didn't seem like such a horrible thing to open your heart, even for a queen.

I liked to believe that as Starling, we simply recognized a good person when we found one.

And Andreas was a good man.

An easy infatuation with a kind, generous, and handsome man didn't seem like a curse.

In another life, I'd stop letting him sleep in that chair and invite him to share the bed with me instead.

Divine, I wished I could draw. When I left this cabin, I wanted something to remember him by. Maybe a sketch of him in the kitchen, sleeves rolled up his honed forearms as he kneaded dough for bread. Or maybe a drawing of him chopping wood, his muscles straining against the fabric of his shirt as he swung the ax.

Mostly, I wanted something to help me remember his tawny eyes. Andreas looked at me and the rest of the world would fade to gray.

It didn't seem fair that our time was coming to an end.

As quickly as I could move, I reached for the sketchbook.

Except I wasn't fast enough. Andreas snapped it closed, though not before I caught a glimpse of my face. He'd drawn me in his chair.

His grin made my stomach flip, and his laugh filled the tiny room.

It was as enchanting as the man himself. And another

reason that it was time for me to move on. If I didn't go soon, I might never leave this cabin.

"Are you hungry?" he asked, setting the sketchbook aside to rake a hand through his sandy hair.

"Yes." Hungry to touch his hair. To thread it through my fingers. To press my lips to his and find out if they were as soft as they appeared.

I would give almost anything to feel the strength of his arms wrapped around my body. I wanted to kiss the hollow below his throat and taste his skin.

When I met his gaze, it was hungry. His tongue darted out to lick his lower lip.

My mouth parted, and my breath hitched.

He cleared his throat, eyes dropping to the table.

As much as I wanted to give in to this attraction, to let the tension between us snap, if I surrendered now, there was no way I'd leave.

So I spoke the words I'd been dreading for suns. "I have to leave, Andreas."

The room went silent save for my pounding heart.

The desire from a moment ago vanished from his gaze. With one fluid motion, he stood, the backs of his knees sending his chair scraping across the floor. "Nelvi'o."

No.

He spoke it in the old language so there would be no doubt of what he was saying.

It was exactly what I wanted to hear. And the opposite of what I needed to do.

"I must find my cousin."

Andreas paced the width of the room, running a hand over his face as he shook his head. "It's too dangerous."

"I'm stronger now than I've ever been." Strong enough to leave.

Something had changed within my body since I arrived at the cabin. My vision was crisper, so clear I could make out veins on a leaf from ten paces away. Whenever Andreas left the cabin, I could hear his footsteps on the road well after he'd disappeared from sight. And there was a strength in my hands and arms and legs that had not been there before.

In Showe, I would have struggled lifting Andreas's ax and swinging it over my head. It was a heavy and cumbersome tool, made for someone his size, not mine.

"You're stronger because you've healed," he said. "You've rested. But you're no match for a monster."

Monster.

We didn't have that word in Nelfinex.

Nor did we have a word for the black beast that Xandra had become.

After I'd described them to Andreas, he'd told me they were called bariwolves.

Xandra had said she wanted to shift into an animal with more bite than a swift. Well, she'd chosen wisely. Bariwolves were feared all across Calandra.

"I will be cautious," I told him. "But it is time for me to leave."

"No, not yet. There is still so much we can learn from each other. I want to know more about Nelfinex."

Andreas had never heard of my continent or any other before, and he'd been shocked to learn just how far across the Marixmore I'd traveled. To his credit, it hadn't taken him long to accept that the world was bigger than he'd once perceived.

Part of what made him so undeniably attractive was his acceptance. He'd believed everything I'd told him.

I'd told him of the continent Kenn and the country Nelfinex. I'd told him that his old language was similar to a dialect from Beesa, another country in Kenn. I'd told him I'd made this journey with my cousin and that we'd been separated because of bariwolves.

In our short time together, I'd shared with him enough

to satisfy his curiosity about my homeland while gleaning everything possible about his world.

And while he was beautiful and kind and compassionate and charming, Andreas and I were closer to strangers than friends. So I'd kept much of my life a secret. If there were shapeshifters in Calandra, I hadn't asked. Maybe, if we'd had more time together, I'd have told him everything.

Instead, I'd say goodbye.

"Andreas." I crossed the room, standing in his path as he paced. When he stopped in front of me, eyebrows knitted in concern, I forced myself to stay on my heels, not to rise up toward his mouth. "I cannot stay."

"You *will* not stay. There's a difference."

I gave him a sad smile. "I will not stay."

He let out a frustrated growl, jaw clenched as he glared at the wall. Then he closed his eyes and sighed, his frame deflating as he took my face in his hands. "Caspia."

I loved hearing him say my name. Almost enough to stay. Almost.

His eyes searched mine before they dropped to my mouth.

Kiss me. Please. I wanted just one kiss before I left.

A first kiss. And our last.

He shook his head, his teeth grinding as he let out another of those frustrated growls and dropped his forehead to mine. Then he let go of my face and hauled me into his arms. A first and last hug, too. "Can I change your mind?"

"Nelvi'o." I turned my nose into his chest, breathing in the crisp scents of wood, his botanical soap, and his own masculine spice.

Andreas smelled like the best parts of Showe and Calandra combined. Like two worlds colliding in a dream.

I breathed him in, soaking in the warmth and strength of his arms. Then I let him go and walked to the kitchen, picking up the drawing from the counter that he'd made me while explaining the five kingdoms.

A map.

"When will you leave?" he asked.

"Tomorrow." Before I lost my courage to walk away.

"And where will you go?"

"I don't know yet. I'll search for Xandra until I find her. And while I'm here, I'll explore your continent. Maybe I'll go all the way to Turah."

"Why Turah?" he asked.

I shrugged. "It's the farthest kingdom from here, isn't it?"

"Yes."

"Then by the time I travel all the way there, I'll have crossed most of Calandra. And if I still haven't found her, then I'll turn around and come back."

It was a half-truth. A veiled lie.

Andreas didn't know of my visions, either. He'd presumed that my cousin and I had come here by mistake while sailing, and I hadn't corrected his assumption. He didn't know that I'd seen Emery's death or that the ritus had called us here. Just like the truth of the Starling, I was afraid that if I told him about the visions and he didn't believe me, well...

I'd had enough heartbreak since leaving Nelfinex.

When I left here, Andreas would be a flawless memory. Untarnished and infallible for the rest of my life. If I failed at everything else, if I didn't find Xandra or avenge Emery or return to Nelfinex, then at least I'd have the memory of this perfect man to cherish.

I was going to Turah because he'd told me many of their people were lumbermen. In my vision of Emery's death, she'd been in a fortress with towering walls made of thick, fallen trees. It seemed as good of a place as any to search for the silver-eyed warrior.

"In my family, the women have a tradition. We have a rite. We leave home and travel into the unknown to find the person we were meant to become."

"And this is your rite?"

"Yes." Even if I never shifted, I knew in my heart this journey would change me forever.

Lifting the map he'd drawn me, I plotted my course.

"Tell me again about the starbursts. What are the colors?"

"Amber for Quentis. Green for Turah. Magenta in Laine. Blue in Ozarth. And here in Genesis, it's persimmon." The color of the fruit that grew on a tree outside the cabin.

"But no silver."

"No."

"And everyone in Calandra has starbursts?"

He nodded. "Everyone. I've never seen a person without them until you."

Maybe the silver-eyed warrior was from a different continent, too. If his eyes were truly unique, then it should make finding him easier. People would talk.

Now that Andreas had taught me how to speak Calandran, I could begin asking questions and understanding their answers.

"Thank you. I vow to repay your kindness."

"Stay alive," he said. "That's payment enough."

"Maybe I'll come back here. I'll bring you a more interesting book and a fresh sketchbook."

He gave me a sad smile. "Then you'd better make your way to Quentis."

"Why Quentis?"

"Because when you leave here, I'll return home."

Then I guess we'd both be saying goodbye to this tiny cabin.

"Quentis." I touched the center of my forehead with two fingers. "I vow it."

"I'll pray to Ama and Oda to guide your path. And to the Six to watch over your journey."

I shook my head. "Nothing good comes from the number six. Pray to the Divine."

"I don't know your god."

"Then I'll have to find you in Quentis and teach you about the Divine's grace."

His eyes crinkled at the sides. "I hope our paths cross again, Caspia."

"So do I, Andreas."

He lifted a hand, like he was about to reach for me. But before his fingertips could brush against mine, he backed away.

And when he walked outside, when the door closed behind him, I knew we'd just had our goodbye.

18

ODESSA

The village beyond the cave ginger bogs didn't have an official name or permanent spot on a map. But according to Sryker, some called it Middle, since it was almost exactly in the center of Ozarth.

The people who lived here were mostly farmers who went into the bogs to harvest the berries from their plots. Most would leave Middle once the growing season was over, returning to their hometowns and their families. And when the next season began, the village's location would likely have moved.

Huts and tents were scattered across the grassy plain. The structures were flimsy and small. Temporary. Nothing that would survive the migration.

There were no developed roads, just paths of dirt that grew wider depending on the popularity of the place to which they led. The path in front of the mercantile was as wide as the shanty itself. So was the path to the shed that served as a tavern. But most trails were only wide enough for a single rider.

The boom of male laughter carried from somewhere in the village, probably the tavern.

Just like the camps on the Harrow River, there was no urgency or panic about the coming migration. Why wasn't word of the scout spreading faster?

We'd arrived at the village just before dark, and there'd been enough time before the sun went down to pick a campsite, secure the horses, and build a fire.

After a quick meal, Evie had rested her head on my lap and fallen fast asleep. Faze was tucked tightly under her arm.

My stomach was so knotted from today's journey, I still hadn't eaten anything.

"Is it always like that? Traveling through the bogs?" I asked Sryker.

"Today was...unusual." He sat beside me, the scars on his face illuminated by the campfire's flames as he poked and prodded at the coals with a stick. "I've never seen that many alligasks try to break through the fences."

Nine monsters had tried to break through the bars on today's ride. Thankfully, only the one had made it through. Still, it had been a harrowing day.

If the attacks on the fence were unusual, then it had to be my fault. In Ellder, it had just been a theory that monsters were drawn to me. But I couldn't keep ignoring the signs.

There was something about me that attracted these creatures.

Ransom had refused to let me test our theory. Well, this journey was test enough.

How many people would die simply because they were unlucky enough to be in my company? The list of names in my mind, the people who'd been killed by monsters, was growing.

Sariah, the woman from a tavern in Ashmore.

Witt, a boy from Ellder.

Luella. Zavier. Jocelyn. Brielle. All killed the night of the crux. Was I the reason the scout had attacked the fortress?

The pressure that had been building in my chest all day made it nearly impossible to breathe.

I couldn't take Evie to Quentis alone. I wouldn't be able to live with myself if her name was on my list.

"Oda blessed us by having the Mavins nearby," Sryker said, glancing toward the band of warriors at the campsite beside ours.

There were eleven men and one woman—Thora—in this crew of Mavins.

According to the rumors Sryker had heard, there were hundreds of Mavins in Calandra, though no one knew exactly how many. They were loyal to no king or kingdom but had pledged their allegiance to gold.

I hoped they didn't expect to get paid for their services today.

The Mavins had ridden with us through the bogs, swinging blades and axes at the alligasks that had battered against the fences.

"You should find out where they're going," Sryker said, setting down his stick and pushing to his feet. "See if you can ride with them. Stay safe, Odessa. May Ama and Oda protect you on your journey."

"Wait." I shifted, carefully moving out from beneath Evie. "Are you leaving? In the dark?"

"It won't be the first time I've ridden through the bogs at night. Though I do think it will be the last. But if I leave now, I'll make it home for Edda's breakfast."

"What about the monsters?"

"They'll leave me alone." He flipped up the hood of his alligask coat.

"Sryker." I moved closer. "You should leave the riverside. Take shelter soon for the migration."

"But it's not time. It's not supposed to come until spring."

"There was a scout seen in Turah."

His forehead furrowed. "I've heard no warning."

No one seemed to have heard a warning. Why? King Ramsey should have sent his pony riders or soldiers with missives to every king on the continent.

"Please, just trust me."

He studied me, then nodded. "All right. Goodbye, Odessa."

"Goodbye, Sryker. Thank you. For everything." I watched

as he walked away until I could no longer see the lime green of his clothes.

I bent and pulled the blanket higher over Evie's shoulders, then squared my own and walked to the Mavins' camp.

If Stryker was right about the Mavins, maybe they could deliver Evie and me safely to Quentis.

The warriors lounged around the fire in a circle made from their saddles. Two of the Mavins were playing dice. One was reading a tattered book. The others seemed content to sit on their bedrolls and stare at the flames in silence. Thora sat with her legs crossed on a blanket and sharpened her ax on a stone.

They looked as comfortable here, beneath a roof of stars, as they would have in a cozy sitting room with a warm hearth.

Each of them had lines across their nose, either one or two. Jodhi was the only man with three. And Thora was the only one with five plus the dots on her forehead and line down her chin.

Did the lines indicate their rank with the Mavins?

Jodhi lounged against his saddle, his hands clasped behind his head, his legs stretched long with ankles crossed. Unlike his companions, he wasn't looking at the fire.

He stared at me, wearing an arrogant smirk.

It reminded me so much of Ransom my heart ached, and I traced the scar on my palm.

In another life, I might have found Jodhi attractive, but there was only one man who made my pulse flutter.

"Look lively, boys," Jodhi said. "We've got a visitor."

The men spared me chaste glances, then went back to whatever it was they were doing.

Thora glanced up, sneered, and continued sharpening her blade.

She seemed like the person I'd have to ask for help, and the first person to tell me no.

"What can we do for you, doll?" Jodhi asked.

I forced a smile, ignoring the endearment, and stopped at the edge of their circle. "I was wondering where you're traveling."

A few shared looks between themselves, letting out quiet laughs.

Jodhi jackknifed to a seat, his grin spreading. "We travel wherever the coin leads."

Exactly the answer I expected. "We need to get to Quentis. I will pay you to take us."

"How much?"

"Name your price."

That drew the attention of a few others. The men playing dice set their game aside.

Jodhi looked me up and down, skepticism filling his dark-brown eyes. "Sorry, doll. I don't think you can afford us."

"One thousand zillahs. Each."

They'd each need a chest to carry that much coin. A zillah was ten times the value of a darric, and that much gold would make them all wealthy.

The offer should have been enough for me to be taken seriously, but all eleven men burst out laughing.

"You've got twelve thousand zillahs in those saddlebags?" Jodhi asked.

"Well, no. I'll have to pay you once we arrive in Roslo."

"We get paid up front. No exceptions," he said.

"I-I don't have anything."

"You've got a rather fancy sword."

"Yes, I do. And I'll be keeping that fancy sword for myself."

Jodhi steepled his fingers beneath his chin. "How about that pet?"

Faze? My nostrils flared. "Absolutely not."

"Then we can't help you, doll."

"Odessa," I corrected, hands fisting. "My name is Odessa."

"Your name could be Queen Kasan, and it wouldn't

matter. We don't do anything for free. And we don't do anything unless we get paid first."

The man with auburn hair, Mathias, chuckled. "We've got pockets to fill before the migration."

Well, you won't have to wait long. I turned to retreat to my own fire.

"Stop." Thora's voice cut through the silence. "What did you say?"

Damn. I'd said that out loud, hadn't I? I cringed before spinning to face the Mavins, and this time, I had their undivided attention.

Jodhi patted the ground beside him. "Have a seat, doll."

It wasn't a suggestion.

A hush settled over the group.

It hadn't taken me long to tell them about the crux scout that had attacked Ellder. There wasn't much to say.

It came. It killed. I left.

"How long ago was this?" Jodhi's teasing tone and arrogant smirk had vanished the moment I took a seat at his side.

"Twenty days, I think? Give or take a few." The days had blurred together since we left Ellder.

"Fuck." A bulky man with Genesis starbursts and spiked blond hair leaped to his feet and began packing up his things.

"Mose. Don't." One of the men playing dice stood and went to stand in front of Mose as he picked up his saddle. "If he finds out…"

Who was *he*? And what was *he* finding out?

"I don't care," Mose snapped. "Get out of my way."

The other man didn't move.

"At least wait until dawn, Mose," Jodhi told him. "You'll travel faster in the day."

"My family needs to be warned. To hell with the rules. I

need to get them to shelter. I'll be lucky to get there in time as it is."

"Let him leave," Thora ordered, and the other man moved. "Good hunting, Mose. To bloody blades."

Mose gave Thora a nod, then stalked off into the night to fetch his horse.

"Is it dead?" a man with smooth brown skin asked. "Did the Guardian kill the scout?"

"I don't know," I whispered.

All I could see was the crux flying into the night with Ransom in her talons.

"Why haven't we heard anything about this?" Jodhi's jaw clenched. "People need to be warned. Fucking Turans and their fucking secrets."

I shot him a glare. Maybe Jodhi was right about the Turans and their secrets. But in this, I couldn't believe King Ramsey wouldn't send word to the other kingdoms. I didn't particularly like Ransom's father, but at the very least, he'd prepare his own people for the migration.

And if the Turans were preparing, others would take notice.

"The Turans aren't purposefully keeping the scout a secret. This happened in a very secluded part of the kingdom. And that monster killed more than survived. Spreading news doesn't happen overnight."

"Well, thank the Goddess Daria we were lucky enough to save your ass today," Jodhi deadpanned.

I really didn't like this man.

Yes, the Turans kept a lot of secrets. Yes, it was infuriating. Jodhi wasn't wrong. Not that I'd ever admit it. And maybe Ramsey hadn't acted as quickly as another king in his position would have, but I refused to believe *Ransom* was keeping the scout a secret.

The only reason he wouldn't have sent word was a reason I wouldn't consider—that he wasn't alive to deliver the message.

He's alive.

"You're sure it was just the one scout?" Jodhi asked.

"Yes, I'm sure." As long as I lived, I'd never forget the monster's piercing scream.

"There should be others," he said, speaking to the Mavins. "There's always more than one scout. The Turans might stay quiet, but other kingdoms won't."

"Agreed," another man said. "And Salem would have sent word. Besides, the migration isn't supposed to happen until next spring."

I didn't know the name Salem, but I did recognize the disbelief on the Mavins' faces. My heart dropped. "You don't believe me."

Jodhi shrugged. "Not really."

Asshole.

I huffed and shoved to my feet. "Why would I lie about this?"

"To try to guilt us into escorting a woman and child to Quentis, since they can't pay."

I opened my mouth. Closed it. *Wow.* "You think I'm manipulating you?"

"Don't take it personally," he said. "I learned a long, long time ago not to trust a beautiful woman who bats her eyelashes and begs for help."

I did *not* bat my eyelashes.

Without a word, I stalked away from the fire, more than ready to return to Evie and Faze. I could see her from where I'd been sitting, but I still didn't like leaving her alone.

"Stop." Thora's order thwarted my plan.

I crossed my arms over my chest and turned, giving her my best glare.

She arched an eyebrow.

This couldn't be the warrior Brother Skore had meant for me to find. Not this woman. There had to be someone else. Someone who would *help* me keep Evie safe.

We were running out of time. They could all pretend like the migration wasn't happening, but I knew the truth.

Thora set her knife and sharpening stone aside, then stood, rounding the fire and stepping outside the ring. She walked to me and stopped an arm's length away. "Who are you?"

A Quentin princess.

The Gold King's daughter.

The Sparrow.

None of those seemed like the right answer.

I was Ransom's queen.

"Odessa Wolfe."

She stared at me, studying my eyes. "All right, Odessa Wolfe. We'll take you to Quentis."

The air rushed from my lungs. "Thank you."

"Thank me with a thousand zillahs." She looked over her shoulder to the men. "We leave at dawn."

And just like that, I was traveling with the Mavins.

19

CASPIA

May Daria grant you luck on your journey. Stay alive, Caspia.
 Until Quentis,
 Andreas

The note, written in Andreas's neat script, was on the table beside a leather satchel. Inside was a loaf of bread, a pack of dried meat, a handful of persimmons, and a pouch filled with gold coins.

I wasn't sure how much it was worth in Calandra, but it was likely more coin than he could afford to lose.

Beside the satchel was a new map, the lines cleaner and crisper than the one he'd originally drawn for me. He'd noted towns and cities and rivers as well as areas to avoid, like the bogs in Ozarth and the vast desert in Laine.

He must have drawn it sometime in the moon, after I'd given up waiting for him to return and fallen asleep. Then he'd snuck back into the cabin and left it all for me to find before dawn.

The cabin was empty and quiet. I took one last look around the room, grateful he was gone.

We'd had our farewell. And without him, there was no temptation to stay.

So I pulled up the hood of my cloak, covering my hair, and slung the satchel across my body. Then, before I lost my nerve, I walked out the door.

"Until Quentis."

...

The narrow trail that led from the cabin came to a juncture with a road. In the suns that I'd spent with Andreas safe in his cabin, I'd forgotten the intense vulnerability of walking through a forest alone. Even on the road, I'd never felt more exposed.

Every few paces, I touched the knife strapped to my thigh.

The temptation to turn back made every step heavy and slow, but I kept putting one foot in front of the other, tracking the sun as it moved over the treetops in a sweeping arch.

I missed Andreas already. I missed his quiet surety and steady strength. I missed his soft smiles and resonant voice. And I already missed his cabin, almost as much as I missed Showe.

It was strange to long for a person I'd known less than a lune.

But Andreas was a man not easy to forget. I didn't really plan to try.

This walk had given me plenty of time to think about my suns in his cabin. About my aunt. About this predicament. About where I was going.

Turah.

It was going to be a long walk.

There was a dampness to the air that made my skin feel sticky, so I stripped off my cloak and tied it around my waist. Then I bound my hair in a knot atop my head to keep the curls out of my face.

The road was narrow, only two tracks that cut through the wood with a mossy strip of green between them. I stepped over the occasional horse hoofprint in the dirt, but there was no sign of other people.

Birds chirped as they flew overhead, winging from branch to branch. I'd spotted a chipmunk earlier, skittering across a fallen log. Every few steps, I scanned the forest, searching for any sign of predators or danger.

Was this the same road that Xandra and I had been on?

Would I find her paw prints in the earth? Would I stumble upon my lost pack?

I tapped my pocket, feeling Emery's elfalter rings. At least I hadn't lost them.

How much would they bring in Calandra? If I hired a ship to take me home, would I be able to find my way to Nelfinex? I should have paid more attention to Cap's charts while aboard the *Cirrina*.

If only I could shift. Flying over this continent as a swift would make my task so much easier. But with every passing sun that the thrum of the ritus didn't return, I lost another sliver of hope.

Maybe I'd be trapped in Calandra. Maybe that wouldn't be such a bad thing if I was in Quentis with Andreas.

A low snarl yanked me out of my thoughts, and I slowed, sweeping my gaze left to right, right to left, searching for the source of the noise.

Don't be a bariwolf. Please, don't let it be a bariwolf.

I turned in a circle, my pulse racing, as another snarl carried through the trees.

When I faced forward again, a fenek stood on the road, its tusks gleaming white.

"Oh, thank the Divine." I exhaled and pressed a hand to my pounding heart. Then I dropped to a knee, holding out a hand to the beast, palm up. "Hello, pet."

The fenek snarled and took a step forward.

"Come here," I cooed, waiting as it took another step.

The cinnamon fur on its throat vibrated as it snarled again. It bared its teeth, dropping its head and shoulders lower like it was going to pounce. Its ears were tucked back tight.

"Easy," I murmured. "I won't hurt you."

The fenek snapped and growled, prowling closer and closer.

The hairs on my arms stood on end as I stared into its mint-green eyes.

Fenek in Nelfinex were sweet, gentle creatures and our most beloved pets. Except this animal didn't seem interested in getting a scratch behind its furry ears. All I saw was predatory hunger and primal rage.

A chill ran down my spine as I slowly rose to my feet. "By the Divine, I vow not to hurt you."

The fenek opened its mouth, those tusks ready to sink into my flesh.

No. This could not be happening. Those of the Starling bloodline could calm and soothe the beasts of this world. We could tame and ride. A tutor once told me I had a way with animals the likes of which she'd never seen before.

I wasn't going to run from this creature. So I held the fenek's gaze, refusing to cower as it snarled. "You don't scare me, little friend."

The beast stopped, tilting its head to the side. It lifted its ears and pointed them forward as it rose from the crouch. One swish of its bushy tail, but it was enough to give me hope that not all was lost.

"That's better." I smiled, dropping my shoulders from my ears as I held out my hand again.

The attack happened in a blink.

The fenek leaped toward me, jaw wide with teeth and tusks ready to tear my body to slivers.

I moved faster than I'd ever moved before, twisting to the side so the beast flew past me. It crashed into the ground with a yelp, then its claws scratched at the dirt as it regained its footing and once more came at me with a ferocity I'd only seen once.

With the bariwolves.

Once more I dodged the little beast as it jumped for me, planting both hands on its ribs and pushing it away.

My knives stayed in their sheaths. I'd made a vow not to hurt this beast. The Starling kept their vows.

I spun around and ran. My boots thudded on the dirt, and

though I was somehow faster in this land than I had been in Nelfinex, I was no match for the fenek.

It snarled as it chased me down the road. With a leap, it hooked its tusks on the hem of the cloak tied around my waist, pulling hard enough to jerk me backward and nearly drag me down.

But my feet seemed to work of their own volition, stepping and spinning, as I tugged the knot free and let the cloak fall away.

It was tangled in the fenek's tusks. While it shook and thrashed, trying to loosen the fabric, I made my break. With one arm pumping and the other holding the satchel so it didn't bounce against my hip, I ran fast and hard.

A familiar snarl made my stomach drop. When I glanced back, the fenek was after me again.

My hand went to a knife, ripping it free.

The beast's paws seemed to float over the ground, its lithe body moving with such fluidity and speed, it was a streak of orange against a backdrop of green.

"Stop," I screamed as tears filled my eyes.

I didn't want to break my vow. I didn't want to kill this creature.

But if it meant my life, then so be it.

The growl at my heels was murderous.

I tightened my grip on my blade and turned, ready to slash the fenek's throat.

It bounded off the ground, but before we could collide, the whistle of an arrow shot through the forest and the bolt lodged into the fenek's heart.

The beast squealed as it slammed into the ground, landing with a sickening crack. Its legs kicked, like it was still running, even on the brink of death. Then the air puffed from its black nose and it slumped, lifeless, on the dirt.

"No." A fenek was good fortune. Its blood should not be soaking the earth.

"Caspia!" Andreas ran through the forest, a crossbow in one hand and spare bolts in the other. The worry on his face nearly broke me in pieces.

I opened my mouth to speak, but all that came out was a sob.

He slid to a stop beside me, dropping the crossbow and bolts as his hands roamed my body, searching for injury. "Are you hurt?"

"No." I shook my head, sucking in a ragged breath.

"Ama and Oda." With his hand, he made a sign in the air, twin teardrops that joined over his heart. Then he pulled me into his arms, holding me tight to his chest.

Andreas had told me that gesture was called signing the Eight.

It was a show of reverence to his gods. To the Mother and Father and their children, the Six, who'd cursed Calandra with monsters.

Monsters like the fenek.

Divine, take me from this place.

"Are you all right?" he asked.

"No." I squeezed my eyes shut, not able to look at the dead fenek. "Where I come from, they are not monsters."

They weren't vicious or bloodthirsty. They didn't attack or bite. They were gentle and smart and steadfast. We let children pick their favorites from every litter because the fenek were loyal companions, through life and into death.

"I had a pet fenek. His name was Helvi'op."

"Helvi'op," Andreas repeated in Nelfinex. "Hop?"

I nodded, clinging to him through another wave of tears.

Never in my life had I cried as often as I had since arriving in Calandra. *Vexx.* What a mess I'd made of this life. Of Xandra's.

All because of a vision.

Maybe I should have listened to my aunt, done as she'd

done, and forgotten all about Emery. Except I couldn't forget.

Because if our roles were reversed, Emery would not forget about me.

I sniffled and leaned away, wiping my face dry. Then I turned my back on the dead monster and started walking down the road.

"Where is your cloak?" Andreas asked, picking up his crossbow as I sheathed my blade.

"Ruined." Even if I could wear the garment again, I wanted nothing to do with it now.

It could stay on this road forever, lost to me like the rest of the belongings I'd brought to Calandra.

By the time I left here, this continent would have stripped me bare.

"Caspia." He put his hand on my arm, stopping and waiting until I faced him.

The lure was too great. My gaze drifted past him to the brownish-orange body on the side of the road.

I crumpled, burying my face in both hands as a sob escaped.

"You're okay." Andreas hauled me into his arms, holding me close as he murmured reassurances in my hair. "It can't hurt you now."

On the contrary. Its very death was the reason my heart ached. But Andreas only knew these animals as monsters. To him, they were only useful if dead.

I took a moment to grieve, then stood tall. "Thank you."

"Come on." He took my hand. "There's a village along the road ahead. If we keep a good pace, we'll make it before nightfall."

"We? You're coming with me?"

"Yes. We'll go together."

I wasn't going to argue, not after that attack. "I'm sorry."

"Don't be." He tucked a curl behind my ear. "I haven't been to Turah since I was a boy. It will be an adventure."

I blinked up at him, sure I hadn't interpreted that correctly. "Turah? But—"

Andreas pressed a finger to my lips. "You said the women in your family have a tradition. A rite. You leave home to discover the person you're meant to be. Well, I'm rather fond of the woman you are now. I think I'll be rather fond of the woman you become, too."

He spoke it all in the Beesan dialect, his "old language." It was faultless, like he'd spent hours rehearsing exactly what to say so I wouldn't miss a thing.

I fisted the front of his shirt and pulled him to me, taking the kiss I'd wanted for suns.

He smiled against my mouth, giving me a moment to discover the softness of his lips. Then he took control, wrapping those strong arms around me as he hauled me off the ground, my toes dangling as he kissed me until I was breathless.

I memorized the warm heat of his mouth, the softness of his lips, and the taste of his tongue. And when I swallowed his groan, the vibration trickled all the way to my toes.

When Andreas finally set me down, I was dizzy and my body felt as if it had grown wings.

Maybe I'd never shift into a swift. But with Andreas, I'd still know what it felt like to fly.

"Ready?" He clasped my hand.

"Ready."

Together, we set off to explore Calandra.

20

ODESSA

Traveling through Laine's dry, harsh plains was as torturous as my childhood harpsichord lessons.

We were too exposed in the desert. Too vulnerable. And time was running out. Whether the Mavins wanted to believe it or not, the migration was coming, and this journey was taking too long.

My days were spent listening for piercing screams and searching the horizon for black wings. But all I saw was an empty sky and a vast expanse of rock and sand.

We'd crossed through Ozarth days ago and were now riding through the heart of Laine. If I'd thought traveling with the Voster had been exhausting, four days with the Mavins had redefined that word.

We left at dawn each morning, only stopping to give the horses a break. Camp was usually made at dusk.

"It's so hot." Evie pushed a lock of sweaty hair off her face. "Can we stop?"

"Not quite yet." We were both drained, but I wasn't about to ask the Mavins for a break.

Where our bodies touched, her back to my front, our clothes were sticky. Faze panted from his carrier, equally as uncomfortable.

The sun beat down on us, and as much as Evie wanted to roll up her pant legs and push up her sleeves, I made her keep her skin covered so it wouldn't burn.

My lips were dry and cracked. The split in the center was bleeding.

"I hate Laine," she said.

"Me too."

All around us were rock formations. Most were weathered, beaten and rounded by the wind. Some had been worn through the middle to create arches of different sizes, probably from ancient rivers that had long since evaporated. The ground was dotted with the occasional patch of dry, brittle grass. And otherwise, there was sand.

Sand that blew into my eyes. Sand that I couldn't shake out of my boots. Sand that I tasted on my tongue, its grit stuck in my teeth.

I loathed sand.

Shades, I wanted a cold bath. I wanted to rinse away the sweat, wash my hair, and burn these clothes.

Jodhi rode up beside us, wearing his ever-present smirk. The magenta starburst in his gaze was brighter, like his eyes recognized he was in Laine. There wasn't a single bead of sweat on his brow. How was he not sweltering dressed in all that black? "Not enjoying the desert, doll?"

"Not especially," I muttered. "We're too exposed."

"This desert is mild. Be grateful we're not in the dunes to the east."

"I meant we're too exposed to the crux."

"Ah. Yes, the crux. The migration should be starting any minute now, according to you."

Asshole. He still didn't believe me.

In the past four days, we hadn't encountered many people on the road, but every single merchant or traveler we passed, Jodhi made sure to ask if they'd heard anything about a crux scout in Turah.

Not a single person had heard the news.

Jodhi's smirk had been growing for days.

I wasn't anxious for the migration, certainly not until we

were safe in my father's castle in Quentis, but I was looking forward to watching that smirk get wiped off his face.

A drop of sweat dripped down my temple, and I wiped it away with my sleeve.

"Take off your shirt."

My jaw dropped. "Excuse me?"

"Your shirt. Laine is not the place to wear a wool tunic. You've got something on underneath, right?"

A thin camisole that was none of his business. "My shirt is fine and staying exactly where it is."

He shrugged. "Just trying to help."

"I'm fine." If *fine* meant miserable.

"Do what you want, doll. I will say, that pink flush to your cheeks is rather lovely." He flashed me a white, handsome smile. A smile I was certain had lured more than one woman into his bed.

I rolled my eyes. "Go. Away."

He winked and stayed beside me on the road, turning his attention to Evie. "Need me to take that pet, pet?"

Evie growled. Or maybe it was Faze.

Neither liked Jodhi. Both were excellent judges of character.

Maybe traveling with the Mavins had been a mistake. We hadn't seen a single monster since the cave ginger bogs. The biggest danger we'd faced was getting lost. But the road was fairly well established, one that Evie and I could have traveled alone.

"Wouldn't it be faster to ride to the coast and sail across the Krisenth?" I asked.

"Faster. Expensive. We debated it the other night while you were asleep."

My lip curled. "Too bad I missed that discussion. You could have woken me up."

"We tried. Thora kicked you. And you just kept snoring."

No wonder my leg hurt the other day. "So why are we not sailing?"

"In case you are telling the truth about the crux scout, none of us wants to be trapped on a ship in the middle of the Krisenth at the start of a migration."

"I am telling the truth," I gritted out, wasting my breath. "So we'll have to go through the Evon Ravine."

"Yes. Have you ever been?"

"No."

The Evon Ravine cleaved Genesis from Quentis. The chasm cut so deeply into the earth, it was said to be nearly black at the bottom. So dark that nothing could survive except obsidian and the chiropti—the bat-like monsters that called the Evon home.

"You're in for a treat," Jodhi muttered.

I wanted to ask if it was as terrifying as I'd heard, if the chiropti were as deadly as marroweels and bariwolves, but Evie was listening.

"So…why Quentis?" he asked.

"You asked me that question yesterday."

"And I didn't like your answer yesterday. Let's try again."

Yesterday when he'd asked, I'd told him that I was sick of the snow and wanted to experience a milder winter. "My husband is in Quentis."

Jodhi arched his eyebrows. "Now she has a husband? How convenient. And he is in Quentis while you're traveling alone with a child, on the cusp of a migration. You're not a very skilled liar, are you?"

"I guess not." I squeezed my thighs and urged Freya into a trot. If Jodhi wouldn't leave on his own, we'd do it for him.

We settled behind Golding, a mountain of a man with warm brown skin, a bald head, and two stars tattooed at his temple. His weapon of choice was a mace.

From what I'd gathered, Golding and Jodhi were traveling companions but not friends. They never rode together or camped side by side. And I had yet to see them speak a word to each other.

Which made Golding my new favorite person.

"Dess?" Evie asked, her voice quiet. "Why did you lie to him?"

"To Jodhi?" I didn't, not really. I was holding out hope that Ransom was in Quentis.

"Yeah. Papa is in the shades, not Quentis."

This girl picked up on more than I realized. She believed, like everyone else, that Zavier was my husband.

It felt wrong to be the person to tell her the whole truth. It felt like something Ransom should do. But he would have other truths to give her. I could explain this one.

"You know how you have to keep secrets," I said, bending so low that only she could hear. "About Papa and being a princess."

She nodded.

"I have to keep some secrets, too. And my secret is about Ransom. Your papa was a very special friend, but I love Ranse. He is my husband. But we don't tell anyone."

She looked up, worrying her bottom lip between her teeth. "You're married to Ransom?"

"Yes, I am."

Ransom and I were always careful to hide our relationship. In public, I was the Sparrow, married to the crown prince. He was the Guardian, famed warrior of Turah.

I'd kissed him in Ellder before taking Evie away to the dungeons. Maybe she remembered. Maybe not. It didn't matter. This was already more than a four-year-old should have to understand.

"Oh." Her shoulders sagged, and then she sniffled and her body began to shake. "But if you're not married to Papa, then you can't be my mama. Where do I go?"

"Oh, Evie." My heart cracked, and the pain made it hard to breathe. I held her close, bending to kiss her hair. "With me. Always with me. No matter what. Okay?"

She nodded as the tears kept falling.

Someday, I hoped this would all be a distant memory. I hoped she'd smile more often than not. I wasn't her mother, but I'd hold a mother's hope that this beautiful girl would overcome her grief.

And she might not know it yet, but she wasn't alone. She had her brother.

I touched my scar as I hugged Evie tighter.

We rode until the sun touched the horizon.

Thora, always at the front of the Mavins, broke off from the road, taking a path to a nearby outcropping of rock with a cluster of sparse trees. Only when she swung off her horse did the rest of us bother to do the same.

By nightfall, the roaring campfire was surrounded by saddles.

Evie and I had taken Mose's place after he left the Mavins in Middle. Five of the bedrolls were empty, the men having spread them out before riding off to hunt.

While the days were scorching, the nights were cold. I folded our blanket in half, the bottom to keep us out of the sand, the top barely enough to keep us warm.

"Not too far," I told Evie as she played with Faze outside of the ring of saddles. Then I took a seat, brushing the cursed sand from my pants.

"You said your last name was Wolfe," Jodhi said from his place across the fire. No matter which spot in the circle I chose, he was always in the spot directly across from mine so that whenever I looked up, he was there. Taunting me seemed to be his new favorite hobby. "Is that your husband's last name?"

"Yes."

"And what was your last name?"

"Why does it matter?"

He shrugged. "Call it curiosity. A woman who can pay a thousand zillahs for each of us should have a fairly recognizable last name."

"Shut up, Jodhi. Your voice is giving me a headache."

Thora was sharpening a knife. "Besides, you already know her name. Stop tormenting the Sparrow."

My jaw dropped.

Jodhi grinned. "Thora always ruins my fun."

"You knew?" I gaped at them both. "How?"

"The Mavins make it their business to keep tabs on the happenings of each royal family. You're the only Princess Odessa in Calandra. And if you were in Turah, you must have gone as the Sparrow instead of your sister."

Well, she wasn't wrong. "Why didn't you say anything?"

"I don't give a damn who you are, Princess. I'm after the Gold King's coin. I have a debt to settle, and he's going to help me do it."

I was simply a means to an end.

For the past four days, I'd convinced myself that I'd taken back some semblance of control. That I was no longer being manipulated by the Voster. I was even proud of myself for hiring the Mavins and making it all the way to Laine in one piece.

Except I was still just a pawn. Control was an illusion.

Thora would use me for her own gain.

Fair enough. I was using her, too. All I cared about was getting Evie to Quentis and finding Ransom.

Jodhi crossed his arms over his chest, his gaze shifting past my shoulder to where Evie was still playing with Faze. The cunning gleam in his eyes was enough to make my stomach drop. "You weren't much of a mystery. But I still haven't figured out who the girl is yet."

"Mine." I reached for the sword at my side, lifting it into my lap.

Jodhi could pester and annoy me to his heart's content. But if he so much as looked at Evie the wrong way, I'd drive this blade through his heart.

Thora laughed. It was a raspy sound, a laugh rarely used. "I like her."

"Any other questions, Jodhi?"

"Not tonight, doll." He dipped his chin, then pushed to his feet, dusting his hands on his pants. "I'm going—"

Before he could finish, the thunder of horses bounced off the rock, and the five Mavins who'd gone hunting stormed into camp.

Golding came into the light first with a dead creature in his grip. He tossed it at Thora's feet.

Thora sat taller, frowning at the dead beast. "I'm not skinning that."

"We're not eating that." Golding fisted his hands on his hips.

I straightened, eyes wide as I took in the monster.

A kaverine.

They were nocturnal animals who lived in Laine's sand dunes and could see almost perfectly at night. Its body was covered in thick brown-and-black fur, and its teeth and fangs and claws were snow-white. So were the two spiraling horns that extended from the creature's skull.

Their dung was called korakin. When boiled to mush and reduced to a paste, it was the strongest hallucinogen in Calandra. It was another ingredient in Luella's elixir that had led to the creation of Lyssa.

"We killed this one and another," Golding said as the other Mavins joined the circle. "We'll need to keep watch tonight in case there are more."

"Evie, come here." I waved her back toward the fire.

She scooped up Faze and came running.

Jodhi scoffed. "A kaverine isn't going to come near a fire."

Golding flipped the monster over, revealing a cut that traveled the length of the monster's belly.

It seeped green, putrid blood.

Lyssa. The kaverine's eyes should have been yellow, but even in the dim light, I could see the milky-white tinge.

Dair, a tall and lanky man with shaggy blond hair, came to stand beside Golding. "Are you all right?"

Golding nodded, bending to inspect the tattered remains of a pant leg. The leather was shredded and coated in blood. Red blood.

He snatched Thora's knife and sliced away the fabric. His calf was covered in claw marks. "It came at me in the dark. Left a few gashes on my horse, too."

"Kaverine are vicious," Jodhi said.

"Nothing like this." Dair marched to his saddle to retrieve a healing kit. "The other one was just as bloodthirsty. I cut off its horns and a leg with my ax. Still kept coming."

My gaze was locked on Golding's legs. "Did it bite you?"

Everyone's attention swung to me at once.

Thora shifted to her knees, standing slowly. "Why do you ask?"

"Did it bite you?" I repeated.

"No."

The air rushed from my lungs. "Good."

"All right, Princess." Thora crossed her arms over her chest. "What do you know?"

Maybe this was a story I shouldn't share. Ransom had always kept Lyssa a secret because he'd feared it would only cause a panic.

But people should panic. About this and the migration.

Besides, there was a very real chance the Mavins wouldn't believe me anyway.

I swallowed hard. "It's an infection. And it's called Lyssa."

21

CASPIA

"Caspia?" Andreas slipped his arm behind my shoulders. "Are you all right? You've been quiet today."

"Yes," I lied. "Just tired."

Tired of last moon's vision running through my mind on a loop.

...

Bodies litter a courtyard walled by towering logs. Fires rage all around me, smoke billowing like clouds.

A chorus of growls and clicks mingles with harrowing screams.

"Xandra." Tears stream down my face as I watch death prowl over puddles of blood.

This is not my cousin. This is not a Starling.

Andreas's lifeless body lies at my feet. His throat is missing. The ring I gave him during our wedding glows in the firelight.

I close my eyes as death snarls.

And let the Divine call me home.

...

Every time I closed my eyes, I saw his dead body.

I burrowed into Andreas's side, willing the image of his death out of my mind, as I stared at the fire he'd built for camp.

We were curled against a fallen log, our legs extended and covered by a blanket to ward off the cold. It was dark, the two moons obscured by a thick layer of clouds. Dark enough to hide the tears swimming in my eyes.

What did that vision mean?

Never in my life had a vision been about me. And never in my life had I seen a glimpse of the future. It was always the past. Always events that had already taken place for other people.

It wasn't a dream. It had the same crisp, clear edges as a vision. The same lasting image that I'd remember until the end.

"You're shivering." Andreas pulled the blanket higher.

My entire body trembled, but it had nothing to do with the stormy weather. "It's cold tonight."

"The seasons are changing," he said. "It will be winter soon."

"Winter?" I didn't understand that word.

"The coldest of the four seasons. Summer. Spring. Winter. Fall."

"We don't have seasons in Nelfinex."

"It's not my favorite, but I love spring in Quentis," he said. "It's beautiful. Lush and green and bright. You'll see when I take you there."

Would he? If we kept going on this path, traveling to Turah, would Andreas survive? Or was this vision a gift from the Divine? This could be a warning that I was on the wrong path. What if I found Xandra, but rather than me saving her life, she took ours instead?

Another shiver ran through my bones.

We'd been traveling across Calandra, and though the suns had been long and grueling, they were worth it for the moons we'd slept beneath the stars.

Except there were no stars. Was that another omen of the death that awaited us at this journey's end?

We'd followed the road through the forests of Genesis to Coraness, the capital situated at the base of the Elroose Mountains. The city was a cluster of buildings with tall, pointed roofs. From red to blue to yellow to green, each structure was painted a bold hue. Even some of the city's stone streets were stained with color.

Coraness was a place I could have explored for summers, but we'd only taken one moon's rest at an inn on the outskirts of the city before buying two horses and leaving the capital behind.

But it had been nice to see that there were cities in Calandra. It was still unsettling how much open space there was between towns. How few people lived on this continent. Or maybe they simply resided in other places, like Quentis.

We'd ridden north, traveling along the foothills until we crossed into Laine. So far, this country seemed as sparsely populated as Genesis. It was so different from Kenn and Nelfinex.

Trees had given way to barren rock. It wasn't exactly like the landscape in Showe, but it was similar enough to make me homesick.

When I'd asked Andreas why there weren't more towns, he'd told me that people tended to cluster in cities, where they'd be safer from monsters.

We had yet to see another monster since the fenek. And while Andreas had gone to buy our two mounts in Coraness, I'd asked the innkeeper if he knew of a silver-eyed warrior.

He'd asked me, in turn, if I was drunk.

Andreas lifted his hand to my face, dragging his knuckles along my cheekbone, stealing me away from my thoughts. "Tell me about your family."

"I have two sisters. Emery and Saskia."

"And your parents?"

"My father died five lunes before I was born."

Emery and Saskia remembered him enough to tell me stories. He'd been the captain of the Royal Blades, nearly twenty summers older than our mother. He died in his sleep one moon.

"And my mother is...gone. She left us when I was a baby. We were raised by my aunt."

"Ah."

"Do you have sisters?" I asked.

"Only a brother. Arick."

"Do you get along?"

"Nelvi'o." Andreas used the old language when he was finished with a topic.

I tilted up my chin and forced a smile. "I'm ready for a real bed."

"So am I. Maybe we'll spend an extra day or two in Skanshon when we get there. There's an inn I've stayed at before with the best clam stew you'll ever taste. And each room comes with a bathtub large enough for two."

I hummed, snuggling closer.

Every moon, Andreas would kiss me until I was dizzy, but before it went any further, he'd pull away. In Coraness, he'd gotten us separate rooms at the inn.

I hoped the mention of a bathtub meant we'd be sharing a room, and a bed, once we arrived in Skanshon. "You've traveled often, haven't you?"

"I have. Once I came of age, my father felt it was important for me to see as much of Calandra as possible. My family is wealthy, and I was fortunate that they could afford to let me explore the realm."

"You're wealthy?" I sat up, trying to match this new piece of information to the man who was stealing my heart.

"Yes. Does that change how you see me?"

"No." Rich or poor, he was still Andreas. "Why were you in that little cabin?"

"To prove to myself I could walk away."

"Walk away from what?"

"The wealth. My father. We are not on the best of terms. I haven't spoken to him in a year, not since I left Quentis. I wanted to live a lifestyle that he'd loathe, so I chose a place I'd never been. The cabin belonged to a man from Clefton. I met him a long time ago, when I was just a boy. He offered to sell it to me. I accepted."

"Will you miss it?"

"Yes." He nodded. "It served its purpose. I'll come back to visit someday, but I won't live there again. I can't avoid Quentis forever."

"What's it like?" I asked, curling back into his side. "Quentis?"

He toyed with a strand of my hair, twining the lock around his finger. "There's an openness to the countryside. Fields of wheat and grain that make a man feel small. It's like being on a ship in the middle of a golden sea. My favorite cities are on the coast, where you can hear the ocean waves from every open window. Where it smells like salt and sand and every spice imaginable."

Like Showe.

The way Andreas talked about Quentis, with affection and adoration in every word, was the way I felt about my home.

Maybe I'd find a piece of my Nelfinex here in Calandra. Enough to fill the void in my heart in case I never returned.

"You miss it," I said.

"Every day."

"I miss my home, too."

"Nelfinex." He spoke the name often, always with a curious lilt in his voice. Any time I told him of my country, he soaked in every word. For all he knew, it could be a string of lies. But there was never a doubt, never a question that I was telling him a tale.

His trust was as beautiful as his smile.

The guilt of keeping the truth from Andreas had started to gnaw at my insides. He was risking his life to take me across this continent, and he didn't know why.

"There is something I haven't told you," I said.

His body stiffened.

"Xandra and I came to Calandra to avenge my sister's death."

"What?" He looked down at me, forehead furrowed.

I took a deep breath, shied away from his warmth, and told him my truths. "My aunt is the queen of Nelfinex."

His eyebrows lifted. "You're royalty."

"Yes. I am Starling."

"What does that mean?"

"It means I'm a Nelfinex princess." As for the rest of what being Starling entailed, well…that was for another sun. "My family and our bloodline have many traditions."

"Your rites."

"Yes. We call it a ritus. And another we hold dear is vengeance. To kill a Starling is a death sentence. I believe my sister Emery's murderer is here, in Calandra. A warrior with silver eyes. And I believe he is in Turah."

Andreas's jaw clenched as he turned his attention to the fire, his gaze fixed on the crackling flames. "That's why you're going there. Not to explore and find your cousin."

"I do want to find my cousin. And also the silver-eyed warrior."

"Why didn't you tell me this at the cabin?"

"I was leaving and didn't think I'd see you again."

"Then what about all this time together?" He flung the blanket off his legs, pacing in front of the fire. "You've had days to tell me the truth, Caspia."

"I'm sorry. It wasn't a secret intended to hurt you." I sat on my knees and closed my eyes. "I was afraid you wouldn't believe me."

"That you're here for vengeance? You might be from Nelfinex, but that is a concept we have in Calandra, too."

I gave him a sad smile. "No, I was afraid you wouldn't believe how I know Emery was killed by a silver-eyed man. And how I know it was in Turah."

He stopped pacing, crossing his arms over his chest.

"I don't have dreams, Andreas. I have visions."

He blinked, then came to sit on the log.

And listened as I told him about my sister's death.

I'd learned enough about Andreas's expressions to know that the clench in his jaw and intensity in his tawny eyes meant he was surprised. And Andreas was not a man who enjoyed a surprise.

He'd been quiet as I told him about my visions of Emery being killed by the silver-eyed warrior, and how I knew they were not dreams but glimpses of the past.

It was strange how something that had haunted me for so long hadn't taken long to explain. It felt bigger than mere moments.

Probably because I'd left out a few details. I hadn't told him that she'd been in a swift's form when she died.

"I would give all the elfalter in the world to know what you're thinking," I whispered.

"Elfalter?"

I fished my necklace from beneath my tunic, letting the orange metal glint in the firelight. "You have gold in Calandra. We have elfalter in Nelfinex. It's the purest and cleanest of all metals. It's impossibly strong, yet it can be molded under exactly the right conditions. It's as precious to us as any gem or jewel."

Andreas studied the pendant, taking it from my hand and turning it to inspect the silver wing. "What is this symbol?"

"The crest of the Starling."

He studied it closely before setting it against my chest. His eyes searched mine, his amber starbursts glowing. His expression was still too serious, too contemplative.

"Do you believe me?"

I wouldn't blame him if he didn't. But it would be the end of us.

I wasn't ready for the end.

"Yes."

For a heartbeat, I thought I'd imagined the word. "You do?"

Andreas shifted off the log, kneeling in front of me. He took my face in his hands, his thumbs dragging over my cheeks. "I believe you."

"Why?"

He bent and kissed the corner of my mouth. "Are you lying?"

"No."

"Then I believe you."

I'd never had such faith from another person, even Emery. Even Xandra.

Tears filled my eyes. Divine, I was tired of crying. "*Vexx*," I muttered, blinking them away.

Andreas caught one that escaped. "*Vexx?*"

"Oh, it's just a curse."

He thought about it for a moment, then grinned. "Here, we say 'fuck.'"

"I like your version better."

"So do I." He sealed his mouth over mine, his tongue dragging over the seam of my lips.

I gasped as he slid inside, slanting for a deeper taste.

His hands moved from my face into my hair. They skimmed over my shoulders and down my spine, settling on the curve of my ass. He groaned, tearing his mouth away.

"Don't stop," I pleaded, fisting his shirt.

"Caspia, there are things…" He trailed off, dropping his forehead to mine.

"What?"

He sighed, easing away. "Nothing."

I let the lie stand.

He wasn't the only one at this campfire with secrets. Sooner rather than later, I'd have to tell him what it meant to be Starling. But not yet.

"Do you want me?" I whispered.

"More than anything in this realm."

I urged him backward, until he was resting against the log. Then I crawled to straddle his hips, taking his face in my hands. "Then I'm yours."

"You are mine, darling."

The endearment made my belly flutter.

I freed the clasp on his pants as I pressed my lips to his. And as we stripped each other bare beneath a blanket of stars, as our bodies became one, I let my other secrets get lost in the dark.

22

ODESSA

For two days, I'd answered countless questions about Lyssa, most three or four times.

Where Thora had mostly avoided me after the cave ginger bogs, she was my constant companion now, riding at my side as we traveled through Laine toward Genesis. From sunrise to sunset, as the mountains on the horizon grew larger, she'd interrogate me for information.

My father would undoubtedly reprimand me for being so forthcoming with a woman whose allegiances were entirely unknown. But I had a feeling even the Gold King would find Thora intimidating.

I couldn't have ignored her questions if I'd tried.

I'd told her about each of my encounters with an infected monster, from the marroweel on the Krisenth Crossing, to the pack of bariwolves wreaking havoc on the Turan people, to the tarkin mother that had abandoned her cubs. And I'd told her about the Guardian's hunting parties and their futile effort to purge their kingdom of the infection.

Thora knew everything I was willing to share.

But she didn't know that the Guardian, the crown prince, and my husband were all one and the same. She didn't know that Evie was King Ramsey's daughter. And she didn't know that Luella was responsible for the very elixir that had contributed to the infection.

I still believed Luella's intentions had been pure. She'd set out to create a medicine to protect her children, to make them stronger. If Ransom hadn't been bitten by that bariwolf, she would have succeeded.

"I'm not sure if I believe you about the migration," Thora said. "But I do believe you're telling the truth about Lyssa."

"Thanks?"

That might be the closest thing she'd ever given me to a compliment. I'd take it.

Thora held up a hand, slowed her horse. I did the same as she brought her fingers to her lips and whistled.

The Mavins circled around us, their expressions stern.

"Jodhi, Mathias, Golding, and Dair, with me. The rest... you have your orders."

Orders? What orders? My eyes widened as one by one, the Mavins scattered, leaving only six horses on the road.

"Um, where are they going? They're coming back, right?"

"No. They have another task," she said. "Though I expect your father to pay their thousand zillahs as if they'd escorted you to Quentis. It's not their fault the Turans have been concealing a plague."

Damn. I really liked the idea of traveling with eleven warriors, not five.

"Don't look so worried, doll." Jodhi chuckled. "We'll keep you safe."

"Let's go." Thora jerked her chin toward the road and mountains in the distance. "I want to get to the edge of the skeleton forest before dark."

What in the shades was a skeleton forest?

I swallowed that question as we took off riding.

Thora took the lead, riding alone. Apparently, her interrogation was finished.

Jodhi and Mathias went behind her while Evie and I followed with Golding and Dair watching our backs.

It was nearly dark when we crossed the invisible border of Laine into Genesis.

Thora led us toward a towering formation of rocks with

a split down the middle, the opening creating a cave. There was already a fire ring in its center and a stack of branches left behind. We weren't the first to spend a dark night in this place, and I doubted we'd be the last.

Our campfire circle was considerably smaller with only six saddles, but at least we had shelter.

Thora and Mathias sat to my right. Golding and Dair to my left, their bedrolls touching. And Jodhi across the fire. Always watching. Always smirking.

Faze sat beside me, gnawing on a piece of dried meat.

Evie was asleep and curled into my side, her body shivering.

Each night seemed to get colder than the last.

"Here. Use this. Dair and I will share." Golding tossed me a thick pelt.

A ruby-red pelt with pink stripes. A tarkin pelt.

These pelts were prized among the rich. But I doubted Golding had paid the lofty price to buy this hide. No, he'd likely killed a monster and skinned it himself.

It took everything I had to spread the fur blanket out over my lap and cover Evie. In the morning, I'd make sure it was folded and returned to Golding before she woke up. "Thank you."

Dair laughed at something in the book he was reading. He leaned closer to Golding, holding out the page. The two bent their heads together, sharing an intimate smile, and then Dair put the book aside and rested his cheek on Golding's shoulder.

I hadn't realized they were a couple. Every other night, they'd kept their distance, sleeping on opposite sides of the camp circle.

Except now the other Mavins were gone. And maybe this meant they no longer had to hide.

"It is forbidden," Thora said, gaze locked on the fire, reading my thoughts. "When we join the Mavins, we vow to give up all ties. Past. Present. And future. But some bonds cannot be broken or ignored."

The night I told the Mavins about the migration, one of the men, Mose, had left to warn his family. He'd said to hell with the rules.

"What are the Mavins?"

"Mercenaries, doll," Jodhi answered.

I had a hunch that name was simply part of their illusion, intended to keep people at a distance. "Who are you really?"

"Shackled," Mathias answered, running a hand over his auburn hair.

"To who?" A king? The Voster? "Salem?"

Jodhi's mouth flattened. "If you know what's good for you, you'll forget that name. And you'll never speak of what you're told or what you see tonight."

Meaning, I'd never tell anyone about Golding and Dair.

"Salem gives...incentives," Dair said. "For keeping one another on the path."

"You mean the other Mavins would tell him about your relationship?"

"Yes. If it meant their own debt was lessened."

"Oh." So much for loyalty among companions.

I couldn't imagine any of Ransom's rangers betraying the trust they had with one another. Tillia knew Zavier wasn't truly the crown prince, and that was a secret she would be willing to take to the grave.

"Who is Salem?"

Jodhi stretched out his long legs, crossing his ankles as he laced his hands behind his head. "Our employer, for all intents and purposes. We are each indebted to his service. And until that debt is paid, we are his to command."

"What does he make you do?"

"Whatever his black heart desires," Golding muttered. "The bastard."

"You hurt people for him?"

Jodhi chuckled. "You really are naive, aren't you, Princess?"

I guess so.

"I've been with the Mavins since I was fourteen," Mathias said. "My mother worked at a brothel. She had the misfortune of servicing Salem one night and fell pregnant. He isn't the fatherly type. So he went to kill my mother before the baby was born. I stopped him from cutting open her womb. Begged him to spare her life. He agreed, but only if I paid him a thousand zillahs. I didn't have even a darric to my name. But he offered me a deal for repayment. I earned this star tattooed on my face and have been in his servitude since."

"I'm sorry."

Mathias shrugged. "It's not all bad. He uses my mother and sister to keep me in line, which means it got her out of that brothel. I don't see them often, but whenever he threatens to kill them, at least I know they're still alive."

"And from time to time, Golding and I have nights like this," Dair said. "Nights when we don't have to pretend."

They might not have had loyalty and secrecy from all the Mavins, but they did from Jodhi, Mathias, and Thora.

"We all have our own stories," Golding said. "But you get the idea."

"Do you owe a thousand zillahs, too?" I asked.

"Two." He touched the stars on his cheek.

"Does this mean that once you receive the payment from my father, you'll be free?" I asked Mathias.

Jodhi laughed, the sound so loud it made Faze sit up straight. "Salem takes a cut. You give us one thousand zillahs, we'll be fortunate to see even half of that."

"Enough talk of Salem." Golding kissed Dair's temple, then leaned back against his saddle and closed his eyes.

Salem had no intention of letting them go, did he? And I suspected if he found out about Dair and Golding's relationship, they'd each earn another star on their face.

Jodhi had three. Thora five.

In the journal, I'd read that she abandoned her armor and leather in the desert. Did that mean someday she'd be free of the Mavins? Did that story have anything to do with Brother Skore telling me to find a warrior?

"Do you know any of the Voster?" I asked.

Thora turned to stare at me, her persimmon starbursts glowing in the firelight. "Never speak of the brotherhood in my presence again."

So...yes.

She stood and, without a word, stalked out of the cave.

Dair went back to reading as Jodhi kept on smirking.

Gods, I was tired of the constant attention. Of the staring and scrutiny. "What?"

"How do you like that pelt? I assume you know it's tarkin?"

I ground my teeth together so hard my jaw hurt. Why couldn't he have been one of the Mavins to leave?

"You can't keep him," he said.

I reached for Faze, stroking the soft fur between his ruby ears as he kept chewing on the meat. "It's not your concern."

"If it's for the girl's sake, she'll only get more attached. And like it or not, doll, he's a monster. Get rid of him before he does something you can't undo."

Jodhi was wrong. There was more to Faze than claws and fangs.

He wasn't a mindless beast, dominated by the instinct to hunt and kill. There was magic in my little monster. Magic in the comfort and love he gave to Evie. Magic in the way he seemed to understand my moods and emotions.

Faze could have escaped into the wilderness countless times on this journey, but he'd stayed, tucked and squished in his carrier as our companion.

"I don't expect you to understand," I said. "And like I said, it's none of your concern."

Faze's ears turned, and he straightened, his meal forgotten.

Jodhi opened his mouth, ready to wield his sharp tongue, but before he could speak, a faint sound came from the distance.

A series of clicks.

My heart stopped.

Bariwolves.

Jodhi pressed a finger to his mouth, standing as Dair nudged Golding, and then the pair of them did the same. Mathias picked up his bow and quiver of arrows.

I reached for my sword, hand trembling as I shifted out from under the pelt and got to my feet.

We stood, motionless, ears trained to the night, but the clicks never came again.

"You heard that, too, right?" I whispered.

Dair and Golding both nodded.

A moment later, Thora stepped into the cave, returning from the forest. Her expression was stone, her eyes hard.

"Bariwolves?" Jodhi asked.

"I fucking hate Genesis. This godsdamn kingdom is crawling with wolves." She snatched her ax from beside her saddle. "I can't tell how many. They're too far away. Stay close to the fire. Let's see if we can't bring the horses inside."

I gulped as Golding, Dair, and Mathias followed her out of the cave.

A fire might keep a normal monster away, but if these wolves had Lyssa, not even the flames would scare them off.

I signed the Eight and sank down beside Evie.

"Don't worry, doll. You're safe."

No, we weren't.

I closed my eyes and traced the scar on my palm.

And as Evie slept, I spent the night praying that Ransom would find us.

Before it was too late.

23

CASPIA

The world was bathed in blood.

Xandra's roar rattled the fortress walls.

A mother wept over her slaughtered child. A man tried to push his guts back inside his body, dropping to his knees as they all spilled free.

Everywhere I turned, there was another bariwolf. Xandra commanded them like an army of death.

She was a monster. Her fangs dripped with Andreas's blood.

I looked to his lifeless body at my feet.

And welcomed the Divine's embrace.

...

I woke with tears swimming in my eyes.

It took a moment for me to remember where I was sleeping.

Ozarth. Skanshon. A suite at Andreas's favorite inn.

We'd spent so many moons beneath the stars that the gauze sheeting around this bed was almost suffocating. Even though I could see the rest of the room through the sheer fabric, it still felt too much like walls.

There was a reason our palace windows in Showe had no glass panes to keep out the elements. Those of the Starling bloodline did not like to feel caged.

A sheen of sweat covered my face, the bedsheets sticky against my skin.

Andreas's arm was draped over my hips as he slept soundly on his stomach. He seemed so at peace, so utterly handsome and relaxed.

It never took him long to fall asleep. He'd pull me close and bury his face in my hair. Then before I could count to ten, he'd have already dozed off.

I envied him that. The more often I had the vision of his death, the more I feared sleep.

It had come six times.

I loathed the number six.

The details became clearer and clearer as the vision repeated.

His hair was shorter when he died, cut above his ears. There was a thin scar on his chin. His gold wedding ring was inlaid with amber jewels, the same color as the starbursts in his eyes.

Where had he gotten that scar? How long had he worn that ring?

Were we happy before that gruesome end?

I slipped out from beneath his arm, careful not to wake him as I climbed out of the bed and pushed beyond the canopy. The robe I'd worn after our bath last moon was draped on a chair. I pulled it on, tying the sash around my waist as I tiptoed from the bedroom.

The inn's emblem—twin crescent moons faced together to form an elongated circle—was laid in the sitting room's floor with emerald tiles. Two navy velvet chairs sat opposite a plush sofa made of the same fabric. The air smelled like orange peel and rose. A pitcher of fresh water sat on the small writing desk beside a new bouquet of burgundy mums. The sheer white curtains floated from the breeze that drifted in from our balcony.

I stepped onto the platform, holding tight to the wooden rail, and breathed in the cool air of dawn as tears pricked the corners of my eyes.

"Fuck," I whispered, dabbing them away.

Even when I was alone, I found myself using Calandran more often than not. If I stayed here long enough, would I forget Nelfinex? If I left here now, if I found a way to sail home, would it change the future?

How did I save him?

I pressed my palms to my eyes, pushing in so hard that white and black spots blanked out everything but the sounds of the city.

We'd been in Skanshon for four suns. Each morning, Andreas would ask if I was ready to continue our journey on to Turah. And each morning, I'd kiss his mouth and drag him back to bed, where we'd stay, naked and entwined, for hours and hours.

How could I continue to Turah when it might mean his death?

There was a clarity to this vision. It was sharper than any other. The only vision I'd seen with this much focus was Emery's death.

If it was repeating, it had to mean something. But what?

I gripped the balcony's rail, digging my nails into the wood. It reminded me of the suns aboard the *Cirrina* when I'd stood at the bow and done the same. Even this morning, with my head spinning, the floor seemed to tilt below my feet like I was aboard the ship again.

What would Xandra do? I wished I could ask her.

The bed rustled inside, the sound so faint it was something I shouldn't have been able to hear. Footsteps shuffled across the floor before Andreas walked onto the balcony, a white sheet wrapped around his waist.

Two strong arms enveloped me as he molded his body around mine. "You're not sleeping enough."

Sleep was a dangerous concept at the moment. "I'll rest later."

He held me tighter, his body keeping me warm.

"Is it always this cold in Ozarth?" Now that the fear from the vision was fading, the chill of the morning was sinking in, raising bumps on my arms and legs.

"If you think this is cold, we'll need to get you warmer clothes before we travel to Turah. It will only get colder until we reach the winter solstice. There might already be snow in the mountains."

"Snow." I repeated the word, sounding it out slowly. "What is snow?"

"Like sand but made of ice. It falls from the sky like white rain."

The vision I had lunes ago of the man riding a horse with that young girl. They'd been in a field beside mountains capped in white. I'd thought it was sand or stone.

But it was snow.

"There is no snow in Nelfinex." No winter.

The suns were almost always the same. We had times when it would rain from dawn to dusk, and while the storms carried a chill, when the clouds parted, the warmth would return as though it had never left.

A cart rolled through the narrow alleyway beneath our balcony, the driver coughing into his fist as he urged on his horse.

Andreas and I hadn't spent much time beyond the walls of this room. All I'd seen of Skanshon had been the road through the city that led us to the Emerald Crescent Inn.

Since we arrived, each meal had been delivered to our sitting room, and if we longed for anything, Andreas would simply go downstairs, gold coins in hand, to make our request to the clerk.

"Do you want to leave today?" he asked.

"No," I murmured, resting the back of my head against his chest. "Not yet."

"Then I want to show you the city. But first, come back to bed." He bent to press his mouth to the juncture of my neck and shoulder.

The kiss was featherlight and sent tingles down my body, desire pooling in my core.

He lifted me off my feet and carried me inside, parting the canopy to lay me down on the mattress.

I slid my hand down his rippled stomach as he crushed his mouth to mine, our tongues tangling as I untied the sheet from his waist.

He settled into the cradle of my hips, his weight pinning me to the bed as he kissed me until I was breathless.

I reached between us and took his length in my fist, lining him up at my entrance.

He rocked us together, slowly, torturously, until he was rooted deep.

"Yes." The stretch of my body around his made my toes curl. I arched into him, my pebbled nipples dragging along his hard chest.

Andreas tore his mouth away, kissing a trail along the line of my jaw until he reached my ear. "Shades, I love to fuck you."

Fuck, I was learning, had many meanings, but this was my favorite.

I hooked my ankles around his hips and dug my fingers into the hard muscles of his shoulders as he eased out, then thrust inside.

He hit the spot that made me melt.

His strokes were quick but deliberate. His hands roamed with intent, leaving sparks in their wake as they moved over my breasts and ribs and thighs. He stared down at me with enough desire to make me come undone.

And when he pressed his finger to my center, I shattered, my body breaking into a thousand brilliant pieces.

The chill of the morning was long gone by the time we collapsed, boneless, onto the bed, our legs twined and his body curled around mine.

Andreas fell asleep instantly, a soft smile on his lips.

I stared at him, memorizing every part of his face, from the sharp corners of his jaw to his strong chin to the dark crescents of his eyelashes, until my own fluttered closed.

The vision came immediately.

This time, I saw the broadsword in the dirt at his side. I saw the crest on his silver armor—a crossbow woven with leaves and stalks of wheat. I saw the gore and blood from where his throat had been torn open by jaws.

I woke in time to slap a hand over my mouth to keep from retching on the sheets.

The streets of Skanshon were made of gray stones, and every road seemed to lead to a bridge. The city was built at the mouth of the Harrow River, where the water flowed into the Krisenth. Instead of a single, wide channel, the water broke off into countless tributaries, like the branches of a willow tree.

The larger channels were full of boats and ferries shuttling goods up- and downstream. The smaller streams gave people a place to wash clothes or cast a fishing line. The water was as blue as the Ozarth flags hung from balconies and posts. As blue as the starbursts in the countless gazes we'd passed since Andreas and I left the inn to explore.

We'd wound through a neighborhood of homes made with the same gray stone as the streets. Each had a roof covered in metal spikes. And above those spikes was a grid of iron bars that were mounted on posts driven into the ground.

It was strange architecture, but most of the grids had certain squares filled with a colored film that cast the homes beneath them in hues of soft blue or green or pink. Maybe the bars were Calandran art, like the sculptures and fountains in Showe.

We walked at a leisurely pace to a nearby market, exploring the stalls and carts. Andreas's fingers stayed threaded through mine as we peered into shop windows and perused display tables. Every other merchant was selling some sort of weapon.

Swords and knives and blades. Every shape and size imaginable. I hadn't seen so many blades since I left Showe.

My hands itched to touch them all.

"Is it dangerous in Skanshon?" I asked Andreas.

"No more than most other cities. Ozarth is known for their iron mines," Andreas said. "It's heavily traded with other kingdoms. Lumber from Turah. Spices and gold from Laine. Oil from Genesis. Grains and livestock from Quentis. Most of the iron mined here is sent raw, but some of the finest blacksmiths in Calandra live in Ozarth. They craft weapons and bring them here to sell."

"Ah." I nodded.

"Would you like one?" Andreas asked, gesturing to a table covered with a plum velvet cloth and an assortment of swords and knives. "Take your pick."

It was easy.

I chose a kukri to replace the one I'd lost in Genesis. The pommel was inlaid with a gleaming amber jewel that reminded me of Andreas's eyes. The grip molded perfectly to my palm, and the silver cross guard was etched with swirls and lines that reminded me of waves.

With the weapon secured across my back, we kept winding our way through the streets, moving into the area of the market where the tables were crowded with fruits and vegetables.

Andreas stood head and shoulders above most. His height seemed to intimidate people in the market, and wherever we walked, they moved out of his way. Or maybe it was simply his commanding presence that sent them scurrying to clear a path.

His confidence was catching, and for the first time in a long time, I felt like the princess I'd been in Showe. The woman who held her head high.

We came to a congested area that smelled of flour and spices and yeast. When I spotted a baker's cart, my stomach growled. The clam stew we'd eaten for our noontime meal was delicious, but I was hungry again.

"Can we buy a loaf of that bread?" I asked Andreas, pointing to the cart.

"Of course." He dropped a kiss to the top of my hair.

The baker smiled as we approached, waving a hand to his offerings.

I opened my mouth, about to ask for a loaf with a leaf design in its crust, when a yelp came from Andreas's side.

He dragged a boy with olive skin and straight black hair out from behind us, keeping hold of the child's arm.

The boy, possibly around Graciella's age of six summers, thrashed and pulled against Andreas's grip.

"Stop," Andreas barked.

The child obeyed, blowing a puff from his mouth to force the hair from his dark eyes. Then he glared up at his captor, his blue starbursts flashing. "Lemme go."

Andreas arched an eyebrow as he dropped to a crouch in front of the boy. "Give me back my coin purse."

"What coin purse?"

The corner of Andreas's mouth twitched. "You're good, little cutpurse. But not good enough."

Andreas plucked his teal coin purse from where the boy had stuffed it in the back of his pants. Then he looked up to the baker. "Two loaves, please."

The baker gave him a sideways glance but picked out two loaves, wrapping each in a thin cloth before handing them to me. "Two darrics."

Andreas fished two small coins from his purse and handed them to the baker. Then, still holding the child's arm, he took a loaf of bread from me. "One day, you will steal from a man who won't be kind when you're caught. Quit stealing before that day comes."

The boy's eyes bounced between Andreas and the loaf. Then he seemed to notice me watching. He met my gaze and shied away, like he was scared for the first time. With a quick swipe, he took the loaf from Andreas, who finally let him go.

The child scampered off, hugging the bread to his chest as he disappeared into the crowd.

Gone. Until I blinked and saw him again.

...

The boy whips open the flap of a tent. The fabric is so dirty and faded it is impossible to discern its true color. Tan or cream or white. The sun is setting, the sky alight with pink and yellow and pale blue.

He glances over his shoulder, making sure he is alone before slipping into the tent. Once the flap is closed, he sits on a pallet in the center of the cramped space. His tattered blanket is a discarded Ozarth flag from the marketplace. He plops down on his makeshift bed, taking a bite from his loaf, chewing as he sits alone in the near darkness.

He signs the Eight, circling a hand from his forehead to his heart and back.

When the tent opens again, a flash of light illuminates the dusty, cramped space. The boy takes a bite so large his cheeks bulge. Crumbs escape his lips. He chews with ferocity, trying to hide the bread behind his body, swallowing too soon. He chokes.

The larger child who burst into the tent rips the bread from the boy's hand.

The tent flap opens again. Closes again.

And the boy, empty-handed, hugs his knees to his chest as tears fill his eyes.

...

"Caspia." Andreas shook me by the shoulders.

I snapped out of the vision with a gasp.

"Are you all right?" His hands came to my cheeks, tilting my head back as his gaze roved my face. "What happened? You were staring off at nothing. I kept saying your name, but you were..."

Lost in a tent somewhere in this city, where a starving child needed another loaf of bread.

"We must find that boy," I told Andreas, taking his hand and pulling him in the direction that the child had run.

"Caspia, what is—"

"Please." I kept pulling, my grip on his hand tightening. "If we hurry, maybe we can catch him."

Maybe we could keep him from starving.

"Caspia." Andreas stopped, tugging on my hand until I faced him. "What the fuck is going on?"

"I saw him in a tent. Another child took his bread."

Andreas stared down at me, his forehead furrowed. "What do you mean you saw him?"

"In a vision." The only vision I'd had while awake. A vision of the future.

And if I could change that boy's fate, maybe I could change Andreas's, too.

24

CASPIA

The boy and his bread were swallowed whole by the crowd in the Skanshon marketplace. His tent could be anywhere in this city, and I had no clue where to look.

"Excuse me," I said, pushing past people, searching past legs and bodies for the child.

"Wait." Andreas's hand had slipped from mine, but I didn't stop.

This boy, this vision, could change everything.

"Have you seen a boy?" I asked a woman selling beaded jewelry in a tarped stall.

She met my gaze and shied away.

"A boy with black hair and a loaf of bread. He's this tall." I held out my hand to the top of my hip. "Have you seen him?"

She signed the Eight and ducked under the tarp's flap.

I slammed my fist on her table, then moved to the next.

The man held up a clay vase. "You won't find a finer potter in this city than me. I'll make you a deal."

"Have you seen a boy?"

His smile dropped, and he shook his head.

I was about to move to the next stall when two strong hands took hold of my shoulders, spinning me around.

"Caspia." Andreas's eyes were panicked. "Stop."

"We have to find him, Andreas. Please."

"You said your visions were about the past."

"Not this one. It came while I was standing right beside

you. Right next to the baker. And I saw the boy with the loaf of bread." I sucked in a calming breath. "I need to know what this means. Why the vision was different."

He sighed, dragging a hand through his hair.

I held my breath, waiting for him to tell me no. For him to finally admit he didn't believe I had visions. That there was no such place as Nelfinex and I was simply some delusional woman he wished he hadn't rescued from the Coraness River.

There were times when I struggled to believe my own reality.

I wouldn't blame Andreas if he turned away right now and left me in this market.

"Okay." He took my hand. "I'm guessing this is a regular place for the boy to pick pockets. We'll ask around. The baker didn't seem surprised when I caught the boy. It's likely he's seen the child before. Maybe he'll know where we can find him."

Never a doubt. Never a hesitation.

I didn't deserve this man.

But I was keeping him all the same.

"Thank you." I lifted onto my toes, kissing the underside of his jaw. Then I followed him back to the baker's cart.

It took the remainder of the sun to find the boy.

At first, I'd thought people's reluctance in the market to speak to us was because we were clearly not from Skanshon. That maybe they protected their orphans from outsiders.

Except then I realized it was me they shied away from. When Andreas approached the market stalls alone, he was met with a much warmer welcome. It was me who made people shy away.

Like the boy, they'd take one look at my golden eyes, searching for starbursts to tie me to a kingdom, only to find they weren't there.

After a while, I kept my eyes on my feet, studying my boots as Andreas did the talking.

When the sun began to set and the sky took on a palette of pastel hues, I was certain we'd failed. That we'd lost the boy and any chance I had of changing his future.

But at the very last stall in the market, a woman selling embroidered slippers pointed across a bridge toward a cluster of buildings on the river's opposite shore.

They were incomplete, their windows without panes and their walls without plaster.

"The man putting them up ran out of coin," the woman said. "They've been abandoned since the summer solstice. I see the children from time to time, though they're good at avoiding adults. I'd wager the boy you're looking for carved out a spot for himself amidst the junk over there."

Andreas bought a pair of slippers in my size, paying her twice the asking price. Then we raced across the bridge, quietly navigating the wreckage.

A swish of black hair caught my eye as we made a lap around the second building. The boy walked with his back to us, his loaf of bread tucked under his arm. He was limping, careful not to put too much weight on his right foot.

Was that why he hadn't eaten the bread already? Had he gotten into a fight? Had he been caught trying to steal from someone else?

Andreas and I spotted him at the same time, sharing a look as we followed him, keeping enough distance not to be noticed but staying close enough not to lose sight of him.

When we found the tent around the corner of a half-constructed building, the boy had already ducked inside.

The tent was exactly as I'd seen in my vision. Filthy. So small only a child could fit inside. It was tucked close enough to a wall that most would walk past thinking it was a covering, not a shelter.

Andreas held up one finger, gesturing for me to wait as he walked to the tent on silent steps and whipped up the flap.

The boy scrambled backward on his pallet, his cheeks bulged with bread. "You."

"Me." Andreas dropped to a crouch. "What is your name?"

The child curled his lip and glared.

Andreas threw his head back and laughed, then stood, grabbing the boy by the back of his collar and yanking him to his feet, too. "You need a bath, urchin. And more to eat than bread."

The boy struggled against Andreas's hold but couldn't work himself free. His bread was still gripped tight in his fist. "Don't call me that."

"Then tell us your name." I crossed my arms over my chest, arching an eyebrow.

He stopped fighting, noticing me for the first time. He shied closer to Andreas, giving me a wary glance.

"Your name?" Andreas repeated.

The boy looked to the ground. "Kos."

I walked over, bending low until I was eye level with the boy. "My name is Caspia. This is Andreas. You're going to come with us, and you're going to behave."

It wasn't an order. It wasn't a threat. It was his future.

Because as I stared at Kos, I realized he was a dirtier, scrappier version of a boy I saw in a vision lunes ago. A vision that had come to me aboard the *Cirrina*.

The vision of a boy with floating books.

It wasn't a vision that kept me from sleep. It was the boy sleeping on the sofa in the sitting room.

Kos looked like a different person after a bath and hot meal. He seemed younger. He was too thin.

Like he'd done for us, Andreas had ordered the boy new

clothes from a nearby shop. Kos was dressed in a sleep shirt and pants, both of which draped on his scrawny frame.

But even with the hollows under his cheekbones, he was actually quite adorable without the angry scowl on his face.

I hoped eventually, we'd actually coax him to smile.

Moonlight spilled through the open balcony doors, and a cool breeze ruffled the sheer curtains.

I'd woken earlier from a dreamless sleep and slipped out of Andreas's arms to check on Kos. The moment I saw the balcony doors open, I was certain I'd find the sitting room sofa empty. That Kos had climbed down the balcony and escaped. But he was right where we left him, tucked beneath a tufted quilt.

Maybe he struggled with the feeling of being closed in, too.

Kos's dirt-smudged bread was hugged to his chest.

Neither Andreas nor I had risked trying to take it away.

I pulled the blanket up over Kos's shoulder, then walked to the balcony, staring up at the navy sky.

The wind pushed puffs of clouds overhead, blotting out pockets of stars. But the two full moons glowed so brilliantly even the clouds could not block out their light.

Somewhere across the Marixmore, were my aunt and my sister flying beneath the stars? If I closed my eyes, I could still hear the sound of their beating wings.

What would Oleana say about Kos? Would she still dismiss my visions as dreams?

This ritus might have been a failure, but the Divine was leading me down a path. Now I knew that I had the power to change the future.

I could save Andreas.

Maybe I could still save Xandra, too.

All I had to do was give up revenge for my sister. Her killer would walk free. I'd sacrifice justice for the man who'd won my heart.

The floorboards creaked inside, and when Andreas wrapped me in his arms, I leaned against his bare chest.

"I was sure we'd wake up and he'd be gone."

I smiled. "Me too."

"I'm going to send him to my family in Quentis. They'll care for him until we return from Turah."

Except if Andreas came with me to Turah, he wouldn't return. That wasn't our path, not anymore.

I tilted my face to the stars. And changed our fate.

Forgive me, Emery.

"I don't want to go to Turah."

"What?" Andreas let me go, spinning me to face him. "What about finding your cousin and the silver-eyed man?"

I put my hand to his cheek, his stubble gently scraping my palm. "I'm giving up my quest for vengeance. I want to go with you to Quentis. I want to take Kos ourselves."

His eyebrows knitted together. "You saw something. You had another vision."

"Yes," I admitted. Now that he knew about my visions, there was no point in denying them.

"Tell me."

"It doesn't matter." I pressed a kiss to his chest and breathed in his clean, woodsy scent. "I couldn't save my sister. But I can save that boy."

And I could save Andreas.

"Take me to Quentis," I murmured with another kiss. "Please."

His jaw clenched, his frame locked tight. But by the third kiss, his arms wrapped around me once more, his hands molding to the curves of my hips. When he slid his palms over my ass, I knew he wouldn't argue.

The next sun, I stayed with Kos at the inn while Andreas made arrangements for us to leave.

And by dawn the following morning, we were on a ship bound for Quentis.

25

ODESSA

The skeleton forest.

As far as I could see, there was nothing but black, leafless trees and scorched earth.

When Thora mentioned it yesterday, I'd thought maybe the road would be made of bones. But now I understood.

The skeletons were the trees themselves, entirely lifeless and dead. They stood like giant, charred sticks stuck in the dirt. Only a few had branches, as black as their trunks. The rest had probably been singed away.

The ground was mottled with black and gray patches. Flecks of white ash floated on the breeze. The storm clouds above blotted out any sliver of blue sky. It was as if all color had been leached from this place.

There wasn't a road that cut through the forest. We didn't need a road. We could weave in and out of the trees without bushes or branches getting in the way.

I reached out and brushed my fingers along a nearby trunk. It was as hard as stone and as cold as ice. My hand came away clean, not covered in soot or ash as I'd expected.

"What happened here?" I asked Jodhi.

He rode by my side, his posture stiff and his jaw clenched. "Some say it was an ancient fire. Others think it was a curse from Izzac himself. That the God of Death used the trees from this forest to build his throne in the shades, and when he left, he took all the life with him to hell. No matter how much rain comes, no matter how many seeds are planted, nothing here survives."

A shiver ran down my spine, like I could feel Izzac's gaze on the nape of my neck. I glanced over my shoulder, searching the trees, but beyond the Mavins riding at our backs, there was nothing but skeletons.

We'd left the cave at dawn after the Mavins had gone out to search for signs of the bariwolves. Other than the one instance, we'd heard nothing else during the night. But wherever that pack had gone, they'd left no tracks to follow.

Still, I rode with the crossbow Sryker had given me tucked under my arm.

There was no chatter or laughter with the group this morning. Not that the Mavins were ever a rowdy bunch, but everyone seemed on edge, speaking in hushed voices.

Thora rode alone at the front of the group. Her white hair, gray clothes, and steel armor blended in with the black-and-white surroundings.

Evie was shivering and had been since we woke up this morning. I couldn't tell if it was from the morning chill or this eerie forest. Probably both.

I kissed her hair. "How about a story?"

She nodded, reaching inside Faze's carrier. This was a new habit of hers, holding his paw as we rode.

I let the crossbow hang by its strap as I pulled Luella's journal from my satchel. Then I opened it to a page and passage I'd read by firelight last night in the cave when I hadn't been able to sleep.

"'A woman with long black hair threaded with silver sits at a little girl's bedside,'" the story began.

...

The girl wears white casts on both of her arms. The woman wears a layer of colorful necklaces around her throat and stacks of bright bracelets on her wrists. Her beaded earrings are so long they brush the tops of her shoulders.

She has a pair of turquoise glasses in her hair. A pair of red glasses perched on her nose. And three pairs tucked into the neckline of her dress. White. Yellow. And pink. She dips a brush into a pot of purple ink and dabs it on one of the girl's casts, adding to the flowers she's already painted. A garden for the little girl to help take away the pain.

...

"What do you think happened to the girl's arms?" Evie asked.

"I don't know. Maybe we'll meet her someday and you can ask." I flipped the page. "The next one is about a boy. Want to hear it?"

"Sure." She nodded, hand still locked on Faze's paw. Body still shaking.

...

A boy with light hair holds tight to a roll of string that stretches into the sky. At the other end is a paper bird with orange feathers and a long tail of blue, green, red, and yellow. He laughs as he releases more string, letting the bird fly higher.

The trees around him do not rustle or shake. The grass blades at his ankles are still and straight. The wind blows only for his colorful bird.

He lets out the rest of the line, and when he reaches the end, he blows a kiss to the bird and sets it free. It soars, disappearing from sight. The boy is sad for only a moment.

A puppy with curly black hair and floppy ears races to him, wagging his tail as he licks the boy's face. "I decided on your name," the boy says to the dog. "I am going to name you Telvi'i-telfus."

...

"Telvi'i-telfus?" Evie laughed. "That's a silly name."

It was in the old language. "I guess it should be—"

"Titus," Jodhi said.

When I glanced over, his eyes were locked on the journal. He knew the old language?

"Interesting book, doll. Where did you get it?"

"Um, a friend of mine found it in an apothecary." I closed the cover and tucked it into my satchel, not liking the way he looked at the book.

"Which friend?" he asked, gaze finally lifting.

"No one you know." I faced forward, wishing I had left that book in the satchel. I was about to urge Freya forward, to move up to ride beside Golding, when Faze growled.

"What's wrong?" Evie asked him, reaching into the carrier with her other hand, like she was about to lift him out.

"Wait." I put my hand on hers just as Thora held up an arm.

We all slowed as she turned, staring into the trees. Slowly, she took her ax from where it was strapped across her back.

My breath lodged in my throat as I followed her gaze, searching through the tree husks.

I heard them before I saw them. Five sharp clicks. Then a bariwolf stepped out from behind a trunk.

"No." My body went rigid.

Our entire group went still, frozen in a moment of shared terror.

Three other bariwolves emerged, each prowling our way, fangs bared. With every step, their large feet and white claws sent up small puffs of ashen dust.

If this place was cursed by the God of Death, then these monsters must be Izzac's creation. The fur on the front half of their bodies seemed darker in this forest. Their pointed scales shone in the morning light, glinting like a thousand silver blades.

Five more wolves came into sight, spread out through the forest.

A pack of nine hunting their prey.

"Fuck," Jodhi hissed, taking his sword from its scabbard.

I fumbled to grab a bolt from the pouch and fit it into the crossbow.

Evie whimpered, gripping the saddle's horn with all her might. I hated that she knew her life was in danger. That her survival depended on how hard she clung to this horse.

Thora snarled and steered her horse toward the bariwolves.

She swung her ax in two circles, the blade cutting through the air with a resounding *whoosh*.

Jodhi rode past me as the other Mavins followed, the warriors forming a line.

A barricade.

"Golding and Dair, you've got the four on the left," Thora said. "Jodhi and I have the five on the right. Mathias, nothing gets through the middle."

Mathias spat on the ground, nocking an arrow into his longbow. "Good hunting, Mavins."

"To bloody blades," the others said in chorus.

My hands were shaking so badly I feared I'd drop the crossbow.

One of the bariwolves growled, a sound so loud and ominous it sank into my skin.

Evie's shoulders shook as she cried.

"Be brave, little star."

"If I say ride, then you ride," Mathias ordered, sparing me a quick glance. "Understood?"

I gulped and nodded.

The tension in the air coiled tighter and tighter, like a string being pulled too tight, and before I was ready, it snapped.

The monsters lunged in unison as the Mavins surged ahead, blades swinging to strike.

Thora was the first to kill by throwing her ax at a charging wolf. She released the weapon so quickly, the heavy handle and steel head were only a streak before it cleaved the beast's snout down the center. Exactly how she'd killed the alligask.

Even if the bariwolf had tried to dodge the ax, it happened in a blink.

She pulled a scimitar from a sheath on her belt and lifted out of her saddle, rising so that as the next bariwolf leaped and lunged, her blade was already coming down onto its neck.

The beast landed with a sickening thud in the dirt.

Jodhi killed a wolf at the same time Golding cut down another.

But Golding had turned his back to a different beast, and the moment the monster saw its chance to strike, it came at him with open jaws, leaping into the air as it tried to sink its teeth into his broad shoulders.

One moment, I was sure we'd watch Golding fall. The next, the beast yelped as an arrow shot through its neck.

Golding startled, eyes wide as he stared at the monster. Then he turned to Mathias, offering a quick bow of gratitude before he spurred his horse to go after the two wolves converging on Dair.

But Dair didn't seem to need much help. He used a crossbow to fire at one monster while using a broadsword to slice at another. Neither hit took down the wolves, but it slowed them enough that Dair could slice and hack at them until they were black heaps on the ground.

When I looked to Jodhi and Thora again, they'd already killed the last of the wolves.

"By the mother," I murmured.

Nine monsters dead in a moment.

The Mavins were as lethal as the monsters they were slaughtering. For a heartbeat, I relaxed. I breathed and lowered my crossbow, thinking we would survive this attack.

I should have known better.

A series of clicks mingled with the chaos as a dozen other monsters emerged from the trees, every bariwolf sprinting for the Mavins.

"Fuck me." Mathias raised his fingers to his lips and let out a whistle to alert the others. "Ride. Now."

I didn't need to be told twice. With a shout, I gave Freya the reins, and my darling, terrified horse tore off through the trees.

Clinging to Evie, holding on for our lives, it was like being back in a dark forest with the Voster. Like being chased by a pack of wolves with Brother Skore. But this time, there was no magic to keep us safe.

I heard the snarl a moment before a black bariwolf came at us from the side, pouncing with claws and fangs ready to sink into Freya's flank.

It missed.

Ama and Oda were watching over us because the bastard missed. Its body swished her tail, then crashed into the ground.

But after a quick roll, it was back on its feet, giving chase.

I aimed the crossbow behind us, bouncing wildly in the saddle, and let a bolt fly. The snarl that came next was enough to know I'd missed.

But the pounding of hooves sounded next, and when I glanced back, the Mavins were flying to catch up.

Mathias slowed just enough to stand in his stirrups, raise his bow, and kill the bariwolf on my heels.

The Mavins caught up too quickly, each of them slowing to match my pace as they surrounded Freya.

The pack of wolves was close behind.

Thora, having rescued her ax, raised the weapon and veered off course, cutting through the trees as she rode away from the others. Three of the wolves ran after her. Golding did the same, drawing another two in the opposite direction.

Jodhi and Dair stayed with Mathias, all three of the men between me and the monsters.

But there were too many, and we were too few.

A bariwolf ran close enough to Mathias to slam its body into his stallion, those needlelike scales digging into the horse's flesh.

Mathias went down in a cloud of dust and limbs, his horse rolling over his body. He staggered to stand and raised his bow, but it was too late.

"No," Dair cried out, whirling to fire his crossbow.

The bolt plunged into one wolf's eye just as another monster slammed into Mathias.

And ripped out the Mavin's throat.

"Faster," Jodhi shouted.

The other wolves were gaining, a horde of black on our heels.

Dair cut one down as it jumped for him, and Jodhi did the same.

The men slowed even more, both lagging to fight off the wolves still giving chase.

Freya pushed harder, putting some distance between us and the others.

A flash of black came from the corner of my eyes as a wolf broke past the Mavins, and with a burst of speed, it was beside us. The monster was smaller than Freya but not by much.

I reached for my sword, yanking it free and swinging it wildly toward the beast, and the blade caught it across the eyes.

The creature stumbled, rolling as it howled in pain.

But the damage was already done.

The monster had slammed its scales into Freya's hip, shredding her flesh.

Time slowed to a crawl.

Her back half couldn't keep up with the front, and it dropped, her knees buckling. Then we were falling to the side, the ground rushing up at us too fast.

Twisting so hard my muscles screamed, I flung my sword away and grabbed Evie, tucking her into my chest as our momentum took us forward.

Freya collapsed.

My shoulder slammed into the dirt, my head a heartbeat later. Pain exploded through my body as we skidded to a stop. It took a moment for the world to stop spinning.

"Evie," I gasped, sitting upright.

She was shaking, all color drained from her face as she stared at Freya.

My horse's belly rose and her chest heaved with labored breaths as she lifted her head, trying to stand. But her body was broken. I couldn't see the wound, but the smear of red on the dirt was enough to know my precious Freya was dying.

Jodhi galloped for us, holding out his arm. "Get up."

Dair was still on the road, battling the remaining wolves. But there were too many. Two had made it past him and were running our way at full speed.

I climbed to my feet, picking up Evie. "Take her. Go."

"Odessa, get—"

"There are too many. Go. Now. Please."

He knew I was right. That not all of us were going to survive this.

Realization dawned on Evie's face, and she started to kick, squirming to be put down. "No," she shrieked, tears streaming down her cheeks as she reached for me. "Dess!"

"I love you, little star." I lifted Faze out of his carrier, practically throwing the tarkin in her arms. "Go with Jodhi."

"No." She sobbed. "Dess."

"I will see you again."

Here. Or in the shades.

I tore my eyes from her precious face and ran for my sword, picking it up from the dirt. Then I hurried to Freya, using her body as a shield, not letting myself watch as Jodhi rode away, Evie's scream still ringing in my ears.

"I'm sorry." I stroked Freya's cheek one last time and looked into her pretty eye. "I will see you soon."

If the monsters were truly drawn to me, this end was inevitable.

With a choked sob, I drew my sword across her throat.

Her eyes flared, horrorstruck. And then the life bled from her body.

Tears streamed down my face as I watched Dair ride into

the trees, drawing off two wolves. His leg was shredded, the blood from the cuts painting his horse's white coat in red.

I held up my sword, the blade dripping with blood, and fixed my gaze on the two monsters running my way.

"Mack, give me strength," I prayed, hoping the God of War would dare to visit this place of death.

One of the monsters lifted its neck and clicked to the other. A team working to bring down their target. The other wolf changed paths, moving around a thick tree so that it could come at me from the side.

"I love you, Ransom," I whispered, looking to the sky.

Was he waiting for me in the shades? I hoped he'd be there when I arrived. I hoped he'd open his arms and together, we could watch over Evie from above.

A growl brought me back to the forest, to the black beasts drawing closer.

My sword wobbled, and I clutched it with both hands.

There were hooves in the distance, a rider barreling this way. Thora or Golding or Dair. But by the time they made it back to the road, it would be too late.

The wolf in front of me growled, its lips curling away from white fangs. It smiled at my death.

Well, I had no plans to go down without a fight. I tightened my grip, ready to slash the moment it pounced.

But it didn't attack. A whirl of gleaming metal came from the side, a sword driving through the monster's heart.

Then a black horse thundered through the trees.

Not a Mavin.

A warrior with silver eyes. The man who owned my heart. My husband, here to escort me to the shades.

Ransom.

26

ODESSA

It was a dream.

Ransom rode Aurinda straight for me, his silver eyes locked on mine. He stretched out an arm, like he was going to pick me up and together, we'd ascend to the shades.

Finally. He'd found me.

And I could be done with this fight.

Tears spilled down my cheeks. I sank to my knees, my sword lowering.

And then it was gone. As Aurinda bounded over Freya's dead body, Ransom snatched the weapon from my hands.

I jolted.

Not a dream.

Be real. Please be real.

I snapped back to reality as he brought my sword across the bariwolf's throat. The monster was close enough that blood sprayed over Freya's body.

Green blood.

The monster collapsed, sliding on the dirt.

"Run, Cross," Ransom shouted, turning Aurinda around.

I pushed to my feet and leaped over Freya's legs as another growl sounded behind me, coming from the trees. But I didn't look back, my eyes locked on Ransom, my heart in my throat, as I raced for Aurinda.

His eyes widened as he looked past me, and then, with a snarl, he urged Aurinda to sprint, both of them breezing past me, my sword raised in the air.

I whirled as a massive wolf jumped for him, trying to knock him out of the saddle.

Ransom kicked it away before its jaws could sink into his thigh. He sent the beast sprawling, making sure those spines didn't get anywhere near Aurinda. In a fluid leap, he flew out of the saddle and was already running when his feet hit the ground.

The bariwolf reared up on its hind legs, but before it could strike, Ransom ran the sword the length of the beast's underbelly. The monster gurgled and lunged, not realizing it was already dead as its organs began to spill from its open abdomen. A heartbeat later, it collapsed by Ransom's boots.

He turned in a slow circle, scanning the trees for another beast. His grizzur-hide vest was coated in blood. His chest heaved as he breathed. When he finally looked to me, it was with swirling, silver eyes.

In a blink, they turned my favorite shade of moss green.

A sob escaped my lips.

And then we were running.

We collided, my arms looping around his shoulders as he hauled me off my feet. My legs wrapped around his hips. One of his hands cupped the back of my head as he buried his nose in my hair.

"You found me," I sobbed into the crook of his neck, breathing in his scent. Leather and wind and earth and spice and Ransom.

He was alive.

"You found me."

"I found you," he breathed, dropping to his knees.

Tears spilled down my cheeks as the crying turned to laughter, and I leaned away, cupping his face in my hands. "Took you long enough."

His smile was a thousand glittering stars. A hundred dazzling sunsets. "Sorry to keep you waiting, wife."

I laughed again and crushed my lips to his, kissing him

for all the days we'd spent apart. For the doubts that had tormented me since Ellder. I poured every emotion into the kiss, the worry and joy and heartache, and as his soft lips moved against mine, as our tongues tangled, the fear began to subside.

He broke the kiss, his eyes closing as he dropped his forehead to mine. "Shades, I missed you."

Weeks of terror vanished at the sound of his voice. Finally, we'd be safe. Finally, we were together.

A shout tore us apart. Hooves pounded on the ground, and Aurinda shifted behind us, a warning that someone was approaching.

Ransom kissed me again, hard and firm. A kiss that would linger, even after we moved apart.

I shifted, about to stand. To put some space between us so that whoever was riding this way wouldn't find me on his lap.

Except before I could push to my feet, Ransom's arms banded around my waist, trapping me in place.

"They'll see us."

"That's okay." He pushed the curls from my face. "No more pretending."

No more lies. No more hidden crowns.

No more Guardian.

This was Zavier Ransom Wolfe.

My husband.

He'd lost so much in Ellder. His warriors. His cousin and best friend. His mother. And now his anonymity.

There was so much to talk about, so much to say. But it would have to wait.

I gave him a soft smile and pressed my hand to his heart. "If you're sure."

"I'm sure." He kissed my temple, then looked over my shoulder.

I twisted, following his gaze.

Thora rode straight toward us, drawing her horse to a stop

beside Freya. Her eyes were hard, her ax in one hand, its blade coated in blood. She glared down at Ransom, her lip curling. "You."

They knew each other? That shouldn't have surprised me, but it did.

"Fuck." Ransom gave me a flat look. "Only you would get tangled up with the Mavins."

"Hey." I frowned. "If not for them, I'd be dead."

"If not for them, I would have caught up to you in Laine," he grumbled and lifted me off his lap, helping me stand.

My legs were wobbly now that the shock of the bariwolf attack was beginning to fade. I swayed on my feet, like this cursed forest was sucking the life out of my body through the soles of my boots.

Ransom looped an arm around my waist, lending me his strength as he turned his attention to Thora. "Where is Evie?"

She looked him up and down before her gaze dropped to his hand splayed across my hip. As far as she knew, the Guardian was *not* my husband. When she looked at me, there was an accusation in her fiery eyes.

Something else we'd deal with later.

"Jodhi has her," I said as the sound of more riders echoed through the trees.

Golding and Dair rode toward us, both breathing heavily but alive.

"Find Jodhi," Thora ordered.

Dair nodded and, with a parting look to Golding, galloped away.

"Mathias," Golding breathed, shaking his head.

The two Mavins shared a look, a silent conversation.

"To bloody blades." Golding dipped his chin and rode off in the same direction as Dair.

"That was the largest pack of bariwolves I've ever seen," Thora said. "And they all had Lyssa."

Ransom's body went rigid.

Damn it, Thora. She'd delivered that statement like a punch to the gut. Probably the goal.

"I, um, told her about the infection."

"You don't say," he grumbled.

"It's spread too far." I looked up at him, pleading with him to understand. "We can't fight it alone."

His irises shifted colors into the hard, stony hazel that meant we'd be discussing it later. "Did either of you see a wolf with only one eye?"

My jaw dropped. Was that why this pack was so big? Was that why he and Zavier hadn't been able to track the one-eyed wolf in Turah? Because it had come to Genesis instead?

"I didn't notice," Thora said. "I was too busy trying to keep them from eating the Sparrow."

"Do you really think it's here?" I asked.

"Maybe."

"What does a one-eyed bariwolf have to do with this?" Thora asked.

"Later," Ransom said. "How many in this pack?"

"I can't be sure," she said.

"At one point, I counted twenty-one." I closed my eyes and leaned into his chest.

Was this my fault? Was I the reason for this enormous pack?

If not for the Mavins, if Ransom hadn't come, if Evie and I had been out here alone...

I shuddered at the thought.

"It's all right," Ransom murmured. "I found you."

He wrapped me in his arms, holding me tight. I could feel the strength in his embrace, hear the steady beat of his heart. But a part of me was certain that when I looked up, he'd be gone.

That this was a dream and I'd wake up in the shades.

Ransom dropped his arms before I was ready. He looked

over his shoulder at the sound of riders. A strangled noise came from his throat before he took off running.

Jodhi galloped toward us with Evie in front of him on his saddle.

Sobs racked her body while her face was buried in Faze's fur.

Jodhi tapped her shoulder so she'd look up.

She blinked, staring at Ransom like she wasn't sure he was real, either. But when it sank in, the corners of her mouth turned down and her little body collapsed forward.

She would have fallen if not for Jodhi.

He kept her in the saddle, taking Faze by the scruff of his neck, until Ransom was close. Then Jodhi let Evie go so she could crash into Ranse's arms.

Safe. Now, she was safe.

He held her to his chest and closed his eyes as he rested a cheek on her hair.

Evie's legs and arms wrapped around him as she cried, harder than any other time she'd broken down on this journey. All her grief, all her sorrow, she gave to Ransom.

Because like me, she knew he could carry the load.

My hand came to my heart as it pinched, tears filling my eyes, too.

Faze squirmed free from Jodhi's grip, dropping to the ground on all fours. He gave the Mavin a hiss, then bounded beneath the horse to Ransom's legs, winding around his ankles.

I sniffled and wiped away the tears as Ransom turned and carried Evie to me.

He murmured something in her ear as they walked, Faze trotting close behind.

Jodhi rode ahead of them, coming to a stop beside Thora.

"Thank you," I told him.

He gave me a single nod, then looked at Thora.

"I won't bury Mathias in this place." Her voice was empty and cold. "Continue ahead. I'll catch up."

Jodhi stayed silent as she left to collect their friend's body.

"I'm sorry. About Mathias."

"So am I." He kept his gaze on Thora's back.

"Dess." Evie ran for me the moment Ransom set her down.

I dropped to a knee, arms wide open, as she crashed into my chest. *Thank you, Ama.*

Ransom walked to us, bending to kiss both of our heads. Then he went to Freya's body, carefully taking off my saddlebags.

I didn't want to leave her body here in this skeleton forest, but I didn't want to risk the bariwolves coming back if there were others nearby.

"Is Freya..." Evie couldn't finish her sentence.

"She's in the shades."

She nodded and started crying again, burying her face in my shoulder as Ransom moved our things to Aurinda. When it was loaded, he came over and picked up Evie, lifting her into his saddle.

"We should go in case there are other wolves," Jodhi said, still not looking at me.

"What about Golding and Dair?"

"Gone."

I opened my mouth, about to ask why they'd leave, but another question came to mind. "What will happen to Mathias's mother and sister if he's not alive to pay his debt?"

"If we're lucky, Golding and Dair will get to them before Salem finds out Mathias is dead." Jodhi finally looked at me. "Any other questions, doll?"

Yes, but that was not an invitation to ask.

He pulled on his horse's reins to turn it around.

As he rode away, I took one last look at my pretty blue roan.

It was a lifetime ago that I met her on the shores of Turah. We'd come so far together. From Treow to Ellder to Ravalli. From a burning fortress to a watery cave.

This horse had saved my life. Without her…

I tilted my face to the sky, knowing that she'd found her way to Arabella. That in the Goddess of Love's shade, she would feel no more pain.

A sob broke free as Ransom's arm slid around my shoulders.

"Damn it." I sniffled, trying to pull myself together, but the frayed pieces were beginning to unravel. "I really loved that horse."

Ransom took my face in his hands, his thumbs catching my tears. "Can you keep going?"

"Yes." I nodded, still crying.

Yes, I'd keep going. Just like Freya, I'd keep going even when I so desperately wanted to stop.

He kissed my forehead. "There's my queen."

27

CASPIA

The ship carrying us from Ozarth to Quentis had no name.

Kos and I were calling it *Snail* because of the crawling pace at which it crossed the sea.

"I'm bored." The boy threw a chunk of orange peel over the back of the ship and into the turquoise water. He groaned, popping a piece of peeled fruit into his mouth. "There's nothing to do."

"I thought you were learning how to sail from the captain so that when we got to Quentis you could steal your own boat and never see Andreas again."

The two had gotten into an argument after Andreas had caught Kos rifling through the first mate's cabin, attempting to steal a brass spotting scope. Andreas had reprimanded Kos, forcing him to swab the deck with the crew. As Kos had furiously scrubbed at a stained board, he'd told me about his plan to steal a boat and leave.

Maybe he would run away. But for now, he was trapped on this ship with the rest of us.

We'd been traveling for suns, winding our way along the coastline of Calandra.

It would have been much faster if we had gone straight through the Krisenth Crossing, but the skies had been angry since we left Skanshon, and Andreas hadn't wanted to risk a storm that might capsize our ship.

Better to take our time than drown.

Last evening, the captain had steered us into a bay to drop

anchor as we'd weathered a storm. As lightning had split the sky and thunder boomed, Andreas and I had spent our time in bed, naked bodies entwined while the rain disguised our moans.

Since the moon I asked Andreas to take me to Quentis, I hadn't seen the vision of his death again.

I hoped that meant I'd made the right choice. That I'd changed his future like I'd changed Kos's.

I hoped that Emery would forgive me from her place beside the Divine in Gloree.

Vengeance would have to wait. By some luck, my path would eventually cross with the silver-eyed warrior's. And then, I could have my revenge.

As Kos finished eating his orange, I began peeling my own, breathing in the sweet scent and savoring how it mingled with the salt in the air.

Divine, I'd missed the smell of the sea. It was as close to the scents of home as I'd found since coming to Calandra.

"Are you gonna eat all that?" Kos asked as I kept peeling.

"I might. Or I might find Andreas and share it with him."

The boy's lip curled, making me laugh.

"You knew the rules when we boarded the ship. No more stealing."

"I got a blister from all that scrubbing." He held up his small hand, showing me his tiny wound. "I was just looking at that spotting scope anyway. I wasn't gonna take it."

"Better not let Andreas hear you lie, or he'll stuff a bar of soap in your mouth again."

Kos harrumphed and kicked the ship's wall. He waited until he thought I wasn't looking before he checked over his shoulder, making sure Andreas wasn't anywhere close enough to hear.

No stealing. No lying. No leaving.

Andreas had given Kos three simple rules. And like most children, Kos was testing the boundaries of those limits.

He reminded me more and more of Graciella with every passing sun. Together, they'd be terrors. I almost wished she were here so I could see the trouble they'd make.

I ate four slices of the orange, then handed the rest to Kos to finish.

He inhaled it like he did most of his meals. This boy had flourished with decent meals and sleep. His body was beginning to fit his clothes, and his cheeks were no longer hollow.

"What?" he asked, wiping at a dribble of orange juice on his chin.

"Nothing."

"You stare at me a lot," he muttered.

"I could say the same for you." I tapped his nose. "Brave enough to ask me about my eyes yet?"

Kos blushed and looked away.

I'd caught him staring at my eyes countless times since we set sail, but he had yet to ask why they were different. At least he'd stopped giving me wary glances.

Kos stayed quiet, and after a few long moments, I was certain he'd run off to another corner of the ship. But then he spoke, so quietly I barely heard his voice over the noise of the waves. "Why don't you have starbursts?"

"Because I was not born in Calandra."

"Then where were you born?"

"On the continent of Kenn. In the country of Nelfinex. In a city named Showe."

He scrunched up his nose. "There is no Kenn and Nelf…"

"Nelfinex," I finished.

"There's no such place." He scowled. "You're the one who needs a bar of soap in her mouth for lying."

I laughed as he stomped away, probably to go find another snack.

Maybe it was better that people didn't know of Kenn. Maybe life would be simpler if I forgot all about Nelfinex.

Not a single vision I'd had since coming to Calandra had been of home.

I wasn't returning to Showe, was I? And neither was Xandra.

It hurt, but for her sake, not mine. I was oddly at peace with never returning home. With not becoming Starling.

My ritus had failed, but that didn't mean I had to stop living.

A yawn tugged at my mouth as I stared over the sea to the shore. In the distance, I spotted mountains of blue and green.

Andreas had told me at breakfast that we were sailing past Genesis. Somewhere beyond those peaks, I hoped my cousin was still alive.

"There you are." Andreas came up behind me, wrapping his arms around my waist. "Kos just informed me that you are a liar and I should be getting out a bar of soap."

I smiled. "I told him I was from Nelfinex. He didn't believe me."

Andreas chuckled. "He is a stubborn one, that child. But curious, too. I bet after he ponders it for a day or two, he'll have a string of questions for you about Kenn. Considering I've never heard of your continent, it's no surprise he hasn't, either."

"How is that possible?" I looked up, finding his eyes. "I can't believe I'm the first to ever voyage to Calandra."

"I don't know." He shrugged. "But in all my travels, I've never encountered anyone from beyond Calandra. I've never read about it or learned about other continents."

"What about in history books?"

Andreas shook his head. "None. I've read my fair share. Not to say something doesn't exist, but it's certainly not common knowledge."

That seemed impossible.

There had to have been other voyagers in the past. Other pirates like Cap willing to test the limits of his ship and crew in the spirit of discovery.

Andreas let me go, moving to stand at my side. He bent at the waist, dropping his elbows to lean on the ship's wall. His expression turned serious, a look I'd seen countless times.

"All the elfalter in the world for your thoughts."

"When I was a boy, my mother gave me a children's book full of myths and legends. There was one story about a woman. I can't remember her name now. But the story goes this woman sailed across the realm, leaving Calandra for a hundred years. When she finally returned, she brought with her animals unlike any we'd ever seen. She said they were gifts from a god more powerful than the Eight."

The Divine.

"She set these animals free from their cages, and they turned on her, devouring her until nothing remained, not even her bones."

I shuddered. "Monsters."

"Vengeance from the Six. The story served as a lesson to young boys and girls to be devout to the gods who rule over Calandra. For they are the true creators of monsters. Of power. We are nothing compared to our gods, and our duty is to bow to their will."

These gods of his, the Six, sounded like monsters themselves.

Andreas waved it off, shaking his head. "It's just a children's tale."

"What if it isn't? Either no other person from Kenn has ever set foot in Calandra, or the truth has been hidden away from the people here, history hidden in children's tales."

"Except I don't know why it would be hidden. There's no reason for it."

Fear. Fear was a reason.

What if other Quiescents had felt the ritus call them to Calandra? What if they'd shifted like Xandra and slaughtered everything in their wake?

What if they'd become monsters?

Like Emery.

If there was even a chance I might shift if the ritus returned, then Andreas should know the truth. The whole truth, this time.

"There's something I need to tell you about being Starling. It means more than being royalty." I took a deep breath. "The Starling are gifted by the Divine. Those of our bloodline go through the rite I told you about."

"To become the person you're meant to be."

"Yes, but it's more than a mindset or temperament or perspective. We literally change. To be Starling means you can shift."

He turned to face me, forehead furrowing. "Shift?"

"Shapeshift." My voice dropped to a whisper. "Once we go through our ritus, a Starling can take on the body of any beast."

Andreas rocked back on his heels.

"My cousin and I left Nelfinex not only to avenge my sister. I felt the call of the ritus. So did Xandra. It called us here, to Calandra, to go through the shift. To become Starling."

"So you can…" He swept his hand up and down, staring at me in disbelief.

"No." I shook my head. "I can't shift. My ritus failed."

He stared at me, eyes wide.

Was this the limit of what he'd believe about me? First Nelfinex, then the visions. If he could just believe me now, in this one last secret, then there'd be nothing else between us.

Andreas glanced over my head, making sure we were still alone. Then he shifted closer, dropping his voice. "What you are talking about is magic."

"Magic," I repeated. "I don't know that word."

"It means impossible."

I gave him a sad smile. "Not for the Starling."

He raked a hand through his hair. "Anyone in your family can become an animal?"

"The Starling only have daughters. The gift is for the blood of women. And once a daughter of the Starling goes through her rite, then yes, she can shift."

"And coming to Calandra was your rite?"

"Yes. And Xandra's. But hers didn't fail. She shifted into a bariwolf and attacked me. The only reason I escaped was because I jumped off a cliff."

"And into the river," he murmured. "That's how I found you."

"Yes."

"You told me you wanted to find your cousin. But she could be out there, as a bariwolf."

My heart ached as I looked toward Genesis. "Or human. She should be able to shift back. If she survived the ritus. Some don't. There's also a chance she's trapped in the monster's body."

It was a theory I'd been contemplating ever since I woke up in his cabin. Saying it out loud made it too real. Too devastating.

Andreas leaned on the ship's wall again, hanging his head as he sighed. "So you can't shift."

"No."

"And if you did?"

I shrugged. "I don't know."

He pounded a fist on the top rail, standing tall. "If there's even a slim chance that you might get trapped in a monster's form, then you can't shift, Caspia."

It wasn't a statement or observation.

It was an order.

"Promise me, Caspia." He took my face in his hands. "Promise me you won't shift."

"You believe me," I whispered.

He traced a thumb across my cheek. "When have I not?"

I collapsed into his chest, snaking my arms around his waist. "Thank you."

"Promise me you won't shift, Caspia. Make your vow."

"I will not shift." I leaned away and pressed two fingers to my forehead. "I vow it."

He closed his eyes, dropping his forehead to mine. "We'll be sailing to Roslo. It's the capital city of Quentis. The castle there has a library with more books than a person could read in two lifetimes. Maybe we'll find something about Kenn in there. Maybe someone has encountered a Starling before."

"I hope so." For my sake. And Xandra's. "Maybe I could find something to help Xandra so she can fly home."

Andreas stood tall, eyes narrowing. "Fly home? You mean become a bird?"

"Yes. Most Starling prefer to shift into the swift. They're beloved in Nelfinex."

"A swift?"

I nodded. "They can grow to be half the size of this ship. The females have the most beautiful black feathers. The males are just as striking but are a shade of rich red."

His face went white. "What you call a swift, we call a crux."

Crux. I'd heard that word murmured in our travels. First, in Coraness. Then again in Skanshon. But I hadn't thought enough of it to ask. I'd simply assumed they were another type of monster we didn't have in Nelfinex, like the bariwolf.

"You have swift in Calandra?" Why hadn't I seen one yet? Did they live in other kingdoms?

Andreas swallowed hard, rubbing both hands over his face. "Fuck."

"What?"

"They migrate here once every generation," Andreas said.

Well, at least that was one mystery explained. The swift did come here to breed.

"And when they come, they kill every living being in their path."

PART II

DISCOVERY

28

ODESSA

"So you're the Guardian." Jodhi was in his usual place at our campfire, across from mine. And even though he spoke to Ransom, he stared at me.

His hands were clasped on his stomach, legs stretched long with his ankles crossed. He was the epitome of relaxed and carefree, despite today's bariwolf attack.

Did he ever get tired of putting up this cavalier front?

"He's the Guardian and the crown prince, Jodhi," Thora said, running her sharpening stone over the blade of her ax. "The Turans do love their secrets and political games."

Ransom scoffed. "The Mavins know a thing or two about secrets and games, don't they, Vale? Or do you prefer to go by Thora these days?"

Her stone slipped off the blade's edge as her eyes blazed. "Call me that name again, Guardian, and we'll see just how good you are in a fight."

Jodhi's laugh was low and menacing.

"How, exactly, do you two know each other?" I asked.

"We don't." Ransom and Thora spoke in unison.

"Okay," I drawled.

Another item to discuss with Ransom when we finally had a moment alone.

Evie hummed as she slept tucked under one of his strong arms. She was practically stuck to his side, and since their reunion, she'd refused to let him out of her sight.

I'd claimed his other arm and held Faze on my lap, sleeping in a ball as I stroked the orange scales on his spine.

If I never set foot in the skeleton forest again, I'd die a happy woman.

While Evie and I had ridden on Aurinda, Ransom had chosen to walk. We'd reached the edge of that cursed place at dusk, and I'd never been so happy to see green grass in my life.

We'd made camp against a cluster of boulders, the rocks large enough to provide a bit of shelter from the wind that blew inland from the Genesis coast. We were closer to the sea than we'd been in weeks, and the hint of salt in the air gave me hope.

It wasn't Quentis, but we were getting close.

Close to the safety of my father's castle. Close to a shelter for the migration. Close to healers and alchemists who could help me find a cure for Lyssa.

Thora set down her ax and stared up at the stars, whispering something I couldn't quite hear. Then she stood, walking past the fire and into the night.

A moment later, Jodhi did the same.

"It's customary for some in Genesis to bury their dead at night," Ransom said. "They believe that under the light of the twin moons, the Six can see a soul more clearly to place them in the correct shade."

"For Mathias's sake, I hope that's true." I leaned my head against Ransom's shoulder and sighed.

"Jodhi is in love with you."

I scoffed. "No, he is not. Everything about me irritates him."

"Trust me. It's a ruse. He is infatuated with you. I should know. We share the same affliction."

There was no way Jodhi had feelings for me, but even if Ransom was right, it didn't matter. My heart belonged to my Guardian.

"How do you know Thora?" I asked.

"I know *of* her. Or I should say, I know of her as Vale. But we've never met in person. She is Cathlin's niece."

My jaw dropped as I sat up straight. "What?"

That explained the white hair.

"Cathlin's family died in the last migration, but her brother's wife survived. The woman was pregnant at the time, and shortly after her husband was killed, she went to Genesis. Cathlin stayed in loose contact with the woman, exchanging letters from time to time. When Cathlin learned that Vale was part of the Mavins, she asked my mother if she could pay Vale's debt for her freedom."

"And your mother said no?" That didn't sound like Luella.

"She agreed. No questions asked. It was Vale who refused." Ransom frowned. "She insisted on paying the debt herself, vowing to take nothing from Turah. That was years ago. I don't know the specifics. I don't think Cathlin does, either. But Mother asked me, if I ever crossed blades with the Mavins, to show mercy to a woman with snow-white hair."

"Has Cathlin ever met her?"

"No, I don't believe so."

I turned and stared toward the darkness. What had Thora done to become indebted to Salem and earn so many stars tattooed on her face? I hoped that the entry in Luella's journal would someday come true, for Thora's sake.

And for Cathlin's. And that maybe, someday, the librarian would get to meet her niece.

I sank into Ransom's side, my gaze shifting to the flames. As much as I wanted to fall asleep, this was our moment alone.

"What happened in Ellder? With the crux? I saw it carry you away and..." My throat closed, unable to finish.

"It's dead." He inhaled like there was more to say. But then he closed his mouth and looked to the fire, his eyes swirling between green and silver.

"What?"

"Nothing." He lifted one of my curls off my shoulder and twisted it around his finger.

What wasn't he telling me? Did the scout have Lyssa? Had it killed someone else I loved?

He dropped the curl and rested his chin on my head. "I think she planned to carry me high enough and drop me. I drove my sword through her heart instead. She took the brunt of the impact as we fell, but I was thrown hard enough that I didn't wake up until dawn. By the time I got to Treow, it was empty. My father and his remaining troops rode through. Nearly everyone left to follow him to Allesaria, but Mariette was still there. When she told me you never made it, I knew something had gone wrong."

"Brother Dime was waiting in the dungeon with Freya." I took a deep breath, then told him about that night. From the fight with Banner to Zavier's death to finding the priest in the hidden passage out of Ellder.

"Well, that explains why it was so difficult to pick up your trail. He must have disguised it somehow," Ransom said. "Probably to hide you from my father."

Or the High Priest.

It was on the tip of my tongue to tell him about Brother Skore and the waterfall, but the Voster's warning about Ransom's loyalty and how my father's life was in danger made me pause.

Later. We could talk about that later.

"How did you find us?" I asked.

"It took a while. I figured you'd go to Quentis with Evie. I went to Perris first, assuming you'd sail the Krisenth. But not a single dockmaster had any recollection of seeing a woman with golden eyes and wild red hair traveling with a little girl. So I rode east, and when I got to the Harrow River, I questioned every ferryman I could find. You made an impression on one."

My nostrils flared. "He was a pig."

"Then you'll be happy to know I broke his arm."

"Good." The asshole ferryman had probably made a lewd comment.

"He told me you crossed paths in Northern Ozarth, near Norcrest. But he said you were alone, that he never saw a Voster."

"Brother Dime met up with another priest. His name was Brother Skore. Dime left not long after that, and Skore led us along the Axmar Mountains. We were chased by some bariwolves"—made a stop at a waterfall—"then he left us near Norcrest. He told me to find a female warrior. I assumed he meant Thora and he knew the Mavins were in Ozarth."

"He left you? Alone? With Evie? And only your sword?" Ransom's entire body tensed. "This Brother Skore had better not cross my path."

"If it's any solace, I was glad to see him go."

"Doesn't matter. He shouldn't have left you."

No. But it was in the past. And with any luck, I'd never see Brother Skore again.

It didn't take long for us to put the rest of our journeys together, both of us weaving through Ozarth and Laine. He'd passed a merchant on her way to Emrist who told him that a woman with curly red hair, riding with a little girl, was traveling with the Mavins.

If not for Thora's breakneck pace, he would have caught up long before the skeleton forest.

"I've never ridden so hard as I did after I saw the bariwolf tracks. I don't know what would have happened if I'd been a day later." He closed his eyes. "An hour."

"But you weren't." *Thank Arabella.* I believed the Goddess of Love had gifted Ransom and Aurinda divine speed so he could be there in time to save my life.

I couldn't imagine what it would have done to him if he'd found us dead. He'd already lost too much.

"I'm so sorry about your mother. And Zavier."

He glanced down at Evie, swallowing hard. "Healer Geezala found him. She heard your whistle. I don't know if he survived, but when I left, he was still alive."

"W-what?" I gasped so loud it woke Faze. He was alive? Zavier might still be alive? My hand trembled as I brought it to my mouth. "Oh, gods."

"I asked Cathlin to send word to Quentis. It should be waiting when we arrive."

"Don't tell Evie. Not until we know."

"Agreed. Does she know about Mother?"

I nodded. "She asked if Luella was in the shades. I told her yes, but that was the extent of it."

He stroked her small hand with his thumb. "Someday, when she's older, I'll tell her the rest. She should know a mother, even if it's only a memory."

It was more than I had of my own.

"I want to go home." I wound a hand around his waist, snuggling closer.

Not to Quentis, but Turah.

I wanted to hide away in a treehouse in Treow with Ransom for months, ignoring the chaos that seemed to be gathering like thunderclouds over our heads.

"Tomorrow, we'll ride to the coast and find a fishing village. We'll hire someone to sail us to Roslo."

"Will we make it before the migration?"

"We'll make it."

"Ranse, no one we met on the road coming here had heard of the crux scout. No one seems to be panicked. The Mavins didn't believe me when I told them. Why hasn't news traveled faster? Why aren't people finding shelter? They need to be warned. Your father wouldn't keep this a secret, would he?"

"No. Thora was right about Turans. We have our fair share of secrets. But this isn't one he'd keep. When we get to Quentis, I'll find out if there have been other scouts."

"Lyssa is spreading across Calandra. The migration is months and months earlier than the scholars predicted. It's never been during a winter before. People won't have stored enough food or found a place to hide. It feels like the realm is on the brink of collapse, and we're trapped in the middle of a firestorm. What do we do?"

"Stay together." He brought his hand to my face, cupping my jaw and tilting it up as he stared down into my eyes. "No matter what. Stay together."

Ransom captured my mouth, his lips a soft press against my own.

I parted for him instantly, our tongues tangling as the embers from the fire floated into the night.

"Hope I'm not interrupting." Jodhi's voice cut the kiss short as he strode into the circle, plopping down on his blanket and brushing the dirt from his pants. "Thora didn't want company."

He stretched out his legs and resumed his relaxed posture, crossing his arms behind his head. "Lovely night, isn't it?"

Ransom growled.

I sighed, relaxing into his side, grateful that tonight, I'd get to sleep on his chest.

Stay together.

If only the realm weren't trying to tear us apart.

29

CASPIA

There was a mural of Bisten in the castle at Roslo.

Bisten, the temperamental, cantankerous male who lived in the palace mews at home. Xandra's favorite swift with auburn feathers that shone like gold in the early-morning light.

The artist who'd crafted this mural had captured Bisten's likeness perfectly. Except the painting was a lie. Bisten was prickly but not violent. Not bloodthirsty.

There had to be a mistake. Because this mural was of a monster.

And this mural would haunt me until the Divine called me to the afterlife.

The gallery was crowded with other tapestries and paintings, but I couldn't seem to tear my gaze from the largest in the hall.

A male swift—I refused to believe it was Bisten—had severed a man in two. There were entrails hanging from the creature's open beak. Blood and shredded flesh clung to his pointed horns. Beneath his foot was a woman, her body crushed and heart punctured by his piercing talon.

The male's ankle was scarred. Three white lines slashed through black, scale-covered skin. There was a notch in his beak. A chip in the sharp edge.

Bisten had those scars. He had a chip in his beak. Those were his glossy, auburn feathers and reddish-brown horns.

Not my Bisten.

Not my swift.

"Who painted this?" The question sounded more like an accusation.

"A fairly renowned painter. He was a young man during the last migration. Foolish enough to risk death to get a glimpse of the monsters. But somehow he survived and has been painting the crux ever since."

It was a lie. They were all lies.

My hands were trembling so fiercely I balled them into fists to keep from tearing every piece of art from these walls. My teeth gritted so hard they cracked. I was afraid that if I opened my mouth, I'd scream.

I'd sailed across the Marixmore and into a moon terror.

This had to be a hoax. I needed this to be wrong.

My heart broke as the anger vanished, chased away by a sorrow that came from the marrow of my bones. My stomach roiled, and I raced for a potted plant against the wall, dropping to my knees as I lost this morning's breakfast in a fern.

"Caspia." Andreas rushed to my side, running a hand up and down my spine. "I'm sorry. I shouldn't have brought you here."

Tears filled my eyes as I sank back on my knees, wiping my mouth with my sleeve. "No, I had to see this myself."

I had to see how the Calandrans viewed the swift.

Not swift.

Crux.

Monsters.

Andreas had told me all about the migrations during our voyage aboard the *Snail* to Quentis. At first, I'd wanted to argue and tell him he was wrong. That it was impossible for the crux to be so vicious. They wouldn't destroy buildings and cities. They wouldn't slaughter and decimate.

But Andreas had never doubted my truths, so I'd listened and accepted his. And when he'd asked if I wanted to see, for myself, what happened during the migrations, I'd agreed to come with him to this gallery in the Quentin castle.

"The buildings in Skanshon with the spikes and iron grids over their roofs. Those are for protection during the migration, aren't they?" I asked.

"Yes. Most cities and villages have their own unique defenses. Here in Roslo, we have migration chambers built beneath the castle. There are other tunnels and cellars built into the cliffs around the city, too."

"Do you fight them? The swift—crux?" Maybe if I started thinking about them as crux, it would be easier to accept them as monsters.

"Most kingdoms bolster their legions and recruit soldiers as the migrations draw near. Did you notice the catapults and large crossbows mounted on the castle's ramparts when we came in?"

"No." I'd been too taken by the gold plating and lofty towers that glimmered beneath the sun. This castle oozed wealth and indulgence.

It wasn't nearly as large as the palace in Nelfinex, but the castle was a sight. The Starling were immensely rich in elfalter, but we didn't flaunt our status by adorning our towers with opulence. Maybe because we had no need to brandish our wealth.

Our most valuable asset flowed through our veins.

Still, the Quentin castle was a sight to behold. It was more gold than I'd ever seen, and as we walked inside, I hadn't noticed much else.

"We do our best to kill as many crux as possible when a migration begins," he said. "It's done as a defense to buy people time to get to shelter. But the sheer number of the monsters means it's impossible to defeat them. All we can really do is hide and wait until the migration has passed."

Andreas had told me the migrations lasted lunes. Less than two if Calandra was lucky. More than three if they were not.

"This is why there aren't many people," I murmured. Why we'd traveled so far and encountered so few.

Their population was decimated every generation.

"When you told me of Nelfinex, I assumed you were plagued with migrations, too," he said. "No one knows where they come from. I figured that they always flew around the realm, leaving death and destruction in their wake."

"No one has ever tried to find out? To follow them from Calandra?"

"We have voyagers who've explored the Marixmore. Most who leave and return find nothing. Some leave and don't return. But if you lived through this"—he motioned to the paintings—"would you be in a rush to follow a crux out to sea?"

No. My chin quivered, the weight in my heart so heavy I feared I'd never be able to get off this floor.

Once the crux left this continent, all the survivors could do was rebuild.

There were treaties between the five kingdoms to ensure peace during the years when there were no crux. Those treaties also guaranteed trade so that each kingdom had the resources necessary to rebuild.

"I don't want to believe this," I whispered, staring at Bisten's mural. "In Nelfinex, at the palace, there is a massive vestibule. The ceiling is painted with a portrayal of every Starling queen. Most choose to have their likeness be of the swift they become. I can't make sense of these murals with the paintings I spent hours admiring as a child."

"I'm sorry, darling."

My eyes filled with tears as he helped me to my feet. "So am I."

"Let's go home."

My stomach was in a knot as we made our way out of the gallery and into a vast, open lobby in the castle. Every hall, every room, was as lavish as the exterior.

The ceilings were vaulted with gilded beams. Crystal chandeliers caught the light from the arched windows, casting sparkles across the marble floor.

The clip of Andreas's boots echoed through the empty space while my feet were entirely silent. The slippers he'd given me felt too soft, too flimsy compared to my boots. But women in Quentis did not wear black cloaks or pants with knives secured to their thighs and wrists.

To visit the castle, Andreas had urged me to look the part. So I'd donned these blue-green slippers and a gown in the same shade with a skirt that swished at my ankles.

Aunt Oleana would love this gown but loathe the slippers.

My necklace was hidden beneath the high neckline, and though they weren't mine, I wore each of Emery's elfalter rings. Not to claim my status as Starling, but to remember where I came from.

"Where is the library you told me about?" My voice echoed in the cavernous space. "Is it in this castle?"

"Yes, but we can visit another day."

"No." I shook my head. "I'd like to see it now."

"Caspia—"

"I must understand, Andreas. I must make sense of this."

It was no longer a mystery where the crux came to breed. Was this violence and bloodlust a part of that process? Or was there something about Calandra that made them different?

Had it made Xandra's transformation different?

Was it the reason it was forbidden to follow the crux when they migrated, because of the horrors they became? Or because our ancestors had known that we'd become as monstrous as the beasts themselves?

How much did my aunt know of Calandra? How many truths had she hidden from her people? From the Starling?

Was this where my mother had flown?

The questions made my head spin so fast I nearly retched again.

"Caspia." Andreas frowned, sensing my discomfort.

"I'm okay." I waved him off and kept walking. "I want to see the library."

Andreas must have read the determination on my face. He sighed, dragging a hand through his hair. Except the long strands were gone.

After we'd docked in Roslo and gotten settled at Andreas's house, he'd brought in a seamstress to tailor gowns and clothes for me. While I was poked and prodded, Andreas and Kos both got haircuts from the valet who'd fitted Kos for a wardrobe.

Andreas's hair was so short that I could only thread my fingers through the longer strands on top. His clean-shaven face didn't tickle when he kissed me. He looked as handsome as ever, yet so different from the man I'd met in that tiny Genesis cabin.

I had the suspicion that I was seeing the real Andreas, the Quentin version, for the first time. The wealthy nobleman.

"I will show you the library," he said. "But we're not staying long. You need to rest."

"You're the one who kept me up all night." We'd taken advantage of his massive bed with room to play.

"That's not what I'm talking about." He stopped walking, staring down at me with enough worry in his gaze to make my heart squeeze. He tucked a curl behind my ear and ran his thumb over my cheek. "You had another vision."

Yes.

While he'd slept, I'd spent my moon staring at the ceiling, praying that the Divine would make the visions stop.

I saw Emery's death every moon. I saw her killed by the silver-eyed warrior over and over and over again. Was this my penance for abandoning my quest for revenge? If this was the price I paid to keep Andreas alive, to change his fate, so be it.

Still, seeing her death hurt every time. Would these visions torture me forever for not going to Turah? Maybe that was the point. Or maybe the Divine was trying to tell me something.

Emery was a swift in my vision. I hadn't thought much about it until now. Was that why she'd been killed? Because she was a crux?

"I promise to rest later." I touched my fingertips to his forehead.

He loosed another sigh, then took my hand, leading me down a series of passages.

"You're quite familiar with the castle," I said.

"When I was a boy, I was tutored here with a class of other noblemen's children. I learned to read and write in the library, and I was instructed by the castle's weapons master in the training center." He turned another corner, and we emerged into a grand foyer with ceilings nearly twice as tall as the last lobby.

People crowded the vast space, voices and laughter creating a dull murmur.

Three women, each dressed in a bright gown, climbed the base of a sweeping staircase. Guards dressed in teal coats with gold buttons, wearing swords and knives sheathed at their belts, stood watch beside columns and pillars. A brawny man with brown skin and wire-framed eyeglasses passed in front of us. When he spotted Andreas, he looked twice and came to an abrupt stop.

Andreas did not.

He ignored the attention, the curious looks and quiet whispers, keeping his chin held high and his grip on my hand unyielding as we marched through the foyer. His hold on my fingers only loosened when we turned down yet another hall.

"The man with the eyeglasses recognized you," I said when I was certain we were alone.

"Yes. He is a workfellow of my father's."

"You didn't want to speak to him?"

"Not today." He stroked my knuckle with his thumb. "I want to show you the library. Then we'll return home. There will be time to make pleasantries with old acquaintances another day."

"What exactly does your father do?"

Andreas's jaw flexed. "He spends coin that is not his to spend."

Before I could ask for more of an explanation, we approached a pair of gilded doors with inlaid swirled carvings.

Two guards stood before the doors, barring the entrance.

Andreas walked to them, and with a single nod, they shifted out of the way. One opened a door for us to enter, bowing as he murmured, "My lord."

Was that Andreas's title? He was a lord? When my head stopped spinning, I'd have to ask more about Quentin politics and how his family fit into the scheme.

But once we stepped into the library, all thoughts faded away as I took in the enormous, round atrium bordered by shelf upon shelf. Three floors filled with countless books.

Andreas had told me this library had more books than a person could read in two lifetimes. I'd wager all the elfalter in the world it would take me three to comb through this many tomes.

It was nearly as vast as the palace library in Showe.

Past the entrance were tables and chairs arranged in neat rows, all unoccupied. Beyond them, the shelves formed columns and stacks that stretched so far I couldn't see the end of the room.

"There are so many," I murmured. "Where do I even start?"

"The bibliosophs will help narrow your search."

I didn't understand that word, but as Andreas led me toward a desk, I assumed he meant the scholars or curators of this collection.

"Why is no one here?" I asked as we weaved past empty tables, inhaling the scents of sage and paper and cinnamon.

"You need to be granted permission to use this library. The king hoards books the way he does gold."

"Why?" I asked.

Andreas sighed. "I don't know. Under his rule, Quentis has become a wealthy kingdom. But King Cross has many secrets. He is a stern, stubborn man who associates less and less with his people. It's fueled rumors about what he's hiding in this castle."

A chill skated down my spine.

A guard stood on the second-floor mezzanine, staring at us with an unreadable expression.

"Why were you given permission?" I asked.

"My former tutor is now the head bibliosoph. He's the one who taught me the old language. I wrote him a message yesterday when we arrived, asking for permission. It is his to grant." Andreas gave me an encouraging smile. "He will help us. If there is any information about Nelfinex or the Starling in this library, we'll find it."

By the grace of the Divine.

When we reached the desk, Andreas knocked on its top with his knuckles.

Beside it on the floor was a stack of three empty crates.

Andreas touched one with the tip of his boot. "During a migration a few generations ago, the crux got into the library and destroyed many of our books. Now, the most important tomes are stored belowground. The bibliosophs keep a catalog and can bring them up as needed."

A moment later, a short man with long, gray hair and a beard that stretched all the way to his navel emerged from behind a shelf, his arms laden with books.

He was dressed in cream linen pants and a matching tunic. Over his shoulders, he wore a teal scapular cinched at the waist with a matching cord. He had a convex nose, and upon seeing Andreas, his green eyes with their Quentin amber starbursts brightened.

"Oh, Andreas." The man rushed to set down his books, then rounded the corner of the desk, pulling Andreas into a tight hug. "You've returned. Oda, bless us."

"Hello, Faxon." Andreas clapped the older man on the back.

"I've missed you, boy." Faxon leaned away, taking in Andreas, head to toe. "You look well."

"I am well." Andreas put an arm around my shoulders, pulling me into his side. "This is Caspia."

Faxon's eyes widened for a brief moment before he bent at the waist in a bow. "My lady. A pleasure to meet you."

"And you." It felt like another lifetime that I'd been given a bow and formal title. Not that I'd ever been called "my lady" before.

Faxon straightened, giving Andreas another once-over. "Have you spoken to your father yet?"

"No."

"You cannot avoid him forever, Andreas."

Andreas nodded. "We'll talk eventually. But not today."

"All right." Faxon's eyes flicked my way. "Your missive mentioned a project. How can I be of help?"

"Caspia is looking for information about her heritage." Andreas bent, lowering his voice. "I will ask for your secrecy in this. And your trust, old friend."

Faxon gave Andreas a curious look before focusing on me. On my golden eyes. He seemed to notice them for the first time, but he didn't appear to be wary. There was more curiosity in his expression. "You have my silence. Whatever we discuss will be between us."

"Thank you." Andreas bowed. "Please give Caspia whatever she desires. And I have one last request. We've taken in a boy from Ozarth. He needs tutoring. He's an orphan, and I don't believe he's ever been taught to read or write. I'll warn you, though. He is...strong-willed."

"Ah." Faxon chuckled. "I had a student like that once."

Andreas smiled. "Kos will put me to shame."

"Then I look forward to the challenge. Give me two days to make arrangements. I'll tutor him myself."

"Thank you, Faxon."

"Welcome home, boy." Faxon's green eyes softened as he stared up at Andreas. There was pride in his expression. Love. "It's good to see you safe. When so much time passed, I was worried that you'd been taken to the shades."

"Not yet. And with Daria's luck, that won't be for some time."

Daria. One of the Six. The Goddess of Luck.

Andreas didn't mention his gods often, but one moon aboard the *Snail*, as he was staring into the stars, he told me about Ama and Oda. About how the Mother and Father were the stars and their children, the Six, made up the shades in between.

Faxon signed the Eight, then gave Andreas another firm hug. Then he bid us farewell as Andreas and I left the library.

We didn't dally in the foyer as we weaved through the crush and made our way outside. Beyond the castle's sweeping entrance and massive doors was a wide stone path. With my hand in his, Andreas led me to the castle's gates.

Once we were outside the wall, Andreas seemed to breathe easier, his hold on my hand relaxed, and his pace slowed.

We walked past homes and shops, making our way toward Andreas's house.

"I don't like the castle," he said. "I avoid it whenever possible."

"Why? Because of your estrangement with your father?"

"No. Because of what it represents. You saw all the gold. How much of the gold used for ornaments and embellishments could have gone to rebuilding after the last migration?"

I was still learning the value of Calandran wealth, but I agreed with his point.

"It's not just the gaudy decoration. I hate that castle for what it did to my brother. You asked me once if Arick and I got along."

And he'd given me a definitive *nelvi'o*.

"We used to. He's two years younger, but that age difference never mattered. For most of our childhood, we were inseparable. We were tutored together. Learned from the same weapons master. Had riding lessons every day until we were thirteen. We spent too many nights at taverns, drinking ale and chasing women. He was my best friend. Until he died a year ago."

A year ago, when he'd left Quentis. "I'm so sorry."

"So am I." He gave me a sad smile. "During the last migration, my mother's family was killed. They lived in Saltmore. It's a city on the other side of Quentis. We traveled for the funeral. My brother and I chose to ride our horses rather than in my mother's carriage. On the journey, Arick's horse was spooked by a snake. He would have been thrown, but his boot got caught in the stirrup. He was dragged, and by the time I caught up to stop his horse, his leg was shattered."

"Andreas," I gasped, staring up at him, my heart aching at the pain on his face.

"He survived. Though that's up for interpretation. Arick was never the same again. He spent months and months in bed, in agony. The healers gave him korakin to numb the pain."

"What is korakin?"

"It is the dung of kaverines."

"I don't know that creature."

"It's a monster. Smaller than some. Similar to a wolverine but twice as ferocious. They live in the deserts in Laine."

Kaverines sounded like the giant weasels in Beesa.

"I'll sketch one for you," he said. "Healers and alchemists will take their dung and boil it into a mush. Then it's reduced to a paste. When it's ingested, it will numb any pain. Usually the person who takes it will hallucinate. But it is often used in infirmaries for people who need a surgery or amputation. It works well. Except it's highly addictive."

We didn't have korakin in Nelfinex, but there were powders and potions that would ensnare people until they craved their next dose more than food or water. "Arick became addicted."

"It ruled his life," Andreas said. "He learned to walk again, though he required a cane and brace. But it took years of him working with a healer to get to that point. Whenever Arick complained of pain, the healer's answer was more korakin. The healer exploited my brother's addiction, gladly taking coin whenever Arick begged for more. Until finally, I intervened and sent the healer to the other side of Quentis, paying him never to return. Except by then, it was too late. My brother was resourceful. And that castle is crawling with people who have no qualms about the harm they do if it means a purse full of gold."

Andreas cast a glare over his shoulder to the spires that loomed above us. They gleamed even beneath a cloud-covered sky.

The palace in Showe was built for the same function. A stronghold for the Starling. A shelter for Nestlings. A home for Quiescents. A place to safeguard knowledge and history.

Yet it wasn't meant to cast such a stark dividing line between the powerful and powerless.

The stone wall around this castle's grounds was a clear boundary for those who were welcome and those who were not. As were its golden gates.

"My parents turned a blind eye," Andreas continued. "They refused to believe Arick had a problem. They never questioned why he was always short on coin or why he never missed a party or ball at the castle. They made excuses when he was passed out in his bed for days and days on end."

"It's why you're estranged from your father."

"I begged him to do something before it was too late. But he wouldn't listen. And then a year ago, Arick was at a party. He was drunk and out of his mind on korakin. He collapsed and fell down a flight of stairs. He broke his neck."

"I'm sorry." I hugged his arm, holding tight as we kept walking.

"Even after Arick's funeral, my father refused to admit it was the korakin. He said Arick's cane broke. That's why he fell. I couldn't stay and listen to the excuses. So I left."

"And went to Genesis."

"It was worth it. Giving up everything for a time." He stopped walking to face me, brushing a lock of curls away from my temple. "It was worth it to find you."

I leaned into his touch, and for a heartbeat, everything in my life made sense. I was here, in Calandra, for Andreas.

But then the next heartbeat came and my world pitched sideways.

A *thrum* vibrated through my body, spreading from my heart to my hands and feet. A thrum I hadn't felt since the *Cirrina*.

The thrum of the ritus.

As Andreas bent to kiss my mouth, I closed my eyes and pretended I did not feel its pull.

30

ODESSA

Thora sat on the ship's railing, one leg dangling over the edge as she stared across the gray-blue sea to the setting sun.

Her hair, like mine, was washed and clean. The flecks of dried green blood from the bariwolf attack were gone, leaving nothing but smooth white strands that fell in sleek panels past her waist.

She looked younger. Lonely. Like she was seconds from toppling over the edge of the ship and sinking into the ocean's depths.

Thora hadn't spoken a word since going to bury Mathias last night. As we rode to the coast at dawn, she stayed at the back of our small procession, even giving Jodhi a wide berth. And when we reached a small village on the Genesis coast, she disappeared.

While Ransom hired a fisherman and crew to sail us to Quentis, Evie and I went to a bath house. After we were clean and wearing fresh clothes, we met Ransom and Jodhi on this ship. Thora was nowhere to be seen.

I'd truly believed she'd left. That she'd sent Jodhi with us to collect payment for her and the rest of the Mavins from my father. But then I came up from belowdecks, where I'd been situating Evie's tiny quarters, and Thora's colorless hair had caught my eye.

She was dressed in a simple pair of leather pants and a gray tunic, the same clothes I was wearing—the village merchant's only variety had been in size. Gone were the leather, armor, and weapons, but she was still as intimidating as she had been the day we met.

I tamped down a rush of nerves and walked closer, the heels of my new boots sharp on the wooden deck. "Hi."

A blink was the only indication she'd heard me.

"I'm sorry about Mathias. I didn't mean for any of this to happen. But I am grateful to you, and to him, for saving our lives." Something I should have told her yesterday.

The splash of waves against the ship's hull filled her silence.

I took a step away, having said what I'd come to say.

"Odessa." She looked to me with red-rimmed eyes, her expression empty. "His death is not your burden. It's mine."

As she shifted her attention back to the sea, a tear glistened on her cheek.

I left Thora to her grief and turned to see Ransom.

He stood in the middle of the ship, his hands behind his back.

The four-man crew was on deck, too, most looking bored, staring at the water like they should be fishing, not shuttling warriors and horses to Roslo. But I suspected that the money Ransom had paid was more than enough to compensate them for their time.

My pulse quickened as I took in my husband.

He'd had a bath, too, and the beard covering his jaw was shorter than it had been this morning. His hair was neatly combed, just begging to be tousled by my fingers. His tan tunic was open at the throat, revealing a hint of taut skin. The fabric stretched around his broad shoulders and the wide plane of his chest. His leather pants hugged his bulky thighs.

He was, without question, the most beautiful man in all of Calandra. And he was mine.

Ransom's green eyes crinkled at the sides as I licked my lips. His perfect mouth turned up at a corner.

My heart skipped.

Shades, I'd missed that smirk.

I hoped that no matter how many years passed, it would never fail to take my breath away.

That smirk was a dozen stolen moments. A hundred precious memories. A single promise of a lifetime together.

I stopped a few feet away.

He frowned, swept out a hand to catch my wrist and pull me closer. "No more pretending, remember?"

"Sorry. Habit." I'd spent months convincing the realm—and for a time, myself—that I wasn't in love with the Guardian.

Not that I'd been very convincing. I was a horrible liar.

Or maybe the way I loved Ransom was simply impossible to disguise.

"What's behind your back?" I asked.

He brought forward two knives.

My knives.

I gasped, reaching for them. But before I touched their hilts, I stilled.

The last time I saw these knives, they were in Brielle's hands. She'd pulled them from Banner's dead body after I killed him. And before she'd been taken by the crux, she'd dropped them in the street in Ellder.

Ransom must have found them. I sort of wished he hadn't.

"Is it strange that I don't want to touch them?"

"No, Dess." He shifted both knives into one hand so he could pull me into his chest.

I wrapped my arms around his waist, breathing in his scent. With one inhale, it was wind and leather. The next, a masculine, citrus spice that mingled with the salt breeze.

It was chaotic and ever-changing, like his eyes, but beneath it all was Ransom, and I'd recognize it anywhere.

"Do you know what I don't understand?" Jodhi sauntered up beside us. "How does one convince an entire kingdom he is not their spoiled crown prince but instead a famed warrior? Are Turans really that gullible?"

Ransom's body went rigid, but before he could use my knives to slice open Jodhi's neck, I took them from his hand.

They molded to my palms, their weight familiar and comfortable. The blades were clean and shiny. Ransom had probably sharpened them as he'd rinsed away any trace of blood.

These knives had saved my life, and yet all I wanted to do was toss them overboard.

"Careful with those, doll. They look sharp."

I leveled Jodhi with a glare as I rolled a wrist, the knife's blade giving a *whoosh*. "Go away."

The Mavin grinned but left us alone, strolling toward Thora. He didn't join her on the railing, but stayed back, giving her space.

"He's baiting you," I told Ransom, my voice quiet.

"Yes, he is." He sighed. "Don't worry. I won't take it. I hate the bastard, but he kept you and Evie alive. So I won't rip out his tongue. Yet."

I rolled my eyes and handed him the knives. "Here. Don't get rid of them. But I don't want them back quite yet."

"Whenever you're ready." He brushed a kiss across my forehead.

Evie and Faze emerged from the stairwell that led belowdecks. She had his leash coiled around her wrist, pulling him along, his claws leaving marks in the wood. "Come. On. Faze."

"You're supposed to be sleeping," I said.

She was dressed in a new nightshirt with a scalloped hem that tickled her bare toes. It was too big for her, but at least it was clean. We still had her nightshirt from Ellder, but she'd stopped asking to wear it.

"He doesn't like the crate," she said. "And he won't stop growling. Can he please just sleep in my bed with me?"

"Sorry, Evie." Ransom knelt beside her. "He'll get used to it. I promise."

The fisherman had taken one look at Faze and refused to allow him on board the ship. He'd only changed his mind after Ransom gave him the last of the zillahs he'd had in his saddlebags and a promise that Faze would be leashed during the day. At night, he'd be locked in a slatted crate.

It was probably a good thing. I had a feeling that Margot would have rules for the tarkin when we arrived in Roslo, too.

"I don't like this ship." Evie pouted.

I didn't particularly like it, either. The quarters were small and smelled of fish. But it was big enough for the horses, and the crew had agreed to sail without delay.

"I'll take you back to your room." Ransom reached for Faze, but the tarkin hissed and swatted at him with a paw, leaving three thin scratches on Ransom's forearm.

The skin began to heal almost immediately, but not before a few drops of dark green blood appeared.

Evie bopped Faze on the nose. "No, Faze. That's bad."

The tarkin immediately cowered, nuzzling against her as he silently begged for forgiveness.

I stared at Ransom's arm, at those tiny beads of blood and the bite scar beside them. And I felt Jodhi's presence over my shoulder, his gaze as intent on that blood as mine.

Ransom swiped the blood away with a quick brush of his hand, then scooped up Faze and stood. "Come on, Evie. Time for bed."

With the monster draped over one arm to hide the scar and my knives in the other, he marched across the deck.

Evie huffed but walked behind him, and together, they disappeared down the stairs.

My heart was in my throat as I took a step to follow.

"Odessa." Jodhi's voice made me stop.

I looked over my shoulder, expecting a snide comment, but all I saw was pity in his gaze.

"If that's what I think it is, then you'd better take those knives back." The gentleness of his warning made it all the worse. He left, returning to stand watch at Thora's side.

While I lifted my heavy heart and went belowdecks.

Ransom's quiet voice drifted from the open doorway of Evie's small room.

I left them to talk and ducked into our quarters, plopping on the edge of the bed. Then I rolled up my shirtsleeve, unclasping the cuff that I'd worn over my forearm since Ellder.

My fingers traced the notches and grooves. My palm slid over the smooth leather.

The light in the room shifted as Ransom filled the doorway, leaning against its frame.

"What do we do?" I whispered.

"I don't know." He stepped inside, closing the door behind him before crouching in front of me, his hands on my knees. His eyes were a brilliant emerald green.

"Here." I lifted the cuff. "You should take this back."

He shook his head. "I trust you."

That trust was more precious to me than every piece of gold in Calandra.

"My father is desperate to find Allesaria before the migration, but I don't know why. He says it's the only way to stop the crux, and maybe that's true. Or maybe he was simply manipulating me to become his spy."

Father would probably kill for this cuff if he knew what it meant. Months ago, I wouldn't have hesitated to hand it over. To tell him anything and everything he wanted to know simply to earn his trust. His faith. His confidence.

To no longer be the daughter he dismissed and ignored.

But months ago, the trust I'd had in the Gold King had been unwavering. I wanted to believe he was a good man. That he had the interests of his people at heart. But my trust in Father was cracking apart like a stone hit one too many times with a hammer of doubt.

Now, all I really wanted was to stop the infection from spreading in Ransom's veins.

Where there is poison, there is a cure.

The words from the old woman with the snake bite echoed in my mind.

"I don't know how he plans to break the Shield of Sparrows treaty. I don't know how he thinks he can go against his blood oaths as king. I don't know if he's planning to start a war or if this is all some scheme for more power." I gave Ransom a sad smile. "He's my father, but I don't know if I can trust him."

And I didn't know if he'd listen to me when I begged for help in finding a cure for Lyssa.

This cuff could be my bargaining piece. It could mean Ransom's life.

"You should take it back." I pushed it into Ransom's chest.

He eased it away. "I trust you."

"What if I make the wrong choice?"

"You won't."

"How can you have such faith in me?"

He lifted a hand to my face, cupping my jaw. "Because you're my queen."

My heart swelled. "I love you."

"Yes, you do. Don't forget." He leaned in, capturing my mouth with his.

I liquefied as he licked the seam of my lips, letting the realm's troubles disappear to a far corner of my mind where they'd wait until it was time to dredge them up again.

With deft fingers, Ransom refastened the cuff around my wrist all while his mouth moved over mine. Once it was fastened, I wound my arms around his shoulders, shifting closer until my chest was pressed against his, the warmth from his body radiating through my shirt. My nipples turned to hard peaks beneath my clothes.

His tongue fluttered against mine before he delved deep, tasting every part of my mouth.

Heat swept through my veins. Desire pooled between my legs. A steady pulse vibrated through my core.

Ransom's arms banded around me as he hauled me off the bed, lifting me off my feet and turning to pin me against the nearest wall.

My legs wrapped around his narrow hips, rocking against his hardness. My body ached for more.

He trailed his lips along my jaw, bending to kiss the length of my neck as my hands slid into his hair. "Shades, I missed you."

"Never again." I closed my eyes. "Wherever we go, we go together."

Ransom sucked on my pulse, and that ache in my center spiked. "Together."

His hips held me against the wall as his hands roved up and down my ribs before they slipped under the hem of my shirt. The rough calluses of his palms and fingers were impossibly tender, their scrape like heaven against my skin.

I tugged at the back of his tunic, drawing it higher and higher, bunching it into my fists as his lips continued to explore the column of my throat.

His hands cupped my breasts, and his thumbs flicked my pebbled nipples. "Gods, I need to fuck you."

"Yes." My moan was wanton and desperate as he thrust his hips against mine, his cock rocking against my clit.

Ransom set me on my feet, and with a quick yank, my shirt was off and falling to the floor.

I reached to unclasp his pants, except before I could free the buttons, a knock pounded on the door. It was too loud to have come from Evie.

My hands stilled as Ransom dragged in an angry inhale.

"What?" he growled, a sound more monster than man.

I almost felt bad for the person on the other side of the door. Almost.

The person knocked again. Clearly, they had a death wish.

Ransom's eyes flashed to silver as he stomped to the door, ripping it open only enough to speak to our visitor but not to expose me as I collected my shirt from the floor.

"You'd better see this." Jodhi's voice came from the hall.

Ransom slammed the door in his face. "Fuck."

I pulled on my shirt as he took a few calming breaths, his jaw flexed and his hands fisted. But by the time I was ready, his eyes had shifted to hazel. Still pissed but not murderous.

Lucky for Jodhi.

Together, we made our way to the deck, where the evening light had nearly faded. All that remained was a sliver of orange on the horizon as the stars twinkled overhead.

Jodhi was standing beside Thora at the ship's railing. He only spared me a hard, cold glance as we joined them.

Maybe Ransom was right about Jodhi's feelings, but at the moment, I had bigger problems.

Out over the waves was another ship, sailing our way.

Standing on that ship's bow was Brother Dime.

31

CASPIA

The golden castle of Roslo blinked out of sight.

My fingernails dug crescent grooves into the ship's wall as the captain shouted orders to his crew. As the white fabric of the mainsail caught the wind, tears dripped down my face, falling into the sea as I floated away from the man I'd left on Quentis's shore.

...

"Caspia." Kos pinched my arm.

"Ouch." I winced and rubbed at the spot.

"Sorry," he mumbled, staring at the table.

I followed his gaze to the grooves in the wooden surface. Scratches from my fingernails. *Fuck.* "Oh, um...sorry."

"Are you okay?" he asked.

"Just tired, sweetling." I forced a smile and covered the marks with my palms.

I'd started calling him the same endearment I'd given Graciella. The more I learned about Kos, the more I realized how different he was from my niece. Yet they were also so similar it made me miss her that much more.

Kos picked up his spoon, scooping a bite of his oats and milk from his bowl.

My own breakfast stayed untouched, my appetite having vanished over the past few suns. Ever since I felt that thrum in my chest, I hadn't been hungry.

The visions of Emery's death had stopped. For two blissful moons, I'd slept soundly on Andreas's chest from dusk to dawn. But I should have known the visions wouldn't stay away for long.

Last moon's vision played through my mind on a loop.

What did it mean? Why had the thrum returned? Was this my body, my blood, preparing to shift? Had my ritus not actually failed?

Was this a different call? Was I meant to return home? How was I supposed to walk away from Andreas? How could I leave Xandra behind?

The unknown was eating me alive.

Kos's spoon froze in midair, his gaze locked on my hands.

They were shaking. I slipped them onto my lap beneath the table.

"Are you excited to start lessons today?" I asked.

Kos nodded, taking his bite. A dribble of milk escaped the corner of his mouth. His feet kicked at the legs of the chair. He was never great at sitting still, but today, his energy couldn't be contained.

Faxon had sent a message to the house last evening that Kos could begin his lessons.

While Kos ate, Andreas was upstairs getting dressed. Then he would take the boy to the library.

"Do you know how many summers you are?" I asked.

"Summers?"

"Years," I corrected myself.

Kos only shrugged. "Don't know."

"Do you remember your mother or father?"

He shook his head. "I had a sister. She looked out for me when I was little."

Kos was still little—though he'd likely kick anyone in the shin if they said as much. As far as he was concerned, he could take care of himself. Unfortunately, it was mostly true.

If he decided to run away, I had no doubt that he'd survive

on the streets of Roslo like he had in Skanshon. But he didn't have to simply survive, not anymore.

In addition to lessons with Faxon, Andreas had arranged for a nanny to live with Kos. They were sharing the bedrooms on the first floor of the house. There was a cook who made all of our meals, and now that the boy was beginning lessons, I suspected his life would fall into a routine. Much like the Nestlings in Showe.

Would I be here to watch him grow? The pit in my stomach, the thrum in my chest, was answer enough.

Andreas walked into the dining room, adjusting the lapels of his coat. "Ready?"

Kos leaped out of his chair and, abandoning the rest of his breakfast—he never left food behind—ran through the house for the front door.

I laughed. "He's excited."

Andreas bent over the back of my chair to kiss my forehead. A crease formed between his eyebrows when he saw the scratches on the table. "Are you all right?"

"Fine." I stood, rising onto my toes to kiss his jaw. "You'd better go before Kos leaves you behind."

"Caspia."

"Go. I'll see you later." I cupped his face and offered the most reassuring smile I could summon. Then I slipped past him, hurrying to the staircase and our bedroom on the upper floor.

I hovered at the largest window, listening for the door to open and close, watching as Andreas set off down the street with Kos at his side.

The castle loomed in the distance, the morning rays reflecting off the golden exterior. Teal Quentin flags stitched with the royal emblem hung from its towers.

It was mesmerizing. As impressive as it was bold.

But when I closed my eyes, all I could see was it winking out of sight.

A shudder ran over my shoulders as I turned away, crossing the room to the balcony that overlooked the city.

Andreas's house was perched atop a hill, and the balcony gave me an unobstructed view over the city's buildings to the aquamarine waters of Roslo Bay.

There was a line of ships docked in the port, but my eyes caught on one with collapsed white sails.

My breath caught in my throat.

The ship from my vision.

The thrum that pulsed through my veins made me want to vomit.

What did these visions mean? Why was I seeing myself, my future, after a lifetime of only seeing the past?

Was there someone on that ship I was supposed to meet? Was there a reason I left Andreas? It would have to be life altering. It would have to be my only option. A last choice.

I pushed off the balcony's railing and raced through the suite, stepping into the slippers I'd left in the dressing room. With my shoes on, I hurried downstairs to scribble a note for Andreas. Then I hurried out of the house and along the road.

After disembarking from the *Snail*, we'd taken a carriage from the docks to Andreas's house. I hadn't planned on returning to the docks, so I hadn't paid attention to the route.

I should have paid attention.

Countless wrong turns and dead ends later, I finally stumbled onto a road that was cluttered with people and smelled like salt, fish, and brine.

The wooden-planked walkways of the docks were bustling with visitors and traders. The crowd ebbed and flowed through the various paths leading to a cluster of market stalls.

It reminded me of Skanshon, with merchants selling all types of goods from vegetables to herbs to fish to tonics. A man carrying a basket of carrots bumped into my shoulder, not sparing a backward glance as he barreled through the masses.

"You need a bracelet, love," a woman called from behind a table cluttered with metal jewelry.

I offered a kind smile but kept walking, standing on my toes to try to see past others. I pushed through the crush, moving toward the water, scanning masts until I found the ship with white sails.

Ducking off the main walkway, I followed a line of boats tied to pylons until I reached the ship at the end of the row. It was secured with thick tan ropes, rocking gently as water lapped against its hull.

"Hello?" I called, searching the deck for a crew member.

A figurehead was carved into the bow, a woman with flowing hair and an ample bust. Beneath her body was the ship's name. The *Malynn*. That name meant nothing to me.

"Hello," I called again.

Boots thudded on the walkway, and a man with tanned skin and glossy black hair dressed in a tailored cream coat approached. "Can I help you, miss?"

"Is this your ship?"

"I'm its captain." He crossed his arms over his broad chest. He was so tall I had to crane my neck to meet his gaze. The amber starbursts in his eyes seemed to glow beneath the sun. "Why?"

He wouldn't believe me if I told him the truth. "What's your name?"

His eyes narrowed. "Let's start with yours."

"Caspia."

"Caspia what? What's your last name?"

We didn't have last names. There was no need in Nelfinex, so I gave him the only answer I could think that fit. "Starling."

"Caspia Starling," he said. "You seem rather keen on my ship. Why?"

Because this ship may or may not take me across the Marixmore. "What has been your longest journey?"

"These are strange questions, Caspia Starling." His mouth flattened into a thin line.

"Sorry. I'm just curious."

He frowned but answered, "Two months, nine days."

"That's not enough," I murmured.

"Pardon?"

I sidestepped past him, walking away as I replayed the vision.

"Oi," he called to my back. "What do you mean it's not enough?"

I ignored him and retreated along the walkway until I was swallowed up by the people in the marketplace.

Why would I get on that ship? Why would I leave?

Was it for Xandra? She was the only reason I'd leave Andreas and return home.

If we could even make it home. Unless the thrum was calling me to Showe, there was a good chance we'd be lost at sea.

My head began to throb as the noise in the market grew louder. Men shouted. Women yelled. It was so crowded that every other step, someone knocked into me, sending me off-balance.

A young man, lanky and tall, bumped into me from behind as he tried to push his way past.

I jammed my elbow into his ribs and shot him a glare.

One look at my eyes, and he shied away.

Divine, I needed out of this market. The crowd parted ahead as a street came into view. I exhaled and quickened my steps until the chaos and smells of the dock began to fade. Then I picked up the skirts of my gown, lengthening my strides as I searched for a familiar building.

In Showe, we had street names. But the buildings in Roslo only had numbers, and I didn't understand the arrangement.

A man leaning against the open door of a small office with square-paned windows dipped his chin as I approached. "How about a paper, miss?"

"I'm sorry, I don't have any coin." I kept walking.

"Here." He pulled a folded paper from his back pocket and pushed off the doorframe, stepping into the street to block my path. He didn't move out of the way until I took the paper from his outstretched hand. "Read it. When you want a subscription, you know where to find me."

Considering I didn't know how to find my own house, it was doubtful I'd be back at this office again.

"Good day, my lady." He grinned, then whistled a tune as he ducked into his office.

I tucked the paper under an arm and marched forward. But just before I came to a corner, the hairs on the back of my neck stood on end.

The man stood in his open doorway again, his whistle carrying along the street.

Something about the way he'd looked at me, the familiarity in his gaze like we'd met before, made me take the paper from under my arm. I unfolded it and skimmed the front page.

Andreas's name was inked at the top of a full-page article.

I read every word.

When I was finished, I crumpled the paper into a ball. Then I put one foot in front of the other, moving through the pain. I didn't try to understand the numbers on buildings. I didn't bother finding a familiar street.

I walked aimlessly through Roslo.

Because the last place I wanted to go was home.

My slippers dangled from my fingers as I stood in front of a pile of rubble. Strange that such delicate shoes could cause such awful blisters. My heels were shredded.

I'd taken the slippers off when I reached this neighborhood of cobblestone streets.

I studied the stains of my dark blood. Mixed with the dust from the dirt roads, the shoes were unsalvageable. Like this heap of wood and stone.

The houses on each side of the ruined house were small but cozy. One was painted white. The other slate blue. They were lovely, adorable homes with desolation in between.

Grass sprouted in patches amidst the rubble. Moss covered the stones. A tree with yellow and orange leaves grew through a section of the collapsed roof. The entire structure was caved in at its center, like an enormous rock had fallen from the sky.

Except this house hadn't been cratered by a rock. A crux had likely destroyed this house during the last migration. And it had been left like an open grave.

How many lives had been lost with it? Why hadn't anyone rebuilt or carried away the remains? Maybe there was simply no one left to care.

Even after all that Andreas had told me, after visiting that art gallery, I still struggled to make sense of this devastation.

Was there a way to stop the crux? Was it possible to change their migrations so they'd breed somewhere else?

That was a question for Aunt Oleana, a queen on the other side of the world.

While I was lost somewhere in Calandra.

A throat cleared.

I blinked, tearing my eyes away from the ruined house.

An older woman walked my way, her steps cautious, like she was approaching a wild animal. Her face was lined with wrinkles. Her short hair was frizzy and gray.

The memory of a vision from aboard the *Cirrina* wasn't

quick to resurface. It floated, more than popped, into my mind.

...

A woman stands at a washbasin, her forehead dewy with sweat. She rinses a green liquid from her hands, the color so dark it's nearly black.

A younger woman with yellow hair rushes for the basin, dunking her hands into the dirty water. "Hali, the blood—"

"Quiet, girl," Hali hisses. "Remember the agreement."

The blond woman nods, staring at the murky water.

Hali finishes washing and dries her hands, then rushes out of the room.

"What kind of monster is this?" the young woman whispers. Then she gets to work cleaning her hands.

...

"Can I help you, miss?" the old woman asked.

I blinked, letting her features come into focus. *Hali*. This was Hali.

"I seem to be lost." I offered her a small smile. "I was walking around and came upon this house."

She turned to face the rubble and crossed her arms over her chest. The sleeves of her tan dress were rolled up her forearms. A white scarf was tied at her neck. Her shoes were sturdy with thick soles.

I'd have to ask Andreas for something more like those shoes than these awful slippers.

"Was this destroyed in the migration?" I asked.

She nodded. "Most of the houses on this street were ruined. Mine is three down. It took a year to rebuild. The woman who lived here left Roslo. She was a nice lady, but she lost her daughters and husband. I believe she moved to Saltmore. It was better for her to leave."

"I suppose so."

"Do you need help finding your way?" the woman asked.

"No, thank you." I still wasn't quite ready to see Andreas. The woman nodded, then walked away.

I stared at the house and pressed a hand to my chest as the thrum pulsed in time with my heart.

"Not yet," I whispered and threw my slippers, one at a time, into the wreckage.

By the grace of the Divine, not yet.

32

ODESSA

"Wow," Evie whispered, resting her head against my shoulder.

She was too little to see over the ship's bow, so I'd propped her up on the railing, holding her close as we sailed across the calm waters of Roslo Bay.

The city's lights twinkled and shimmered over the waves. The gold castle, lit by lanterns and torches and the unfiltered light from the twin moons, was aglow tonight.

Evie's gray eyes sparkled with its reflection as she stared in wonder at the Quentin capital. For a moment, I saw my city from her perspective. Grand and marvelous. Glitzy and alluring, especially for a little girl. It was a world apart from the Turan fortresses and treehouses.

Roslo was said to be the finest capital city in all of Calandra. Ransom might disagree, since he'd actually seen every capital city. Maybe I'd change my mind if I ever saw Allesaria. But even I was awed by the city of my birth.

The gold plating on the castle was my grandfather's doing. He'd been prone to spending Quentis's wealth on extravagance. There were nobles who still spoke of his indulgent parties and galas, some with longing, others with contempt.

My father was a more practical ruler. He used Quentin resources wisely, and during his reign as king, he'd amassed a fortune for our kingdom. Enough to earn his moniker.

The Gold King of Quentis.

But Father always grumbled at the nickname. I'd heard

him gripe more than once over the excess in the castle, from the gold utensils he found beside his plate at every meal to the myriad of jewels inlaid in the banister of the staircase that led to his private chambers.

The castle was excessive. Magnificent. It was intimidating in its splendor and beauty. It was home.

Home.

That word didn't fit Roslo the way it used to. Maybe if we'd arrived during the day, if my cliffside had been more than shadows, I would have felt more at home.

Behind us, the crew hurried around the deck, preparing us for port.

The closer we came to the city, the tighter my stomach twisted. I'd been a jittery mess for days thanks to Brother Dime's magic, and now that we were fast approaching the city, I was about to lose my roast chicken and potato dinner overboard.

How was Father going to handle this unplanned homecoming? Would he be angry when he learned that Ransom and the Guardian were not only the same man, but that the Turans had fooled us all during my wedding? Would he be willing to help me find a cure for Lyssa?

Would he finally tell me his secrets?

Shades, I wasn't ready. We were supposed to have another day on this ship before we arrived in Roslo, and damn it, I could use another day to bolster some courage.

Brother Dime always seemed to thwart my plans. *Bastard.*

The evening we'd crossed paths, he'd left his ship for ours. Then he'd used his fluid magic to manipulate the water and wind to send us speeding through the ocean. The entire ship seemed to vibrate with his power, setting me completely on edge.

What little I'd eaten earlier churned in my gut. I'd barely slept since he boarded.

The priest had taken Evie's room, and the flimsy wall

between us hadn't been enough to block out his magic. Not to mention the bed in our chambers was not designed for three.

Evie had slept between Ransom and me. Her wiggling combined with Faze's never-ending protests from his crate and the constant sting of Voster magic had rubbed me raw.

Still, I'd take another sleepless night on this smelly ship if it meant avoiding my father for one more day.

Ransom's arm slid around my waist as he came to stand by my side. While I'd been with Evie on deck, he'd been stowing our things and saddling Aurinda. "Ready?"

"Nope." I looked up and found eyes of swirling silver.

The color matched the circlet he wore over his brow. The band was simple, a twist of metal threads woven together, its ends disappearing into the dark strands of his hair.

No more pretending.

Tonight, he was Zavier Ransom Wolfe, the crown prince of Turah. He'd walk into my father's throne room much like he had months ago, cold and commanding.

Ransom's eyes had been silver since Brother Dime boarded the ship. There was a barely contained fury simmering beneath his skin.

He'd confronted the priest about abandoning Evie and me in Turah, and had Dime not apologized profusely, promising Ransom he'd had no idea that Skore would leave us, my husband might have murdered the Voster.

Brother Dime had offered me the same apology, and while it had sounded sincere, I didn't trust it or the brotherhood.

"Wolfe," Jodhi called. "You're needed below."

Ransom growled. Then he slid his hand around my hip, letting it drop and caress the full curve of my ass.

I rolled my eyes, and while the color of his didn't soften, I caught a smirk before he walked away.

"Let's go rescue Faze from his crate," I told Evie, helping her down from the railing. With her hand in mine, we crossed the deck for the stairs just as Brother Dime emerged, his burgundy robes lifted to reveal his bare feet and bony ankles.

His magic hit me like an icy wind, forcing me back a step as it drove into my skin.

It was nearly impossible to gauge the Voster's expressions with their solid eyes, but something about him seemed harder tonight. As if he, like Ransom, was preparing to face a foe.

I shuffled Evie backward and to the side, making room for him to pass.

Except he stopped, blocking the stairs. "The old language. Did you learn it?"

"Yes."

"Did you finish reading the book?"

"Not yet." There wasn't much left to read in Luella's journal, but ever since Jodhi questioned the book, I'd left it in my satchel.

Brother Dime nodded once, then moved to walk away.

"What is it?" I asked. He probably wouldn't answer, but it was worth trying. "There are stories in that book that came true. They unfolded before my eyes. It's impossible. What does it mean?"

"It means you're on the right path."

That answer wasn't helpful in the slightest. Well, at least I wasn't surprised.

Did that mean Thora was the warrior Skore had intended for me to find? Did that mean I was supposed to be in Quentis for the migration?

I didn't bother asking Dime, instead helping Evie belowdecks and down the narrow hallway to our room, where Faze was clawing at the slats on his crate.

Ransom had already taken our bags to Aurinda, so I strapped on the harness for my sword and slung my satchel over one shoulder, Faze's carrier on the other. Once he was tucked away, Evie and I returned to the deck just as the ship came to a slow, floating stop.

Ropes were thrown to tie us to the dock as a wide plank bridged the gap. The access closure to stowage was opened so Ransom and the Mavins could lead out their horses.

Not a single fisherman or the captain bid us farewell as we walked off the ship.

It took the length of the docks for my body to stop expecting the motion of waves as I walked, and as we reached solid ground, Ransom lifted Evie into Aurinda's saddle.

My hands were shaking, and I was too nervous to ride, so I walked beside Ransom, leading our small procession through the streets.

The city was quiet, most people tucked in their homes. It was impossible to tell with doors closed and window curtains drawn, but it didn't seem like anyone in Roslo was preparing for the migration.

Had anyone started packing? Did they know the crux were coming? That the horde could arrive any day?

If I had to go door to door while I was here, I would give these people a warning.

We continued past familiar buildings and homes until we were standing before mine.

Ten guards were stationed at the entrance. The ornate golden gates were open, which meant there was an event tonight. Normally, they closed at dusk.

Two of the guards stepped forward, both tall, hulking men. One held up a hand, looking right at me as he spoke. "Off you go. Nobility only."

I blinked. "What?"

"You heard me. Nobility only."

He didn't recognize me. None of them did.

I opened my mouth to tell him I was quite noble, but Brother Dime emerged from the shadows first.

The guards all shied away, their eyes wide as they

remembered their courtesies and waved the Voster inside the castle's grounds.

"Send for a stable boy," Ransom ordered, giving the guard a withering glower.

"Of course, sir." The guard offered a quick bow as we passed.

Ransom lifted Evie down from Aurinda, urging her my way. "Why don't you both wait inside? We'll be right behind you."

Brother Dime stayed with Ransom and the Mavins while I took Evie's hand, leading her up the wide cobblestone path that led to the castle's imposing staircase.

"Wow." Evie's eyes were wide as we climbed the steps toward the arched, gilded doors. When we reached the top, her mouth was hanging open. "This is where you live?"

"This is where I used to live." As we crossed the threshold into the grand foyer, I waited for a feeling of peace to hit me. I waited for my nerves to settle. I waited for the exhale that came at the end of a long journey.

But my breath felt lodged in my throat. The castle was familiar.

Yet I felt like a guest in my own home.

The marble floors were polished to a shine. The intricate gold filigree on the pillars and gables reflected the light from the crystal chandelier.

"Miss." A guard marched to us, his bushy gray eyebrows pulled together in a frown.

"Good evening." I couldn't recall his name, but I knew this man. He'd been a part of the guard for years, with enough decorations and medallions on his uniform to indicate a high rank.

"How did you two get in here?" he barked.

Wait. Was he joking? I arched my eyebrows. "We rode on the back of a lionwick."

"Do you expect me to laugh, girl? Off you go. Nobility

only." He took my arm to escort me outside, but I didn't move.

"Let me go," I snapped. "Now."

"Outside."

"I'm not leaving until I speak to my father."

The guard huffed. "And who exactly is your father? The king?"

He didn't recognize me, either. Yes, my clothes were plain and my hair was red instead of dyed brown. But this man should know my face. At the very least, my eyes.

Except there wasn't a hint of recognition. None. He stared through me, not at me.

I was the princess they'd already forgotten.

It hurt more than it should.

Footsteps sounded behind me, and I felt him before I saw him. Ransom took one look at the guard's hand clamped around my elbow, and his face turned murderous. "If you want to keep that hand, let her go. Now."

The guard gulped and released my arm.

"This is how you treat the future queen of Turah?" Ransom sneered.

The guard blinked. Then his hand was gone, his eyes panicked and wide as he looked to Ransom, then me, and back to Ransom. "I'm sorry. I didn't—"

"Just take me to my father." I cut off his apology, not wanting to hear it.

"Of course, Princess." He bowed at the waist, then led us through the castle.

Ransom walked at my side while Brother Dime and the Mavins fell in line behind us.

Music filtered through the halls as we approached the throne room. As the hum of laughter and conversation swelled, Evie's hold on my hand tightened.

"Highness." The guard bowed again and swept out an arm for us to enter the room.

The last time Ransom and I were in this room together, my entire life flipped on its head.

I just hadn't realized at the time that I'd been living upside down.

Ransom and I shared a look as we stood on the outskirts of a crush. The corner of his mouth tugged into that handsome smirk, like he was remembering that day, too.

The party was at its peak, the throne room crowded with guests wearing fine coats and bejeweled gowns. Servants with trays of wine goblets milled around the room as people laughed and gossiped. The room was drunk.

Two women my age, both noble daughters I'd known since my childhood, stood nearby, whispering to each other as they pointed and leered at people in the crowd. A young man was making lewd gestures toward a woman with her back turned.

Gods. No wonder I'd never enjoyed these parties.

Maybe if we were quick, we'd be able to sneak through the crush unnoticed.

A bald man walked by, smiling as he passed. That smile fell as he did a double take at Ransom. "Y-you're the Guardian."

So much for going unnoticed.

Ransom gave the man a deathly glare, but the damage was done.

The whispers started instantly.

That's the Guardian.

Are those Mavins?

Who is she?

The very last thing I wanted was for these people to see me like this, weary and worn. Even if they didn't recognize me as the princess. The urge to duck my chin, to hide behind a curtain of my hair, was tempting, but I held my chin high as I stepped into the throng, holding Evie close as we plowed through the crowd toward the front of the room.

Father sat on his throne, staring toward the windows and

into the night. One of his ankles was kicked up over his knee. He held a goblet of wine in one hand as the fingers on his other drummed on the chair's golden arm. He looked bored. He looked tired. He looked lonely.

Where was Margot? The chair beside Father's was empty.

The noise in the room lessened, even the musicians quieting their merry tune as we arrived at the bottom of the dais.

Father tore his eyes from the glass, his gaze landing on me first. He stood so fast the wine in his goblet sloshed over its edge and onto his hand. A smile pulled at his mouth, his eyes blinking me into focus. He took a hurried step, like he was going to break into a run and haul me into his arms.

Then he blinked again, and it was like a wall slammed down between us. The joy on his face disappeared. The smile vanished. His caramel eyes hardened.

I'd missed my father when I left for Turah, though not often and not much.

Now I remembered why.

He looked over everyone's heads to the doors and snapped his fingers, only once. "Out."

It didn't take long for the music to cease entirely. The crowd stilled as partygoers shared worried glances.

But my father was not one to repeat himself.

People began to shuffle toward the doors, spilling into the hallway.

Only when the room was empty did he move. He walked across the dais and down its stairs to greet not me but the Voster. "Brother Dime. Welcome."

The priest clasped his hands in front of his robes. "I will retire to my quarters. We will meet in the morning."

"Of course," Father said as the Voster turned and swept out of the room on silent feet.

When he was gone, Father still didn't meet my eyes. Instead, he leveled his gaze at Ransom and the silver circlet on his brow.

Ignoring me only ignited Ransom's rage. Anger pulsed off his body in waves.

Or maybe that was my fury, boiling to the surface.

I wasn't going to be ignored. I wasn't going to be overlooked.

"Father, this is Thora and Jodhi." I held out my free hand toward the Mavins. "They saved my life. As did a number of others. Please find rooms for them both and arrange for twelve thousand zillahs to be delivered to them before dawn."

Finally, I got his attention.

He looked to me, eyebrows slowly rising. "Odessa, I will speak with you in a moment."

"No. You will speak to me now." My voice came out too loud, too high-pitched.

Evie shied closer to my leg, and Faze let out a growl as he poked his head from the carrier.

I took a calming breath as Father's attention dropped to my tarkin. "And you will pay them now."

His eyes narrowed as he regarded me, like I was a stranger in his castle. But Father would learn soon enough.

The princess who'd left Quentis, the woman he'd sent to Turah to spy and assassinate the Guardian, was not the daughter who had returned.

Ransom's chuckle filled the room. "King Cross, let me introduce you to my queen."

33

CASPIA

Andreas and Kos were at the dining table when I finally returned to the house after wandering the streets of Roslo.

They were hunched over a sketchbook, Andreas's arm draped around the back of Kos's chair.

Kos's face was the picture of concentration as he drew. His eyebrows were furrowed, and his tongue poked out from the corner of his mouth.

"Good. Now we'll shape the nose." Andreas took the stick of charcoal from Kos's hand, demonstrating for the boy. Then he returned the pencil. "Your turn."

"Like this?" Kos asked as he drew.

"Just like that." Andreas smiled, his eyes crinkling at the sides.

It had been a while since he smiled that way. Unguarded. Content.

Andreas had stripped off his coat to the simple white shirt beneath. It stretched over his broad frame, molding to the honed muscles of his arms and shoulders. Yet with all that strength, he had such a gentleness when it came to me. To Kos.

My heart ached, seeing them together. Seeing Andreas with a child.

He was good with the boy. The parent Kos needed. Patient. Kind. Loyal.

In what version of my life did I get to witness him with a child of our own? What promise would I have to make the

Divine to change my fate? What did I have to do to make this incessant thrum stop?

I loved him.

I loved Andreas more and more with every heartbeat. Every breath.

It wasn't fair that I had to give him up already. But I guess he had never really been mine to begin with.

Maybe all I could do now was find a way home. And do everything in my power to spare the people of Calandra from another migration.

At the sound of my bare feet on the floor, Andreas's eyes lifted and his shoulders relaxed away from his ears. "There you are. I was getting worried."

I feigned a smile.

His gaze shifted to my dirty, bare feet. "What happened?"

"The slippers hurt."

He stood from the chair, smile gone as he came to me. "Where did you go?"

"The docks." I sidestepped around him to peer over Kos's shoulder. "What is this?"

"Andreas is teaching me how to draw." The boy grinned up at me, then went back to his sketch of circles and lines, the foundation of what would become a face.

Beside his sketchbook was a small drawing, an example Andreas must have done.

It was my face.

He'd drawn it from memory.

"Kos, that's enough for today," Andreas said. "We'll practice more tomorrow after your lessons."

The boy sighed and set down his pencil, but he didn't argue as Andreas ruffled his hair and sent him off to his room, where the nanny was waiting.

"Are you hungry?" Andreas asked.

"No." I shook my head and trudged for the stairs, my legs heavy as I climbed.

Andreas followed me, and when we reached the second floor, he steered me toward the bathtub with his hand on my lower back.

I watched as he wordlessly drew a bath, filling the tub with enough water to soak my feet. "You don't need to do that."

"Humor me." He held out a hand to help me step inside.

The water rinsed away the dirt. The wounds had already healed.

"What's wrong?" he asked.

I sat on the tub's edge and pulled the crumpled paper from the pocket of my gown.

"What's—" Andreas didn't finish his question as he unfolded the page. He didn't look at all surprised.

"You've seen this already."

"Yes." His nostrils flared as he recrumpled it into a ball and tossed it across the bathing chamber.

"You are betrothed." My voice was flat. A numbness had settled into my bones as I'd wandered around Roslo.

There were many things in the paper to discuss, but at the moment, before I climbed into his bed again, that seemed to be the most important.

He walked to the closest wall, his hand fisted. For a moment, I was sure he'd punch a hole into that innocent wall, but he simply planted it on the smooth surface before hanging his head. "No. I mean, yes. This was arranged by my mother while I was away."

I'd hoped it wasn't true. I'd hoped that "betrothed" meant something different in Calandra than it did in Nelfinex.

But now the vision made sense. This was why I would leave.

"I'm sorry, Caspia," he whispered.

I closed my eyes, swallowing past the growing lump in my throat.

The paperman must have seen me in the castle. He'd speculated in the article about the mysterious red-haired woman who'd been linked to Andreas and what I might mean to his upcoming wedding, which was slated for the winter solstice.

Well, he had nothing to fear. I'd be gone by then. I'd be sailing away on the *Malynn*.

"Do you love her?"

"No." His reply was instant. "It's simply a contract that I need to find a way to void. This woman has no affection for me, beyond friendship. It's a marriage for political reasons. Nothing more."

"A marriage is still a marriage." I stood in the water, then carefully stepped out of the tub.

"I'm sorry." Andreas grabbed a towel from a hook and brought it over, dropping to his knees to dry my feet. "I've been trying to find a way out of it. But it's…complicated."

"Complications you should have shared with me. I shouldn't have had to read them in that paper."

"I know." He looked up at me, regret brimming in his eyes. "I'm sorry. There are things to say. I did not expect—"

I pressed my fingers to his mouth.

As frustrated as I was to learn his secrets this way, I didn't have the energy to fight. If our time together was running short, then I didn't want to spend it arguing or apologizing.

We'd have our chance for a goodbye. Soon, I would uncomplicate this situation for him. But I wasn't ready to let him go. Not yet.

So I folded at the waist, replacing my fingers with my mouth.

My lips pressed to his as I kissed them from corner to corner, memorizing the feel of his soft pout.

His hands slipped beneath my skirt to slide up the backs of my legs. A trail of sparks ignited under my skin, and my body came alive beneath his hands.

Andreas touched me, and I knew what it was to fly.

He flicked his tongue against my lower lip, seeking

entrance. The moment my mouth parted, I was lost, the world and everyone in it forgotten.

His palms cupped my curves, squeezing and kneading my flesh until I ached for more.

Taking him by the collar of his shirt, I tugged him to his feet. Our mouths stayed fused until it was him who towered over me.

My skirts stayed bunched around my hips as he hoisted me into his arms. I looped my legs around his waist as he carried me out of the bathing chamber.

The evening light flooded through the windows, casting his bedroom with a gentle peach hue. If I closed my eyes, I could almost imagine it was Nelfinex. That Andreas had come with me on that ship and we'd sailed away from this cursed kingdom.

Away from the woman who would become his wife. A faceless stranger whose name might as well be Envy.

Right or wrong, betrothed or not, he was mine. I wasn't giving up my claim on him quite yet.

I tugged at the laces on his collar, loosening his shirt as he sat on the bed with me perched on his lap.

He kissed the line of my jaw to my ear, nipping at the lobe. "Gods, I want you."

I rocked against his arousal as it strained against his trousers. Desire coiled in my center as I dragged his shirt up his back so I could dig my nails into his skin. "Take me."

He growled against my throat. With a fast twist, he laid me on the bed, tearing at my gown until my breasts came free with the sound of splitting seams. Then he flattened his tongue and dragged it over a nipple.

"Yes," I moaned as he sucked the pebbled bud into his mouth.

Mine. He was mine. The idea of giving him up, of losing him to another woman, made me rage.

I dug my nails harder into his back.

"Caspia," he murmured against my skin, his mouth trailing along my collarbone before he kissed the space over my heart. Almost as if he could feel that thrum. As if he could chase it away. "My Caspia."

"Forever." Even after the Divine welcomed me to Gloree, I would belong to Andreas forever.

We tore at each other's clothes, tossing them on the floor. He lay down, positioning me on top of his naked body. His muscles bunched and flexed as I straddled his bulky thighs, his hands holding tight to my hips.

He kept his eyes locked on mine as I sank down on his length, slowly rocking us together until he was fully rooted.

"Fuck." My breath hitched as my body stretched around him, the wave of pleasure so fierce I nearly came apart.

The cords of Andreas's neck tightened as he closed his eyes, his head thrown back in ecstasy. He thrust up his hips, sending his cock deeper. "Ride me. Hard."

I moaned, cupping my hands over my breasts to toy with my nipples. Then I did exactly as he commanded. I lifted off his hardness only to slam down on him, bringing us together with such force I cried out his name. "Andreas."

His hands came to my thighs, his arms helping as I brought us together over and over. The rippled muscles in his stomach clenched as he stared at our connection, watching as he disappeared into my body. "Fuck, you are incredible."

I bit my lip, my inner walls trembling as I moved faster. Harder. Heat swept through my body, stealing my breath. My heart felt like it was going to beat out of my chest.

I forced my eyes open to memorize his face. I let myself drown in his tawny gaze. If only we had a lifetime of moments like this.

He reached for me, threading his hands into my hair as he took me by the back of the neck, dragging me down for a kiss.

His tongue fluttered against mine as he flipped me on my back and fucked me with long, pounding strokes. "Let go."

"Andreas." I clung to his shoulders as he took me higher and higher. And then I was weightless, soaring to the stars.

Tears pricked the corners of my eyes as the release shattered through my bones and ripped through my muscles. I came apart, head to toe, riding every pulse as Andreas thrust one last time and joined me in oblivion.

We collapsed in a tangle of limbs and thundering hearts.

Andreas wrapped me in his arms, dropping to his side to keep from crushing me with his weight. He buried his nose in my hair and wrapped his large body around mine.

I couldn't seem to catch my breath, the pressure in my chest unbearable. The feeble remains of my strength fragmented, and the numbness I'd found earlier vanished. Pain rushed in like the tide.

A sob escaped before I could stop it, and I slapped a hand over my mouth. But it was too late.

Andreas lifted onto an elbow, staring down at me as I broke. As I cried for the life I'd thought we would have together.

"I'm sorry." Andreas held me closer. "I'm sorry, Caspia. I'm so fucking sorry."

He whispered his apologies in my ear as I cried myself to sleep.

And when I woke to a dark room, to his body still curled around mine, I left him to sleep while I silently moved to the balcony.

I spent the moon staring across Roslo toward a ship with white sails.

I spent the moon listening to the thrum in my chest.

I spent the moon fighting it with every beat.

Not yet.

34

ODESSA

"Odessa," Ransom murmured as we walked down a long hallway in the castle's west wing. "Say something."

I shook my head, clamping my teeth and lips shut tight.

If I opened my mouth, a string of expletives would come out. And at the moment, I was working very hard to keep my composure so that the stewards leading us to a suite wouldn't leave us to tell the rest of the castle that Princess Odessa had returned and lost her mind.

The plush carpets muffled our footsteps. The hall smelled like jasmine and white tea.

The Mavins walked beside us. Jodhi took in the portraits displayed on the walls and statues featured in various alcoves, but Thora looked ahead and only ahead as we passed door after door.

The three stewards leading us down the corridor parted, one moving to a room on the left, another to the right, and the third at the end of the hall.

"Madam." The steward on the left waved Thora inside her room.

She walked through the door, and when he stepped to follow her inside, she slammed it in his face.

Jodhi chuckled. "Goodbyes aren't really Thora's style."

He went with the second steward to his own suite, pausing outside the door. He winked at Evie, then lifted his gaze, holding mine long enough that Ransom inched closer. "It's been an adventure. Good hunting, doll."

"To bloody blades," I murmured.

"Thank you," Ransom said. "For keeping them alive."

"No thanks needed. Just a thousand zillahs." He smirked, then walked into his room and, like Thora, closed it before the steward could finish his job as escort.

We hadn't been with them for long, but I'd miss the company of the Mavins. Hard and cold as they were, they had kept us safe. Now our agreement was done.

Father would pay them, and by dawn, I suspected they'd be riding away from Roslo.

I hoped that someday, the journal entry about Thora would come true. That she'd find her freedom. And maybe someday, she'd meet her aunt Cathlin.

"This way, Highness." All three stewards escorted us to the suite at the end of the hall and waved us inside. The lanterns in the receiving room were lit. They'd brought in a vase of fresh flowers for the round table in the center of the space.

We trailed behind the stewards as they led us through the short entryway and into a large parlor filled with cozy chairs, sofas, and chaise longues. The space was lit by candelabras, and the sheer white curtains over the floor-to-ceiling windows were drawn. A spread of cured meats, hard cheeses, and dried fruits was laid out on the rectangular dining table.

There was a mirror of this suite in the east wing of the castle on the fourth floor. My sister Mae's suite. It was the suite beside mine.

But Father hadn't sent us to my former suite in the east wing. He hadn't put us in the wing of the castle where his family lived. He hadn't even sent us to the southeast wing, where visiting royalty stayed.

No, he'd sent us to the west end of the castle, where he typically tucked away guests he wanted to avoid.

Two lady's maids, both dressed in plain tan dresses with white aprons, emerged from one of the rooms off the parlor.

One was a blonde. The other a brunette. It was so eerily similar to my former maids, Brielle and Jocelyn, that my chest pinched.

But I didn't recognize either of these women. Maybe they'd been hired after Brielle and Jocelyn left with me for Turah.

"My saddlebags?" Ransom asked a steward.

"We've stowed them in the closet along with fresh clothes, sir."

"Highness," I corrected through gritted teeth. A title my father should have acknowledged. "You will address him as Highness. He is the crown prince of Turah."

"Of course." All three stewards spoke in unison as they offered apologetic bows.

"You may go," I said.

"We've drawn you a bath, Highness, and laid out night-clothes," a lady's maid said, her voice timid and soft.

"Thank you." Hopefully the water was lukewarm, because I was raging hot after that reunion with Father. Maybe tepid water would cool my temper.

"Go." Ransom urged me forward. "I've got Evie."

I lifted Faze's carrier off my shoulder and set him on the floor to squirm free.

Faze, still miffed about the crate and leash, let out a *rawr*.

A collective gasp rang out as the stewards shied away. The blond maid gave a tiny scream before she pushed the brunette in front of her, using her body as a human shield.

I'd wager we'd have at least one new maid by morning.

"Everyone, meet Faze."

I emerged from the bathing chamber clean and slightly less angry.

Evie and Ransom had sampled the snacks, and the splash of water drew me to the other bedroom's bathing chamber, where Evie was in the tub and Ransom was toweling off an angry wet tarkin.

There was a fresh scratch on Ranse's hand that was already knitting itself closed.

"Dess, watch me." Evie went to one side of the copper tub and launched herself to the other, the distance three times the length of her body.

"Nice. Did you wash your hair?"

She nodded, plugged her nose, bulged out her cheeks, and plunged under the water.

Ransom finished toweling off Faze and let him go. "There, little monster. You're free."

Faze shook out the water, then bounded straight to my legs, rubbing against my bare ankles, making sure he had my attention and that I knew he'd been forced into the bath against his will.

Ransom crossed the room and stopped in front of me, twirling a wet curl around his finger as he took in my teal satin nightgown. He looked relaxed, but his eyes were still silver.

It was the longest I'd ever seen them that color.

"Better?" he asked.

"Yes." I nodded to the door. "Your turn. I'll finish up with her."

He dropped a kiss to my forehead, then slipped out of the room. Maybe after his own bath his irises would shift back to green.

It didn't take long to finish Evie's bath and tuck her into bed. When she was snuggled under a pile of blankets with her stuffed rabbit, Merry, on one side and Faze on the other, I turned off the lamps and slipped from the room, ignoring the food as I put out the lanterns in the parlor, bathing the suite in darkness.

I found Ransom in our bedroom, standing at the windows. His hair was wet and combed. A white towel was wrapped around his waist. He'd peeled away the curtains to stare out over Roslo, the city's lights dwindling as the moons rose higher toward the stars and shades.

And in his hands was his circlet.

He didn't turn away from the glass as I approached but stretched out an arm to tuck me against his side.

I sagged against him, and as the last remains of my frustration vanished, I kind of wanted to cry.

Tonight wasn't the first time Father had ignored me. But tonight was different. Tonight, it felt intentional, like he'd wanted to hurt me. I'd traveled so far, I'd changed so much, and he'd barely been able to look at me.

Was this my punishment for failing as his spy and assassin?

He'd asked me to kill the Guardian. An impossible task, considering Ransom and I were bound by a blood oath and forbidden to cause the other harm. Not that I'd ever hurt him, blood oath or not.

I'd explained the ruse to Father, informing him that Ransom was not only the Guardian but also my husband and the crown prince. I'd hoped for a sliver of understanding, maybe a question or two in return.

Instead, he'd dismissed us moments later, not giving us a chance to talk about the crux scout or ask if there'd been any message from Cathlin.

"He didn't seem shocked," I said. "When I told him who you are."

"No."

"Do you think he already knew?"

Ransom sighed. "I doubt it. I think your father has spent a lifetime masking any emotion."

Or maybe there was simply no emotion to show. I was beginning to think I'd imagined his initial reaction. The joy that had lit up his face. Maybe he'd been drunk, too.

"Who's worse? Your father? Or mine?" I teased.

"Mine," he muttered. "No question."

Ramsey was infecting men recruited to his militia with Lyssa. Or a version of Lyssa. He was trying, and failing, to recreate the Guardian in the hopes the Turans would have a fighting chance during the migration.

Instead, the infection was killing his men, burning them from the inside out.

Maybe now he'd stop, since it was too late.

"The nobility should be preparing for the migration, bringing people in from the countryside, not enjoying parties. My father must not know about the scout."

Fucking Turans and their fucking secrets. Jodhi's voice echoed in my mind.

"Ramsey hasn't told anyone."

"No." Ransom's jaw clenched. "He must not have sent the pony riders beyond Turah."

Those riders who normally took letters and missives would tell the Turan people. But if they'd been commanded to stay within Ramsey's kingdom, then there were so many innocent people who'd be left to suffer.

Word would spread eventually. Any traveler visiting Westor or Perris would notice that the Turans were taking shelter. But that would require time. Time the kingdoms didn't have.

Too many would be taken by surprise and slaughtered.

All while Ramsey was hiding in Allesaria. He'd be safe in his secret capital, and when the migration was over, the amount of damage done would be anyone's guess.

The migration normally came in the spring. Were the fall harvests completed? Had people stockpiled their food? They'd need it for both the migration and the coming winter.

"I thought coming here would be safe, but…" After my father's chilly welcome, I was questioning that choice.

"There's nothing that can be done tonight. In the morning, I'll meet with your father. And if we must, we'll go back."

My jaw dropped. "Before the migration? There's no time."

"There might be." He stared down at the circlet, his

eyebrows furrowed. "We might have more time. The scout was…"

I waited for him to finish. "What?"

He shook his head. "Nothing."

"Liar." I knew that nothing. "What aren't you telling me?"

"The scout is dead, and I've heard nothing of others. There should have been others. There's a chance it wasn't a scout at all."

Now he sounded like the Mavins. "What does that mean?"

"I don't know." Ransom exhaled. "But we might have time to return to Turah. Though if we go back, I won't take you or Evie to Allesaria. It's too dangerous, and I don't trust my father. But…"

"You're going to Allesaria."

"Yes. To stop my father."

"And what?" I scoffed. "You'll just drop us off somewhere?"

"You can stay in Perris."

The city on the Turan coast was a mirror to Roslo across the Krisenth. If we sailed the crossing, we could be there in ten days or less.

"And Zavier? If he's alive?"

"Then he'll stay with you, too. I won't let him go to Allesaria, either."

"No." I shook my head, stepping out of his hold. "If you go to Allesaria, then I'm coming, too."

"You're not."

I tossed up a hand. "We came all the way to Quentis to have this argument again."

"Odessa—"

"You can't even act against your father because of all your ridiculous blood oaths." I paced the length of the bedroom and, for the second time tonight, felt the urge to strangle a stubborn, infuriating man. "What happened to us staying together?"

"If something happened to you, I'd never survive."

"That goes both ways." I crossed the room again, putting my hands on his bare torso. "We're stronger together, Ranse."

He tossed the circlet aside. His hands dove into my hair, pushing the curls away from my face.

My gaze dropped to the dark veins that spread out from his sternum, snaking beneath his taut skin. There were more than there'd been in Ellder. The infection was spreading, across Calandra and through his body.

Where there is poison, there is a cure.

What if I didn't find a cure in time? The High Priest had been siphoning the Lyssa from Ransom's blood, but if he'd spent a month searching for me, then he'd gone too long.

My best chance at a cure was using Father's healers in Quentis.

We needed to stop Ramsey from infecting his militia in Turah.

How could we be in two places at once?

"What do we do?" I whispered.

"We worry about it in the morning." Ransom hooked his finger under my chin. Then he bent and sealed his mouth over mine.

One sweep of his tongue, and the chaos in my mind vanished. The noise quieted until all I could hear was the soft hum from his throat.

I wound my arms around his waist, splaying my hands over the hard muscles of his back.

He kept my head in his hands, slanting his mouth over mine to deepen the kiss.

Gods, he tasted good. I could spend my lifetime kissing this man and it wouldn't be enough.

He licked every corner of my mouth with long, languid strokes of his tongue that made my knees go weak. He sucked on my bottom lip until my nipples pebbled beneath the satin of my nightgown, pressing against his hard chest.

A throb settled in my core as I let my hands roam over his skin, feeling that incredible strength beneath my fingertips.

There were still moments when it didn't feel real. When I was afraid I'd open my eyes and he'd be gone.

He trailed his mouth along my jaw and cheeks and temples and forehead, like he was trying to convince himself this was real, too. The light scrape of beard on skin made me shiver.

Ransom's fingers came to the thin straps of my nightgown, peeling them over my shoulders until the fabric slid down my body, pooling at my feet.

I untucked the fold in his towel, letting it drop.

His tongue darted out and licked his bottom lip as his gaze raked over my naked body, head to toe. His throat bobbed as he swallowed hard, and then his mouth stretched in a slow smirk. "The things I want to do to you."

A flush warmed my cheeks. "Tell me."

"I want to lick every inch of your skin. I want to come on those pretty nipples. I want to fuck you all night. I want to make you see stars and forget everything except the fact that you're my wife."

Those promises, that final word, made my sex clench.

His hand snaked up my bare hip, his fingertips leaving a trail of tingles along my ribs as he dragged them higher and higher until he traced the swell of my breast. He tormented me for another moment, his cock thick and hard between us.

My core throbbed, and my breath hitched.

"I love you." I waited, breath held, for him to say it back.

Ransom's eyes were darkened with lust, but they were green. A rich, mossy green that reminded me of the Turan forests. "Don't forget."

He crushed his mouth to mine, the tenderness and teasing from a heartbeat ago gone as he swept me into his arms and crossed the room with a few long strides, laying me on the bed. There was an urgency to his kiss as he came down on top of me, a hunger for more.

His teeth scraped my lips. His hands dug into the soft flesh of my hips as his weight pinned me to the bed.

Ransom was everywhere at once, and if there was even a small thread of my consciousness tied to reality, he severed it the moment he slid inside my body, filling me so completely I cried out his name.

A string of incoherent sounds escaped my mouth as he made good on his promises, tasting my skin and fucking me into oblivion.

Stroke after stroke, thrust after thrust, he brought us together in a frenzy until I was a writhing, trembling mess beneath him.

My fingernails dug into his shoulders, hard enough to leave marks, and then I shattered, coming apart so entirely my vision was nothing but white as tears leaked from the corners of my eyes.

"Odessa." Ransom spoke with his lips against my throat, my name murmured in a voice that was mine and mine alone. His body quaked as I clenched and pulsed around him, the piston of his hips never pausing until I was entirely wrung out.

I was still reeling with the aftershocks of my orgasm as he pulled away and came all over my nipples, his release hot and sticky and so erotic I liquefied.

Once he was spent, he sank back on his knees, his face tipped to the ceiling as he closed his eyes to regain his breath.

Never in his life had he looked so at peace. Even with those dark veins spreading from his heart, he was perfect. Mine.

Ransom cracked his eyes open and stared down at me and the mess he'd made. The cocky grin that stretched across his lips was breathtaking as he rubbed a hand over his beard, covering his mouth as he gave a soft laugh. Then he hoisted me up, pulling me against his chest as he tugged me off the bed.

We barely made it to the bath before he was inside me again. He made good on every promise, fucking me all night long.

And by the time dawn kissed the horizon, I was fast asleep in his arms.

35

CASPIA

A baby boy with rosy cheeks and flaxen hair. A giggle of pure joy. Andreas lifts him toward the sky, eyes crinkling as he smiles up at his son.

...

The *Malynn* was still docked in the harbor.

For eleven suns, I'd awoken at dawn, hoping that when I stepped onto the balcony, it would be gone. And for eleven suns, its bright white sails had cast a gloom over my mood.

Roslo was beautiful this morning, the air crisp and cool. The clouds had parted enough to let in the sun, and Andreas's city sparkled like a jewel. I might have actually enjoyed the view if not for that fucking ship.

If I waited long enough, would it float away? Except it couldn't leave, could it?

Not without me.

The thrum was relentless. As unwelcome as those white sails.

"Fuck." I pounded a fist on the balcony's metal railing and spun around, about to storm inside, but instead, I collided with a broad, strong chest.

"Whoa." Andreas steadied me with an arm around my waist. "Sorry. I thought you heard me."

"No." I righted my feet and shifted out of his hold. Then I put an arm's length between us.

He dropped his chin but not before I saw the flash of regret cross his expression. Andreas had apologized more times than I could count, but this distance between us only seemed to grow.

My doing.

I'd spent eleven suns nursing a wounded heart, mostly alone. I left in the mornings for the castle's library, where I'd sit at a table in a secluded corner and pore over the books Faxon brought me.

By the time I returned to the house each evening, I was so mentally drained I barely had the energy to ask Kos about his lessons. The moment dinner was finished, I'd come upstairs and collapse in bed.

The only good thing that came from being so exhausted was that my visions had stopped.

For now.

Nothing in the library had proved helpful, and there were just so many books. Maybe if they'd been in my language I could have made faster progress, but as it was, it took time for me to translate and read.

My head ached constantly. My heart was heavier than it had ever been. And beyond the first conversation about his betrothal, Andreas and I hadn't talked about the paper.

We hadn't really talked about anything.

Instead, I was avoiding him. Hurting him.

It wasn't so much the betrothal his mother had arranged. It was the secrets. I'd shared so much with him. The cuts from his silence were still bleeding.

I sighed. "I'm sorry. I'm…upset."

Last moon's vision of Andreas with his child, a baby that I knew with every fiber of my being was not mine, was salt on a gushing wound.

The Starling only had daughters.

"Don't apologize. This is my fault." He reached for me, his hand cupping my face as his thumb traced my cheek.

I lost his touch too soon as he handed me a folded slip of paper.

"Faxon sent that message this morning. There is someone in the city he believes might be able to help. He's invited him to the library. When you're ready, we'll go together."

"All right. I'll get dressed."

With a nod, he turned on a heel and crossed the bedroom.

I waited until the sound of his footsteps on the stairs faded before I breathed. "Damn."

Another Calandran expletive I found myself using more often. Except no amount of cursing seemed to accurately convey my mounting frustration.

I'd never felt this angry before. I was mad at Andreas. I was mad at this continent. I was mad at Xandra for leaving me alone. I was mad that I couldn't read faster. I was mad that it rained so often.

I was mad.

Mostly, I was mad at myself.

These visions had me in a stranglehold. They were a plague, and I was their victim. Ever since I'd started seeing the future, nothing had been the same. My life was forfeit to the images in my head. They'd twisted me into a knot and stolen my free will.

This had to stop.

Before they cost me everything.

Rushing into the dressing room, I traded Andreas's shirt, the one I slept in each moon, for a navy gown. Then I went downstairs, where Andreas was waiting with an apple—my breakfast. The house was quiet, Kos having already left with his nanny.

"Do you know who we're meeting?" I asked as I pulled on my boots.

He'd bought me other shoes, five pairs, each sturdier than the slippers I'd ruined. But I'd gone back to wearing my boots, not caring if they were in style with Calandran fashion. They were pieces from home, like my elfalter necklace and Emery's rings.

"He is a priest and an emissary to the king." Andreas's forehead furrowed. "When you see him, do not be frightened of him. The priests are…intimidating. But he will help us if he can."

Priests. I didn't know that word. But rather than have him explain, I simply nodded. I'd learn soon enough.

Andreas took my hand, bringing it to his lips to kiss my knuckles. Then he placed the apple in my palm. "Eat. Please. You haven't been eating enough."

I was too angry to eat. There was too much on my mind. "I'll try."

He moved in close, his hands framing my face as his eyes searched mine. "I don't know what brought you to me, but I thank the gods for every moment we have together."

Spoken like a man who knew the end was near.

Spoken like a man who would let me get on that ship.

I bit the inside of my cheek to keep from crying. "We should go."

He nodded, then squared his shoulders and straightened his coat. He might not be in a soldier's uniform, but he looked like he was preparing for battle.

Who was this emissary? Or was Andreas's tension simply from yet another visit to the castle?

We set out on the road, walking briskly through his neighborhood. For every person we passed, Andreas dipped his chin.

I nibbled on my apple, taking small bites even though my stomach protested, until it was gone. Then I tossed the core in a bin when we reached the castle's open gates.

The grounds were busier than normal, with visitors milling around manicured lawns, courtyards, and fountains. People who were normally clustered inside must have come outdoors to enjoy the sunshine.

Every head turned our way as we marched for the entrance. Gilded pillars, colorful stained glass windows, and the ever-present Quentin flag greeted us at the top of the sweeping staircase.

The moment we passed the threshold, Andreas's hand clasped mine. His grip only loosened once we stepped into the library.

The scents of parchment, lilies, and wood filled my nose as we weaved through the atrium. The light streaming through the windows caught the crystals in the chandeliers, scattering rainbows through the room.

Even though it was overwhelming, the sight of all the books still made my breath catch no matter how many times I visited.

Andreas might hate this castle for what had happened with Arick, but even he had to be awed by this beautiful library.

Kos's familiar giggle echoed from past Faxon's desk.

And a strange, crawling sensation prickled on my forearms.

I let go of Andreas's hand, wiping at my wrist.

"What?" he asked.

I lifted a shoulder. "A bug must have crawled up my sleeve."

Andreas stopped, pushing up my sleeve to inspect my skin, turning my wrist over as he searched for a bite.

"It's fine." I waved him off, righting the fabric even though the prickling was still there. I wouldn't wear this dress again.

The giggle sounded again.

Kos loved his lessons with Faxon, and Faxon adored his new pupil. In the few interactions I'd witnessed, Faxon beamed with pride over the speed with which Kos was learning to read and write.

The bibliosoph's desk was empty, but we followed the sound of Kos's laughter around a lofty bookshelf.

Faxon stood on the highest rung of a ladder, shelving books as they floated up to him.

Kos sat on the floor, surrounded by a pile of books. His legs were crossed and his smile wide as he picked up a book and tossed it in the air, only for it to float on an invisible wind to the librarian's waiting hands.

"Floating books," I whispered, coming to a stop.

My skin prickled, not only on my arms but over my entire body. The sensation was so sudden and overpowering I grimaced, slowing as Andreas continued forward.

I shook the skirt of my gown as the sensation worsened, like invisible needles and pins were stuck in the fabric. I rubbed at my arms and neck, fighting the imaginary spiders crawling beneath my dress.

Andreas stood behind Kos, smiling as he watched the books float to Faxon. He didn't seem at all surprised or shocked. When he realized I wasn't at his side, he came over and held out his hand.

"What is this?" I asked, still scratching at my arms. "Is that Faxon's doing? Or Kos's?"

"Neither. Come. Meet the priest I told you about. You'll understand."

Except I couldn't move. Every step was agony, the sharp stinging spreading from my scalp to my toes.

A figure emerged from behind the stacks, passing by Faxon's ladder. His burgundy robes swished at his bare feet and the grooved nails that covered his toes.

My gasp drew his attention.

Impossible.

Magic.

He set down his hands, and with them, the books floated to the floor.

Faxon climbed down his ladder as Kos hopped to his feet.

I stared, unable to breathe, as the priest walked with an unnatural grace to stand by Andreas. The pain in my body radiated into my bones, and my frame began to tremble. A pounding rhythm beat behind my eyes, like a blacksmith striking his hammer to my skull over and over and over again.

"Brother Nold. This is Caspia." Andreas swept a hand my way with the introduction.

The priest bowed. He stood taller than Andreas, and even though his robe was loose, it couldn't hide his bony shoulders or lanky frame. His skin was a pale white, his lips thin and ashen. Without hair or eyebrows, his solid greenish-black eyes seemed to bulge from his skeletal face as he stared down the line of his pointed nose. His fingers were tipped in the same clawlike nails as his feet.

The energy around him crackled against my skin. My sight blurred at the edges, the world spinning too fast. My legs wobbled, and the apple I'd eaten threatened to come up.

"Velvi'os-telfer," I whispered.

I'd heard rumors of their unique appearance, but few people in Nelfinex ever encountered their race. They'd become all but a myth in Kenn.

And their history a warning for other countries.

Ages ago, they'd lived in a country that bordered Beesa. The fifth country in Kenn. A country that no longer existed. The Beesans had invaded and waged a war against the Velvi'os-telfer, persecuting them for their religion.

After a hundred summers of fighting, the Beesans were victorious. The Velvi'os-telfer had been slaughtered, their homeland stolen. Those who'd survived had fled into hiding. Most lived deep in the wilderness, though the Beesans still hunted their people.

But they must have fled to Calandra, too. When? How many had come here? How had he made those books float?

My head was throbbing so fiercely I couldn't think. I couldn't breathe.

"Caspia." Andreas's voice sounded muted, like he was at the other end of the library, not at my side.

The stinging on my skin, the agony tearing through my veins, was too much to withstand.

By the grace of the Divine, make it stop.

I toppled forward, the strength in my legs giving out.
Andreas reached to catch me.
So did Brother Nold.
The priest touched me first.
A scream tore from my throat.
And the world went black.

36

ODESSA

Evie's scream woke me from a dreamless sleep. I kicked off the sheet tangled around my legs and jumped out of bed.

Ransom was already running into the dressing room.

I snagged my teal nightgown from the floor and dragged it over my head. The satin was cold as it skimmed over my body and I ran for the door, yanking it open.

Evie stood in the middle of the parlor, still dressed in her nightshirt. Her teeth were bared, her hands balled in small fists. Faze stood between her legs, wearing a similar expression.

Her gray eyes and his violet blazed as they glared at the intruder on the opposite side of the room.

"Mae?" I rubbed the sleep from my eyes.

My half sister was dressed in an embroidered teal gown. A sparkling tiara was woven into her golden hair. If not for the daggers in each of her hands, I might have mistaken her for Margot, she looked so much like my stepmother.

"What is going on?" I skirted around a couch to stand behind Evie.

"That little monster bit me." Mae accentuated the last two words with a stab of a knife in the air.

Oh, gods. *No.*

Faze had been more aggressive lately, mostly with Ransom. But he'd never tried to bite anyone before. A swat of his paw was as violent as he'd get.

Regardless, if he'd attacked Mae, then it was over. We'd

have to set him free. Maybe if we were careful and kept him locked in this suite, we could keep him a while longer. The idea of setting him loose in Quentis made my stomach churn, especially if we were on the brink of a migration.

"Are you all right?" I didn't see any blood. Maybe he hadn't broken skin. I bent and scooped Faze from the floor. "I'm so sorry. He's never bitten anyone before."

"Not him." Mae flicked her knife's tip toward Evie. "Her."

"Back up. *Evie* tried to bite you?" I blinked, and as Faze wiggled free, I let him fall back to the floor.

He immediately returned to Evie's side, standing guard, snarling at Mae.

"Yes," my sister seethed.

I looked down at Evie, eyebrows raised. "You bit her?"

Evie crossed her arms over her chest, and in that moment, she'd never looked more like Ransom.

"Why would you— Mae, would you please put the knives away so we can discuss this without weapons?"

My sister's lip curled as she kept her glare locked on Evie.

"Mae," I snapped. "Knives. Down. Now."

"Fine." She huffed but lowered the blades, tucking them back into the jeweled sheaths on her belt.

"Thank you." I pushed my curls away from my face and took a deep breath. "Okay. Let's start at the beginning. What happened?"

"She was gonna take Faze," Evie said. "And when she wouldn't give him back, I bit her on the leg."

"Demon." Mae planted her fists on her hips.

Evie stuck out her tongue just as Ransom walked into the parlor, still fastening his leather pants.

His tunic molded to the honed muscles of his arms and chest. His hair was a mess, thanks to my fingers last night, and the ends brushed his shoulders. His feet were bare, and the morning light caught the sharp angles of his face. Beneath his beard, his jaw was locked. His circlet kissed his brow. Even scowling and irritated, he was gorgeous. He radiated power and authority.

Mae's gaze raked over his body, and she smoothed a lock of sleek blond hair away from her face as she offered him a demure smile. "You're more handsome than I remembered, Guardian. Or should I call you Prince Wolfe?"

Well, it hadn't taken her long to learn of Ransom's true identity, had it? Did she have spies hidden in the walls of the throne room? It wouldn't surprise me.

"Ransom, you remember my sister, Mae."

He stopped in the center of the room, hazel eyes hard as he glared at her. "Is there a reason you're in our suite this early in the morning?"

"She was trying to take Faze." Evie picked up Faze and carried him to Ransom.

Mae's sickly sweet smile only widened. "I was simply curious about your cat."

"Please. I don't believe that for a second." I knew that malicious gleam in her blue eyes. "What are you scheming, Mae?"

"Nothing." She feigned innocence.

Liar. "Touch him again, and I'll tell every paperman in Roslo that you have a fungus growing on your toes."

"Odessa." She scoffed, her facade disappearing. "That's very...*me* of you."

"You will not touch him again." I raised my chin, pinning her with a glare. "Have I made myself clear?"

She flicked her wrist. "He's not even cute."

"He's adorable, and you know it." I crossed the room, and even though she hated hugs, I gave her one anyway. "Hi."

She squirmed, and when I only tightened my hold, she relaxed, finally hugging me back until I let her go. Then she gave me a sideways glance. "What happened to you? You seem different."

"Well, I married the Guardian, set sail for Turah, was

almost eaten by a marroweel, lived in a treehouse, was almost killed by a pack of bariwolves—a few times—adopted a tarkin, moved to a fortress, killed a man who was trying to kill me, and that's only the beginning. It's barely dawn. I'm tired. And you should have knocked. Don't sneak into this suite again."

Mae looked at me like I'd sprouted wings.

"You're right. I'm different." And she'd realize soon enough that the dynamic in our relationship had changed.

A knock came at the door.

"Come in," Ransom called.

A steward cleared his throat as he stood at the mouth of the entryway. He offered a deep bow before speaking. "The queen requests that you join her at breakfast. Presently."

Presently, as in right now.

I guess we'd get all of the reintroductions done this morning.

"Thank you," I said, dismissing the steward.

As much as I wanted to crawl back into bed, the sooner we told my father about the crux scout, the better.

"Let's get dressed." Ransom steered Evie toward her bedroom as my sister turned to leave.

"Mae?" I said, waiting for her to pause and look back. "I missed you."

Not terribly. But I'd missed her.

She didn't say it back before she swept out of the room.

I sighed, my shoulders slumping. Well, that reunion had gone better than mine with Father, but not by much. Someday, I needed to stop wishing my sister were a different person.

That I had a sister who liked my hugs. A sister who'd break into my suite because she wanted to see that I was alive and well. A sister who was like me.

But Mae was Mae. And wishing for her to change was as pointless as wishing to touch the stars in the shades.

I trudged to the bedroom to get ready for the day. My brother was somewhere in this castle, and if he wasn't at breakfast, then I wanted to see him soon.

The maids had only brought me gray gowns and slippers from my former wardrobe, and the idea of wearing them again felt too much like stepping into the past, so I pulled on yesterday's clothes, wishing I had something clean. My shirt still had the faint aroma of fish from the ship.

But I wasn't facing my father in gray.

After quickly plaiting my hair and donning Ransom's cuff under my sleeve, I returned to the parlor, where Evie and my husband were waiting.

Evie was dressed in yesterday's clothes, too.

"She didn't want to wear a dress," Ransom said.

"Neither did I."

As I pulled on my boots, Ransom donned his vest and weapons. Then the three of us set out for the first floor of the east wing.

The doors to Thora's and Jodhi's rooms were both open, the servants already cleaning them for future guests.

The Mavins had probably left before dawn.

The castle staff we passed on the way gave us a wide berth. Ransom drew most of the attention, followed by Faze, then Evie, and, finally, me. Word must have traveled through the palace that I'd returned, because a few of the servants bowed and addressed me as Highness.

Margot's preferred dining room was in a corner of the east wing. Buttery sunlight streamed through the windows that bordered the space on two sides. A servant stood next to a table laden with food. The smells of pastries, fruit, spiced meats, and poached eggs made my stomach growl.

My stepmother, looking as regal as ever, sat at the foot of the table, sipping tea from a hand-painted cup as she read a paper. Her ocean-blue eyes, bright with the amber Quentin starburst, lifted as we walked into the room. One look at my clothes, and her face soured. "Pants?"

"Pants." I stopped at the nearest chair, staring down the length of the table at my stepmother.

Ransom pulled out a seat for Evie, helping her sit. Then he dropped Faze on her lap and took the chair beside hers.

The servant immediately began bringing them food while I stared at the only mother I'd ever known.

If Margot had missed me, it didn't show.

"Your hair." She set down her cup and the paper.

"What about my hair?"

"It's lovely." Her indifferent demeanor cracked. Slightly.

My shoulders dropped from my ears. "Evie, this is Margot. She's my stepmother and the queen of Quentis."

"Hello, Evie." It was the most genuine, kind hello I'd ever heard from Margot's lips.

Evie gave her a shy wave, then hugged Faze closer.

Margot looked to Ransom and dipped her chin. "Your Highness."

"Majesty. Thank you for your hospitality." He sounded more like a prince than ever.

Somewhere in the shades, Luella was smiling down at her son. At the loyal, polite, steady man she'd raised.

"Welcome back to Quentis," Margot said. "Please let me know if there's anything I can do to make your stay more comfortable."

"Clothes," I answered for him. "Specifically, pants."

Margot grimaced, but there was humor in her eyes. "We will find you pants. Now, eat. You're skin and bones."

I took the chair beside Ransom's and did as my stepmother ordered, eating until my belly was fuller than it had been in months.

"Ah, there he is." Margot sat taller, smiling at the windows as a streak of blond hair raced by the glass.

"Arthy?" I rose from my chair as my little brother ran through the grass in the garden outside the dining room.

He'd grown while I'd been gone. His hair was shorter. How could his face have changed in just months? The chubby cheeks he'd had since he was an infant had all but disappeared. Now he looked less like a toddler and more like a boy. Still, his smile made my heart swell.

"Dess." Evie tugged on my shirt, her eyes wide. "The bird."

I'd been so fixed on Arthy's face I hadn't noticed the kite tucked under his arm.

It was a bird with orange feathers and a long tail of blue, green, red, and yellow.

Exactly as the journal had described, and carried by a boy with light hair.

My stomach pitched, my breakfast roiling, as Brother Dime walked into the garden. His hands were clasped behind his back, his robes swishing with his strides.

Arthalayus lifted the kite in one hand as he held tight to its string in the other. Then he took off running, giving the kite a swift throw into the air, high enough that Brother Dime's magical wind lifted it into the sky.

The bird flew higher as Arthy laughed, letting out more string.

The trees in the garden didn't rustle or shake. The grass was still and straight. The wind only blew for my half brother's paper bird. And when he reached the end of the string, Arthy set the bird free.

He blew it a kiss and watched until it was out of sight.

"Titus," Evie whispered as a black puppy with floppy ears and curly hair came bounding through the garden, tail wagging.

I stood and walked away from the table, my heart racing as I approached the windows.

How was this possible? Every time a story from that

journal found me in real life, I felt like the realm was tilting sideways. Throwing me off-balance.

What was that godsforsaken book?

"Hey." Ransom came to my side, concern furrowing his brow. "Are you okay?"

"Fine," I lied. "Just Voster magic."

We needed to talk about that journal, especially since it had been his mother's. But now wasn't the time.

"Who is that?" Evie asked, joining us at the window.

"That's Arthalayus. My brother."

Margot came to stand beside us, a soft smile on her lips. She looked at Arthy with a devotion she saved just for him. Since the day he was born, that boy had owned her heart.

"He's been making kites," she said. "But the weather has been too rainy to fly them. Today is lovely but calm. When Brother Dime offered to help, you should have seen Arthy's face. It's always a fight to get him to eat breakfast, but today, he practically shoveled his food into his mouth. He left right before you arrived."

"When did he get the puppy?" I asked.

"Just two days ago. He's still deciding on a name."

Titus.

Arthy dropped to his knees, and the puppy licked his face. He spoke to the dog, and even though I couldn't hear him, I knew exactly what he was saying.

Elvi'i elvi'am gelvi'o-elfing telvi'u nelvi'aim yelvi'u Telvi'i-telfus.

I am going to name you Titus.

Evie looked up to me, her lower lip worried between her teeth.

I bent to whisper in her ear, "We'll talk about it later, okay?"

She nodded, taking my hand as the other kept a firm grip on Faze's leash.

Arthy ran off through the gardens with the puppy as a man dressed in a legionnaire uniform strode into the dining room.

His blond hair was trimmed short and speckled with strands of white at the temples. He was tall with a trim, fit physique and a slightly crooked nose. Behind his wire-framed glasses, his hazel eyes gave no hint of emotion. His teal coat was decorated with gold buttons and a row of medals above the breast pocket.

The man bowed to Margot. "Majesty."

"General Hawksley."

General? I glanced at Ransom.

This must be the man who'd taken Banner's place after the former general had failed to return from Turah.

"The king requires your presence," Hawksley said. "Immediately."

Margot nodded. "Of course. I'll be right there."

Hawksley held up a hand. There were rings on every finger. "Apologies, Queen Margot. The king's request is for Princess Odessa. She is to come alone."

Margot stiffened.

So did Ransom.

An older woman with short, gray hair and deep wrinkles set in her plump face walked into the room. She took one look at me and beamed. "Princess Odessa. So the rumors are true. You've come back to us."

"Hello, Nathalia." I crossed the room and let her pull me into a hug.

Nathalia was the reason I loved hugs. As a child, her hugs had chased away my nightmares and soothed my lonely heart. She'd been a constant at this castle for years, first as my nursemaid when I was young, then as Mae's. And now as Arthy's.

She knew Father and Margot rarely gave us affection, so she did everything possible to fill that void.

"Finally got rid of that horrible hair dye, I see," she murmured low enough that Margot wouldn't hear. "Good for you."

She pulled away from the hug but held on to my arms to take a long look at me. What she saw made her frown. "You're too thin."

"A few more breakfasts with Margot, and I'll be good as new."

"You see to that, my girl."

The pounding of footsteps came a moment before Arthy raced into the room with Titus giving chase. His giggle nearly brought me to tears. "Mother, did you see—" He gasped. "Dess?"

"Arthy." I rushed to him, dropping to a knee as he flew into my arms. "Oh, I missed you."

"I missed you, too." He squeezed me so tight it almost hurt. "Want to meet my puppy? I just named him Titus."

"Yes, I'd love to meet Titus." I laughed, brushing a tear from the corner of my eye. "Want to meet my tarkin?"

His jaw dropped. "You have a tarkin?"

Father's throne room was frigid, empty, and utterly silent. The heat and noise from last night's party had been sucked out of the room through the row of open windows.

Hawksley marched across the marble floor, leading me to Father.

He was outside on his sprawling balcony, overlooking his capital.

The general waved me through the balcony's doors, and after a succinct bow, he turned on a heel and left.

I waited for Father to turn and greet me. When he didn't, I squared my shoulders and took a place at his side. "Father."

My gaze drifted to the cliffside next to the city. My cliffside. My sanctuary. A place I'd visited countless times to escape the stifling expectations in this castle.

The grass was turning brown, the green fading as the season changed. Gray storm clouds gathered on the horizon, and though it was still sunny, I'd spent enough time staring out over the ocean to know those clouds would be coming our way.

"Report," Father ordered, like I was one of his legionnaires, not a daughter. "Did you find the road to Allesaria?"

"Maps are forbidden in Turah. And to enter the city requires a blood oath to keep its location a secret."

"That doesn't answer my question. Did you go to Allesaria?"

"No." It was the truth.

A muscle in his jaw twitched as he stared at a large ship with white sails tied to the docks. The boat we'd arrived on last night was nowhere to be seen.

"The Guardian is the prince. That was…unexpected."

It was oddly comforting that Ransom had managed to fool not just me but Father, too. At least I wasn't the only Cross who'd been deceived. "Ransom had his reasons for the deceit."

"And what else has *Ransom* told you?"

"Don't," I clipped. "You don't get to spit his name. Not when he's told me all of his secrets and you have yet to share yours."

Father tore his gaze from the harbor, looking down at me. Bewildered? Impressed?

I'd never seen this expression on him before. "There was a crux scout in Turah. It came a month ago. Ransom killed it, but I don't know if there have been others. You need to warn people to prepare for the migration. It's coming sooner than they think."

Father's face hardened, and he turned his gaze to the horizon, like he could see all the way to Turah.

"There's more." I took a deep breath. "I need access to your healers."

"Why?"

"There is an infection spreading through the monsters in Turah. It's called Lyssa. I want to find a cure."

"Yes, I know of this infection. It is not Quentis's problem."

"It's spreading, which makes it a problem for everyone in Calandra. I want access to your best healers."

He frowned. "You've done nothing but make demands since you arrived."

"And you've done nothing but make me want to leave again." My voice was too loud, the emotion and anger bleeding through. "The west wing? Really? That's where you sent me? Like I'm a bothersome guest, not your daughter? Did you send Mae to my suite this morning?"

"You brought a monster into my castle. I asked her to deal with it."

I hated that I was jealous of the faith he put in Mae. "I brought a pet who shows me more love than you ever have."

"Fine. You may use the healers." Maybe it was my hopeful ears, but I heard a hint of regret in his voice. "Now please ask Prince Zavier to join me. He and I have things to discuss."

"We're not done talking." I crossed my arms over my chest. "You don't get to dismiss me yet. Why did you want me to kill Ransom?"

Father stayed quiet.

"What is in Allesaria that can stop the migration?"

Silence.

"Will you ever trust me with the truth?"

He didn't hesitate to break my heart. "No."

37

CASPIA

The world returned with a fuzzy focus as I awoke to shouting. Rainbows from the crystal chandeliers sparkled on the ceiling. The light reflected off the swirls painted on the ceiling in gold. So much gold.

Andreas's angry voice carried across the library. "What the fuck did you do to her?"

"Andreas." Faxon was calm but firm. "Your anger is not helping the situation."

"Answer me, Brother Nold," Andreas barked.

"I did nothing." The priest's tone was soft and enthralling. As smooth as a silken sheet. It was like a lullaby threatening to lure me back to sleep.

Except with that voice came the prickle on my skin and a dull ache through my head. It wasn't as overpowering as it had been earlier, but it was strong enough to rouse me fully awake.

I pushed up off the stiff divan where I was lying, taking in the quiet alcove. It was a reading nook with shelves built into the walls. Across the space was a window overlooking a row of trimmed hedges in the castle's gardens. And in the center of the room was a small desk with a high-backed velvet chair in the same coral shade as the divan.

Kos sat on the opposite end of the sofa. At my movement, he straightened and cupped his hands over his mouth. "She's awake."

I winced as he yelled, the noise only making my headache worse.

"Are you okay?" he asked.

"Yes," I lied as Andreas rushed into the alcove, his expression panicked and worried.

He dropped to his knees beside the divan, taking my face in his hands. "You're all right?"

I nodded, gritting my teeth against the constant sting. I was too cold and too hot. Lightheaded and queasy. "The Velvi'os-telfer. Where is he?"

Andreas didn't need to answer. As the awful sensation spiked, I knew Brother Nold was coming this way.

"Stop." I squeezed my eyes closed. "Please. Don't let him come any closer."

"I will not let him hurt you," Andreas said. "You're safe."

I shook my head. "No, it's…"

The magic. It had to be the magic making me sick. It felt like poison sliding over my flesh, flowing through my veins.

I forced my eyes open, but the world was spinning too fast. Then I lowered my voice, not wanting Kos to overhear. "It hurts to be close to the priest."

Andreas's forehead furrowed, but he didn't argue. He twisted over his shoulder as Faxon approached with the priest not far behind. "Go back to the desk. Both of you."

Brother Nold backed away immediately.

Faxon hesitated, then nodded, motioning for Kos to follow him out of the nook.

I waited until we were alone, until Andreas shifted to sit on the divan at my side, then breathed. The pain was still there but bearable now that the priest was gone.

"All this time, I've wondered if anyone from Kenn has come to Calandra. I thought it would be a Starling or explorer. I didn't expect it to be the Velvi'os-telfer. Or I guess here you'd call them…"

"Voster," Andreas finished for me. "You know them?"

"I've never met one myself. They are nomads, and most live in hiding. They were driven from their homeland ages ago after they lost a war with the country Beesa."

Was that how the Beesan dialect, Andreas's old language, had come to Calandra? From the Voster?

"According to our history books, the war started because of their religion. Their beliefs did not align with that of the Beesan king, and for that, he decided they were an abomination. Mostly, I think he was a power-hungry tyrant who saw an opportunity to expand his country. His descendants are ruthless."

Religious persecution was simply the guise for slaughter and invasion. I didn't know much about the Voster faith and who they worshiped. As Nestlings, our focus in education was about our own traditions, our own beliefs, not forgotten cultures.

"Who do they worship in Calandra?" I asked Andreas, though I suspected the answer.

"Ama and Oda." He signed the Eight. "And the Six."

How long had the Voster been here? Had they adopted the Calandran religion or brought their own to this continent? How had they escaped Beesa?

How did they have magic?

"I must talk to Brother Nold." The notion of being in the same room as him made my insides twist, but there was no other way.

"No, not if it hurts you."

"It's better with some distance. I can't feel it now that he's gone."

"Feel what?"

"I don't know. In Kenn, the Voster don't have powers. At least, not that I know about." I couldn't imagine they would have lost the war otherwise. "I've never heard of any being that could make a book float in the air."

"The priests have fluid magic. They can manipulate water and wind and blood."

Magic. I was really starting to hate that word. "That must be what I can feel. It's like insects crawling on my skin. Like being poked by a thousand needles."

If I could feel it but the Calandrans couldn't, then it was either because I was a Starling or because I came from Nelfinex. Maybe what gave them their starbursts protected them from the Voster magic.

Andreas put his arm around my shoulders, hauling me into his side. He kissed my hair, then stood, helping me to my feet, steadying me as I swayed. "We're leaving. I don't want you around him."

"Not yet. I must speak with him."

"Caspia—"

"I have to understand." I clutched Andreas's arm. "I could spend my life in this library and never find answers. Brother Nold might be the only way."

Andreas dragged a hand over his face. "All right. Let me talk to Faxon."

I sank to the edge of the divan, hands clasped in my lap as he left the alcove.

Did the Voster in Calandra know their people across the Marixmore were all but extinct? Did my aunt know they lived here, too? That they had magic?

It didn't take long for Andreas to return. He walked to me, holding out a hand. "Faxon has an idea. Come on."

He led me through the library toward an iron spiral staircase in a dim corner. We climbed to the second-level mezzanine, passing column after column of bookshelves as we circled the atrium, only stopping once we hit a wall.

Below us were the gilded double doors, both closed. We stood at the railing, staring out over the library below, until Faxon emerged across the atrium with Brother Nold.

They took up a position mirroring ours. The prickling sensation returned, but with the open air between us, it was tolerable.

"The acoustics are strange in this part of the library," Faxon said. "It's nice that when I need a text from over there, I don't have to yell."

He was far enough away that he should have had to shout. But at his normal volume, I could hear him as if he were standing at my side.

"I'll leave you to talk." Faxon nodded to the priest, then disappeared into the stacks.

"I am sorry for any pain and discomfort I have caused." Brother Nold pressed his hands together as he bowed.

"Would you mind if I asked you some questions, Brother Nold?"

"Ask, child."

I took a deep breath and looked up at Andreas. "I need to speak to Brother Nold—"

"Alone." He finished my sentence and kissed my temple. "If you need me, I'll be downstairs."

My heart started to race as I stared at Brother Nold. "You know I am from the continent Kenn."

"Yes."

"How?"

"It has been a long, long time since I heard anyone call me Velvi'os-telfer."

"How long?"

"Since the war. So many summers I have lost count."

The wars had started over four hundred summers ago and had lasted generations. "How is that possible?"

Brother Nold looked to his side, to a table with two wooden chairs. He lifted his hand, and one of the chairs rose from the floor. He floated it close and set it down. Then he took a seat, his burgundy robes pooling to cover his feet. "How did you come to Calandra?"

"On a ship."

"You were called here, weren't you? The ritus. You are

Starling. It has been a long, long time since I've seen someone with a Starling's gold eyes."

"Yes." I nodded. "But my ritus failed. I didn't shift."

"You will." It sounded like an omen of death.

What I'd wanted for so long, to become Starling, now seemed like my doom.

"The journey from Kenn to Calandra is impossible for most. This land is small compared to Kenn. Any error in navigation means a sailor could pass by without even knowing it's here. Without your ritus call, I suspect you would not have found it, either."

"Is that how you came here?"

"I am Voster. We have no ritus. But we escaped the wars thanks to the help of three of your Starling ancestors."

"They came here. And left?"

"Only one. The other two… Their Starling lives were claimed by this land."

My mind raced at how they might have died. No, not died. *Their Starling lives were claimed.* "They shifted. And could not shift back."

Brother Nold cocked his head to the side. "You did not come here alone."

"No," I whispered. "My cousin, Xandra, came with me. She changed into a bariwolf. Then tried to kill me."

"Ah."

"What happened to them? The Starling who led you here?"

"There was no choice. It was our death or theirs."

I swallowed hard. "And the third?"

"She flew away and left us to our peace."

"As a swift?"

Brother Nold nodded.

"So there is hope." I pressed a hand to my heart as it swelled, the hope in my chest bringing me nearly to tears.

"Do not hope," he warned. "She was an old and powerful Starling, yet even she could not shift back to her human form. She killed for months. Every human she encountered was sent to the shades. We do not know that she returned to Nelfinex. We only gave thanks when she was gone."

She must have returned to Nelfinex. She must have found a way home.

And she was likely the reason it was forbidden for Starling to come to Calandra. Because hundreds of summers ago, a Starling came to this continent and became a monster. A crux.

She was the catalyst for our law.

What else had she started?

"Did the crux migrate to Calandra before you arrived?" I asked.

"No."

By the grace of the Divine.

The swift had a keen sense of smell. They were territorial birds with a deep connection to the Starling, more so than any other creature on Nelfinex.

Something about that journey to bring the Voster here must have changed their migration patterns. My ancestors had led them to a new breeding ground.

Here, the crux were terrors. Here, the Voster had powers. Here, the Starling were monsters.

Why? What was different about Calandra?

Magic.

"You made those books float," I said. "How?"

"How is it the Starling blood allows you to transform? I do not know why we were gifted this magic when we reached this land."

"Have you ever returned to Beesa?" I asked.

"No." He dropped his chin. "We cannot return. It is sworn."

"To who? The Calandrans?"

Brother Nold ran a finger the width of his pale lips and didn't answer.

"Andreas said that you are an emissary to the king."

"Yes, child. The brotherhood strives to ensure that what has happened in Kenn does not repeat itself in Calandra."

"You mean the war and the persecution of your people."

He nodded.

I wanted to ask more about his magic. About his role in Quentis and what exactly it meant to be a part of the brotherhood. But the sting of his magic was beginning to sink deeper beneath my skin. The ache in my head was returning with a vengeance. "Why does your magic hurt?"

"Because you are Starling. You are not meant to be here."

"But I'm not Starling. Not yet."

"Yet you feel it."

I nodded and pressed a hand over my heart and the thrum within.

"Go, child. Leave Calandra. Before it's too late." Brother Nold stood and bowed, then was gone. When the prickle of his magic faded and I could breathe fully, when my head stopped spinning, I knew he'd left the library.

And I knew, without question, I would not see him again.

38

CASPIA

Blood coats a marble floor. Burgundy swirls over glossy white. Swords and arrows lie scattered around lifeless bodies. Sunlight streams through windows tinted with blues and greens and yellows.

Through the wide balcony doors, a wind sweeps into the large, echoey room. It ruffles the feathers on my wings. It stirs the metallic tang of death. The tang I taste on my tongue.

A man stands before me, his sword dangling from a hand as the other clutches a gash in his side. Bloody tears drip down his face. "Please, Caspia."

Caspia.

Somewhere, deep inside, the woman named Caspia screams. She rages to be set free. To be unleashed from the torment and the fire burning through her veins. But her scream is nothing compared to the pain and madness and craving for more blood. More death.

There is no Caspia.

I release my own scream, the sound shaking the walls.

The man drops his sword and closes his eyes. "I love you."

Somewhere, deep inside, the woman named Caspia cries. Begs. Fights.

But the man becomes just another dead body on the cold marble floor.

...

The sky was on the razor's edge of dusk. My eyes were too full of tears to make out the stars from Andreas's balcony.

Was that how Xandra had felt after she became the bariwolf? Had she been trapped inside the beast, forced to watch every gruesome act?

We were not meant to be here.

I didn't want to heed Brother Nold's warning from the library and leave. But if that vision was the alternative, if I stayed and killed Andreas, I would never survive it.

Why had the Divine called us here to this cursed land?

There had to be some reason. I had to believe it wasn't simply to slaughter innocent people.

Maybe soon, I'd understand. But for that to happen, I knew in my heart it was time to leave.

Losing Andreas was inevitable. I realized that now. We were destined to end.

The thrum pulsed through my veins.

The light of the two moons seemed to shine particularly bright on the ship with white sails still docked in the bay, like a beacon calling me home.

I was not meant to be here.

It was time to say goodbye.

Wiping my cheeks dry with my palms, I filled my lungs and tipped my face to the sky.

By the grace of the Divine, take this pain.

Part of me wished that I hadn't been born to my family. I wished the gift had passed me over. I wished my blood was simply blood.

But the other part of me couldn't regret this journey. Not if it meant finding Andreas.

"Will I always find you out here in the middle of the night?" Strong arms wrapped around my shoulders. Andreas set his chin on my head, the heat from his bare chest warming my back.

I took hold of his forearms and closed my eyes. "Not always."

His body tensed.

I should have known he'd hear the truth behind two simple words. That they meant more than my inability to sleep through the moon.

"You're leaving."

Yes. I couldn't say it. My heart was in pieces, and admitting it would only make me cry.

He buried his nose in my hair, folding his body around mine. "We didn't have enough time."

A lifetime wouldn't have been enough. But Andreas wouldn't ask me to stay.

There was too much working against us. The realities we'd been ignoring, the differences in our lives, hung over our heads like a rain cloud. Whether we were ready or not, it was going to storm.

"There is a ship in the harbor." He pointed to the ship with white sails as if I hadn't been staring at it for suns. "It was named after my mother and belongs to my family. The captain is a good man. He's been working to help me restructure our fleet."

Now it made sense why the ship hadn't sailed away. When Andreas left the house for his business affairs, he was meeting with its captain. Of course his family owned the *Malynn*. Normally, the irony would at least earn a dry laugh, but I wasn't in the mood for a laugh.

"There's no one else I'd trust to take you home."

That ship would need to sail farther than it had ever gone before, but that was a detail I'd share with the captain. I'd let him decide if it was possible and make the necessary provisions.

"I can't go with you," Andreas murmured. "But gods, I wish I could."

I would take Andreas to Nelfinex. I would show him my city and castle. I would keep him there for the rest of my life. But if the Starling and Voster changed in Calandra, there was a chance it wouldn't be safe for Andreas in Kenn.

Besides, we both knew he wouldn't leave. He had too many obligations. Too many complications.

I tilted my face to the sky. "When I'm home, I'll look up at the two moons and know you can see them, too. And even though we are an ocean apart, you'll be with me."

His hold tightened. "Fuck, I hate this."

"So do I." Turning in Andreas's embrace, I rested my head against his chest, listening to his heart. The thrum pulsed so strongly in my own I was sure he could feel it, too.

Elvi'i lelvi'ov yelvi'u.

I love you.

When a Starling gave her heart, she gave it for life. No other man would take Andreas's place. No other man would share my life.

All while he would go on with his. He'd marry that woman, his betrothed. He'd sleep beside her each moon. He'd have children who shared his tawny eyes and perfect smile.

I hated that future. I hated that woman. I hated that those children wouldn't be mine.

"Kiss me," I said, swallowing the lump in my throat. Ignoring the sting in my nose.

I'd have moons aboard that ship to cry.

Andreas took my face in his hands, searching my eyes. Then he sealed his mouth over mine, carrying me to his bed. And we gave each other one last moon to not think about tomorrow.

The Roslo docks at dawn were eerily quiet. The walkways were empty, the market stalls shut behind tarps, and the shops closed and dark. The air smelled sweeter, still chilled in the small hours of the morning. The ocean waves smacked against the pylons of the docks, and the sky on the horizon was as dark as the clothes I'd donned this morning.

Gone were my gowns and slippers. It was fitting that I was dressed in the same pants and vest that had brought me across the Marixmore. Now they would take me home.

The pants were thinning at the knees. The sole of my left boot was coming loose. And my vest's hem was frayed.

The elfalter rings were warm on my fingers. So was the necklace worn above my heart.

The only piece of Calandra I was taking with me was Andreas's coat. I'd stolen it from his dressing room this morning while he was asleep. The sleeves were far too long, and it might as well have been a gown of its own for how it fell nearly to my knees. But it smelled like him, like wood and soap and spice.

The captain hadn't seemed surprised when I'd walked up to his ship this morning. He'd been at the stern, sipping a drink from a chipped cup.

Maybe he was a man who wasn't easily shocked. Or maybe Andreas had told him to be at the ready for the sun I arrived. I'd ask later. We had plenty of suns ahead.

He still hadn't given me his name, but he had agreed to take me wherever I told him to go. He'd asked for an hour to gather the necessary supplies, and then we would leave Roslo.

I'd wandered the docks for that hour before turning back. Every step down the walkway toward the *Malynn* was heavy, like I was wading through mud that came up to my waist.

Three men carried barrels across the plank between the dock and ship. A woman with short, spiked blond hair fitted her fingers between her lips and whistled to a bald man on the dock. He nodded and went to one of the thick ropes keeping the ship tied to a post.

There were five ropes left to untie. Five ropes, and we'd sail to the horizon, the crew following nothing but my instruction.

I pressed my hand to my heart.

And stopped.

The thrum was gone.

All I could feel was my heartbeat. I pressed harder, closing my eyes, waiting to feel it again.

Nothing.

If there was no thrum, then I had no way to find home.

No, that couldn't be right. I'd felt it last moon on Andreas's balcony. And I'd felt it this morning, hadn't I?

Except I didn't remember feeling it as I studied his face in the dark. I couldn't remember the thrum when I slipped out of his bed to silently dress. I hadn't felt it while I wrote a note to Kos before leaving the house and navigating the dark streets of Roslo.

Walking away had been excruciating. The pain must have masked the call.

So why couldn't I feel it now? What did this mean?

I couldn't get on this ship if there was no pull in my chest. I'd condemn us all to death. But if I didn't leave, what did that mean for Andreas?

Would this mean his death? Would he even want me to stay in Quentis? I closed my eyes, torn between wanting the thrum to return and cheering that it was gone.

By the grace of the Divine, show me the path.

A wind, cold and sharp, blew the ocean spray against my face. A shout carried over the noise of the sea.

"Caspia."

I turned away from the ship and toward the city.

Andreas ran down the dock, long legs eating up the distance between us. His hair was unruly, his shirt untucked. His eyes were wild and panicked. He didn't stop running until I was in his arms. Until his nose was in my hair and my face was tucked into the crook of his neck.

Was this why the thrum was gone? Andreas had changed his mind. It was never me who'd had to decide. This was always Andreas's choice to make.

"Stay with me." He leaned away, taking my face in his hands. "Don't go. Stay with me."

"What about—"

"It doesn't matter. None of it matters."

Tears flooded my eyes as a laugh or a sob, I couldn't tell the difference, broke free. "Are you sure?"

This would change everything.

"Stay with me. My Caspia. Please."

I threw my arms around his shoulders. "Until the Divine calls me home."

PART III

DYNASTY

39

ODESSA

I sat on my cliffside with my knees hugged to my chest, staring toward the storm brewing on the horizon.

The afternoon breeze had quickly turned into a gusting wind, whipping my hair into my face. The cold cut through my clothes. The scent of rain filled my nose. Lightning sparked and popped with white flashes.

In the east, the sun was still fighting to be seen through the gray, billowing clouds, but it was losing that battle.

I could relate.

After the awful meeting with Father, I'd needed to escape the castle. *His* castle. My feet had walked themselves out here, and now I couldn't seem to make them go back.

All this time, I'd hoped to earn his trust and confidence. But he was never going to tell me his plans. Maybe, deep down, I'd known he'd never let me in and that's why I hadn't told him how to find Allesaria. I hadn't given him Ransom's cuff.

I hadn't earned Father's trust.

And he'd shattered mine.

"There's my queen." Ransom dropped to a seat at my side, his shoulder brushing mine as he draped his arms over his bent knees.

We sat together, wordlessly watching as the rain began to fall over the ocean, blurring the line where the sky met the sea.

"Where's Evie?" I asked.

"With your brother. The nursemaid promised to watch her and Faze."

The nursery with Nathalia was the safest place in the castle. And I hoped that Evie would find a friend in Arthalayus. Even if our time in Quentis was short.

"Did my father find you?"

"Yes. He wanted to know about the crux scout. He sent his new general to expedite preparations."

Well, at least he was taking the migration seriously. "Did he ask about Banner?"

"No."

I sighed and leaned my head against Ransom's shoulder. "They want me to be the woman I was, and I don't know how to go back."

Ransom bent and kissed my hair. "You were always this woman. I knew it the day I watched you jump off this cliff. You were always my queen. It's not your fault they weren't paying attention."

Tears filled my eyes as the ache in my heart spiked. "I don't want to stay in Quentis. If we set sail tomorrow, do you think we could make it to Perris before the migration? Take shelter there? You said we might have more time."

Leaving meant I wouldn't have access to my father's healers, but that didn't mean I had to give up on a cure. I'd just find healers in Turah.

Ransom shifted to dig something from his pocket. A letter, the envelope folded in half. He handed it over, letting me pull the parchment from inside. "This was waiting for me when I finished meeting with your father."

The handwriting was feminine and crisp. "From Cathlin?"

He nodded.

"I don't want to read it if it's bad news." If it meant reliving Zavier's death.

"He's alive."

My entire body exhaled as I signed the Eight. "Thank the gods."

"They're sailing here. For Evie."

No surprise. Zavier wouldn't be apart from his daughter during a migration.

"Cathlin sent this from Ellder with a pony rider," he said. "They were leaving the same day it was sent but knew a rider and trade ship would reach Quentis first."

"When will they arrive?"

"I don't know. This was sent a week after I left. She wasn't sure how quickly they could travel with his injuries. But soon. If I had to guess, they will likely be here within the week."

"Then we'll have to wait for them."

"Yes." Ransom nodded.

A week seemed like no time at all. It wasn't. Except a week could mean the start of the migration. A week meant we might not have time to get back to Turah.

Damn.

It had been more than one month but less than two since Ellder and the crux scout. We were living on borrowed days unless Ransom was right and we had more time. There'd been no word of other scouts yet.

"Okay, we wait." For Evie's sake, and Zavier's, I'd endure my family. And use every resource at my disposal. "Then while we're here, I'm going to task my father's healers with finding a cure for Lyssa."

Ransom's frame locked. "Odessa, this is wasted effort."

"Not to me. I know you don't believe it's possible, but I can't watch those dark veins spread from your heart and do nothing. If it fails, then at least I can say I tried. Your mother believed in a cure. Let me believe in it, too, even if you don't."

The hopelessness in his green eyes, the way he'd already accepted death from this infection, made my heart ache.

"Please. Don't ask me to give up hope."

Ransom closed his eyes and exhaled. "How often do I tell you no?"

I curled into his side, hugging his arm. "Thank you."

"Do you trust your father's healers?"

"I don't know them very well." But I also didn't know if we had another choice. "I'll meet with the head healer and give him a vial of your blood. I'll say it came from an infected monster."

Until I knew I could trust the healers, the source of Ransom's gifts would remain a secret. The last thing we needed was another king following in Ramsey's footsteps, trying to recreate the Guardian while killing people instead.

"Just until Zavier and Cathlin arrive," he said. "If there's still no word of another scout, we're going home."

Home. Not Quentis. Not even Turah.

Ransom was my home.

"Deal." I rested my head against his arm, neither of us making a move to leave.

Together, we watched the storm move closer and closer.

Knowing there was no escaping the rain.

The castle's infirmary reminded me of the stables. The rooms were like stalls that lined a straight walkway, their walls only as tall as my chin. White curtains hung from the ceilings and could be pulled closed for privacy, but most were left open so the staff could peer into their patients' rooms from the hall.

A nurse led me down the walkway, his legs so long and pace so quick I had to jog every other step to keep up, keeping hold of my satchel as it bounced against my hip.

In one of the rooms we passed, a legionnaire had a gash on his arm that was being stitched closed. In another, a scullery maid was being treated for a burn on her hand.

Whenever I'd needed a healer, they'd come to my rooms.

But as a child, I'd snuck into the infirmary a few times to explore or avoid a tutor.

The infirmary was mostly used for castle staff, but if the city's larger facility was full, they would open this to the public. Even though these halls only held a few patients each day, there were at least one hundred rooms. Most of the beds had been empty for nearly thirty years.

Once the migration started, it wouldn't be big enough. They'd likely cram two to three patients in each space.

It was built below the castle's foundation, just like the city's infirmary. I prayed to the Eight that the crux didn't find their way past the rock and stone, scenting out the blood that would stain these clean, white rooms.

Nerves rocked my empty stomach like churning waves as we neared the end of the hall. I clutched the glass vial in my hand tighter.

Ransom had given it to me this morning.

Yesterday, after he agreed to let me talk to the healers about a cure, we hadn't spoken of Lyssa again. We'd returned to the castle, drenched with rain. Then we'd collected Evie and spent the rest of the night locked away in our suite.

There was a very good chance that Father's head healer, a pudgy man named Geoff, would dismiss me completely. I'd known Geoff since I was a young girl, and while he'd always been kind, he shied away when he looked at my golden eyes.

My lack of the Quentin starburst was something he could not explain—therefore, he kept his distance.

But he had the most experience, and if we were going to find a cure, I needed the best healer in the kingdom.

The nurse turned a sharp corner, leading me down a series of hallways. We took a staircase down to a lower level, then another. The temperature dropped as my heart climbed into my throat.

One final stairwell and short hall led us to an arched wooden door with a round gold knocker.

The nurse thwacked it twice, then, without a word, left me standing alone.

"Thank you?" I said to his back.

He was already taking the stairs two at a time.

I braced as footsteps sounded on the opposite side of the door.

A short, stocky man yanked it open. "Yes?"

"I'm looking for the head healer?" I glanced past him, but the room at his back was too dim to see far.

He stepped out of the doorway and waved me inside. "All the way back."

"Thank you."

He left, pulling the door closed behind him, as I inched along the entryway.

"Hello?" I cleared my throat. "Um, Geoff?"

No answer.

The scents of burning sage and rosemary hit my nose as I made it to the end of the hall and stepped into a cluttered, windowless room.

Bundles of drying herbs and flowers hung from the ceiling. Jars of liquids and tonics crowded wooden shelves. Books overflowed from the case where they were stacked, the excess piled on the floor.

The table in the center of the room was a jumbled mess of leaves, stems, and dried flower petals. Someone had set out a cutting board and chopping knife.

I didn't remember Geoff having an underground apothecary.

A woman breezed through another doorway from a side room, drying her hands on a white towel. She stared at me over the frame of her purple spectacles. There was another set perched on top of her head, those red. And hooked into the neckline of her dress was a third, the frame a vivid magenta, nearly the exact shade of the starbursts in her black eyes.

She had long, black hair threaded liberally with silver and gray. Her tan skin was flawless and smooth, her upturned nose perfectly balanced between her rosy cheekbones. Her beige dress was embroidered with orange flowers. She wore ten different necklaces, as thickly layered as the bracelets on both wrists. Her beaded earrings were so long they brushed the tops of her shoulders.

My jaw hit the floor.

The woman in the journal who'd painted flowers on a little girl's casts. This had to be her.

The healers typically wore sterile clothing in varying shades of gray. I'd always thought my wardrobe fit perfectly in the infirmary. This woman was as vibrant as a spring garden.

"Can I help you, dear?" she asked, tossing the towel on a table.

"I was looking for Healer Geoff." Though I wasn't anymore.

Brother Dime had told me the journal meant I was going in the right direction. This was the woman I was supposed to find.

Maybe every entry in that book was meant to lead me here. To a woman who could cure my husband.

"I'm sorry, Geoff is no longer here." Her voice was smoky and peaceful, a voice I'd want to hear if I was in the infirmary. "He moved to Kolmberg this summer to be closer to his grandchildren before the migration. My name is Alore. I'm the new head healer. Can I help you?"

I squeezed the vial in my palm. "Yes, I think you can."

My hand felt empty as I walked through the castle. It hadn't been easy to give that vial of Ransom's blood to Healer Alore, but all I could hope was that I'd made the right decision.

We'd spent hours talking in her workshop, as she called it, sipping her own blend of ginger-and-spearmint tea.

Alore had only been in Roslo for a few months. She was originally from Laine, and she'd spent most of her career at the largest infirmary in Ostan. But female healers, no matter their skill or qualification, were typically overlooked for promotions if there was a viable male candidate around.

After being passed over again and again, she'd finally had enough. She praised Daria for the timing of her move to Quentis. The Goddess of Luck had brought her to Roslo just as Geoff had been preparing to leave.

My father had hired her to take Geoff's place.

The Gold King had many flaws, but he didn't discriminate against women. Father wanted the best and the brightest in his employ.

I think he'd found that in Alore.

She was kind and smart. Eager and ambitious. She had something to prove to her former colleagues back in Laine.

I hoped the challenge she craved was a cure for Lyssa.

I'd told Alore everything over a second cup of her tea. From Luella's elixir to the bariwolf bite. Of how we believed the infection began and how it was spreading to monsters across Calandra.

She knew Ransom had Lyssa, that it was the source of the Guardian's special abilities. She knew King Ramsey was attempting to give Lyssa to his militia but it was killing his men instead. She knew I was desperate and that we were running out of time.

I'd given her Luella's alchemy journals, two books I'd carried with me across Calandra. And I'd left Alore with the vial of blood and a growing curiosity.

I was counting on that curiosity.

Maybe it was a mistake to confide in her. Maybe she'd run to Father and tell him everything.

It was a risk I had to take if it meant saving Ransom's life.

The foyers and halls were swarming with castle visitors as I walked toward the east wing. Noblemen and city officials streamed through the front entrance, presumably for a meeting with Father about the migration. There were five times the usual number of legionnaires and guards in the palace, their marching bootsteps charging the atmosphere with a sense of urgency.

It was the energy I'd been wanting to feel since leaving Turah. That sharp edge of panic and foreboding danger I hoped would spread across the continent like wildfire.

The crux art gallery was unsurprisingly empty when I arrived. No one came into this hall except for me.

The paintings and tapestries and murals that depicted past migrations had always been gruesome, but now that I'd seen a crux with my own eyes, witnessed its destruction, I was glad I'd skipped breakfast.

The migration was coming, and we weren't ready. *I* wasn't ready.

Was there any way to stop it? Or had Father only used that as a motivator for me to do his bidding?

I turned in a slow circle, taking in the artwork. A prickle on my skin had me spinning back toward the entrance as Brother Dime walked into the gallery.

He bowed. "Hello, child."

"Brother Dime." Was he here to talk to me? Or could I leave?

I took a step.

"Stay," he ordered.

Right. I guess I'd stay.

He glided to the largest mural, staring up at the gory depiction of an auburn male crux. "Magic is intent and consequence. Take, for example, a blood oath. The intent is in the spoken word. In the vow itself. Magic makes it real by consequence."

"Okay," I drawled. "Good to know?"

He turned and stared at me.

"Is that supposed to mean something to me?"

No answer.

That meant yes.

Intent and consequence. What was his consequence? "Are you telling me this because you can't tell me something else?"

He smiled. Well...sort of. He gave me the Voster equivalent of a smile. Then he looked around the gallery. "Magnificent creatures, the crux."

"If 'magnificent' means horrific."

"Keep an open mind, Odessa."

"To what?" Calling the crux magnificent was as laughable as it was cruel.

"The truth." He walked from the hall, pausing beside a potted fern. "But remember, the truth is rarely gentle. To hear. Or to speak. Your mind is full of questions. Stay. For this is where you'll find answers."

Then I guess it was a good thing we were staying in Quentis.

40

CASPIA

Ink stained my fingertips. The scrape of my quill against parchment mingled with the sound of the fire crackling in the hearth.

In the suns since the *Malynn* had sailed away from Roslo, Andreas and I had been inseparable. We'd spent most of our time at the house, locked away and wrapped in each other's arms. But we couldn't hide from the world forever, and at dinner last evening, a missive had come, marking the end of our isolation.

The missive had come from his father, a summons to a meeting. Something about preparations. The castle was busier than normal today. So while I was spending my sun in this alcove of the library, Andreas was in a meeting room somewhere in the castle, dealing with his family.

As much as I missed spending countless hours in his bed—*our* bed, as he reminded me daily—it was time to get started on a task of my own.

It was time to tell my story.

Maybe there was a book in this library that described the continent of Kenn. A book that mentioned Nelfinex and Showe. If there was, neither Faxon nor I had found it yet.

So I was writing one of my own.

This journal would be a record that a world existed across the Marixmore. And maybe the next Starling who was called to Calandra for her ritus wouldn't feel so lost.

Summers from now, maybe everyone in Calandra would

know of Nelfinex. Maybe a voyager would set sail across the ocean in search of my beloved city, Showe. Or maybe this journal and the other on this table would spend generations in this library collecting dust.

All I cared about at the moment was penning my memories, my beliefs, and my culture onto these blank pages.

Since the thrum had stopped, my mind felt quieter. It made sifting through the memories easier. My visions had lessened, too. I'd only had one in the eight suns since the morning on the docks—a vision of Faxon speaking to Andreas about adopting Kos.

I flipped the page of my journal and dipped my quill into my ink pot.

Queen of the Starling

But before I could begin the tale of my aunt's rise and reign, Faxon swept into the alcove, his arms laden with books.

"Here we are." He set them on the edge of the table, wiping the damp from his brow with the back of his sleeve. "Some of those are quite heavy. If you'd like to take any of them with you when you leave, I'd be happy to escort you and carry them."

"Thank you." I closed the journal, set my quill aside.

I'd asked Faxon for any books about Calandran lore and history as well as accounts of past migrations. Maybe if I scoured enough books, I'd learn why Calandra was different than Kenn. I'd learn why the Voster had magic. Why I'd been so sick when I first arrived. Why a Starling got trapped in her shifted form.

Maybe I'd find a way to save Xandra.

If she was still alive.

I reached for the book on the top of the stack. It was small, slightly larger than my hand, and more of a novel than a tome. "What's this one?"

"Well, you asked me for anything about Calandra's history.

That is more a storybook than a history, but I thought you might find it interesting."

I opened the cover to the title. *Sonnet's Ninety*.

Faxon took a seat on the edge of the table. "It's a collection of ninety stories written by a man named Sonnet. He was once a famed gladiator in Laine, never bested by man or beast. Because of his skill, he earned favor with Mack."

Mack. Which god was he? The God of Death. Or maybe Izzac was the God of Death and Mack was the God of War? I got the Six jumbled up more often than not.

"Sonnet wandered the desert for ninety days during a migration," Faxon continued. "He had no magic or shelter or weapons. He should have been easy prey for the crux, but Mack took pity on him and gave him stories to tell the crux. For ninety days, Sonnet whispered those tales of magic and monsters and wars and legends. And when the crux finally left Calandra, he returned home to write this book. It's more lore than fact, but it's significantly more entertaining than some of these others. And it's easy to carry around."

"Thank you." I set it with my journals. "Then I'll take it home to read tonight."

Faxon stood, smoothing the front of his scapular and adjusting the cord tied at his waist. He shifted from foot to foot, opening his mouth only to close it before speaking.

"What is it, Faxon?" I asked, though I already knew the answer. This was what he'd already spoken to Andreas about.

"Lady Caspia." He squared his shoulders. "I will understand if you refuse. I realize you may consider this an overstep. But I would be remiss if I didn't ask. I would like to ask your permission to adopt Kos. My husband and I have often talked about having children, but we wanted it to be the right child at the right time. Enough years passed, we both thought maybe that time would never come. Then Kos arrived, and, well…we've both grown quite fond of the boy through our teachings."

Faxon's husband, Gable, was the weapons master in the castle. He, like Faxon, had once taught Andreas, too. And now Kos was their student. It didn't surprise me at all that the boy had stolen their hearts.

"I realize we're getting on in age." Faxon's forehead furrowed as he clasped his hands together. "But our home is well established. Our family is simply missing—"

"Kos," I said.

He nodded. "Andreas had no objection. But he urged me to ask you."

"And you have my blessing." I stood, walking to the bibliosoph to take his hands.

Tears filled Faxon's eyes before he pulled me into a tight hug. "Thank you."

I laughed, hugging him back. "By the grace of the Divine, Kos is lucky to have you both."

"Bless Daria for her luck and Arabella for her love." He let me go and wiped his cheeks dry. Then he waved to the stack of books. "I will let you return to your work while I find Gable and share the good news."

As he hurried from the alcove, I returned to my seat, a smile on my face. It had been a while since a vision had made me happy. Maybe in time, I'd forget the horrible futures I'd seen, the glimpses of death and loss. Maybe those visions would be overshadowed by those of love and life.

I shuffled through the books, picking one from the middle of the stack.

Migration Defenses: An Analysis

I opened the cover, then turned the title page only to have the paper's edge slice into the pad of my finger.

"Damn." I hissed, pulling away to inspect the cut.

A drop of blood welled on my fingertip. Dark-green blood.

My blood in Nelfinex was red.

The first time I'd seen this green blood was the sun I

wandered through the streets of Roslo and got blisters from my slippers. I'd spent countless hours pondering how this was possible. How so much of my body had changed.

This had to be part of why the Starling were different in Calandra. Maybe the reason I'd been so sick when we first arrived was because every fiber of my being was altered, including the color of my blood. It had to be from the magic.

Had the Voster's blood changed, too, when they came from Kenn? Or had they simply been gifted magic? As painful as our initial meeting had been, I'd endure it ten times over if I could have the chance to speak to Brother Nold again.

Every book I read just left me with more questions.

The sound of thudding boots made me hide my hand beneath the table just as Andreas strode into the alcove, his jacket unbuttoned and the ties beneath his throat loosened.

He looked frayed and frustrated, but his eyes crinkled as he gave me a soft smile, rounding the table to stand behind my chair, then bending to kiss my forehead. "Hello, my heart."

The endearment was something he'd been using since the docks. I'd go through all the pain and anguish again just to hear him call me "my heart."

"Long day?" I asked.

"Very. And unfortunately, not over quite yet. But I had a moment and wanted to see how you were doing."

"I'm good." I nodded to my stack. "Faxon brought me plenty of books."

"I see that." He chuckled. "Did he talk to you about Kos?"

I nodded. "Yes. I gave them my blessing."

"I knew you would." Andreas settled his hands on my shoulders. "I'm happy for them."

"So am I."

Andreas and I weren't looking to give Kos away. We both cared deeply for him. But there'd never come a moment when I'd considered myself his mother. Andreas was not his father.

We loved him. But we were not his parents.

Kos was special, and the bond he'd formed with Faxon and Gable was unique. They belonged to one another. We'd simply been the link to unite a family.

Andreas sighed and kissed my forehead again. "I'd better go and finish my obligations for the day. How much longer will you stay?"

I shrugged. "I don't know. I'd like to read for a while."

Neither of us loved being in the castle. Andreas had his own reasons. I simply tired of the hushed whispers and gossip that seemed to follow me through the halls. But if I stayed hidden away in this alcove, I could pretend I was reading somewhere else.

"Some of these look heavy. Don't even think about carrying them home."

"Just the small ones," I promised. "The rest can stay here until tomorrow."

"Good. We can read some together tonight."

Andreas was as eager as I was for answers about why the Starling and Voster were different in Calandra. While he was working during the sun, I muddled my way through these tomes. But after sundown, it was much faster for him to read, as I still stumbled over certain Calandran words and phrases.

He kissed the corner of my mouth, lingering long enough to send a shiver down my spine. Then he was gone, refastening the ties of his collar and buttoning his jacket as he left the alcove.

I waited until the sound of his footsteps faded before I lifted my hand from beneath the table. The bleeding had stopped. The cut was already healed.

My stomach knotted as I wiped the last hint of green on my skirt.

Even if it took me a lifetime, I would find the truth. I pressed two fingers to the center of my forehead. "I vow it."

"What do you vow?" Kos bounded into the room, wearing a teal scapular that was clearly made for adults. It was bunched and rolled at the waist, and the cord was wrapped around three times to keep the fabric from pooling at his feet.

"Look at you." I laughed. "Are you my librarian now?"

"No, I'm the bibliosoph." He puffed up his chest, claiming the title of head librarian. "Do you need any books from the tall shelves? I can find the ladder and get 'em down."

"I think you'd better leave those to Faxon, sweetling."

Kos pouted. "He won't let me climb up anymore since I almost fell, and he says I would have broken my neck if he hadn't been there to catch me."

"He's probably right. Besides, don't you have to go to weapons training soon?"

The boy tugged at the cord around his waist, freeing its knot. The scapular puddled at his feet as he wiggled free. "Want to come? I bet Gable can teach you how to use a sword."

"Who says I don't already know how to use a sword?"

"Do you?" He gave me a sideways glance. Always skeptical, my Kos.

Maybe in the future, he'd read my book about Nelfinex. And decide to find it for himself.

41

ODESSA

There was a jar of brown hair dye on the counter in our bathing chamber, delivered by a maid while we were sleeping.

Ransom walked into the room, stopping behind me. Through the mirror, his reflection went from sleepy to sneering in a blink. "That better not be what I think it is."

I bit the inside of my cheek to keep from crying.

It was our third morning in Quentis, and I had yet to get new clothes. The closet was still full of gray gowns and slippers.

Now I knew why.

Margot had no intention of getting me pants.

She'd been so lovely during our shared breakfasts. She'd asked about my time in Turah, her interest seemingly genuine. She'd been sweet to Evie, and just yesterday, she'd said how nice it was for Arthy to have a friend in the nursery.

I should have known it was all a show for Ransom's benefit.

My chin quivered.

"Fuck." Ransom wrapped his arms around my shoulders as I looked to the floor, hiding my face with a curtain of my hair. He kissed my shoulder. "I'm sorry."

Last night, I'd had a sinking feeling in my stomach when I returned to the suite to find nothing had changed in my closet. Ransom, Evie, and I had spent another evening locked away, dining alone, since we'd received no invitation to join my family.

After our meal, I'd washed my tunic and pants in the tub,

setting them out to dry on a chair in our bedroom. Thank the gods I hadn't left them in the bathing chamber. The maid who'd delivered the dye had probably been instructed to snatch them away.

I sniffled, blinking back tears. If I cried, Margot would win. If I wore a gray dress, she'd win. If I put Evie in the dresses in her own closet, Margot would win.

Margot was not going to win.

We needed coin, and I wasn't about to ask my father. But I wasn't destitute, not yet.

As tempting as it was to sell the gray dresses, they wouldn't bring as much as the set of knives in the closet.

And I couldn't bring myself to touch them again. Even looking at the hilts took me back to Ellder. No matter how clean, I'd always see Banner's blood on their blades.

Knives for pants and a resounding *fuck you* to Margot seemed like a fair trade.

I met Ransom's silver eyes in the mirror. "Would you be upset if I sold my knives?"

Ransom's mouth pulled into a smirk. His eyes swirled to green. "Not at all."

Dressed in a new pair of bronze linen pants and a shirt of the same shade, I found Ransom in the castle's training center.

The sound of blades striking blades greeted me as I walked in, the scents of cedar, metal, and sweat filling my nose. There was a group of children on one side of the enormous, lofty room shooting arrows at round targets. A handful of legionnaires were sparring. And Mae was training with Brix, the captain of the guard, in the center ring.

My sister had avoided us completely for the past three days, ever since she broke into our suite to do Father's bidding. It came as no surprise to find her here. This center was Mae's favorite place in the castle.

Brix was older by ten years, but he was Mae's preferred training partner, and lover, because he met her intensity beat for beat.

She moved effortlessly in the ring, her sword arcing and cutting through the air with a grace that reminded me more of a dance than a fight. The skirt of her dress swished around her ankles and calves. The jade sleeves were loose and billowy, the fabric thin to allow for ease of movement.

Gable, the weapons master, watched on from a bench, barking out their mistakes.

There weren't many.

After Gable had deemed me a lost cause, I'd stopped coming to the training center on a regular basis. Eventually, I'd stopped coming entirely, more than willing to concede this space to Mae.

She was as fast and agile as ever, and the longer she sparred against the captain, holding her own, the taller Gable sat. The higher he lifted his cleft chin. Pride beamed from the older man's face as he observed his favorite student.

I slipped into the center, skirting the walls as I walked to the far corner, where Ransom and Evie were working together.

He was training her with a wooden sword. The same wooden sword Mae and I had used when we were children.

Faze was on his leash, tied to the rack of weapons mounted on the wall. He chewed on a bone, more content than he'd been in days.

I bent to scratch his ears as I passed, then joined Ransom.

Evie stuck her tongue out of the corner of her mouth, her eyebrows knitted in concentration as she gripped the sword with both hands. She drew it back over her shoulder, then swung it forward, aiming at his knee.

Ransom let her hit him, feigning injury.

Evie giggled. "I win."

"You win." He ruffled her hair, taking her sword. "Good job. You can take a break."

She skipped away to plop down beside Faze.

Ransom walked straight into my space, forcing me to tilt up my chin to keep his eyes. Silver again.

"Nice clothes, my queen." He brushed his mouth against mine. "I'm looking forward to taking them off you later."

A shiver rolled down my spine.

He grinned against my mouth, then swatted my ass with his free hand. "Grab a sword."

I groaned but walked to the wall of weapons, pulling down a sword the same size as my own.

Ransom retrieved his from the corner, then led me to a training circle adjacent to Mae's.

A snicker carried through the room.

Mae and the captain had stopped their fight. Both stared our way, their heads bent in a whisper.

Gable stood from the bench in front of Mae's ring and came to sit at the one in front of mine.

"Then should we skip this training session, husband?" I batted my eyelashes at Ransom.

"Not a chance, Cross."

Blarg. The last thing I wanted was an audience, especially this one.

Gable had given up on me as his student. He'd grumbled about my poor aim with a crossbow and warned Father that I'd only hurt myself if armed with a blade.

And Mae was, well...Mae.

The moment I fell on my ass, she'd be the first to laugh. And falling on my ass was inevitable.

"Block them out," Ransom said, his voice low and smooth. "Just you and me."

I closed my eyes and pictured a training ring beneath towering evergreens. I imagined the smell of pine in my nose and needles beneath my feet. I drew in a long inhale and opened my eyes. Then I gave Ransom a single nod.

"That's my queen." His smirk was the only warning before he attacked.

I shuffled backward and to the side, barely blocking a strike.

He frowned, eyebrow arched.

"Stand my ground," I muttered. "I know."

But at least I was still upright.

Ransom came at me again, and this time, I didn't retreat but moved to create an opening of my own to attack.

We fell into a familiar rhythm, a dance of our own making, until the rest of the room faded into a blur and all that remained was us. Silver eyes slowly shifted to hazel. And finally, his gaze flashed vibrant green.

I knew I was in trouble when he moved so fast I lost focus on his face. One moment, I was standing. The next, I was flat on my back, the sword tumbling from my grip as he came down on top of me, pinning me to the floor.

"Not fair," I grumbled.

He grinned down at me, a lock of his dark hair escaping the knot at his nape. His hands pinned mine above my head. The weight of his body kept me trapped to the floor. "That was good."

"Was that a compliment? In the training ring? I thought praise was for the bedroom."

He chuckled, bending close. His lips tickled the shell of my ear. "You want praise? Then wait until I fuck that smart mouth of yours tonight. I'll give you all the praise you can handle."

My breath hitched. Heat flushed my already warm cheeks.

He chuckled and kissed the corner of my mouth, then jumped to his feet before helping me to mine.

The rest of the room came into dizzying clarity as Ransom picked up my sword and carried it to the weapons rack.

Mae stood beside Brix with her arms crossed over her chest and a frown marring her pretty face. The captain looked impressed? Before I could read his face, Mae elbowed him in the ribs and he winced.

Gable stood from the bench and joined me in the ring.

I'd forgotten just how intimidating the weapons master could be. Gable was a brute of a man and nearly as unnerving as Father. There was a stiffness to his gait due to the limp of his left leg. His thick, wavy hair was entirely silver, the brown I recalled from my childhood completely gone. The smile lines around his mouth were deeper than before, though, like he'd found something to smile about more often.

He looked down the line of his straight nose and crossed his arms over his barrel of a chest. "Princess Odessa."

"Hello, Master Gable."

He grunted. Or was that a laugh? I'd never heard him laugh. "I always wondered if there was a piece of your mother hidden away inside of you."

I rocked back on my heels, the force of that statement hitting me square in the chest. "Y-you knew my mother?"

"I've never seen anyone as quick with a blade." He looked to Ransom. "Except him."

My mother knew how to fight? That seemed like something I should have known. Maybe, as a child, it would have encouraged me not to give up. "No one speaks of my mother."

"Those who knew her learned a long time ago it was best not to mention her name for fear of your father's wrath." He looked me up and down and frowned. "Your footwork needs improvement. Come back tomorrow. We'll see what we can do."

"You want to train me?"

His eyebrows lifted. Gable wasn't one to repeat himself.

"Tomorrow it is." I had no desire to work on my footwork,

but I'd return and let him boss me around if it meant the chance to ask him more about my mother.

Maybe I'd finally get to learn about her life. And why the High Priest had asked about her.

"Thank you," I said, hope filling my chest.

Except Gable's attention was no longer on me but over my shoulder.

I turned to see Father standing in the doorway, his golden crown catching the afternoon light.

The hard, unforgiving look on his face was aimed at the weapons master.

And when I turned to face Gable again, he was already ambling away.

42

CASPIA

I set down my quill and closed the cover of my journal. The story I'd set out to write was finished, and I suddenly wanted to take it all back. To rip the pages free from the binding and toss them into the fireplace.

Yet as I stared at the book and its companion, this incredible weight lifted off my shoulders.

The burden of the Starling was no longer mine to carry alone.

I hadn't filled either journal entirely. I liked that there was room to add more over time.

But I'd written the story of my life. The story of my people and family. I'd even included things I hadn't shared with Andreas, like how my blood had turned green and that I was stronger and faster than I'd ever been in Nelfinex. That my sight and my hearing had sharpened.

This project had consumed me, but no matter what was to come, at least there was this record.

I stood from my chair, my back and shoulders stiff from the hours I'd been sitting at the table in the library's alcove. With my stack of books clutched to my chest, I left my quill and ink behind and made my way to Faxon's desk.

A pair of wire spectacles rested on the curve of his nose as he sat hunched over a book, squinting as he read.

The library was dim, the light that normally streamed through the windows muted by the thick layer of gray clouds that had settled over Roslo.

I missed the sunshine. I loathed the rain.

Andreas had warned me that as we continued toward the winter solstice, the clouds and rain would be constant. But eventually, the weather would clear and the spring in Quentis would make every gloomy moment worthwhile.

"Faxon," I said, coming to a stop at his desk. "I'm sorry to bother you. But could I ask for a favor?"

"No bother at all, Lady Caspia." He hopped off his stool and removed his spectacles, leaving them to hold the place in his book. "What can I do for you?"

"I was wondering if you might…" My hands held tighter to a journal. *Let it go, Caspia.* "Will you hide this somewhere safe?"

His eyebrows furrowed as he held out his hand. "Of course."

Let it go. I gave him the journal, resisting the urge to snatch it away.

Faxon didn't open the cover. He didn't peek inside. And in my heart, I knew he would honor my privacy.

"And the other?" Faxon pointed to my other journal, a twin to the one now tucked in the crook of his arm. "Would you like me to put it away, too?"

"No, I'll keep this one."

"Very well." Faxon nodded, giving me a slight bow, then disappeared somewhere in the stacks to hide that journal on a shelf where it would be forgotten.

Until it was time for Kos to find it.

The vision of him reading the first page had come to me three moons ago. It had been short and blurry at the edges, almost like it had been cloaked in a fog.

Most of my visions had been like that lately. Like dreams.

A mountain forest covered in white.

Countless graves beyond a fortress wall.

A man with black braids and one leg holding his newborn son.

These new visions felt like fragments of shattered glass, and I had to figure out how they all fit together.

Maybe I'd never see the entire picture.

A yawn tugged at my mouth, a side effect of the dreary weather. I headed for the library's doors, steeling my spine for the walk through the grand foyer.

The novelty of *me* hadn't worn off yet. People loved to whisper about my hair. My clothes. My eyes. Mostly, people didn't seem to understand who I was to Andreas. I'd heard the term *mistress* a few times, and though we didn't have that word in Nelfinex, I understood the concept.

In Nelfinex, he would have been my lover. My consort.

In Calandra, I would need a different title to truly belong.

Wife.

We hadn't spoken of his betrothal contract lately, though I knew he was still working to nullify the agreement. If people were speculating about me, well...I didn't know. I avoided the papermen and their publications at all costs.

Did the library have a rear exit? I made a mental note to ask Faxon about it tomorrow.

I was in the middle of the atrium when the double doors swung open. The guards held them for a woman wearing a navy gown embroidered with silver thread.

Her golden hair hung in sleek panels over her shoulders. Her tawny eyes, accented with amber starbursts, were so familiar I came to a stop.

I knew those eyes. I woke up to them each morning and fell asleep to them each moon.

Vexx. Andreas had warned me that his mother wanted an introduction. He'd made excuses, but clearly, she was done being put off.

This was worse than the papermen and castle gossips. But at least we weren't in the foyer.

The skirts of her gown swished as she crossed the space between us. Behind her, the guards closed the doors. They probably had orders not to open them again until she was done with me.

Malynn stopped at arm's length, her gaze cool and calculating as she eyed me up and down.

White and green jewels dripped from her ears. A necklace made of the same stones hung heavy around her throat. Her face was flawless, her skin accented with creams and powders. She smelled of lavender and rose petals. Her fingernails were polished to a glossy shine. She exuded affluence and authority.

Andreas was not the type of man to flaunt his wealth, and it made it easy to forget this was his life. That his family's wealth meant power and responsibility.

Like the responsibility of marrying a woman his parents had deemed acceptable.

Damn. I should have worn my nicer dress.

Malynn frowned, and for the first time, her cold exterior cracked. Behind it was sheer disappointment.

I think I preferred her icy glare.

"So you're the woman who has corrupted my son."

A storm raged over the sea. Waves with white caps rolled toward the port and crashed against the cliffside next to the city. The ships in the docks rocked back and forth. Sheets of rain fell from the clouds, and lightning flashed.

One. Two. Three. Four. Five.

Thunder boomed before I reached six. Only minutes ago, it had taken until the count of ten for the *crack* to reach the balcony.

The storm was moving closer, and I wouldn't be able to stay out here for much longer, but those angry gray clouds matched my mood.

"On the balcony. We haven't been out here for a while."

Andreas wrapped me in his arms as he joined me at the rail. "What's wrong?"

"I met your mother today," I said through gritted teeth.

His frame locked. "Fuck."

"She came to the library. She's very beautiful."

"Yes, she is."

Malynn hadn't stayed long. She'd finished her assessment, clearly found me lacking, then informed me that, "You will be a problem."

She hadn't even asked for my name before leaving in a flourish of that expensive dress.

I'd marched home and had spent the rest of my afternoon on this balcony, watching the storm.

"I'm sorry." Andreas rested his chin on the top of my head.

"You assume she was rude."

"Oh, I know my mother quite well. She was rude."

My lip curled. "Apparently, I'm going to be a problem."

He pried my hand off the rail and laced our fingers together. "She's upset that I nullified the betrothal contract."

I whirled, looking up at him. "It's over?"

"Yes." He turned me in his arms, hooking a finger under my chin to close my mouth. "The woman she intended for me to marry is the daughter of her closest friend. I met with her after you and Kos were settled. She wanted to marry me about as much as I wanted to marry her, as in not at all. But she asked if I would keep the facade of our engagement in place until her beloved returned from Ozarth. He went to trade a shipment of grain for the gold needed to offer for her hand. She sent me a message this morning, saying he had returned and together they had informed her parents they were engaged and that she was not marrying me. I didn't have the chance to find my mother today."

"She found me first."

"I'm sorry." He twisted a curl around his finger. When he let it go, he dropped to his knees.

Another blast of sound thundered across the sky as I stared down at him. "What are you doing?"

"Caspia." Andreas took my hands in his. "Marry me. Be my wife."

My heart skipped. *Yes.* I wanted to say yes. I would say yes to anything he asked of me. Except I didn't know what it meant to be a wife.

He must have read the confusion on my face because his eyes softened. "It means you are mine. And I am yours. From now to an eternity together in the shades."

I didn't believe in the shades. But I would wait for him in the afterlife. "Yes."

The word was barely out of my mouth before he stood, capturing my lips with his just as the clouds above us burst.

We laughed, not breaking our kiss as the storm soaked through our clothes. As our tongues tangled, I tasted raindrops on his smile.

"Gods, I love you. I don't deserve you. But I'll keep you all the same. Until the end of our days." He pressed two fingertips to his forehead. "I vow it."

"As do I." If all we ever had was this moment, promises made to each other beneath a torrent of rain, it was enough.

He spun me in circles and kissed me until I was dizzy, then carried me inside, a puddle forming beneath our feet as he set me down. "Whatever you desire, all you have to do is ask. We'll find your cousin. We'll avenge your sister. I'll send someone to track down the silver-eyed man. And if I need to trap every bariwolf in Calandra, then so be it."

"No." I threaded my fingers through his hair. "I don't want vengeance, not anymore."

Maybe that silver-eyed warrior had saved countless lives by taking hers. Maybe he'd had no choice if she'd become a monster.

And while I did want to find Xandra, it would mean locking her in a cage.

Maybe it was better to let her roam free.

"I want to keep spending time in the library. Keep searching for clues until I find it."

"Find what?" His forehead furrowed.

I took a deep breath. There was a reason that my sisters and I had been raised by Aunt Oleana. A reason my mother had never returned to Nelfinex. And I had a feeling that reason was tied to everything I'd learned since coming to Calandra.

"The truth about my mother's disappearance."

43

ODESSA

The bed shook so violently it felt like someone had picked up the mattress to flip it over. I jerked away as Ransom kicked at the sheets.

Shades. "Wake up." I popped up to my knees, putting my hands on his shoulders. "Ransom."

My voice only made the thrashing worse. His head rocked back and forth on the pillow as his eyes squeezed shut.

"Ransom." I shook him, then took his face in my hands. His skin was too hot. "Wake up. It's only a nightmare."

His hands balled into fists, and he roared.

I pushed the hair from his sweaty brow, and this time, I shouted. "Ransom!"

He moved so fast I had no time to react. He sat upright, spinning me as he grabbed my wrists and slammed them into the headboard. His body pinned mine to the bed as a snarl tore from his throat.

I yelped, more surprised than pained, frozen in a moment of terror as I looked at my husband's face.

And saw a monster staring back.

Ransom's teeth were bared, and his eyes were as silver as the moonbeams streaming through the windows. There wasn't a hint of awareness that he was growling at his wife.

"Ranse," I whispered, forcing calm into my voice even though my heart was racing. "Come back to me."

He blinked.

Silver morphed to hazel. Wrath became horror. Then my

wrists were freed and he put the expanse of the bedroom between us.

"Fuck." His hands dove into his hair, pulling at the strands.

"I'm okay." I crawled off the bed, rushing to him.

"Dess?" His throat bobbed as he swallowed. Then his shoulders curled inward and he dropped his face into his hands.

"I'm okay." I took hold of his wrists and tugged them down. "Look at me. I'm all right."

He scanned me, head to toe. Then he took my wrists in his hands, gently turning both over to make sure I wasn't lying. The regret in his eyes was a knife through the heart.

"You didn't hurt me. It was just a nightmare."

He closed his eyes, pulling me against his chest as he buried his face in my curls. "I'm sorry. I'm so fucking sorry."

"Don't be." I wrapped my arms around his waist and pressed my nose against his chest, breathing him in as I listened to his pounding heart.

It mingled with the sound of the rain pinging against the windows and the distant boom of thunder from tonight's storm.

"What was it? The dream?"

"I saw her coming for you," he murmured. "In Ellder. She was flying so fast, and I couldn't get there in time. I couldn't save you from her."

I held him tighter.

This wasn't just about a nightmare. It was the Lyssa. The dark veins stretched farther away from his heart than ever, some reaching down to tickle his ribs.

His control was slipping, little by little. How much longer did we have until he lost his grip entirely?

"I can't..." He shook his head, letting me go. He paced the room, dragging a hand over his beard. "I'll sleep on the couch."

"No." I walked to the door, crossing my arms over my chest.

"Dess, I won't put you in danger."

"Don't go. Please." I went to him, putting my hands on his hips. "Stay together, remember?"

He sighed, framing my face. His eyes searched mine, and I knew there was nothing I could say that would change his mind. So I didn't bother talking.

I slid a hand behind his neck and lifted onto my toes, pulling him down for a kiss.

My mouth moved over his, a sweep from corner to corner as Ransom stood motionless, his body locked. Only when I licked the seam of his lips did he finally give in.

Whatever control I'd had vanished as he slanted his mouth over mine, holding me in place as our tongues tangled.

There was a fierce edge to the kiss and the grip of his hands as he picked me up and carried me to bed. He dragged my nightgown up the length of my legs and over my hips.

And then he made me forget everything but the feel of his body moving inside mine. The taste of his tongue and the rumble of his deep voice. He fucked me until I was exhausted, and when I curled into the warmth of his arms, the last thing I heard before falling asleep was a soft apology.

"I'm sorry, Dess."

"I love you, Ranse."

When I woke at dawn, his side of the bed was empty.

So was the couch.

Evie and I were sharing a quiet breakfast in the suite when the summons came.

"The king requests you join him in his study," the steward said. "Presently."

I sighed and scarfed down a piece of toast and sweet

persimmon jelly—a staple around this castle—then took Evie and Faze to the nursery to play with Arthalayus and Titus.

Meeting with Father was not on my agenda today. I had a husband to find. But my foolish, silly little heart held on to a sliver of hope that Father might actually want to see me.

I knew I'd likely be disappointed. But that foolish, silly little heart of mine didn't care.

The doors to the king's study were open when I arrived. I steeled my spine and stepped into the room.

Father cut an imposing figure behind his walnut desk, a quill in hand as he wrote on a piece of parchment. He didn't so much as glance up as he spoke. "I'll be with you in a moment."

A fire crackled in the stone hearth, its light melding with that from the lamps placed around the room. The walls were paneled in the same walnut wood as his desk. Portraits of his parents hung on one wall. The other appeared empty, but when I was a little girl, I'd snuck into his study to steal a mint candy from the jar he kept on his desk.

When I'd heard him approach, I'd hidden beneath the leather sofa in front of the fireplace. And I'd peeked out to see him open a panel to a secret compartment with a brass key.

The panel's door had blocked my view of whatever he kept hidden in the walls. Maybe I needed to try harder to find out.

There was a wall of windows at his back, but the teal curtains had been drawn today. They blocked out the light but not the sound of the drizzling rain.

I inched farther into the room, toward a table and a map spread on its surface. It was the same map Father and I had pored over the night before I left for Turah months ago.

The only preparation I'd had before I became his amateur spy was a single night. My wedding night.

He'd spent hours trying to cram as much information into

my mind as possible, from the information about Turah he'd gathered from professional spies to his theories of Allesaria's location.

The map was different today, with notations and lines across Calandra, not just Turah. There were *X*s in red. Lines drawn in blue. Circles in black.

He'd told me he needed to get into Allesaria. That there was something he wanted in the hidden city. But was that only part of his scheme? I'd thought his interest was just in Turah. But what if he had broader ambitions for the five kingdoms?

A chill raked down my spine as my attention snapped to Father's desk.

His gaze was waiting.

Shit. I walked away from the map toward his desk, clasping my hands behind my back so he wouldn't see them tremble. "You asked to see me?"

"Yes." He steepled his fingers beneath his chin. "There was an incident this morning in the stables with Prince Zavier."

"Ransom," I corrected.

He waved off the name. "He had an altercation with a guard who now has a broken arm."

"Well, then I'm sure it was in self-defense. Ransom doesn't go around breaking arms for sport."

"From the report I received, the guard made a few snide comments. For his disrespect, he'll be punished. But those punishments are for Captain Brix and General Hawksley to deliver. Not a Turan guest. He is your husband and a visiting prince, and as such, I will grant him some leeway. But there is only so much insolence I will tolerate, Odessa. Am I understood?"

I stayed quiet. He wasn't really looking for a reply. But at least now I knew where Ransom had gone.

He picked up his quill and went back to the letter he was writing. "You may go."

My foolish, silly little heart was a jackass for luring me here.

I turned to leave, angrier at myself than Father. But before I made it to the doors, he stopped me.

"Odessa."

"Yes?" I turned, feigning a smile.

His lip curled as he took in my sable pants and belted green shirt. "Stay away from Gable."

"No."

His jaw clenched. "That's not negotiable."

"Then you can tell me about my mother."

The room went so still, even the motes stopped floating in the air. "Leave."

I stood my ground, refusing to let him dismiss me again. "The High Priest asked me about her, and I didn't have an answer. I deserve to know who she was. If you're not going to tell me, then I'll find someone who will."

"Don't make the mistake of testing me."

"Don't make the mistake of threatening me." The words came so forcefully I couldn't have stopped them if I'd tried.

I'd never sounded more like Ransom in my life. Unwavering. Unafraid. Unbelievably fed up with the secrets in this castle.

"Why are there no portraits of her in the castle? Why is no one allowed to speak about her? Did she hurt you? Did she take a lover? Is that why you won't talk about her?"

"Enough, Odessa." He slammed his fist on the desk. Waves of fury radiated off his frame.

Months ago, that rage would have chased me from his study. But I was tired of being left in the dark. He could either tell me the truth or he could live knowing I'd make my own assumptions.

"I heard a rumor that you killed her. Did you?"

A wall came crashing down between us. The emotion in

his gaze vanished. The anger disappeared. There was nothing but empty silence.

He didn't deny my accusation. He lifted his quill, dipped it in an ink pot, and went back to work.

"What are you searching for in Allesaria? How will you stop the migrations? By killing the Voster?"

He kept writing, his voice cold and distant. "If I must."

"Even if it costs you your life?"

"It won't. You are dismissed."

Always dismissed. That wasn't anything new. "Why are my eyes gold? Why don't I have starbursts? Did my mother have gold eyes? Why can I feel Voster magic? Could she feel it, too?"

The quill clattered as it fell from his fingers. Father looked up, the color slowly draining from his face. "You can feel their magic."

"Yes." I crossed my arms over my chest.

"You never told me that."

"Well, I guess I learned how to keep secrets from the best. What does it mean?"

He stood, slowly, palms flat on his desk like he was using it to keep his balance. "It means you need to stay away from the Voster."

"That's not an answer."

But it was all the answer he was going to give.

Without a word, he rounded the desk. And since I wouldn't leave his study, Father walked out instead.

44

CASPIA

The hem of my dress was soaked with rain and ice. When I left the house this morning, my hair had been dry, but even though I wore a hooded cloak, the weather had seeped through the fabric.

My teeth chattered as I walked through the castle's grand foyer.

"Caspia Starling," a man called as he pushed off a pillar where he'd been leaning. Waiting.

I walked faster, eyes aimed forward.

This made the fourth sun in a row that he'd been waiting for me at the castle. *Twelvi'ot*. It took everything I had not to fling the insult his direction, but not only would he not understand the language, it would only earn me another feature in his paper.

I loathed this paperman.

It was the same man who'd given me a free copy of his trashy paper, throwing Andreas's family ties and betrothal in my face. His name was Chapman Leek. As ridiculous a man as the lies he printed each week.

According to Chapman's paper, I was a spy from Laine sent by the royal family to steal books from this castle, a brothel owner from Genesis looking to start a franchise in Roslo, or a pirate from Ozarth who'd lured Andreas into her bed so she could commandeer his family's fleet.

Did he know the meaning of accuracy?

"May I have a minute, Caspia? Can I call you Caspia?"

My lip curled as I kept walking.

He was undoubtedly here to ask me if Andreas and I were married. Chapman wasn't the first paperman to catch me on my way to the library, but he was the most obnoxious.

He fell into step at my side. "Are congratulations in order? I'd love to be the first to print the happy news."

There were rumors swirling around Roslo that Andreas had married the mysterious Caspia Starling, but we had yet to make an announcement. I certainly wasn't telling him or any other paperman first.

Andreas's parents didn't even know yet.

The ceremony had taken place the morning after Andreas asked me to become his wife. We'd gone to the sanctuary in this very castle and been married without witness by a cleric who'd promised his discretion.

Andreas had cemented that promise with a sizeable donation of gold.

Riches clearly wasted on a cleric who couldn't keep his mouth shut.

But Andreas had warned me our secret wouldn't last long. It was only a matter of time before someone discovered the marriage scroll tucked away in the sanctuary's archives.

If Chapman wanted to print the truth for a change, he could go down to those dark, dank archives and do some damn research.

"Are you taking another trip to the library? That's five just this week."

"I do like to read."

"What are you reading?"

I lifted a shoulder, walking even faster. "Whatever strikes my fancy."

He jogged past me, spinning to walk backward so I could see his face. "Where did you say you were from?"

"I didn't," I snapped, stepping around him as I kept marching. "Good day, sir."

"So formal. My name is—"

"Unnecessary."

The guards stationed at the library saw me coming and opened the doors.

I breezed through them, knowing the guards wouldn't let Chapman follow. No papermen allowed.

King Cross was onto something with that royal decree.

As the doors were pulled closed behind me, I exhaled, finally able to breathe. I stripped off my wet cloak, then draped it over my arm and walked across the atrium.

Faxon was in the alcove, crouched beside the hearth, adding a log to the fireplace. "Lady Caspia."

"Hello, Faxon. How are you?"

"Cold." He stood, wiping the dust from his hands. "This storm feels infinite."

"It sure does." I hung my cloak on a hook to dry, then walked to the fire, holding my hands toward the warm flames.

"Here are the books you requested yesterday." Faxon nodded to the stack on the table. "I hauled up a crate with a few others. If I find anything of interest, I'll bring it in."

As much as I wanted to start searching for clues that my mother had come to Calandra, I had no idea where to start. Neither did Andreas.

Crux sightings in the past twenty-five summers? Death records from the city's crematorium noting a woman with no name and curly red hair?

Aunt Oleana had told me my mother was a dreamer. I had a feeling her dreams were visions, like mine. Did I put an advertisement in with the papermen asking for any and all information about Calandran seers?

Until we had a better idea of how to narrow down that search, I'd keep scouring books on Calandran history and magic, searching for a way to free Xandra from this curse.

"I've also brought you a gift." He picked up a

package—judging by the shape, a book—wrapped in brown paper and tied with a satin ribbon.

I smiled and unwrapped the present, revealing a familiar cover and tattered pages.

Sonnet's Ninety. A book I'd read more than any other since coming to Quentis. "Faxon. Thank you."

"You, my dear, are welcome. I know you love it. Now it's yours."

"But this is the library's copy. Will you get in trouble for giving it to me?"

"That copy was from my own personal collection. I lent it to the library. They've borrowed it long enough. That book was meant to be yours."

I hugged it to my chest as I kissed his cheek. "I love it. Thank you."

Faxon blushed, then clapped his hands. "Now, I shall leave you to your reading. I'll be back in a bit to check on the fire."

I smoothed a hand over the book's spine as he passed, about to disappear from the alcove. "Faxon?"

"Yes?" He turned.

"Have you ever wondered if the tales in this book were real?" I asked. "If they were more than mere stories?"

"What do you mean?" He came closer, his smile fading.

"What if Sonnet did not whisper these tales to the crux? What if he wrote them during a migration to tell Calandra's history? What if he disguised the past in these tales?" I flipped the book open to a story I'd read more times than any other. "'The Ancient Battle.'" I cleared my throat, then continued.

...

There was once a great battle between the Six and an evil pythoness. She fought with a legion of female warriors more powerful than any amassed in Calandra.

The prophecies given to her by the darkness gave her an unnatural advantage in the war. And even though the Six were gods with immense power of their own, against thousands, they were outnumbered. The battle raged from one summer solstice to another. Until finally, on a field soaked in blood, in a moment of desperation, while his siblings were being chained and burned, Mack took up his broadsword and struck down the pythoness, cutting off her head.

Though the battle was won, the Six were forever changed. Their bodies broken, they chose to retreat to the shades, taking up their place between Ama and Oda in the stars.

...

Faxon hummed. "It has been a long time since I've read *Sonnet's Ninety*. I must confess that I forgot that bit of folklore."

I didn't think it was folklore. I had no evidence, no proof, other than this feeling about that story. That this book was more than it seemed.

"Why can't I find a history of Calandra before the five kingdoms?" I asked.

"I don't know that it exists."

"Don't you find that strange?" There was a stack of books on the table that proved Calandrans, at least Quentins, were meticulous with their recordkeeping. "I read that the first king of Quentis was named Magnus Cross. I wanted to trace his lineage, but I can't find anything before the first migration. Three hundred summers is a long time, but it's not ancient. When did Magnus rule? Was there a king before him?"

"I don't know. The migrations are incredibly destructive. It's quite likely that any history from before that time has been destroyed or lost."

"Or erased."

Faxon blinked, stunned momentarily, before he glanced over his shoulder, checking to ensure we were alone. "What are you saying, Lady Caspia?"

"I don't know."

I'd spent so much time in this library, flipping through tomes and texts. So far, I had yet to come across any mention of the Starling or the continent of Kenn. Not entirely surprising.

But it was the lack of Calandran history that made me wonder. Other than a single mention of Magnus Cross, any written history began with the first migration, caused by my ancestor three hundred summers ago.

With every passing sun, I was beginning to feel that the lack of information was intentional.

"I just find it odd that—" My words were cut short as a prickle of energy shot up my forearms.

The sensation spread so fast I gasped, backing away from the alcove's open entrance. But there was no escaping the spike of pain that zinged through my body as a Voster walked into the room.

Faxon shifted in front of me, but his body could do nothing to block the waves of energy that rippled off the Voster's frame.

The priest was not dressed in the same burgundy robes as Brother Nold. He wore pale blue that only accentuated the colorless shade of his skin. He stood at the entrance to the alcove, hands clasped behind his back, staring at me with those dark-green eyes.

My heart climbed into my throat as I waited for him to speak.

But the Voster did nothing. He simply stared.

He looked similar to Brother Nold, yet there was a difference in his magic. It felt sharper. Stronger.

"Can we help you, Brother?" Faxon asked, still standing in front of me.

The Voster pursed his lips, then brought a book out from behind his figure. He crossed the alcove and walked straight into Faxon's space, forcing the librarian aside.

All so he could stand in front of me.

I winced at the harsh bite of his magic, taking a step backward.

The Voster cocked his head to the side.

Then, in a blink, the pain was gone.

My body sagged. The breath I'd been holding rushed from my lungs. I swallowed the lump in my throat and met the priest's gaze.

His jaw was clenched, and there was a tightness around his eyes, like my pain was now his.

He tossed me the book. It hit me square in the chest before I caught it. Then he held up a single pointed finger with a gnarly, grooved nail, pressing it against his puckered lips.

I gulped.

Without a word, he spun and left, his robes swirling around his ankles and bare feet as he breezed out of the alcove.

The prickle returned a moment later, uncomfortable yet bearable. And then it was gone along with the Voster.

"Are you all right?" Faxon asked, his hand coming to my elbow.

"Who was that?"

He shook his head. "I don't know. I've never seen him before."

I looked to the book and the dingy, gray leather. The corners were worn and bent. The spine was cracked. The pages were more yellow than white and frayed at the edges.

"What do you know of their magic?" I asked Faxon.

"Little. The brotherhood is incredibly secretive. We know they can manipulate fluids. They seal treaties signed in blood with their magic. Every king in Calandra has sworn at least one blood oath on the Shield of Sparrows treaty. But as far as the inner workings of the brotherhood, you won't find anything in this library about them. Trust me, I've looked."

I made a mental note to read about the Shield of Sparrows treaty and any other blood oath on record.

"What happens if a king breaks a blood oath?"

"Death."

A shiver rolled down my spine.

I carried the book to the table and took a seat.

Faxon came to stand behind my chair, peering over my shoulder as I carefully peeled back the front cover.

The first page was blank. I touched the parchment, and a stab of pain shot up my arm to my elbow.

"Ah." I yanked my hand away as I hissed, giving the sting a moment to fade.

"Would you like me to touch it?" Faxon asked.

"No, I'll do it." I took a deep breath and turned the page, expecting another shock. But the energy was gone, and all I felt was the rough texture of the old, thick paper.

"The old language," Faxon murmured as he scanned the page. "Felvi'or thelvi'ee Stelvi'r-lelfing. Do you need me to interpret this for you?"

"No." My heart stopped. "I know what it says."

For the Starling.

45

ODESSA

My butt was going numb thanks to the hard, cold floor in the crux art gallery. I'd been sitting against the wall for hours, tucked beside a stone pillar with a bronze crux sculpture on top.

Luella's journal was open on my lap. My sketchbook was tucked beside my knee.

Father loathed my obsession with this gallery, and that seemed reason enough for me to spend more time here before we left Quentis.

There were a thousand places to read in this castle and all colossally more comfortable than this floor. But those places all had people. And after the meeting with Father in his study this morning, I simply wanted to be alone.

This empty, quiet hall gave me room to think. To lick my wounds in solitude. To read and reread this journal, cover to cover, from the story of the poisoned woman, to the man with a lionwick claw, to a warrior with white hair shedding her armor in a desert.

They were lovely, vivid stories that made absolutely no sense.

I closed the journal on a sigh, trading it for my sketchbook. Before I forgot the details of her face, I wanted to draw Freya. I wanted to capture her as she'd been before that awful day in the skeleton forest. As I flipped through the book for an empty page to give my horse, I paused on a drawing I'd done of Ransom.

He leaned against the railing of his treehouse in Treow, staring up at the shades and stars. His profile was an artist's dream, strong and balanced with sharp, clean lines. But there was an exhaustion to his features, a hollowness to his cheeks. I'd shaded dark circles beneath his eyes.

I'd drawn him exactly the way he'd looked that night after the tarkin attack in Treow.

The night after the High Priest had siphoned some of the Lyssa from Ransom's blood in the encampment's infirmary to lessen the effects of the infection. To keep it from taking my husband's life.

Ransom wouldn't break a guard's arm unless he was defending himself. I didn't care what Father said. He was wrong. The guard must have attacked Ransom first. But the leash on his temper was getting shorter. The Lyssa was taking control.

I traced the scar on my palm.

We needed the High Priest.

I flipped to the next page. It was a sketch of Faze not long after we rescued him from death. He was curled on my pillow, so tiny and new.

This book was nearly full with sketches of Treow and monsters. Of ships and mountains. Of friends, like Tillia and Samuel Hay, who we'd left behind. Of Luella, lost to the shades.

Maybe someday Ransom would want a drawing of his mother. He didn't talk about her, but when he was ready, I'd listen.

Each page was decorated with ornaments and patterns at their edges. They were seemingly random swirls and lines. But if they were aligned with the others, arranged in exactly the right way, it would show a map of Turah.

An incomplete map. The road to Allesaria was missing.

It wouldn't take much to finish. All I'd have to do was spread these pages across this cold, hard floor and add a series of lines leading to the Axmar Mountains.

I took the sketch of Faze from the book. But rather than lay it on the floor, I tore off the edges until all that remained was a drawing of a baby tarkin. Then I crumpled the torn strips into a ball, destined for the first fireplace I found.

Before I could move on to the next page, the sound of footsteps pulled my attention to the entrance as Margot walked into the gallery.

She grimaced as she took in the nearest painting, then turned her back to the artwork. Her gaze skated over me on the floor, then snapped back so fast it had to have hurt her neck. "Odessa?"

I gave her a finger wave and closed my sketchbook. "Hi."

"What are you doing in here and on the floor?"

"Reading." I didn't bother getting up. Moving meant she would win by scaring me out of my hiding place.

And my mantra from yesterday was still firmly locked in place.

Margot wasn't going to win.

She took in my unbound curls and pants and scuffed boots. Her frown of disapproval was as familiar as the back of my hand. "You've changed."

"No, I haven't. This is who I've always been. You just didn't want to see me."

Margot pondered that for a moment. Then the disapproval vanished and her eyes softened. She almost looked proud. Almost. "You *have* changed. It's his influence."

"Yes, it is. He makes me better. Stronger. Braver. Happier. He doesn't ask me to blend into the walls or change the color of my hair. He sees me for me." Something she never did.

I expected a pointed, exasperated retort. Instead, she wrapped her arms around her waist and studied the floor.

When she finally looked up, there was an apology on her face. Maybe someday, she'd speak it, too.

Margot spun in a slow circle. "I hate it in here."

"Then why are you here?"

"These paintings serve their purpose. They're a reminder of what is to come." She walked closer and reached for the statue on top of the pillar at my side, stroking the crux's metal beak. "My father was a sailor who drowned in the Krisenth when I was young. His ship went down in a storm. My mother raised me on her own after he died."

I sat straighter, glued to her every word. Never, in twenty-three years, had Margot spoken of her family.

"Mother took a job in the castle as a washerwoman to afford our life. She insisted I go to school so that I'd have better prospects to marry a wealthy man. She worked long hours, which meant I spent long hours alone. Our little home was my palace. I learned to clean. To cook. To order around my imaginary friends. When the migration came, we were assigned to share a chamber with a family of five. One of the children, a little boy, took sick two weeks into the migration. The healers came and locked our door, not wanting his illness to spread through the rest of the tunnels."

I'd heard a story like this before. Luella's story, of how her family had taken ill while they were in a shelter during the last migration. How they'd all died before it was over.

It was the reason she'd created the elixir. So that her children would be strong enough to survive.

"When I got sick, I begged Mother to take me home," Margot said. "I wanted to be back in our house, in my own castle, where I could die in peace. I was fourteen. I knew I wouldn't survive in that chamber. Mother pounded on the door until her fists bled. The healers let us out with the understanding that we wouldn't stay. And so she led me from the castle and into the open."

Margot took hold of the statue's wing tip, her knuckles turning white like she was trying to break it apart. "I've never heard a quiet like the one that greeted us when we left the castle. The streets were filled with rubble and wreckage. Every other house was destroyed. They said Quentis received the brunt of the migration that year, but as we walked, the skies were clear. And by some miracle, our house was standing."

"Did they come back? The crux?"

"No." She released her grip on the statue. "We walked in the door and startled a looter. He hit my mother so hard, she never woke up."

I gasped, my hand coming to my heart.

She dabbed at the corner of her eye, then smoothed her skirts, lengthening her spine and raising her chin. "The migration brings out the worst in people. It's an unfortunate reality of what we're about to face."

"Father says he can stop it."

"Only if you can convince your husband to show him the way into Allesaria."

The ball of crumpled paper felt like a lead weight in my hand. "Ransom is bound by a blood oath."

She swept a hand toward the artwork. "Then I guess we're doomed."

Not if Father shared his secrets. I kept that to myself, because she might know his plans, but Margot would never betray Father.

"I'm so sorry about your mother," I said.

"I took her place in the castle's washroom. Did you know that? The sickness passed, and once the migration was over, I went to work in her stead until I was promoted to a lady's maid."

"And now you're a queen."

"Lucky me." Sarcasm dripped from her tone. "Married to a man in love with a ghost."

I'd heard ladies at parties whisper the same, but this was the first time my stepmother had admitted it to me. "Why won't he tell me about my mother?"

Margot hesitated long enough I was sure she'd leave. But

then she lowered her voice and gave me a sad smile. "When she died, she took a piece of his soul to the shades. He does what he must to simply keep living when his heart is no longer in this realm. It's not meant to hurt you. It's because *he* hurts so much. You are a reminder of what he's lost."

I dropped my gaze to my lap. "Is that why you had a maid leave hair dye in my bathing chamber?"

She shrugged. "You have her hair."

I wasn't going to dye my hair again, but I wasn't as angry at Margot as I had been earlier. "Okay."

Her gaze swept around the room once more, her mouth flattening. "There are more suitable places to read in this castle. Why don't you try the library?"

There were people in the library.

Before I could reply, footsteps came from the hall. "Sorry I'm late, darling."

Margot tensed, and fear filled her blue eyes. The skirts of her dress made it impossible for me to see who'd come into the gallery, but that was not my father's voice.

She backed away from the pillar, clearing her throat. "General Hawksley."

His eyebrows came together, and then he spotted me on the floor. He schooled his expression instantly and bowed. "Majesty. I apologize. I thought you were someone else."

Someone else who wore a crown in her blond hair? Sure.

Now it made sense why Margot would come to a gallery she hated. She, like me, needed a place to be alone.

Hawksley wasn't a king. He wasn't nearly as striking as Father, but he was handsome with a rugged edge. I could see why Margot might find him attractive. I could see why she'd risk this gallery for the chance to be alone with a man who called her "darling."

My father certainly didn't.

"Princess. Please forgive my intrusion." Hawksley bowed again, then, without a glance to Margot, left the gallery.

I collected my books and stood, shaking out the numbness in my legs.

"Odessa." She held out a hand, stopping me before I could leave. "I…"

"Don't worry. I won't say anything."

Margot let her arm fall to her side. "Thank you."

"The secrets in this family will be our undoing."

She met my gaze. "Or our salvation."

46

CASPIA

The king of Quentis sits at the head of a table long enough to seat one hundred nobles. Floral arrangements infuse the air with a sweet fragrance. Golden utensils, crystal flutes, and glass goblets crowd polished stone plates. The guests all laugh and smile as the king shares a look of disapproval with his beautiful blond queen.

The noise in the dining hall is deafening, though not loud enough to hide the sound of Malynn's teeth grinding together from her seat across from mine.

"Wrong fork," she hisses, her nostrils flaring.

I return the wrong fork to the empty space beside my plate. There is a line of forks resting on a crisp, white linen napkin. They are exactly the same. Three tines, each etched with vines.

I'm not hungry enough to test another, so I tuck my hands beneath the table and stare at the floating bubbles in my glass of sparkling wine.

"Teach her, Andreas," Malynn snaps, loud enough that the people sitting around us stop talking to listen. "Before she embarrasses us all."

Andreas drapes an arm across the back of my chair.

And picks up his own wrong fork, stabbing it into the roasted hen on his plate as he glowers at his mother.

Malynn glowers back.

...

The fire roaring in the hearth made this parlor insufferably hot. Sweat beaded at my temples. My stomach growled. My throat was dry, my water glass empty. The light from the overhead chandelier was so bright that the pages of the book in my lap glowed. My headache had moved from manageable to miserable.

Or maybe it was simply the contents of this stupid book.

"Gah." I lifted the book off my lap, about to throw it across the room, but I reined in my temper and snapped it closed instead.

There were too many rules. Too many formalities. I rubbed my temples and closed my eyes. If I slept with this book under my pillow, would these customs sink into my mind so I wouldn't have to read another page?

"There you are." Andreas wore a scowl as he pushed through the parlor's glass-paned doors. "I have been looking for you for over an hour. I was getting worried."

"Sorry." I sighed as he dropped to his knees in front of my chair.

"Why aren't you in the library? Is everything all right?"

"I just needed a change of scenery." In truth, his mother had been in the library when I arrived this morning. I'd been ignoring Malynn's invitations to join her and her ladies for their afternoon tea. Rather than take the hint that I was not interested in the life of a noblewoman, she'd been waiting for me in my favorite library alcove.

Her invitation was an order.

I defied it anyway.

But since I wouldn't put it past her to have the guards escort me to tea when it was time, I'd snuck off to this tiny parlor in a quiet wing of the castle.

Andreas lifted the book off my lap and read the title embossed on the cover. "*Quentin Etiquette*."

Faxon had brought it to me this morning when I'd asked for a book about Quentin decorum, specifically a book for royal dinners.

The vision I'd had last moon of me embarrassing Andreas at that party was the clearest I'd had in weeks. At least it wasn't about death, but it had still put me in a rotten mood.

We were going to a gala in three suns. As much as I'd rather be reading anything else, I didn't want to widen the rift already growing between him and his family.

"I don't want to humiliate you by using the wrong fork," I admitted.

His eyes softened. "I don't give a damn what fork you use as long as you eat and stay healthy."

"But other people care. And they'll be watching."

"Yes, they will." He lifted my hand, kissing my knuckles. "I don't care about any of this."

"But they do," I whispered. "It probably won't kill me to read a book about etiquette."

"Probably not." He chuckled and stood, taking the book to the fireplace. With a flick of his wrist, he tossed it into the flames.

"Andreas." I shot to my feet, but the book was already ablaze. "You get to explain that missing book to Faxon."

"With pleasure, my heart."

As Andreas had predicted, it hadn't taken long for Roslo to learn of our marriage. The dinner and party invitations arrived nonstop. There was yet to be a sun that went by without a sketch of his face or mine in a paper subscription.

Chapman Leek was still a *twelvi'ot*, spreading lies about my background and identity. His competitors were nearly as bad. I was an enigma and therefore the enemy. Most portrayed me as a foreigner with no wealth or status who must have tricked Andreas into this union, because why else would he want me?

"When I was a Nestling, I was the favorite among our tutors," I told Andreas, slumping into the chair. "I was the girl who always behaved. Who never missed an assignment or failed a test. I followed every rule. I was everyone's friend."

"Why does this not surprise me?" He grinned, leaning against a wall and tucking a hand into his pocket.

"It feels like I'm failing." I looked to my hands clasped in my lap, to the rings gleaming on each finger.

"You're not." He pushed off the wall, once more crouching in front of me. He laced his fingers with mine, waiting until I met his gaze. "When I was a boy, I hated being trapped in a carrel."

"I don't know that word."

"A study space with a desk." He tucked a curl behind my ear and cupped my cheek. "Just ask Faxon. I made everything more difficult than it needed to be. If someone told me to do something, my immediate response was *why*. I didn't care if I failed. I was usually the student making jokes and disrupting the class. You would have hated me."

I smiled. "Definitely."

"I grew out of it eventually. Stopped fighting those who were just trying to help me."

"Are you saying I need to learn etiquette?"

"No. I'm saying you don't have to learn it alone. You have me. Always."

I sighed, leaning into his touch. "When we go to this dinner, I need you to tell me which forks to use."

"Done." With a kiss on the tip of my nose, he stood, pulling me to my feet.

I gathered the other book I'd brought with me to the parlor. The Voster's gray book, one I rarely let out of my sight.

"Any progress?" Andreas asked as I tucked it under an arm.

"No." I'd read it three times since the no-name Voster priest gave it to me, hoping with each turn of a page that something would click into place. So far, nothing. I was nearly as frustrated with it as I was the etiquette book. "I started it again today but couldn't concentrate."

"Come on. I have an idea." With my hand in his, he led me from the parlor and through the castle.

The halls were crowded. People gawked as we passed—the stares and whispers, the relentless looks of disapproval, were grating on my nerves. It was probably a good thing I didn't carry weapons regularly.

The library's atrium was empty when we walked through the doors, and the sigh I breathed was loud enough to echo off the ornate ceiling.

Faxon's desk was empty, so we continued through the stacks, looking down each row, until finally we found him with Kos.

The boy was pushing a cart behind the bibliosoph as he shelved books.

"What does eco-monic princips mean?" Kos asked, handing Faxon a book.

"Economic principles," Faxon corrected. "That means the study of commerce. Of supply and demand. Of behaviors that drive the consumption of goods."

Kos scrunched up his nose. "Sounds boring."

"It is, my son." Faxon laughed. "At least to me. What's next?"

Kos picked up another book, this one a bright purple. "Flowers. Also boring."

"Not to gardeners."

"I don't wanna be a gardener."

"And what do you want to be?" I asked Kos as we joined them.

"An explorer," Kos answered without hesitation. "Or a librarian."

The proud smile on Faxon's face was blinding.

"Good answer." Andreas ruffled Kos's hair and winked. "I bet that earns you a sweet tart from the kitchens later."

Kos giggled.

"I'm sure we can visit the cooks later," Faxon said. "But only after you finish your lessons. Off you go. Back to your carrel. Work on your assignment. I'll be over shortly."

As Kos ran off to continue his studies, Faxon pushed the cart aside. "I thought you left for the day, Lady Caspia. How was the book on etiquette?"

"Andreas burned it."

My husband only shrugged when Faxon gave him an admonishing look. "Had to be done. It was as dull as economics."

"I can't argue with that," Faxon said. "Can I help you with something?"

"I don't suppose you have a tutor's carrel available at the moment?" Andreas asked. "It seems my mother has discovered Caspia's alcove, so it's time to find a new hiding spot."

Was it childish to hide from his mother? Yes. But I was absolutely going to hide.

"Andreas, those carrels are cramped and drab. They're for tutors. They're not befitting a lady."

"Humor me. Please."

With a frown, Faxon waved for us to follow him. We weaved through the library, past the desks where young students, like Kos, were hunched over texts and books as they studied.

Several of the other librarians and teachers milled around this section of the library, instructing students. Most gave slight bows as Faxon, Andreas, and I passed their stations. Then we arrived at a row of ten doors.

Faxon fished out a ring of metal keys, flipping through them as he stopped in front of the last in the row. He fitted the key into the lock and opened the door to a narrow space the size of a pantry or closet. He lit the lanterns on the wall, giving them a moment to illuminate the carrel.

I walked inside, skimming my fingers over the wooden desk and the thin sheen of dust on its surface. It was cold and dark. There were no windows, and the chair looked stiff. But it had a door with a lock. "It's perfect."

"Then it's yours. I'll leave you to it." Faxon unfastened the key from the ring and placed it in my palm.

The metal warmed and clinked with my elfalter rings as he left us alone.

I rounded the desk and took a seat in the chair. Stiff. But the wood was smooth, the back comfortable against my shoulders.

A space this cramped, a room that felt like a cage, would normally have me coming out of my skin. But I'd adjust.

Andreas leaned against the doorframe. "I will find you something better. And I will talk with my mother."

"I like this little carrel. And don't talk to your mother. It will only make it worse."

"But—"

"Please?" This was not his battle to fight. In truth, there was no battle here.

My aunt expected everyone in our family to represent our bloodline, whether we were Nestling or Quiescent or Starling. It wasn't unreasonable for Malynn to expect the same from me now that I was married to Andreas.

"Fine," Andreas grumbled. "I'll stay quiet. For now."

I set my book on the desk and ran a finger along its gray spine. "I need to speak to the Voster who gave me this book."

"No."

I laughed. "Yes."

"Caspia."

"Andreas."

He frowned.

I smiled. Each sun, he became more and more protective. It was oddly attractive. "Is there a way to send the brotherhood a message? Maybe through the king's emissary? There is something important in these pages, Andreas. Something I must understand. Maybe a way to save Xandra."

He sighed. "What if it's only a story?"

"What if it's not?"

My third read of the book had been out loud to Andreas. He was as perplexed as I was with the story.

This book was an account of evil magicians and read like a novel. If not for the mention of Starling at the beginning, if not for the Voster giving it to me, I would have thought it was fiction. At first glance, it seemed as if it could have been Sonnet's ninety-first tale.

But it was so detailed, so descriptive, it felt like a history.

The magicians had once been ordinary men of a religion that worshiped Calandran spirits. They lived in a monastery deep in the mountains. One harsh winter, the men found themselves without food. They were near starving and on the brink of death. They prayed to their spirits, begging for help and to spare their lives.

By the time the ice melted, nearly every man at the monastery was dead.

All but six.

Feeling forsaken by their spirits, the men began worshiping demons who reveled in lost and angry souls. And the remaining six men made those demons a bargain.

For magic and immortality, they offered their bodies as hosts.

Possessed by these demons, the men became magicians. They fooled people into believing their power was a blessed gift to save humanity. They were worshiped and revered.

Until all of Calandra bowed at their feet.

"There has to be something significant with the number six," I said, my voice low. "It can't be a coincidence."

Andreas lifted his hand like he was about to sign the Eight, but he changed his mind at the last moment, raking his fingers through his hair instead. "This feels dangerous, Caspia."

I opened the book. "The truth usually is."

47

ODESSA

With every step we took toward Healer Alore's workshop, more muscles in Ransom's body bunched and tensed. His shoulders had practically crept to his ears.

The message I'd received from Healer Alore this morning over breakfast was short and succinct.

My workshop. Midmorning. Bring him along.

The last place he wanted to be was this infirmary, but I'd asked him to come, and he was humoring me at the moment.

When he'd finally returned to the suite last night, well after dark, he'd been quiet and withdrawn, forcing smiles for Evie's benefit. After we tucked her into bed, I asked him about the guard in the stables.

The man had been whipping a mare so violently that the animal had been on her knees, bloody and beaten. Her entire backside had been flayed with gashes.

Ransom went to stop the assault, and the guard, in a frenzy, turned the whip on him instead of the horse. The broken arm was the guard's consequence.

I didn't feel sorry for the bastard at all.

After the son of a bitch was taken to the infirmary, Ransom took Aurinda for a long ride in the countryside. When he returned to the stables, the mare the guard was whipping had been put down.

It was probably a good thing the guard had already been released from the infirmary. I might have stopped by his room and slipped a small dose of fenek tusk powder in his tea. Not that I had fenek tusk powder, but that man deserved a little taste of poison. Not enough to kill him, but enough to make him reconsider every choice he'd ever made.

At this point, I was angrier than Ransom. Mostly because my father had jumped to the wrong conclusion and had the gall to blame my husband.

"Dess." Ransom took my wrist in a hand, giving it a gentle shake so I'd unclench my fists.

So maybe we were both a little tense this morning.

We reached the end of the hallway and Alore's arched door. I tapped the knocker twice, and the same man who greeted me the other day opened the door, waving us inside.

Alore was at her workshop table wearing a maroon frock and canvas apron with countless stains. She had five different-colored pairs of spectacles tucked in various pockets. A set with a white frame sat perched on the tip of her nose. A blue pair was on top of her head.

Her gaze shot straight to Ransom as we walked into the room. "Good. You're here. Sit. Tea?"

"No." He took the one and only stool beside the table.

Alore came to stand in front of him, planting her hands on her hips as she studied his eyes. Silver, like they had been since yesterday.

He hadn't worn his circlet since the nightmare when he pinned my wrists to the headboard.

"This elixir of your mother's, I believe I've managed to recreate it," Alore said. "There's no way to know for certain, but I think I'm close based on the notes in her book."

My mouth fell open. "You've already created the elixir?"

"Don't give me too much credit," she said. "The notes were impeccable once I figured out how to interpret them. We were lucky I had most of the ingredients, and a quick dash to the docks is where I found the rest. But the elixir is the easy part. Now I've got to try to recreate the infection."

"What? No. I said you could research a cure, but we're not recreating the infection." Ransom moved to stand, but Alore planted a firm hand on his shoulder, pushing him back to a seat.

"Odessa told me about your father. Please trust me when I say that I have no intention of weaponizing this infection and giving it to others. Any notes I take in creating Lyssa will be destroyed. You have my word. But I can't make a cure if I can't replicate the infection. I need to start at the beginning."

Ransom's jaw clenched.

Alore rolled her eyes, entirely unfazed. She snatched a glass tube from her table and handed it to him. "Spit. All the way to the top."

He arched an eyebrow. "Spit?"

"You were bitten, yes?"

"Yes," he grumbled.

"And Lyssa seems to travel by bite, yes? I'm getting nowhere with your blood. So let's try your saliva. Spit."

He growled but tipped the tube to his lips.

She crossed her arms over her chest as she looked between the two of us. "You two are intimate, yes?"

My cheeks flushed. "We're married."

"That doesn't always mean anything." She arched an eyebrow at Ransom. "I assume you're not biting her."

Ransom answered that one with a glare.

"Good. Don't. I believe the infection has manifested differently in you than it does monsters, but let's not risk the princess, all right?"

Ranse and I shared a look. Then he kept on spitting.

"Your mother believed the elixir in your blood mingled with the bariwolf's saliva from the bite, thereby creating Lyssa." Alore began to pace the length of the small room. "It's a solid theory. There are many elements about monsters we don't understand and a magic to their bodies."

Alore swept up a book from the table, one of Luella's journals, and traded out the white glasses on her nose for the blue pair tucked into her hair. "She wrote here that the elixir was the fundamental magic for Lyssa and the bariwolf's saliva was the missing piece. She believed a bond formed when the monster attacked. The Lyssa then morphed into one version for the wolf and another for you. Well, I'm doing a few tests. Forgive me, but I borrowed your tarkin from the nursery yesterday."

"Faze?"

"I needed monster saliva to mix with the elixir. Don't worry, he was unharmed." She set the book down, then breezed into the adjacent room, returning a moment later with a small metal cage full of gray rats with pink ears.

"You're giving them Lyssa," Ransom said.

"That's what we're going to test." Alore snatched the tube from his hand and put it in a wire holder. There were already two vials in the tray, one labeled with her name, the other with *tarkin*. "If Luella's theory is correct, the one injected with both the elixir and the tarkin's saliva will develop Lyssa. My saliva won't do a thing. Yours is the question mark."

"And then you'll find a cure?" I asked.

Alore braced her hands on the table. "I'm going to try."

It was more hope than I'd felt in days.

Ransom stood, not waiting to be dismissed as he left the workshop.

"Thank you," I told her.

She watched him stalk out of the room. Then she gave me a single nod and got back to work.

By the time I left to catch up to him in the hallway, he was already gone.

The training center was swarming with people. The center of the room was taken by a dozen sparring guards, and a small troop of legionnaires was practicing archery at the indoor range, escaping the rain outside.

Gable was working with a young boy with black hair, teaching the child how to punch an invisible opponent. His gaze lifted as I walked inside. He gave me the slightest of headshakes and went back to instructing the boy.

My father must have known I'd ignore his order to stay away from the weapons master and in turn made sure that the weapons master would stay away from me.

I swallowed the disappointment and lifted onto my toes, searching past the soldiers in the hope of finding Ransom.

Instead, I saw my sister. Her training partner for today made my blood run cold.

Evie held a dagger in her fist as she stared up at Mae. She nodded intently at whatever my sister was saying.

Maybe if Mae hadn't been so snide and secretive since our return, my stomach wouldn't have dropped at the sight of them together. But then I saw Faze.

He was chained to the wall, struggling against a metal collar much too small that was clamped around his throat.

A jolt of icy panic ran through my veins as Mae unsheathed her own dagger and shifted into a fighting stance.

Children trained with wooden knives and swords, not sharpened blades. What the fuck was Mae thinking? When she was younger, she'd arrive at meals with more than one cut on her arm. But real lessons with real weapons hadn't started until she was bigger, twice Evie's age.

I took off running, pushing past soldiers as they blocked my view.

A man's shoulder slammed into me, nearly knocking me over. "Watch out."

I caught my balance and kept moving, eyes locked on Evie as Mae sliced her knife through the air.

"Stop," I called.

Either Mae didn't hear my shout over the commotion in the room or she ignored me.

Evie backed away and to the side, dodging my sister's blade.

When Mae's blue eyes flicked to me, her smile was full of spite. She slashed, and the tip of her knife cut a long gash into Evie's shirt.

Her favorite nightshirt. The shirt from Ellder. She'd asked to wear it again today.

Evie froze. Horror etched on her face as she took in her ruined sleeve. Then her cheeks flushed a furious red as her grip on the dagger tightened, her knuckles turning white. She lunged for Mae, knife raised above her head.

I swooped her off her feet, pulling her away as she kicked and squirmed. "Calm down, little star."

"She wrecked my shirt!" She screamed so loud the sound filled the cavernous room.

Every soldier fighting came to a stop.

Evie let loose another furious scream before she dissolved into tears, folding forward as the dagger slipped from her hand and clattered on the floor. She twisted in my arms, burying her face in my neck as she sobbed.

"We'll stitch it." I stroked her hair, wishing I could tell her Zavier was on his way. That her father was alive and this shirt didn't matter.

But not yet. Not until I saw Zavier alive with my own eyes.

"What the hell, Mae?" I glared at my sister.

She shrugged. "Oh, I'll buy her a new one. It's just a shirt."

"Not to her." I held out my hand and snapped my fingers. "Give me the key to that collar on Faze. Now."

Mae flipped her hair over a shoulder, then pulled it from her pocket, dropping it into my palm. "He chewed through the rope leash."

"Then find another one."

"So touchy these days. I liked you better when your hair was brown."

"You liked me better when I let you get your way." *The spoiled brat.*

I marched to Faze and dropped to a knee, shifting Evie down. "Can you unlock Faze for me?"

She dried her eyes with her hands, then took the key.

I surged to my feet and whirled on Mae. "You had no right to bring her here."

"Arthy comes nearly every day. I thought she might like it, too."

As much as I loved Nathalia, she shouldn't have let Evie go with Mae. But our nursemaid still had a soft spot for Mae. A soft spot that my sister exploited.

Mae walked to a nearby bench and picked up two swords. She tossed one over. "Was it all just a show?"

"Was what a show?"

"That little performance with the Guardian." She took two quick steps, the sword slicing through the air.

I backed away. "What are you doing?"

"You just stole my training partner." Her gaze darted to Evie. "You can at least take her place."

"No." I scowled. "We're done here."

"Come on. Indulge me." Her blade swung much too close to my face.

I kept my attention on Mae but felt the eyes of every person in this room. "I don't understand why you're doing this."

"No, you don't understand." She held the blade up, pointing the tip at my nose. The haughty, conceited lilt in her voice became hollow and cold. "You never will."

This was not my sister. Something had happened while I'd been gone. Something had changed.

"Mae, what's wrong?"

Before she could answer, the sword was ripped from her hold, Ransom's grip bruising as he yanked it from her hands.

She hissed in pain as he threw the weapon on the floor. Then he stood between us, staring at Mae with an icy fury that sent her back three steps.

But her fear flipped in a blink, shifting to white-hot rage. Quicker than I'd ever seen her move, she took a small knife hidden up her sleeve and threw it at Ransom.

Time slowed, and for a moment, I was back in Ellder, watching Banner throw a knife into Zavier's stomach. I heard Evie's scream from that horrible night. It mingled with her scream in the training center.

Except Mae's knife never hit its mark.

Ransom caught it in midair, spinning it back at her with a flick of his wrist.

Her hair rustled in its wake as the blade flew past her shoulder, embedding itself into the wall.

A collective inhale echoed in the room. Then silence.

"Dismissed." Gable's voice boomed.

The center emptied like a cup of spilled tea.

Even the weapons master slipped away, taking the boy he'd been training through a side door, leaving us alone.

A tear dripped down Mae's cheek.

I couldn't remember the last time I saw her cry.

"I was supposed to be the Sparrow. I should have been the one to leave," she whispered, then fisted her skirts and ran.

"Mae," I called after her, but she was already out the door.

What the hell had happened here while I was gone?

"Take Evie out of here." Ransom's order was almost a growl.

"Ranse—"

"Now, Odessa." He swallowed hard, his hands fisting. His entire body vibrated with rage. "I don't trust myself right now."

He didn't. But I did.

I closed the gap between us, taking his hand and prying his fist apart. Then I flattened the scar on my palm against the scar on his. "I trust you."

He closed his eyes and swallowed hard. "Go, Dess."

Evie sniffled, clutching Faze as she walked over. She peered up at us through tear-soaked lashes. Her little fingers folded around Ransom's other fist.

His shoulders relaxed. His eyes opened. Still silver but not as angry. He stared down at her mouth, pulled into a pout. And then he crashed to a knee and hauled her into his arms. "Are you okay?"

"I wanna go home." She sniffled.

"Me too," Ransom and I murmured in unison.

He reached for me, tugging me down and drawing me into their embrace. "Together."

"Together." I buried my face in Ransom's shoulder, breathing him in.

We held on to each other, even as Faze squirmed to be set free. As the tarkin bounded away, I tracked him through the empty center until movement beyond the doorway drew my focus.

Whoever was watching us was quick to duck away.

But I could have sworn I saw the glint of my father's golden crown.

48

CASPIA

A faint prickle stole my attention from the journal on my desk.

The hairs on my arms stood on end, and the thoughts I'd been recording were forgotten as I stared at the carrel's closed door. I held my breath, the beats of my heart measuring every passing moment until the knock came.

"Come in." My voice was thick, my throat clogged with nerves.

The knob turned, and the door opened slowly to reveal a swish of pale blue robes.

The Voster who'd brought me the gray book eased into the room, closing the door behind him.

It should have been excruciating, having him this close. My carrel was by no means spacious.

But as he took the chair opposite my desk, all I felt was a steady push of his magic, like my clothes were too heavy, the fabric coarse and itchy. It wasn't exactly comfortable, but I didn't hurt.

"Hello," I said.

He folded his hands on his lap. "Hello, Starling."

I'd prayed to the Divine that he'd return. That I could ask him a string of questions. Yet now that he was here, I couldn't think of anything to say but hello.

We stared at each other, the silence in the tiny room growing and pushing at the walls.

Faxon must have told the Voster where I was working.

That, or whatever message Andreas had sent through the king's emissary had included where to find me.

"Your magic is different today," I said. "I can't feel it like before."

"I am channeling it inward." He gave a slight grimace. It was the same pained expression from the first time we met.

"You're holding it inside so it won't hurt me."

"Better me than you." He didn't smile. I wasn't sure if the Voster could smile. But the shape of his mouth changed, just slightly, as if he was trying. "It has taken me some time to learn. To build up an endurance so that we may talk."

"There is a place in the library where we could talk and be separated far enough that you wouldn't—"

"No. We will meet here and only here."

I sat a little straighter at the warning in his tone. Was it not safe to discuss these things outside this room? "Did you receive my message?"

"Yes. Do not send another."

Another warning. I wasn't going to ask why, not when it seemed more important to listen than speak.

"Did you read the book?" he asked.

I nodded. "Yes."

"And?"

"It's a story."

"History is a story."

"So this really happened. There were six evil magicians in Calandra. Are those the Six who you now worship as gods?"

"Who do you worship, child?" he asked.

"The Divine."

He hummed, a note so soft and smooth it could lull me to sleep. "As do I. The Eight are a myth made real by time and magic."

I blinked. "The Voster believe in the Divine?"

"*I* believe in the Divine. Many of my brothers do not.

Much about us has changed in the time since we inherited our...gifts."

He focused on the glass of water on my desk. He lifted a hand and, with a flick of his wrist, spun the water into the air, twirling it into a spiral that stretched thinner and thinner, higher and higher, until it nearly reached the ceiling.

The force of his magic was instant, stinging and sharp like a hundred quills stabbing into my skin. My fingernails dug into the arms of my chair as I gritted my teeth, doing everything to hide the agony. If he could bear it, then I would, too.

But his display of magic didn't last long. He re-coiled the spiral of water, returning it safely to the glass. Then the pain was gone and I could breathe again.

"Would you not question your beliefs if you arrived in a land where you could manipulate wind and water and blood? Would you not embrace the magic of this land and the gods who reign over its people?"

"Maybe," I admitted. "So the Voster became devout to the Eight after coming to Calandra."

"Once, long ago, my people worshiped a god whose name we no longer speak. When he abandoned us in the war, when he left us to die in our darkest days, he was forsaken." He pursed his lips. "Most of my brothers now sign the Eight. But there are some, like me, who have learned the grace of the Divine. Some, like me, who questioned the histories we were told."

The gray book he'd given me rested on the edge of my desk. I placed my palm on its cover, fingertips stroking the worn leather. "I have read countless books in this library, and hardly any mention the Voster. And the written history of Calandra seems to only go back three hundred summers to the first migration. It's...suspicious."

I understood why there was no mention of Kenn or Nelfinex or Beesa. If the Starling who first came to Calandra had caused death and destruction, if she had been the catalyst for the crux migrations, then I wouldn't bring attention to a land across the world, either.

But the Voster were special. They had magic. If I was a historian or author, I would write countless books about that alone.

"You will find nothing *here*," he said. "But that does not mean it doesn't exist."

"Where?"

"Far away from the eyes of humanity."

"It's hidden. Why?"

He reached forward and tapped his grooved, green-tinged fingernails against my water glass. "Did you know that our magic allows us to seal blood oaths?"

"Yes."

The Voster held my gaze but didn't speak.

Or maybe he *couldn't* speak. "You can't tell me. You've taken an oath."

He leaned back in his chair and pointed to the gray book.

A book that was his way of breaking an oath. "Who wrote this book?"

"That is of no consequence."

My mind was whirling as I attempted to make sense of what he was trying to tell me. "If this is a history, then the magicians were real. People began worshiping them as the Six, but they were not real gods. They were granted powers by demons, correct? I can only assume that means the Infernal."

The great enemy of the Divine.

"Good will always battle evil," he said. "Light will always fight the dark. In those moments, you'll learn who you truly are. Continue."

I took a deep breath, letting the far-fetched theories I'd been pondering loose. "The Voster in Kenn do not have magic. But you do in Calandra. And here, the Starling get sick. If we shift, we can't shift back. And when the swift migrate here, they become monsters. They become crux and are nothing like the creatures from home."

He steepled his hands in front of his mouth as he listened.

"This land is cursed. The magicians did something to Calandra. In humans, it's the reason they have starbursts in their eyes. In the Voster, it gives you magic. In the Starling, we lose control over our bloodline's gifts. I don't understand why certain animals become monsters here while others don't. Maybe they were never meant to be a part of this continent, like the swift. But regardless, there is something *wrong* with Calandra."

He said nothing as my words hung in the air.

Maybe I'd spent too much time in this library. Maybe my imagination had run rampant. Now that I'd spoken the idea of a cursed continent out loud, I couldn't deny just how fantastical it seemed.

"Those of us who left Kenn have been here for many, many years," he said.

"You were one of the Voster who came here with my Starling ancestors?"

"Long ago."

"Are you immortal? Is that part of the magic?"

"Not immortal. Long-lived. But yes, I once lived in Kenn. I had a wife and three daughters. My family was killed by Beesans in the war. It has been a long time since I've sat beside their graves. We fought as best we could, for a hundred years. But in the end, we lost. Those of us with nothing left to lose took our chance to flee. But I would return someday, if possible. I would rest beside my beloveds again. *If* I can break the ties binding me to this land."

"The magic traps you here? Or is it your oaths?"

He didn't answer.

"Why are you telling me these things?"

"Because too much has been lost," he whispered. "Too

many have been forgotten. Too many were left behind. What was ours was stolen. It should be reclaimed."

He spoke in a way that seemed to condemn his brothers. For their devotion to the Eight. For their magic. For turning a blind eye to his people across the Marixmore.

"Has a Voster ever been born in Calandra?" I asked.

"No."

"So those of you here…" I trailed off.

The Voster in Calandra had been here for hundreds of summers. They'd witnessed the crux migrations.

"Is there a way to heal Calandra and stop the migrations?"

Silence.

"The first Voster I met was named Brother Nold. Do you know him?"

"Yes."

"He wore burgundy robes. Yours are blue. Is the distinction important?"

Another question he did not answer. Instead, he stood from the chair, bending slightly at the waist. "That is enough for today."

"You're leaving?" I stood, too, panicked that I'd barely scratched the surface of my questions. And he hadn't told me if I was correct. "But—"

His magic bit into my skin, cutting off my protest. It was slipping past his control, no longer wanting to stay locked away. "Fear not, Starling. We will speak again."

"When?"

His gaze traveled up and down my body. "Before it is your time."

My heart stopped. "H-how did you know?"

"Hide your truths as best you can. And tell no one we have met."

Truths that only Andreas knew. Truths I would not be able to hide forever.

"What's your name?" I asked.

He walked to the door, and I was certain it was another question he would avoid. But then he looked back over his bony shoulder. "You may call me Hain."

"Thank you, Brother Hain."

"No Brother. Just Hain."

I nodded, and he slipped from the carrel. A chill snaked down my spine.

A heartbeat after the door clicked shut, Hain lost the hold he'd kept on his magic's leash. It slammed into me like knives. I squeezed my eyes shut, a soft cry escaping my lips. But the pain didn't last long.

Hide your truths as best you can.

I walked to the door and flipped the lock.

49

ODESSA

On silent feet, I slipped out of Evie's bedroom, easing the door closed with a soft click.

After the fiasco in the training center earlier, she'd been quiet and withdrawn. Like those first days after Ellder, rather than tuck her in and say good night, I'd stayed with her until she fell asleep.

We'd both needed to cuddle.

Ransom stood at the windows in the suite, staring over the city's rain-drenched lights. "I keep hoping I'll see Zavier and Cathlin's ship in the bay."

"Soon." I joined him at the glass, looping my arm through his and hugging it to my chest.

Zavier and Cathlin could be here any day now, depending on the trip across the Krisenth. I hoped this rain wasn't slowing them down. I hoped their ship could weather any storm.

And I hoped that ship would be up for a return journey.

We all needed to go home. I only wished we could give Alore more time.

"I've spent too many years in the Turan wilderness." Ransom's frame sagged. "Too much time roaming free. These walls feel like a cage. And there are just so many people in this castle."

The castle had always been a bustling, central hub in Roslo for business and politics. But there seemed to be more people than normal lately. More soldiers and noblemen crowding the halls and foyers.

Maybe it was the migration, drawing people into the castle. Maybe it was the weather, driving people indoors. Maybe there'd always been this many visitors, and I simply hadn't noticed until now.

After my summer spent in the vast Turan wilderness, falling in love with a kingdom and its prince, I was feeling caged, too.

"Is Allesaria not this way?"

"No. It's..." Either he couldn't think of the right words or the blood oath he'd taken to keep Allesaria a secret forbade him to say more. "You'll see. Someday. When it's safe."

Would it ever be safe? The realm felt like it was crashing down over our heads and safety was nothing more than an illusion.

"I'm losing control," he whispered.

"I know."

"I would have killed your sister today. If she had hurt you, I would have snapped her neck. Just like how I broke that guard's arm in the stables." He hung his head. "I am not this man."

"It's the Lyssa."

"What happens when I'm not strong enough to fight it?"

"We'll find a cure."

"What if we don't?"

"What if we do?" I slid my hand down his arm and laced our fingers together. "Alore has already made so much progress. I'm not giving up yet."

"Mother would have loved Alore. She would have set one foot in that workshop and never left." He pressed his free hand to his heart. "I miss her so much it's hard to breathe."

I wasn't sure what to say, so I held on to him, waiting for the grief he'd buried for weeks to come floating to the surface.

"When I was a boy, she insisted on cutting my hair herself," he said. "If I had a nightmare, she'd crawl into bed with me and we'd burrow under the blankets so she could sing me a song. She was a horrible singer. She taught me to waltz when I was fourteen so that I could impress a girl at a gala. Apples were her favorite fruit. She was scared of snakes. Lilies made her sneeze."

The words poured from his lips as he told me story after story of his mother. Like he was using the good memories to erase the sad.

When he was finished, he cleared his throat and blinked too fast. "If something happens to me, promise you'll make sure Evie knows about our mother?"

"Promise."

Gods, I hated this. Ransom spoke as if he were already halfway to the shades. The gods would have to fight me for him. I wasn't finished with my Guardian yet.

"I love you."

He kissed my hair. "Don't forget."

Not at all what I'd hoped he'd say.

Did I believe he loved me? Yes. He'd told his father that I was his life.

Still, I craved those words. To hear them in his deep timbre.

His silver eyes searched mine. He must have seen the disappointment, because his forehead furrowed. "What?"

"Nothing." I lifted onto my toes, pulling him down to kiss the corner of his mouth. "Take me to bed."

"Yes, my queen." He swept me into his arms, holding me like I was precious, and carried me into our room.

"Close your eyes," he said, setting me down.

I obeyed, my pulse accelerating as his heat disappeared. Seconds elapsed, one after another, as I stood, waiting. Listening for any sound besides my heartbeat and raspy breaths. A throb bloomed between my legs, an ache for his touch.

"How are you so perfect?" His voice was closer than I'd expected, a murmur not far from my ear.

Ransom's hands settled on my neck, roaming across my

shoulders and down my ribs. He skimmed my breasts and gripped my waist and massaged my hips. He was everywhere at once, like he'd forgotten the shape of my body and was learning its curves all over again.

I melted beneath his touch, losing myself in the darkness.

His palms splayed across my ass, pulling me close, pinning me to his hard body. He hooked a hand behind my knee, drawing it up until my aching center was pressed against his arousal.

My lips searched for his, but he just held me to him, letting me feel it as he grew thicker and harder, his entire length rocking against my core.

"Feel how much I want you."

"Yes," I panted.

"Only you, Dess. Only you." His mouth slammed onto mine. He swallowed my moan as his tongue delved deep, twisting and tangling with mine as our teeth clattered.

It was a reckless, frantic kiss. Wet and ruthless.

I rocked against him as he bucked his hips closer, but with these godsdamn clothes between us, it wasn't enough. My fingers dove into his hair, pulling and tugging at the strands.

A hand closed around my breast, squeezing and digging into my flesh. His thumb rolled my nipple through my shirt.

The desire flowing through my veins, pooling in my center, bordered on the edge of desperate and painful. My hold on his hair tightened as I fought to get closer, aching for more friction.

Ransom tore his mouth away, breathing hard as he fisted the hem of my shirt, whipping it and the thin camisole beneath over my head. They puddled on the floor as he dropped to his knees to unfasten the clasp on my pants and drag them down my hips and thighs.

The air was cool against my hot skin and the wet slick of my sex.

"Fuck." Ransom sat back on his heels, staring up at me. His eyes were hungry and as dark as the room. "You're perfect."

His hands came to my thighs, stroking up and down my skin, leaving tingles in their wake. Then his mouth was on me, and I nearly collapsed.

"Ranse," I whimpered, my hand diving into his hair to keep my legs steady.

He ran his tongue through my slit before he fluttered it against my clit.

My head was spinning, dizzy and drunk on his tongue. My body went up in flames as he took me higher and higher, driving me toward a cliff's edge.

I exploded on a cry, every muscle in my body quaking when I shattered. My knees weakened, but he held on to me, keeping me balanced as he continued to lick, drawing out my orgasm until I was spent.

He kissed a trail up my stomach and over my ribs to my breasts. He took a nipple in his hot mouth, sucking hard before moving to the other and giving it the same treatment. He let it go with an audible pop.

Then he stripped off his own shirt, and the sound of fabric tearing filled the room. His cock bobbed free as he shoved down his pants. Ransom fisted the shaft, giving himself a few hard strokes, staring down at my naked body. "Look at you."

"Fuck me," I breathed, my hand replacing his. My thumb caught the wet bead at the tip, smearing it over the head of his dick as I stroked. "I need to feel you."

He took my face in his hands, his fingers tangling in my hair. "Your wish, my queen."

Ransom dropped his lips to mine, the kiss languid and torturous. He lifted me off my feet and onto the bed, settling his weight on top of me.

When he brought us together, it was slow and methodical. Inch by delicious inch. Stroke by toe-curling stroke. Until finally, he filled me completely, my body stretching around his length as he thrust as deeply as he could get.

"Gods," I whispered. "I love you."

"Mine." He withdrew and thrust forward, hard, earning a gasp. "You're mine, Odessa."

"Yours." I captured his mouth, kissing him as he fucked me through the night. Every time I thought he was spent, we'd start over again.

He claimed my body until the rain beyond the windows eventually stopped. Until the sun peeked through the cracks in the curtains.

Until the silver bled from his eyes and gave way to magnificent green.

The color wouldn't last. I knew I'd wake to silver, but I'd take whatever little moments I could get. I yawned, collapsing on top of his chest, my eyelids too heavy to keep open. "I love you."

He kissed my hair.

And as I drifted off to sleep, I dreamed that he said it back.

50

CASPIA

Sonnet's Ninety lay open on the desk in my carrel.

I'd finished reading the tale of the ancient battle between the Six and the pythoness for what had to be the hundredth time.

A tale of good against evil. Light battling the dark.

In those moments, you'll learn who you truly are.

Hain's words kept coming back to me as often as I came back to this story.

Was there more to that statement than wisdom? Was he talking about me?

Who, exactly, was the pythoness?

A loud bang sounded from beyond the closed door, and I abandoned my reading, hurrying outside and into the hallway.

Faxon and a female tutor about my age were hurrying to close a large window that had blown open. The wind had been raging for hours, its gusts slamming against the castle. A cloud of dust burst through the open panes, and the taste of dirt spread across my tongue as the grit snuck into my eyes.

"Hurry," Faxon ordered, pushing his side of the window closed as the tutor did the same on hers. The moment it was latched, both sagged against the panes.

Beyond the glass, leaves streaked through the air and the trees whipped from side to side, their branches in a frenzy.

"It's all right," the tutor told her students, who were all

staring wide-eyed outside. "Back to your work. It's only the wind."

Faxon double-checked the window's latch, then came over, still panting from the exertion. "I don't like the wind. There's a reason I am not a gardener or soldier or fisherman. I'll stay inside and out of the elements, thank you very much."

I laughed. "Well, if that window opens again, leave it to me. I don't mind the wind."

The Starling believed that winds were a good omen. My aunt loved to find a strong current and let it carry her to the stars.

"You leave the window to me," Faxon said. "It's bad enough you're in that tiny carrel. I will not have you worrying about the windows."

"I happen to like my tiny carrel."

He sighed, still peeved that he couldn't talk me into somewhere more appropriate for a lady, but we both knew I wasn't going to budge.

With a wink, I left him to return to his duties while I went back to my reading, propping the carrel's door open to listen to the wind outside.

The words on the page of the book blurred together as I let my eyes lose focus and my mind wander.

If the evil magicians from the gray book were in fact the Six, then who was the pythoness? In Sonnet's recount, she'd amassed a terrible army to conquer Calandra.

What if she wasn't the villain in this tale? If the Six were demons of the Infernal, maybe the pythoness was fighting against their magic. Maybe Sonnet had reversed their roles in his story because he'd been a believer in the Eight.

But I was not a believer.

I was a seeker of truths.

A figure appeared in the doorway, crashing into its frame so hard I gasped.

"Hain?" I shot out of my seat, about to rush to his side, but he held up a hand, bony fingers splayed wide.

"I'm all right." The Voster closed the door and shuffled to the empty chair. He collapsed in the seat, and with his eyes closed, he breathed for a few long moments.

His skin was not its normal pale white. There was color in his cheeks, and sweat dampened his hairless head.

"Are you sick?"

He shook his head. "No. But I don't have long."

"Okay." I clasped my hands on the edge of my desk, waiting.

There wasn't a hint of magic in the room, not even a trace of that pressure or its presence.

He was suppressing it again to save me the pain.

"I can endure it," I said, knowing he'd understand what I was talking about.

But Hain shook his head as he swallowed hard, keeping his eyes closed as he spoke. "When we met last, we spoke of magicians."

"Yes. They took their power from the Infernal's demons and became the Six. They cursed this land."

"Was evil victorious?"

"I don't know. I suppose." I glanced between him and the gray book, a constant companion on my desk. "Unless I misunderstood your story."

"It is not my story. It is yours." Every word was pained, his voice hoarse.

My story. How was this my story? I swallowed hard, sliding *Sonnet's Ninety* closer. "There is a tale in this book about the Six. They battled a pythoness and her army. After they defeated her, they went to the shades."

The corner of Hain's mouth turned up. I suspected it was as close to a smile as I'd ever get. "I was right to choose you."

"Choose me? What do you—"

"Who was the pythoness? Who would have opposed the magicians?" he asked.

"You never call them the Six."

"I do not believe in the Six. Answer my question."

I blew out a long breath, sagging in my seat. "I don't know. This is the only story I've come across that mentions a pythoness. Anything else in the library that has tales about soothsayers is fiction."

"Caspia." It was the first time he said my name, and it sent a chill down my spine. "You came to Calandra for a reason, did you not?"

Yes. To avenge Emery and go through the ritus. But I hadn't told Hain about my sister. "H-how did you know that?"

He didn't answer. He stayed slumped in that chair, his head resting against the back. His breaths became deeper, and with his eyes closed, I worried he'd fallen asleep.

But the silence gave me time to replay everything he'd said. To take each word and hold it up to a mirror. To flip it around in my mind, examine it at all angles.

My story. Mine. A Starling who had followed her ritus to this land. And who'd seen a vision of her sister's death. A vision in which Emery had been a monster.

My story.

Not me. My bloodline.

"Was the pythoness a Starling?" I spoke so quietly I was certain he hadn't heard.

Hain's eyes popped open.

"The Starling fought the magicians. Were they victorious?"

"Yes." He nodded, pushing himself up straight. The effort seemed to zap all of his strength, and he leaned forward, resting his elbows on his knees. "There are things I cannot say. I have drained my magic as best I could, but even the frayed remains will keep me bound to the oaths of long ago."

"The wind. That was you?" I looked to the wall like I could see through it to the windows. It had been howling for hours, since long before I awoke this morning.

Just how much power did he have?

"But you still have blood. Isn't that what binds the oaths?"

"Not when an oath is sworn between the brotherhood. We are bound by magic." He closed his eyes again. "You must ask me the right questions. That will be the only way I can answer. I can't speak the words myself."

The right questions.

My heart started to race. I opened the gray book, furiously flipping through the pages. "If the magicians lost their battle against the Starling, something would have happened to them. They would have been imprisoned or... executed?"

Hain sighed. "The Voster send our people to the sea when they die."

"So the magicians were sent to the sea?"

He frowned.

Wrong question.

"What do you do with your dead?" he asked.

"We burn them on funeral pyres, and the ashes are sealed in glass orbits. We keep them in temples." *Oh.* "The magicians were burned and their remains sealed."

Hain's shoulders relaxed.

The right question.

I stared at the wood grains on my desk, letting my mind wander. "But if the magicians were defeated, why would the Starling leave Calandra? How did this continent become cursed?"

He stayed quiet.

So I could answer my own question.

"The magic remained. The magicians themselves were destroyed, but the magic wasn't. It lingered and became a part of Calandra. It is the reason for its wrongness."

And that magic had to be the reason my own body had changed. The reason my blood was now green.

Magic was poison to the Starling. And to the swift.

"From what I have read, it did not happen immediately.

For a time, there was peace." Each word was spoken through gritted teeth, like he was testing the limits of his bond.

"There are books about this?"

"Not anymore," he murmured.

Was it the Voster who had destroyed those books? Or people who worshiped the Infernal?

"Okay." I rubbed my temples. "So the magic must have seeped from their orbits. And as it spread, like a tree taking root, it cursed the land and chased the Starling away."

To Nelfinex.

"When? This must have been countless summers ago. Long before the migrations or the Voster coming here. This would have been…"

The beginning. The origin.

The story of how the Starling came to Nelfinex. The start of my family's dynasty in Kenn.

An age ago.

Divine. It was a good thing I was sitting.

"If the Six were defeated, how are they now revered as gods?" Why would Sonnet reverse the roles of good and evil?

"Just because they were dead does not mean the Six were forgotten. Without light to balance dark, we become children of the night."

The nuance of this story must have taken a new shape over time. Truths had been forgotten. Manipulated. If my ancestors had become monsters, trapped in the form of beasts, it made sense that people would have turned on them.

"So to save themselves and the people of Calandra, they sailed away. They fled these shores."

And magicians were martyred until they were known as gods.

In a way, this meant the myths were true.

The Six had created monsters.

Bariwolves. Fenek. Kaverine. Alligasks. Grizzurs. Tarkin.

But not the swift.

Those, my ancestors had found in Nelfinex. And hundreds of summers ago, after delivering Hain and his brothers to this land, one had returned home, only to leave a trail for the others to follow for migration.

"Why didn't the Starling destroy the orbits, if they feared the magic was still alive?"

"That, I do not know," Hain said.

Maybe it was as simple as not knowing how. "If the orbits are destroyed, will the magic cease?"

Was this how I saved Xandra?

Hain didn't answer—couldn't answer. He simply stared at me.

It was confirmation enough.

All this time, I'd been reading books, searching for clues, questioning Calandra's history. And all this time, it had been linked to my own.

My heart raced. Hope surged. *By the grace of the Divine.*

Could we purge the magic? If the migration came but the curse was gone, then everyone in this continent would see the swift as they were.

I sat taller. "Where are the orbits kept?"

He shook his head.

My mind began to whirl, spinning so fast I couldn't keep my train of thought. If we couldn't find them, then there would be no saving Xandra. No curing Calandra. "If the Starling chose the locations, could a Starling find them?"

"It is possible."

"And that is why you are here, isn't it? Because I am the only Starling in Calandra. You've searched for them. You've tried to find them. And you can't." Other than Xandra, but she wasn't going to be much help. "Let's say that I did find the orbits. That I found a way to destroy them, too. That would fundamentally alter Calandra, wouldn't it? The Voster would no longer have magic. Why would you want that?"

Hain looked to his hands and empty palms. "I cannot remember my daughters' faces. I have forgotten what it feels like to love. To grieve. To live. Light and dark. Good and evil. My people across the Marixmore are suffering, yes?"

"Yes."

"We have ignored it long enough. We let tyranny win by fleeing Kenn." His eyes turned glassy. "You have much to consider, Starling. There will be those who oppose you."

"Your brothers?"

"Among others. Many kings have come to rely upon our blood oaths and treaties. And yes, my brothers will not give up their power willingly."

"Even if it means an end to the slaughter of the migrations?"

"They do not even care about the lives of their people. Why would they give up magic for humans?"

This was the reason for his secrecy. For insisting that I never attempt to contact him again. To hide my truths. The Voster would sooner see me dead than risk the chance of me destroying the source of their power.

"Brother Nold." A bolt of terror raced through my veins. "He knows that I am Starling. He—"

"Is not a threat. But trust no other."

An irritation raced up my forearms. It was more of a burn than the normal sting and prickle of his magic, but I rubbed at it all the same.

"My magic returns." He sounded disappointed. "I must go."

"Will I see you again?"

He was barely able to stand from the chair, and once on his feet, he swayed, nearly toppling over as he shuffled to open the door.

"Let me help you." I stood and rounded the desk, but when I reached for him, he waved me off.

"There is no helping me now, child. This quest is yours."

"Will you be all right? Will your magic return?"

"By the grace of the Divine, I will fulfill my destiny." He clutched at his stomach, wincing at an invisible pain. It passed after a moment, and he stood tall. "Farewell, Starling."

"I—" A lump formed in my throat. I pressed two fingertips to my forehead, silently vowing to make his sacrifice worthwhile. "Farewell, Hain."

He stared at me for a long moment, his gaze difficult to follow, but it seemed to fix on my hair. Then he hurried away with uncoordinated steps, nearly tripping over his robes, until he disappeared around a corner and was lost.

Silence filled the carrel.

When I walked into the hallway and glanced out the windows, the wind was gone.

51

ODESSA

Puffs of steam fogged the bathing chamber as I slipped through the door. The scents of lavender, mint, and eucalyptus filled my nose, the combination clean and fresh.

Ransom's arms were draped over the edge of the tub, his head lolled to the side as he soaked.

Sound asleep.

His beard was damp and his hair wet, the ends tickling his shoulders. A drop of water sluiced off his chest, plopping into the tub with a *plunk*.

Shades, he was beautiful. My fingers itched to trace the straight line of his nose and full pout of his lips. His strong, masculine features and muscled torso would be the next sketch I added to my journal.

The sight of him made my heart skip.

I could stare at him for hours, but I shied away, wanting him to rest. Except before I could sneak out the door, he jerked awake. His eyes were bleary for a moment, like he'd forgotten where he fell asleep.

When he saw me, they closed again and he relaxed deeper into the water. "Spying, Cross?"

"Wolfe," I corrected, walking to the tub to perch on its edge. "I'm thinking about taking my husband's name. But we'll see. I'm undecided."

"Undecided?" The corner of his mouth turned up as he flicked water onto my shirt. When he opened his eyes, they were a soft, mossy shade of green.

If only we could erase the dark veins on his chest.

One of the lines had snaked toward the hollow beneath his throat. If it crawled up his neck, he wouldn't be able to hide it with his clothes.

Ransom followed my gaze, looking down to his heart. "Don't worry. Once we get back to Turah, the High Priest will siphon the Lyssa from my blood. They'll fade."

A sinking feeling settled in my stomach.

According to the High Priest, there was no way to remove it entirely from Ransom's body. The infection and the blood had fused so thoroughly, it would be impossible to separate them completely. So he siphoned enough to temper the effects of Lyssa by diluting it in Ransom's body.

What if we didn't get back to Turah in time? What if the migration trapped us in Roslo for months? We couldn't wait that long. And I still wasn't convinced the High Priest was on our side. All I could hear was Brother Dime's warning about Ransom's loyalty.

Could Brother Dime siphon the infection? Ransom had said once that the High Priest had attuned his magic to Lyssa, so it had to be possible for another priest to do it, too.

"You should rest today. Avoid the chaos in the castle." I drew a circle in the water with my fingertip, ripples spreading across its mirrored surface. "I'm going to find Mae."

"No."

I gave him a sad smile. "She's the only sister I have. And something is wrong. I know you don't trust her. But you trust me, right?"

I'd practiced that all morning. The look on his face said he knew it, too.

"Odessa. No. She crossed a line yesterday."

"I know." I sighed. "But before we leave, I have to at least try to talk to her. If the unthinkable happens during the migration, I don't want yesterday to be how we remember each other."

He frowned. But he didn't tell me no.

"I love you."

He hooked a finger under my chin, pulling me in for a chaste kiss. "Be careful."

"I'm always careful."

"The most terrifying part of that statement is you actually believe it."

I rolled my eyes and splashed water in his face, earning a chuckle, then stood. "I'll take Evie to the nursery."

"No, leave her. We need some time to talk."

I stilled. "Are you going to tell her about Zavier?"

"Not yet. But it's time we start preparing her to lose Faze."

"Not yet." My heart dropped. "He's not ready." *I* wasn't ready.

Ransom sighed. "We can't keep him forever, my love."

"I know." The endearment softened the blow but just barely. "After the migration, I'll set him free. I promise."

"I'll do it," he said.

I shook my head. "No, he's mine."

"Then together."

"Together." I gave him a sad smile, then left him to his bath.

The ache in my chest followed me out of the suite and to the castle's main level. How were we supposed to let Faze go? Ransom was right. Faze was born to roam free. And he was going to hate being trapped in a migration shelter for months. Still, he was our pet tarkin. A part of our family.

I was so busy nursing a wounded heart that I didn't hear the argument in Margot's dining room until I was just outside the door.

"Tell her," Margot snapped. "Or I will."

"Do not threaten me, Margot." My father's voice made my blood run cold.

I'd never heard her challenge him before.

Margot let out a dry laugh. "Or what?"

There was a hopelessness in her voice, like he'd hurt her so thoroughly during their marriage that she had gone numb. That she had nothing left to lose.

"Don't think I am ignorant to what happens in this castle or your bedroom." Father had to mean Hawksley. *Gods.* "I have let you continue with your dalliance, but don't test me. And do not forget your place."

Wait. Was he okay with her having an affair with his general? Maybe they were both having affairs.

"I am well aware of my place." She let out a frustrated growl. "It's by your side. How could I forget? I have stood beside you, dutifully, for decades. I have loved you. I have done everything you have asked. I have stayed quiet, watching you become this shell of a man. I have tolerated every insult you have thrown my way and obeyed every command. And in my place, I have never asked you for anything. I'm asking now. Tell her the truth. Before it's too late."

There was a pregnant pause. Then came the sound of breaking glass, like he'd thrown a goblet against the wall.

I was still reeling, my heart in my throat, when footsteps marched in my direction. And before I could escape, Margot stormed through the door.

She drew up short in the hall, surprised for a moment. Then her expression hardened and she crossed her arms over her chest. "So you did learn how to spy while you were in Turah."

"I'm sorry." My cheeks went hot. "I didn't mean to eavesdrop."

"Of course you did." She pursed her lips, then walked away.

"Margot?" I stopped her, waiting until she turned. "What isn't he telling me?"

Her gaze drifted to the dining room door, and for a moment, I thought she might actually give me an honest answer. Instead, she lifted her chin. "What makes you think we were talking about you? The world does not revolve around you, Odessa."

"Oh. Right. Sorry." *Shit.* "Is it Mae? Is she okay?"

"No, she's not." Without another word, Margot swept away, her posture perfect and regal, the skirts of her teal gown streaming behind her.

A queen making her exit.

I moved to follow her down the hall, but the silence in the dining room lured me back, and before I lost my nerve, I walked inside. This was likely the worst possible time to approach my father, but I needed to find Brother Dime.

I hoped Father would want to get rid of me enough to just point me in the right direction.

He was crouched against the wall, picking up shards of broken glass. Something a servant could do. Instead, he was cleaning up his mess.

I went over and bent down, plucking a large piece off the marble.

His gaze lifted. "You don't need to do this, Dess."

"I'll help." I wished I didn't like it so much when he called me Dess. I wished it didn't give me hope that our relationship wasn't a lost cause.

We collected the jagged pieces of glass, piling them on an empty plate on the table.

As he picked up the final bits, I wiped my hands on my pants. "I came to ask you a question. I need to find Brother Dime. Is he still in the castle?"

Father stilled, his hand hovering over the floor. "No."

That sounded like a lie. "Do you have a way to contact him? I wouldn't ask if it wasn't important."

He stood, not meeting my eyes as he dropped the pieces in his hand on the plate. "No."

And that lie was blatant. "Please."

"Why?" He crossed his arms over his chest.

"It's for Ransom."

Father's lip curled. "The Guardian."

"Don't," I chided. "Why do you do that? Why do you dislike him?"

"I don't trust him."

Fair. The day they arrived in Quentis, Ransom had let Zavier convince us he was the prince. He'd been dishonest to Father from the start. "You don't have to trust him. But can you trust me?"

I regretted the question the moment it was past my lips.

Father's jaw clenched. His silent *no* was as loud as shattering glass.

Brother Dime had warned me that the truth was rarely gentle.

Well, let the suffering begin.

"All this time, I wanted to be good enough for you. But truth is, you were never good enough for me."

He flinched.

I left him with his broken glass.

Later, I'd feel sad. But today, I needed help. Ransom needed help. If Father wouldn't tell me where I could find Brother Dime, then I'd figure it out myself.

The priest stayed in this castle. Maybe there was a maid or servant who could point me to those quarters.

I was rounding a corner, about to duck down a stairwell that would take me to the lower levels of the castle where the staff worked, when a swish of pale blue caught my eye.

It was gone in a blink, but I knew that color.

Brother Skore's robes.

I gasped and changed directions, my boots smacking on the floor as I raced to follow.

Was that really him? Why was he here? Was he searching for me?

Given our last interaction, after the waterfall, I had no desire to be around the priest. But I wanted to know what the hell he was doing in Father's castle.

The hallway opened to a foyer filled with castle guards. They stood in neat rows, all eyes locked on Captain Brix at the front of the room, standing on a small platform, reading from a page as he doled out orders and assignments.

I weaved through the crush, skirting to the back of the space as I stood on my toes, searching for Brother Skore.

His tall, lanky frame and bald head vanished down another corridor.

"Dismissed," Brix called, and the guards scattered, blocking my view of Skore.

I dodged men and women as they moved in all directions, bumping into me as I bumped into them.

"Out of the way," a man barked as I nearly tripped over his foot. He realized too late who he was addressing. "Sorry, Princess."

I ignored him and kept going, finally making it to the corridor.

Empty.

"Damn it." I pushed the curls from my face and ran to the end of the hall, where it branched in three different directions. Straight. Left. Right. Where the hell had he gone? "Brother Skore?"

My shout bounced off the walls. I held my breath, ears straining for an answer.

Nothing.

Maybe it was a different priest. Maybe they were all swapping burgundy robes for pale blue.

"Shit." I took a step down the hall to my left, hoping for once I'd sense the sting of Voster magic. But all I felt was sweat snaking down my spine and a panic that I'd lost my chance. I sprinted the length of the hall anyway, and when there was still no magic, I whirled and ran back.

"Goddess Daria, how about a little luck?" I jogged down a different hallway, hoping I'd made the right choice this time.

It led to an unguarded door that opened to the gardens. I

burst outside, looking both ways, searching past shrubs and trees for any sign of the Voster. But he was gone, likely down another passage in the castle's labyrinth of halls.

"Gah." I fisted my hands, letting out a frustrated grunt.

At least there was a Voster in the castle. If it took me all day, I'd hunt the priest down.

I'd seen Skore pull blood from those bariwolves and drain their bodies to husks. He might be exactly who we needed until Alore found a cure.

Spinning for the door, I was about to retreat inside, when a distant scream pierced the air.

A scream so familiar my heart stopped.

"Evie?" I called her name but was already running toward the sound, racing around a tall hedge and into a round courtyard.

A stone fountain bubbled in its center. Beside it, a guard, dressed in his teal uniform, had blood streaming from his nose.

Ransom stood with his fists clenched, seething at the guard.

And Evie was kneeling on the ground, holding Faze as tears streamed down her face.

I ran to her, picking her up, checking her head to toe for injuries. "Are you hurt?"

She shook her head, sobbing. "I w-wanna go home."

The last word was a wail of heartache.

Gods. What was happening? I stood and eased her behind me, keeping one hand on her shoulder as I took in the guard.

He wiped at the blood dribbling down his chin, then spat a glob at Ransom's feet.

"Leave," Ransom ordered the guard. "Now. Before I do far worse than break your nose."

The guard sneered, but he backed away, flashing me a smile with bloody teeth.

I waited until he was gone, then wrapped Evie in a hug. "What happened?"

"He tried to take Faze." She buried her face in my shoulder.

I looked up at Ransom.

Rage simmered in his molten eyes. "We came outside to let Faze run and play. The guard lured him away with a hunk of meat. Evie whistled for him, and it made him pause enough for me to catch up."

Evie's cooing noise. The birdsong she'd learned from Brother Skore.

Ransom dragged a hand over his face. "These godsdamn guards."

Bastards. This was my father's castle. This was my childhood home. If they were trying to run us out of Quentis, they were doing a damn fine job.

My mind stopped.

Could that be true? I'd never had an incident with the guards before. They were trained to all but blend into the walls. Granted, I'd never brought a baby monster into the castle.

Was this Mae's doing? She'd been so strange since we arrived. And it was a well-known secret she was involved with Captain Brix. Had she enticed her lover to intentionally torment us so we'd leave?

The hairs on the back of my neck stood on end as the feeling of being watched brought me to my feet. I turned in a slow circle, scanning the courtyard and gardens.

But we were alone with the trees and hedges and wind that rustled their changing leaves.

"Let's go inside." I reached for Ransom's hand but froze as my attention swung to the castle.

Brother Skore stood in the window, his tall body framed by the sill. His pale blue robes blended in with the light walls at his back.

I gasped.

"What?" Ransom asked, following my gaze.

I held up a hand, silently begging for Skore to wait.

Except before I could run inside to find him, Ransom stepped in front of me, blocking me from the Voster. "Odessa, get out of here."

"Brother Skore?" Evie rushed forward.

"Stay back." Ransom caught her around the waist before she could go to the glass, pulling her behind him. "*That's Skore?*"

"Yes." I nodded, trying to move past him, but he blocked me again. "Listen, I know you're mad that he left us in Ozarth, but I need to talk to him."

Ransom picked up Evie and grabbed my hand, dragging us through the gardens to leave.

I twisted back to the window, but Skore was already gone. *Damn it.* "Ransom, what's going on?"

"We need to get out of Quentis."

"Why?"

"He's Kennin."

"Say that again?"

"Kennin. They're a faction of zealots. If Dime is associating with Skore, then it's likely he's a radical, too. It means he's a traitor to the brotherhood." Ransom lowered his voice, checking over his shoulder as he walked faster. "Anyone found to be associated with the Kennin is put to death by the High Priest."

"Oh." Well, fuck.

52

CASPIA

Hain rests on his knees at the edge of an ocean cliffside. His pale blue robes pool around his body, covering the rock beneath him. Waves crash, sending sea spray into the air. Wind whips the tall grasses around him.

Blood, as black as death, drips from his nose. His face is gaunt, his cheeks hollow.

He bows his head and whispers a prayer.

A prayer spoken in a language from across the Marixmore. A prayer spoken in Nelfinex.

"By the grace of the Divine, guide them home. By the grace of the Divine, grant these Starling the strength to do what I could not. By the grace of the Divine, welcome me to Gloree."

He lifts his face to the sky and smiles. Blood dribbles from the corner of his mouth as he opens his arms.

He hitches his last breath. Then a blade, silver and sharp, cuts through the air.

And Hain's head tumbles off the cliff.

...

I woke with a gasp, sitting upright so fast I shook the bed.

Andreas was awake in a blink, reaching for me. "What is it? Are you all right?"

A vision.

A horror.

"He's dead." I swung my legs over the edge of the bed and buried my face in my hands, pressing my fingertips against my eyes to blot out the sight.

"Who is dead?" Andreas knelt behind me, his hands on my shoulders. "Caspia."

"Hain," I choked out. "A vision."

"Then it might not happen."

"Maybe not." But something about that vision felt inevitable.

A breeze drifted through the open windows, making me shiver.

Andreas climbed off the bed and pulled on the pants he'd discarded earlier. His naked chest caught the moonlight as he closed each of the windows, then grabbed my robe from the chair in the corner. He draped it over my shoulders, then crouched in front of me, his hands taking mine. "Tell me about it."

I closed my eyes and recounted the vision, translating Hain's prayers to Calandran.

By the grace of the Divine, guide them home.

By the grace of the Divine, grant these Starling the strength to do what I could not.

"He spoke in Nelfinex," I told Andreas. "Not Beesan. Not Calandran. It was Nelfinex."

I hadn't even known he could speak Nelfinex. During our two meetings, we'd used Calandran. And the gray book was written in the old language.

"Guide *them* home," I said. "Grant *these* Starling. Both prayers were plural. He must mean Xandra. But I can't remember if I ever told him about her."

Andreas ran a hand over his face, his palm scraping against the stubble on his jaw. "Maybe he learned it from Brother Nold."

"Maybe." If they were allies, they would have shared our conversations.

There'd been a finality to our last meeting in my carrel. Had he known he was leaving to face his death? "Do you think he died for betraying a magical oath to the Voster?"

"I have no idea," Andreas murmured, standing to pace our darkened bedroom. "I would think that betraying an oath would kill you instantly. Though I don't know anyone who has ever died from breaking a blood oath. Maybe his magic was able to keep him alive longer than it would a human."

It didn't really matter. Whatever the cause, Hain was going to die, if he wasn't dead already. Murdered, probably by the Voster.

The burden of truth was now mine to carry.

Maybe it always had been.

How long had Hain waited for this perfect storm? A Starling descendant who came to Calandra but had not completed her ritus. Any other would be lost, like Xandra.

Was this the reason the Divine had called me here? Was this my destiny?

"I'm going to find the orbits and destroy them," I whispered.

Andreas stopped pacing. "What?"

"It is the only way to save Xandra. And it could stop the migrations from killing so many innocent people."

He shook his head. "You can't be serious."

"Andreas." I met his gaze, knowing what he'd see in mine.

Responsibility. Loyalty. Heritage.

He wasn't the only person in this bedroom with a duty to their family.

"I'm Starling. I can find them." There was no proof but the feeling in my heart.

"No, Caspia." He sliced a hand through the air. "It's too dangerous. You heard what Hain said. The Voster will not want to lose their magic. You cannot win against them."

No, I couldn't. He was right about that. A lifetime spent training with the Royal Blades was nothing compared to magic. But it didn't change my heart.

"You know I have to do this. Or at least try."

"And if I forbid it?"

I arched an eyebrow.

My handsome protector. My strong husband. But even he couldn't change my mind. We both knew that.

His mouth flattened, and he resumed pacing. It took a few moments but not many.

Just like our early suns together, trekking across Calandra, his faith in me was as predictable as the tide. He believed everything I'd ever told him. And he'd never let me go after the orbits alone.

"We will do this my way." He stopped pacing and pointed to my nose. "Or I will lock you in this room and throw away the key."

My heart swelled. I loved this man so much it was hard to breathe.

Knowing Andreas, he'd insist on coming along. He'd hire a legion to keep me safe. He'd plan and plot and spend every gold coin in his family's coffers if it meant my survival.

But we would do this. Together. And by the grace of the Divine, we might actually succeed.

A smile, fueled by hope, tugged at my mouth.

"Do *not* smile when I am angry at you, Caspia."

I bit the insides of my cheeks.

"Obviously, I'm going with you."

"I expected as much." I stood from the bed and walked to him, wrapping my arms around his waist as I pressed my ear to his chest. "I love you."

He exhaled, and a heartbeat later, he wrapped me in his arms and buried his nose in my unbound hair. "I won't lose you. Not to the Voster. Not to this dark magic. The moment I fear your life is at risk, this is over. Please don't ask me to watch you die."

"I vow it."

He held me for a long moment, and when he let me go, his expression was masked with that serious look I'd come to know all too well. His mind was already working, already formulating a plan and assessing possibilities. "Hain gave you no indication of where these orbits might be hidden."

"No." I sat on the bed and hugged a pillow to my chest. "But I would think they'd be in fairly remote locations. If I was hiding the remains of magicians, I'd keep them far away from people."

"Hundreds and hundreds of years ago, there wouldn't have been five kingdoms. Even the landscape could have changed over so many years."

"Someone must have been in power. Too bad any records from then don't seem to exist." Or, more likely, they'd been destroyed by the Voster to hide the truth of their powers.

"If I had to venture a guess, I'd say rulers were more fragmented," he said. "The Cross lineage is known to have always held power in Quentis. But I don't know how far that power extended. Possibly beyond the Evon."

The Evon Ravine acted as a natural border between Quentis and Genesis. It was the reason we'd sailed to Roslo rather than travel by land.

Andreas had told me that it cut so deeply into the earth that only a sliver of noontime sunlight reached the bottom. And the monsters that lurked in its depths were known to be more terrifying than any other, save the crux.

A shiver rolled down my spine.

It sounded like the perfect place to hide a magician's orbit.

"In Nelfinex, after we burn our dead on funeral pyres and seal their ashes in orbits, most are kept in temples. The Starling temple is deep below the palace in Showe, carved into the rock."

I'd only been to the Starling temple once, the sun we put my great aunt's orbit to rest. It had been so cold my teeth had chattered through the ceremony. I'd held back tears for fear they would freeze on my cheeks.

"If the Starling from long ago brought their traditions from Calandra to Nelfinex, then they might have chosen burial places deep in the earth. I think we should go to the bottom of the Evon Ravine."

Andreas scowled. "I was afraid you'd say that."

"Are there other ravines like it?"

"To my knowledge, the Evon is the largest crevasse in all of Calandra. However, there are other places known to be as treacherous. A waterfall in Ozarth that falls into a vast hole. The Grint Mine in Laine has tunnels through a chasm. The cliffs on the eastern shore of Genesis have caves that are rumored to lure people to their depths."

Caves like the one Xandra and I had found after we landed? Could that be why we became so sick? We'd been too close to a source of dark magic? Maybe the Starling had sent the remains to every corner of Calandra.

"All right. We start at the Evon. And we keep searching until we find them all."

"I hate this," Andreas said.

I gave him a sad smile. "So do I. But this is bigger than us. This could mean the end of the migrations. This could mean so many lives saved."

He came to the end of the bed, his shoulders slumping. "Is it selfish of me to care more about your life than that of any other? All I want is to hide you away and keep you to myself."

"But you won't," I whispered.

He shook his head. "No, not when this could change Calandra forever."

I rested my head on his arm. "I love you."

Not only for wanting to protect me, but because he would fight for those who could not fight for themselves.

He kissed my temple. "I love you, too."

"Even though I'm going to drag you to the bottom of the Evon Ravine?" I teased.

"To the bottom of the ravine, my heart." He framed my face with his hands. "To the ends of the realm."

53

CASPIA

The carriage jostled side to side as the driver did his very best to hit every bump in the road.

I gritted my teeth and wrapped my arms around my belly, breathing through my nose. My back ached. My legs were restless. My stomach churned with too many nerves. Too much unspent energy.

Too many layers.

My pants, tunic, and cloak stuck to my sweaty skin, and the open windows only seemed to let in dust.

This carriage was supposed to keep me out of the elements on the journey to the Evon. Andreas wouldn't like it, but after our next stop, I was riding on the supply wagon. This damn carriage could return to Roslo for all I cared. I couldn't be trapped in here for five suns, no matter what agreement I'd made with my husband.

The clop of hooves was a steady companion as our caravan meandered through Quentis fields of wheat and grain. As far as I could see, there were golden hills and sweeping green plains. Not long ago, we'd passed a farmer riding on a horse-drawn plow, tilling a pasture.

He'd stopped and stared as our legion passed.

Andreas had wasted no time in organizing our expedition once we'd decided to search for the orbits. We had four wagons loaded with food, water, and weapons. We'd brought along digging equipment and lanterns in case the orbit was buried. He'd enlisted a healer to accompany us in case of injury. And he'd hired fifty trained soldiers to escort us to and from the Evon, as well as a trader who frequently traveled the ravine.

Seth Hay and his family made their living by transporting goods to and from Genesis. He was one of the few merchants who didn't haul goods to the coast and ship them by boat. Instead, they traveled up and down the Evon every lune.

They had a fleet of narrow wagons specially designed for the steep switchbacks that cut into the ravine's cliffs. Their pack mules were bred for their sure feet and calm temperaments. And the Hays were arguably the most versed in the ravine's monsters.

Andreas was probably paying them more for this single trip to the bottom than they'd make in all their other trips this year combined.

A whistle rang out from the distance, and I swayed forward as the carriage driver pulled back on the horses. The moment the wheels stopped, I was out the door, marching away from the carriage for some air.

"My lady, wait." The young driver leaped from his seat, but I ignored him and kept moving.

I stalked off the road and into a field of grass that tickled the tops of my boots. The ground was uneven and the grass so tall and thick it was like wading through water. But with every step, I dragged in long, deep breaths until my head cleared, and my noontime meal sank back into my stomach from my throat.

I stopped and closed my eyes, tilting my face to the sky.

"My lady." The young driver stopped a few paces away, panting as he looked between me and the carriage. "Are you ill?"

"No. I just needed to breathe." To feel like I wasn't trapped in a cage. I waved him off. "You can go."

"I, um...I'll wait for you."

"Don't worry. I won't be alone for long."

A moment later, Andreas galloped over on his bay horse, swinging off in a fluid motion and tossing the reins to the carriage driver. "Go."

"Yes, sir." The driver bowed, then led the horse away.

"Are you okay?" Andreas scanned me from head to toe, frowning when his gaze landed on my face.

I didn't have a mirror, but I knew I looked a mess. My hair was frizzy, the curls wild from the stuffy carriage. Sweat beaded on my brow, and I'd felt the color drain from my face an hour ago.

"I'm riding on a wagon beside a driver," I told him. "Or you can find me a horse. But I'm not getting back in that carriage."

"All right."

"How much longer will we travel today?" I spun in a slow circle, taking in the area. We'd stopped beside a grove of trees that bordered the road on both sides.

"Another few hours until we reach the village." He put his hands on my shoulders, kneading at the stiffness in my muscles. "I'll send a rider ahead and have a bath ready."

He hated this. It was written all over his face. But neither of us would turn back now, not when so much was at stake.

It would take five suns to reach the Evon. We could make it in four, but if we stretched it to five, it meant we could stop at an inn each moon. And while part of me longed to sleep beneath the stars, curled next to Andreas, I wanted to be as rested as possible by the time we reached the bottom of the ravine.

Tomorrow, we'd reach Arany, the closest city to Roslo, where everyone in our party would be able to stay at an inn. But otherwise, those traveling with us would pitch tents and camp outside the small villages along the route.

"Can you make it until tonight in the carriage? We're about to venture into lionwick territory. They are mostly nocturnal, but I'd feel better if you weren't on a horse or out in the open."

After what I'd read in the library about the monsters, they seemed deadly enough that I'd be wise to heed Andreas's warning. "Fine."

As much as I didn't want to be in the carriage, I didn't feel like coming face-to-face with a lionwick, either. There would undoubtedly be enough surprises on this journey once we reached the ravine.

Andreas bent to kiss my forehead, then took my hand, threading our fingers together. "I'll ride beside you for a while and—"

A man's scream split the air before it was cut short.

Andreas and I both whirled toward the forest as a horse without a rider came racing down the road. Blood gushed from four deep gouges cut into the animal's neck.

"Lionwick!" a soldier shouted, and chaos erupted. Fighters drew swords and notched bolts into crossbows. A handful of them spurred their horses our way, doing their duty to ensure we were safe.

"Go." Andreas gripped my arm, holding tight as we turned and ran for the carriage.

The thick grass slowed us to barely a jog.

A low growl caught my attention, and I looked over my shoulder just in time to see a barbed tail whip above the grass.

"Andreas, down!" I ducked, pulling as hard as I could on his arm.

The tail flew above us in a deadly arc but missed. Barely.

We stood, whirling as we kept moving away. Andreas's hold was unrelenting as he hauled me behind him.

A roar came a moment before a lionwick pounced from the grass, jaws open wide to reveal sharp, black teeth ready to sink into Andreas's flesh.

But Andreas had lifted his crossbow, and with a bolt

already loaded, a quick squeeze of the trigger sent the arrow into the monster's heart.

The beast landed at our feet, nearly toppling us over.

Its chest rose and fell with labored breaths. Blood seeped from the bolt and pooled on the dirt as it gave a final growl. Its front leg twitched once, and then it was dead. Its long, barbed tail slumped over its body like a snake.

"Vexx," I cursed, pushing the curls out of my face.

The soldiers riding for us kicked their horses to a run, their swords raised as they shouted, voices panicked.

A flash of gold caught my eye. The whip of another barbed tail, slicing through the air on its way to Andreas's throat.

I pushed at him as he pushed at me, both of us trying to save the other. He shoved me far enough out of the way the tail missed my face. But the monster was clever, and even though I'd shoved Andreas hard, whatever control it had on that tail was as quick as a bolt of lightning.

The tail dragged across his chest, cutting through his leather vest and shredding the clothes and skin beneath.

"No," I screamed as he dropped to his knees.

Behind us, soldiers charged, but years of training took control. Moving with a speed that was not my own, I ripped Andreas's sword from its scabbard across his back.

When the second lionwick pounced from the grass, I was already swinging. The blade cut clean through the monster's neck, severing its head.

Blood sprayed. Soldiers shouted. I dropped to my knees at Andreas's side.

"Divine." I ripped off the sleeve of my tunic, holding it to the blood coating his chest.

"I'm all right." He winced, his hands covering mine. "It's not deep."

"Help," I barked at the first rider.

"Get the healer!" the man yelled over his shoulder toward

the carriage. Then he barked orders at the other soldiers. "Spread out. Look for more. You three stay here."

I ignored them and focused on Andreas's wound, pressing harder to stanch the blood.

"Caspia." He put his hands over mine. "I'm all right."

I looked up and met his gaze, realizing my own was swimming with tears. "I'm sorry."

"I'm fine." He breathed, letting me feel the rise and fall of his chest. "I'm all right."

"I could have lost you." My chin began to quiver. "What are we doing?"

"Saving the realm from monsters far more deadly than the lionwick."

A woman came hurrying for us, a brown satchel strapped across her chest. A blue scarf covered the tops of her black braids while their ends hung loose. Her eyes stayed locked on Andreas, and only when her hands took the place of mine did I finally move out of the way and let her work.

She frowned up at him and shook her head. "These cuts will need to be sewn shut. But they're not deep. The Six spared your life."

The Six could fucking rot.

I bit my tongue as she dug into her satchel and took out a roll of gauze.

With deft fingers, she wrapped the wound, then stood, helping Andreas to his feet. As they started toward the wagons, I turned back to the dead lionwicks.

Their smooth, leathery coats were as golden as the castle we'd left behind in Roslo, their claws as black as their teeth. These creatures were designed to hunt and kill. Yet they were two of the most beautiful animals I'd ever seen.

Even in death.

I'd never killed before. The sword in my hand felt too heavy, but I didn't let it slip from my fingers.

There were beasts in Nelfinex with fangs and claws and

talons and teeth. Beasts feared by humans. But not the Starling. Never the Starling.

Except whatever bond we shared with beasts had been broken in Calandra a long time ago.

This was what Calandrans faced all the time, wasn't it? That farmer we'd passed earlier. Did he know how to save himself from a lionwick?

This attack hadn't been about food. There was much easier prey with the livestock in the area. They'd come after us for the kill.

For bloodlust.

What would these creatures be like if the orbits were destroyed? Would they be this vicious?

"My lady, may I escort you to the carriage?" The soldier who'd called for the healer dismounted his buckskin horse. His blond hair was combed neatly, and even though he was younger than most, if I had to guess, he was Andreas's age. Like my husband, he carried an air of authority.

"Thank you." I turned away from the carcasses and fell into step beside the soldier, his horse trailing close behind.

His expression remained blank, his eyes locked ahead where Andreas was sitting on the end of a wagon while the healer took out supplies to stitch his wounds.

Another soldier rode up to us, his horse's coat foamy with sweat. "We've checked the area. No signs of another monster, sir."

"What happened to the soldier in the trees?" I asked.

The man atop his horse gulped and shook his head.

"I'm sorry."

"We're all from Quentis," the blond soldier said. "We know the risk of traveling in the countryside."

"Does this happen often?"

"Never more than one at a time." The rider gulped. "They came right for you. Normally they climb up and hide in treetops before—"

"You can return to your position," the blond man ordered. "So can the others. We'll take extra caution with archers as we make our way through the trees."

"Yes, sir." The man rode off to relay the message.

They came right for you.

Yes, they had.

Probably because I'd been out in the open. But what if there was more to this attack? What if that bond between Starling and beast wasn't as broken as I'd thought?

When we reached the road, I didn't stop at the carriage, wanting to check on Andreas.

"Can I bring you a cloth, my lady?" the blond soldier asked before I could walk away.

"A cloth?"

His hazel eyes with amber starbursts dropped to my hands.

To my fingers coated in Andreas's blood.

"No." *Not yet.*

It would serve me well to suffer this blood on my hands.

As a reminder of everything at stake.

54

ODESSA

Traitors. That word ran on a loop through my mind as Ransom hurried us out of the gardens. Brother Skore and Brother Dime were traitors.

By the time we returned to the suite, my stomach was so knotted I was sick.

Evie didn't need much coaxing to take Faze to her room, and Faze didn't try to leave her side.

Were we fools to think we could separate them? Their bond grew stronger every day, and I was kidding myself to think he was my pet. Faze had belonged to Evangeline all along.

I left them on her bed with Merry the stuffed rabbit and a doll she'd taken from the nursery. And in the sitting room, I found Ransom at the windows, staring at the sea.

Waiting for Zavier's ship.

"How do you know Skore is a Kennin?" I asked, taking a seat on a chair.

"The robes. The Kennin wear blue." He moved away from the glass and took the seat across from mine. He leaned his elbows on his knees, his voice low as he spoke like he was afraid the walls were listening. "Generations ago, before the Shield of Sparrows treaty was formed, there was a war within the brotherhood. Few know it happened. Even fewer risk speaking of it. But my father felt it was important for me to know of the Kennin, given Turah's allegiance to the Voster."

"Aren't all kingdoms allied with the Voster?"

"Until today, I would have answered yes." He rubbed a palm across his beard. "But then I saw a Kennin walking through your father's halls."

Halls with more secrets than gold.

"The brotherhood fractured during the war. Those who opposed the Voster's ideals, the zealots, were killed. But some escaped death and, in their exile, formed the Kennin."

"What do the Kennin believe?"

"That they themselves should rule the five kingdoms. That those with magic should be in power."

"I can't see my father condoning those beliefs. Do you think he knows of the Kennin? Until you and the High Priest came to Quentis, the only Voster I'd ever seen in this castle was Brother Dime. And if he's playing both sides…"

"I don't know, Dess. But if the High Priest finds out, if he learns that Dime is working with the Kennin, the Voster will act. Without mercy. If there is any hint that your father has knowingly harbored a Kennin, he will fall. I do not want you here when that happens."

There had to be more to this story. I couldn't imagine Father being aligned with a magical faction that wanted to steal his crown. Unless the Kennin had something to do with his plans.

What exactly had I helped Skore retrieve from behind that waterfall?

It was a mistake to have kept the whole truth from Ransom. I never should have believed the Voster's lies.

Shades. I was in so far over my head I was drowning.

"I need to tell you something." I took a deep breath. Then I told Ransom all the missing pieces. From the journal of his mother's written in the old language to its stories that seemed to come true. To Brother Dime's vague warnings. To the waterfall and its luminescent tunnels.

And the days I'd spent with Brother Skore of the Kennin.

It was dark by the time Ransom returned to the suite. His hair was windswept, and he smelled of rain and salt.

"Well?" I asked, standing from the couch where I'd been reading Luella's journal since putting Evie to bed.

"It's done."

I exhaled. "Is this the right decision?"

"I don't know, Dess." He crossed the room and pulled me into his arms. "But I don't know what else to do."

Ransom and I had talked for hours after I told him about Brother Skore. Neither of us knew what the priest had been after in those caves, but we agreed it was time to find out.

We didn't trust my father. We didn't trust Brother Dime. And while I was hesitant to believe the High Priest had our best interests at heart, Ransom had convinced me the only path to the truth about that magic was through the Voster.

So he'd gone to the docks to find a merchant willing to take a sealed missive across the Krisenth. The letter would go to a ranger Ransom had stationed in Perris. And that ranger would then take the message to the High Priest.

Ransom let me go and paced the room. He stopped in front of the couch, dragging a hand through his hair. When he looked at me, the unease I'd felt all day worsened. It was a look I'd seen before, like he wasn't telling me something.

"What is it?" I asked.

Before he could speak, a knock came at the door.

"Ignore it," I said at the same time he called, "Come in."

A lady's maid slipped inside. She gave Ransom a wide berth as she brought me a folded slip of parchment, delivering it after a curtsy. "A message, Highness."

I flipped it open and read the note as the maid scurried to leave.

I'll be in my suite after dinner.

"It's from Mae." I handed Ransom the note to read. "I'll take Faze to the gardens to pee tonight, then go to Mae's suite so we can talk."

He crumpled it and shook his head. "Will you listen if I tell you not to go?"

I lifted onto my toes and kissed his chin. "Probably not."

He cast his gaze to the ceiling. "Of all the women in this realm, it had to be you."

I smiled, kissed him again, and walked over to where Faze was sprawled on the floor to scoop him up.

After putting Evie to sleep, I'd snuck him out of her room so he could go outside once more. Ransom usually took him this late, but I'd handle it tonight and talk to Mae.

"Don't be long," he said.

"I won't." Hopefully I could coax Mae to come to the suite to talk so Ransom wouldn't have to fret.

Faze bounded at my side as I led him on his leash to the nearest stairs and to the main floor.

The guards stationed in the halls bowed as I passed. When I reached the door that led to the gardens off the west wing, the guard at the exit hesitated before letting me outside.

"Would you like me to escort you, Highness?" the man asked.

"I'll be all right. But thanks."

The night's wind was sharp against my cheeks as we stepped into the dimly lit gardens. I shivered, wishing I had brought a coat. I tugged Faze down a wandering stone path, willing him to be quick about his business.

A gust blew my curls into my face. I tucked my free hand into my pants pocket as my teeth started to chatter. "Are you done?"

Faze answered with a growl. He pulled on the leash, forcing me to turn.

A figure emerged from the shadows.

It was the guard from the fountain earlier. The man with the broken nose, the one Ransom had punched. Blood still stained his unbuttoned coat.

I took a step away, my heart inching up my chest.

Five other men emerged, one with his arm in a sling.

"You're not who we were expecting, but you'll do." The man with the sling laughed along with a few of the others.

Fuck. They'd been waiting for Ransom.

Six men against the Guardian wasn't enough. If Ranse could kill a crux, these idiots would have been child's play. Except Ransom wasn't here.

A skinny, wiry man tipped a brown bottle to his lips, taking a long pull. He wasn't dressed in uniform, but I'd seen him before in the training center with the other guards. The other men were familiar, too.

Guards. They were all guards.

I raised my chin, willing my hands to stop shaking. "Leave. Now."

They all laughed as they moved closer.

"My father will hear about this."

"Not if you go missing in the night," the man with the broken arm slurred.

If they were all drunk, I might be able to outrun them. I bent and picked up Faze, then glanced over my shoulder.

Where three others approached on quiet feet.

My stomach dropped. "What do you want?"

"That tarkin. He'll fetch us more coin than we'll make in a year working at this golden piss hole."

There wasn't a chance I could fight off this many men, even if they were drunk. But I forced as much bravado into my voice as possible. "Touch him and it will be the last thing you ever do."

They laughed in unison, a sound so loud it should have alerted the guards inside. But the wind howled, carrying their cackles and jeers into the dark.

I would run, see if I could break past the three behind me by some miracle. But before I could make my break for the door, my sister sauntered up beside the drunk guards.

She fell into step beside the wiry man with the bottle.

No. Not Mae. Not my sister.

Was this her doing? Was she the reason the guards had been tormenting Ransom?

The guard beside her glanced over, then took a second look.

She gave him a sickly sweet smile. Then slammed the palm of her hand into his nose.

My own laugh bubbled free, but any joy was cut short as the guard with the broken nose pointed at me.

"Get her," he barked.

The men collapsed on us, charging forward.

I kicked the guard who reached me first, my boot slamming into his groin.

He doubled over, groaning in agony.

"You little bitch," a man shouted at Mae as he swung a wild right hook.

She dodged the blow with a quick sidestep, snatched a dagger from her belt, and drove it into his thigh.

A hand fisted my hair from behind, and pain exploded through my skull as a man dragged me back, hard enough I tripped on my own feet. But I caught my balance and used a move Tillia had taught me in a training ring in Treow.

I stepped toward him, loosening the grip on my hair, then ducked and twisted, bringing my knee into his groin.

He let me go, dropping low enough I could drive my heel into his teeth.

The next man who came at me went down after I jabbed him in the throat, cutting off his air.

The attack was sloppy, but we were grossly outnumbered.

Mae whirled and slashed with her knives, but one of the men caught her wrist, twisting hard enough that she dropped the dagger. It clattered to the ground as she stomped on the back of the guard's knee.

I ran for the knife with Faze still clutched against my side, but before I could reach it, an arm banded around my shoulders. And then there was a blade at my throat.

"That's enough out of you." The man's breath was hot on my cheek and reeked of ale. It was the guard from the fountain. "The tarkin. *Princess.*"

"Never." I tossed Faze on the ground, hoping he'd run away.

He growled, landing on all fours as he bared his fangs.

"Get it," the guard barked, and two men chased after Faze, losing him in a hedge.

The guard's other hand reached around my front and came to my breast, squeezing so hard tears sprang to my eyes. His mouth came to my cheek, his tongue licking my face.

I closed my eyes, my neck straining away from the blade as its edge dug deep enough into my skin that I felt the sting of a shallow cut.

Mae was still fighting, her blond hair whipping around her shoulders as she avoided punch after punch.

A guard came flying at her, barreling into her side. They slammed into the ground as he climbed on top of her to pin her down.

"How much gold are you wearing, bitch? Do you keep it on when you're fucking Brix? Maybe I should find out why he's so obsessed with your cunt." He tore the jeweled necklace from her throat as she kicked and bucked against him.

Red coated my vision.

The blade dug into my throat as I struggled in the guard's hold.

A streak of pink-and-red fur came racing toward me as

Faze darted past the men chasing him. He leaped for the guard holding me, his claws sinking into the teal coat.

It was enough of a distraction that I grabbed the man's fist, forcing the knife away from my throat. With all my strength, I bent his wrist backward until his grip loosened. And then I wrenched the knife from his hand and drove it up and into the soft flesh under his chin.

Slick, hot blood sprayed across my hand and gurgled out of his mouth as he staggered away, eyes wide. Then he fell to the ground.

I whirled to help Mae, but before I could move, another guard grabbed my arms, holding me back.

Two other men were on top of my sister, pulling up her skirts to take the bejeweled daggers strapped to her thighs. The guard on top of her leaned in close, his mouth seeking hers.

"Fuck you." She spat in his face.

He licked a glob that landed on his lips, giving her a menacing smile. Then he took hold of her neck, choking her hard enough that her eyes bulged.

"No!" The scream that came from my mouth was so loud it pierced the night.

The sound of a door opening was faint in the distance. The guard who'd offered to escort me outside walked over, slowly at first, until he realized what was happening.

His jaw dropped as he drew his sword. But he wouldn't get the chance to defend us.

Behind him, moving faster than the wind, was Ransom.

His sword sliced through the first man he reached, clean at the waist, severing his body in two.

The man holding me let me go and scrambled backward, tripping over the guard I'd killed. He managed to get to his feet and sprint away into the night.

The other men scattered, trying to escape, but Ransom was a blur of fury and steel, striking them down until the only one left was the man who'd been choking my sister.

Ransom's sword landed hard on the stone as he punched the man, over and over and over. Blood-coated teeth flew in all directions until the man dropped.

Dead.

But Ransom didn't stop. He kept pummeling the man, turning the body into pulp.

Gods, there was so much blood. "Ransom, no," I shouted, rushing closer. "Stop."

He whirled on me before I could touch his shoulder, bloody fist raised. The silver in his eyes flowed like liquid metal. His focus shifted to my neck, to the cut, and his growl echoed through the gardens.

"It's just a scratch."

His gaze fell to his hands. To the blood coating his arms. Then to the corpse at his feet. Horror filled his expression.

I moved closer, but he shied away. "It's okay."

We both heard the lie. Nothing about this was okay.

Ransom took one last look at the guard's body. Then he was gone, disappearing into the night.

Faze walked over, tucking himself between my feet as he rubbed against my leg.

I bent and picked him up, stroking his scales. It was the second time I'd been attacked and he'd come to my rescue. "Thanks."

"Princess." The guard from inside appeared at my side. "Your neck."

"I'm fine." The cut was raw and bleeding, but I waved him off. "Help my sister."

But she didn't want help, either. She pushed herself up off the ground and righted the skirts of her dress to cover her legs. She walked to me with her chin held high and anger blazing in her blue eyes.

"How did you know I was out here?"

"I was coming out of the dining room when I saw you head outside. Glad I decided to follow."

"So am I," I whispered.

She stood above the dead man at my feet, his face unrecognizable. Then she sneered at his corpse.

"I'm sorry." I took her hand, holding it tight. Absorbing the trembling she was trying so hard to fight.

Her gaze lifted to the darkness. To the place where Ransom had disappeared. "And I thought I was vicious."

"He isn't."

She kicked the dead man's boot. "Are you sure about that?"

No.

Not anymore.

55

CASPIA

The Evon was a chasm of black obsidian. The rock absorbed the fragments of light from the sliver of sky above, and even the torches were struggling to win the battle against the dark.

Our group was near silent as we descended into the ravine. Any talk was kept to a whisper. The horses were quiet, too, stifling their whinnies and neighs. But the steady beat of their hooves and the crunch of wagon wheels on rock was enough noise to fill the canyon, every sound echoing above and below.

Seth Hay, the merchant Andreas had hired, walked ahead of me. His shoulder-length brown hair was tied with a leather strap at his nape. The strands were streaked with gray.

He was quite possibly one of the kindest men I'd ever met, with a quiet bravery that reminded me of Andreas.

We'd invited Seth to join us for dinner last evening, getting to know more about him and his family. When his father retired, Seth stepped into the role as head of his family's trading company. He was thirty-five summers and the oldest brother of three. He blamed his gray hairs on the ravine, teasing that the walls were so jealous of the rich, warm brown that they stole bits of the color each time he made this trip.

At this point, I wasn't sure it was in jest.

We'd been descending into the Evon for an hour, and I already felt it sucking the life from my bones. How he did this regularly was truly remarkable.

Seth glanced over his shoulder, making sure I was still a pace behind.

I gave him a nod and kept walking, one foot in front of the other. One hand skimming the stone at my side.

Ahead of us, a rock tumbled over the edge. It clattered and crashed on its fall lower and lower. The sound seemed to go on forever, until finally, it stopped at the bottom.

When we'd reached the ravine this morning, I'd marveled at how wide it was from one side to the other. I'd stood at the edge and lifted my arms, then closed my eyes and imagined beating my wings as I soared across the chasm.

Maybe, if the orbits were destroyed and the dark magic was purged from Calandra, I'd complete my ritus. And I'd fly over the Evon on wings that weren't imaginary.

A shout rang out ahead.

Seth held up his hand, stopping those of us behind him. Then he inched past the others in the line ahead, making his way toward the commotion.

"How are you?" Andreas stood behind me, wrapping his arm around my shoulders.

"I'm all right." I leaned against his chest, careful not to press too hard on his sutures.

The healer had given us herbed poultices to apply each morning to ensure the gashes from the lionwick didn't get infected. He'd promised me that he wasn't in any pain, but from time to time, he'd wince if he moved too quickly.

"I don't feel anything," I murmured. "What if there's nothing down here?"

"Then we'll regroup." He glanced over the edge. "But we've still got a long way to go."

I was already dreading the climb out of the ravine.

Seth had told us we'd be riding out. The switchbacks were so steep and long that hiking would not only be exhausting, but it was more dangerous than trusting a horse or mule. I wasn't an accomplished rider, but Seth had promised the horses we'd be riding had been up and down the ravine numerous times. They knew the way and would bring us home safely.

"Is everything all right?" Andreas asked as Seth returned.

"A few of the soldiers seem to be suffering vertigo." He rubbed at his lined forehead. "It's not uncommon. But I'd rather not see anyone else killed on this journey. My advice is to send them out."

Andreas nodded. "All right. This is your area of expertise. I'll defer to you."

As they talked about who would return, not just the soldiers in danger of falling but those who'd escort them out, I stared across the ravine, squinting as I tried to make out the switchback road on the opposite cliff.

But it was too far. Too dark.

How was I supposed to find an orbit in an area this large? If they were the same size as those in Nelfinex, the glass orb would be slightly larger than my favorite honey melon. Andreas would be able to carry it in one hand.

To find something that small in a ravine so large, we'd be here for summers.

It didn't take long for word to spread through the line that our party was breaking up. Ten men made their way past us, shuffling carefully. The blond soldier from the lionwick attack volunteered to lead the group out, and as he rode his horse past us, he gave Andreas and me a slight bow from atop his stallion.

Once they were gone, Seth faced forward.

And we continued our march into the depths of Calandra.

The stinging pain came at the end of the trail.

At first, I'd thought it was simply the cold and my nerves that had put me on edge. But once we stepped into the bottom of the Evon, I realized it was magic.

Above us, the sky was only a sliver of white between the towering cliffs. Every soldier carried a torch, the glow of the flames tinting the rocks in shades of orange and yellow.

The bottom was narrower than I'd expected. The cliffs tapered only slightly from top to bottom, but over such a vast distance, it meant down here in the depths, a person could cross from side to side in less than one hundred paces.

The ground was rocky and uneven. A path had been cleared between the switchbacks on one cliffside to the next for horses and wagons, but otherwise, it was jagged and rough.

It had taken half a sun to make the descent. Seth Hay said only a fool would sleep at the bottom of the ravine, and normally, they immediately began the climb on the opposite wall.

We had supplies to make camp, though I hoped we wouldn't need to stay that long, especially considering it would be impossible for the horses to accompany us over the rock. The rest of our journey would be made on foot.

Some of the soldiers would stay behind with Seth to watch over our supplies and protect the mounts from monsters. The rest came with us, their weapons at the ready.

Each had tucked either a pick or hammer into their belt. Our horses were all tied to wagons or the larger rocks scattered around us.

Some soldiers looked stoically into the darkness, searching for threats. Others looked wholly terrified, ready to leave the moment they were given permission.

I wasn't going to make them stay any longer than necessary.

The Evon ran sea to sea. On one end was the Krisenth Crossing. On the other, the Marixmore. The switchbacks had been carved closer to the Krisenth side. It would take suns, maybe weeks, to reach the ocean on the other end.

I hoped it wouldn't come to that.

"I can feel the magic," I told Andreas. "It's down here."

Closing my eyes, I focused on the prickle and the way it vibrated against my skin. I walked in the direction of the Krisenth, ten steps, then twenty. The sting lessened, barely. So I turned and followed the magic in the other direction, toward the center of the ravine, and as the sensation gradually grew stronger, I let the pain pull me along.

It was different than the ritus, yet the concept was the same. My blood knew where it was going. Toward danger.

"This way." I lifted the torch Andreas had lit for me and started along the rocky floor, careful to pick my footing so I didn't slip. Most rocks that fell from above had smashed to gravel. But there were stones of every size, all made of the same black obsidian.

"Let me carry that." Andreas took the torch, following close. His other hand remained poised at his sword's hilt.

The soldiers divided, most accompanying us while some stayed with Seth Hay to watch the wagons and horses. Heavy footsteps and dull murmurs followed Andreas and me as we made our way along the ravine.

I blocked out the noise, focusing on that irritating buzz. It didn't take long until we lost sight of the horses and wagons, the darkness swallowing the light from their torches.

We walked and walked, so far that Andreas finally forced me to stop and catch my breath.

"It's getting stronger." My face was damp with sweat. I rubbed at my arms, but the magic's sting couldn't be erased. Where the ritus pulled, this sensation almost pushed me away.

"My lord." A soldier cleared his throat behind Andreas. "How much far—"

Two shrill chirps came from above us, the sound bouncing off the cliffs.

A moment later, a body dropped onto the rocks beside us.

Seth Hay's lifeless eyes were open. So was his throat.

I screamed.

"Run. To the wall," Andreas shouted.

I couldn't tear my eyes away from Seth's face, frozen in horror.

"Caspia." Andreas gripped my arm and hauled me away, pulling me toward the cliffside.

The other soldiers all clustered together, weapons raised, as they searched the dark for whatever had killed Seth.

Andreas set the torch on a rock and pulled me against his body, flattening us against the ravine's wall as another shrill chirp resounded around us.

Then came the beat of wings and a blast of air that blew the hair out of my face.

The monster came at the soldiers like an arrow, swooping down from the dark, its wings as black as the obsidian.

"Down!" Every soldier dropped to a crouch as the beast flew overhead, snapping at them with its massive fangs, two on the top row of its mouth overlapping with two on the bottom.

Its beady, opal-white eyes caught the torchlight as it loosed another chirp. Its short tail had a spiked club at its end. Its long, pointed ears were fuzzy and turned upward, listening for any sound.

The monster missed each of the legionnaires, flying over them and disappearing into the dark.

"Stay against the wall," Andreas bellowed, holding me close to his side as he raised his sword.

"Chiroptus," I whispered, but saying the monster's name aloud still made it almost impossible to believe. Andreas had told me about the giant bats that drank blood.

Seth had warned us both about them before he died.

"By the grace of the Divine." I covered my mouth with my palm to smother a sob.

"Set down your torches," Andreas commanded the men. "Hide as much of the flames as you can. The monsters are mostly blind. They use the chirps to find their victims. Hold completely still when you hear them. Stay out of the light."

My racing heart climbed into my throat as I held my breath, waiting for the monster to return.

I didn't have to wait long.

Three chirps rang out, and then came the beat of wings.

The chiroptus swept down, landing on the rocks beside Seth's body. It was enormous, the size of a young crux. It had four wings, and each was covered in small barbs that flexed up and down as the monster sank its fangs into Seth's body. Slurping, gurgling noises filled the air.

All we could do was listen to the monster drink every last drop of the merchant's blood.

Tears dripped from my eyes. My entire body trembled.

Andreas moved so slowly it took me a moment to realize what he was doing. Inch by inch, he raised his crossbow. With the monster distracted, it didn't notice until the bolt zinged through the air.

It tore through a wing, tearing the leathery membrane.

The chiroptus screeched, the noise so loud I felt it vibrate in my chest.

"Fire!" Andreas shouted as the monster whirled toward us.

The soldiers didn't hesitate. Arrows and bolts rained down on the monster.

It tried to fly toward us, pushing off its short legs, but as it tried to flap its shredded wings, it collapsed.

A soldier beside us let out a fierce cry as he pushed off from the wall. He ran to the creature, driving his sword through its skull.

Everyone on the line exhaled a collective breath as he stood, turning to us with a victorious smile.

The chirp came but a heartbeat before another monster swept down from above.

It slammed into the soldier, and the man's scream was cut short by a bloody gurgle.

The soldiers killed the second chiroptus like they did the first, with a barrage of arrows and bolts. But this time, none risked emerging from the wall to ensure the monster was dead.

"Now what?" I asked.

Andreas bent to pick up his torch. "We'll stay close to the wall. If you hear their chirp, drop and freeze."

I pushed off the cliff, fisting my hands to hide their trembling.

Andreas looked behind us. I wasn't sure what we'd find when we retreated to the wagons, but it wasn't time to turn back. Not yet.

"Greater than us," I murmured.

He nodded. "Greater than us."

I continued on, following the sting.

When the next chirp came, we all huddled against the cliff, dropping to our knees. The chiroptus flew around us, stirring the air with its wings, but we were able to hide enough that it moved on. Probably to finish off the blood from the bodies of the men we'd left behind.

It became harder and harder to worry about the chiropti as the magic grew stronger, overwhelming my senses until all I felt was the sting slamming into me like waves.

My feet were too heavy, like someone had wrapped thick chains around my ankles. I went to step over a rock but tripped instead.

"Caspia." Andreas caught me, holding me steady as tears streamed down my face.

"It's close." I breathed through the pain, gritting my teeth as I took his hand and kept going.

The bottom of the ravine curved slightly, forcing us around a massive rock. As we rounded its edge, I came to an abrupt stop.

Ahead of us was a wall. The cliffs seemed to join together, blocking us from going any farther.

"Fuck," Andreas hissed.

"No." My heart dropped.

This wasn't the end of the ravine. But it was the end of our journey.

The only way past the wall was to climb over it, but it was as tall as the castle in Roslo. Maybe if we'd brought the right equipment, the soldiers could scale the face. But there was no way I could climb.

"Let's get back," Andreas said. "We won't make it up before nightfall, but I'm not risking staying down here with the chiropti."

Except I couldn't move. All I could do was stare at the wall, feeling that push, like the rocks were screaming. *Run, Starling. Run.*

Maybe the Starling from long ago had found another way to the bottom of the chasm. Or maybe...

I stepped toward the wall.

"Caspia." Andreas gripped my arm, but I wiggled free, pushing myself to go faster.

I didn't stop until I was within arm's reach, and only then did I see the gap. It was disguised by the dark, only visible from a certain slant. It opened to a tunnel through the wall.

"Wait." Andreas took my elbow, pulling me behind him. "I'll go first."

With his torch raised high, he led us through the passage, his sword ready at his side.

The moment I stepped through to the other side, the agony spiked. The bread I'd nibbled on this morning came up as I retched against the wall, vomiting until my stomach was empty.

"We're going back," Andreas said.

"Not yet. We have to keep going. We're close. I can feel it."

His molars ground together, but he didn't stop me as I kept walking.

The ravine's floor looked exactly the same as it had on the other side of the wall, the ground covered in rock fragments with only a sliver of light streaming from the opening far, far above.

I looked up, taking a moment to summon my strength. And that's when I heard the faint trickle of water. "Do you hear that?"

"Shh." Andreas held up his hand so the soldiers would be quiet. "There."

He pointed toward the opposite wall, to a section of rock that shimmered in the torchlight. A smooth, colorless waterfall that slicked down the obsidian.

"Water," I whispered. "Of course."

The Voster had fluid magic. They could manipulate water. The magic hadn't seeped from the orbits into the land.

It had started with water.

I hurried for the wall with Andreas close behind. The closer we got to the water, the stronger the magic, but I gritted my teeth and kept moving, refusing to stop when we were so close.

The waterfall was as tall and wide as a man's body. It came from a crack in the rock and flowed to a pool that was the size of a large bathing tub.

I dropped to my knees, the sheer force of the magic weighing me down. Then I peered into the pool to its bottom.

To a glass orbit hidden in the bottom of the Evon Ravine.

"Stay back and on guard," Andreas ordered the soldiers, standing beside me.

I reached for the water, but before my fingers could skim the surface, Andreas snatched my hand, pulling it away. "But it's down there."

"I'll do it." Andreas dropped to a knee, rolled up the sleeves of his shirt, and clenched his jaw. But the water didn't attack as he reached into the pool, pulling out the orbit with both hands.

The water sluiced off the glass, dripping from his hands and the ball.

The outer shell was clear, but its center was a swirl of water and wind. A magical storm trapped inside, raging to be set free.

"We found it." A tear slid down my cheek as my body sagged.

And then the world faded away.

56

ODESSA

"Where's Ransom?" Evie asked the question that had kept me up all night as she pushed the last bite of her breakfast pastry around her plate.

"He's busy this morning. But he'll be back soon."

The lie was more for my benefit than hers.

Ransom hadn't returned to the suite after the attack in the gardens.

I'd spent the night on the couch with Faze on my lap, watching the door, willing it, with every breath, to open. But as dawn lit the windows, as Evie roused from sleep, I gave up my vigil and prepared for a new day.

I'd invited Mae to the suite last night, but she'd declined. Instead, she'd retreated to her own rooms, asking one of the guards to send for Captain Brix.

For Mae's sake, I hoped the captain kept his job once Father found out about what had happened. I would hate for my sister to lose him.

"What are we doing today?" Evie asked, sneaking a piece of bacon to Faze under the table. "Can I play with Arthy?"

"Maybe later. We're going to visit a healer first."

"For your neck? What happened?"

"Oh, nothing." I adjusted the scarf I'd tied around my throat, covering the cut. "It's just a scratch."

*

Alore greeted us at the door to her workshop. She looked down at Evie and Faze over the rim of her turquoise glasses, gave them both a quick hello, then waved for us to follow her down the hall.

"His saliva didn't work. Neither did the tarkin's." She frowned at the cage of rats on her table. "At least not yet."

"But it might."

"It might." She pushed her glasses into her hair. "It's too bad we don't have the bariwolf that bit him."

No, that one-eyed monster was somewhere in Turah, spreading the infection and slaughtering innocent people.

"What's next?"

"I'm not sure." Alore sighed. "Since this hasn't worked…"

"Please don't give up." I let every bit of desperation bleed into my voice.

"Fear not, Princess. I'm not the giving-up type."

The grand foyer was clustered with people as we left the infirmary. The crowd was mostly nobility and their entourages making their way up the sweeping staircase to the second level.

A man with straw-colored hair nodded to Evie and me as he passed by. His caramel eyes locked on Faze tucked under my arm. He nearly tripped on the first step, too fixated on the tarkin to watch where he was walking.

Another man with his bulbous nose stuck in the air cut us off. Two older men, their bald heads bent together as they whispered, nearly bowled us over.

It was like swimming against the current.

"When can we go home?" Evie asked, her hand clutching mine.

"Soon, little star."

The crowd thinned as we made it to the center of the

foyer, and we veered toward the staircase that would lead us to the west wing.

But before we could start up the steps, a woman called my name. Her voice echoed through the space, as clear and resounding as the castle's midday bells.

Evie and I stopped in unison, both whirling around.

A group of travelers stood just inside the doors. Five weary, beautiful, familiar faces stared across the foyer.

Samuel Hay, a paperman and my friend, stood with his son, Jonas.

Geezala, the best healer from the fortress in Ellder.

Cathlin.

And Zavier.

He looked awful. His skin was gray, and he was much too thin. His tunic and vest hung loosely around his frame. The dark circles under his eyes were as purple and blue as bruises. But he was alive.

Alive. And in Quentis.

"P-papa?" Evie's hand slipped from mine as tears filled her gray eyes. "Papa."

"Evie." His voice cracked, his face crumpling with relief.

"Papa!" She tore off through the foyer. Arms and legs pumping. Brown hair streaming.

Zavier rushed for her, dropping to his knees as she flew into his open arms.

She slammed into his chest, her little arms wrapping around his neck as she sobbed, "Papa."

Zavier's shoulders shook as he cried, holding as tightly to her as she clung to him.

Her sobs filled the foyer, crashing into the vaulted ceilings. It was the sweetest music, the sound of a child's broken heart stitching itself together.

"Praise Ama." My hand came to my chest as my eyes flooded.

I let the tears fall as I walked over, straight into Cathlin's waiting arms.

"Hello, my dear."

"You're here." The weight of everything I'd been carrying seemed to press down on my shoulders.

And like she could feel my strength giving way, Cathlin hugged me tighter. "We're here."

A callused hand slipped into mine.

I held to Zavier as he held to Evie and Cathlin held to me.

A family reunited. Not the one of my birth, but the one of my making.

I peered past Cathlin's shoulder, giving Samuel and Jonas a watery smile. And for Geezala, I mouthed, *Thank you.*

She dipped her chin.

Cathlin let me go to dry her own eyes. She ran a hand over Evie's hair, and then her gaze swept through the lobby, searching. "Where's Ransom?"

Zavier sat on the couch in the suite with Evie curled in his lap, sound asleep. She'd drifted off not long after lunch, like it was finally safe for her to rest. Like the sadness couldn't haunt her dreams anymore.

And while she slept, I told Zavier and Cathlin everything that had happened since Ellder.

The gentle lines in Cathlin's face seemed to deepen the more I spoke. And the exhaustion in Zavier's doubled by the time I was finished telling them about last night.

"We can't stay here." Zavier closed his eyes, looking as tired as his daughter. He shifted slightly and winced, his entire body tensing as his hand came to his stomach.

"Are you all right?" I asked.

"You need to rest." Cathlin stood, smoothing the skirt of her tan dress. Her chestnut-brown eyes narrowed on where he clutched his belly. "I'll make you some of Geezala's tea."

The healer was in a suite down the hall, the same suite

where Thora had stayed. Samuel and Jonas were staying in the one where Jodhi had been.

Zavier looked down at Evie, stroking her dark hair. "Thank you. For keeping her safe."

Safe? That word seemed like an illusion. A luxury no Calandran could afford with the migration upon us. "Will you be all right to sail?"

Before Zavier could answer, the door to the suite banged open and Mae barged inside, the skirts of her green dress swishing around her legs.

"Get to the throne room." She panted, out of breath like she'd run the length of the castle.

"What?" I stood, the blood draining from my face. "What happened?"

"I don't know. My lady's maid just told me that there's a rumor going through the castle that Father arrested the Guardian and had him locked in the barracks."

My stomach dropped as my eyes shot to Zavier.

The hard, unyielding mask of a Turan ranger instantly fell over his face. His green eyes hardened as he carefully moved Evie and pushed to his feet. "I'll go."

"No. You stay with Evie." The last time Zavier was here, he lied to Father. Numerous times. His presence in the throne room would probably just make this worse. "We don't have much here, but we should pack."

"You're leaving?" Mae asked.

I gave my sister a sad smile. "We can't stay in Quentis. We need to return to Turah."

"What about the migration?"

"It's a risk we have to take."

She swallowed hard and squared her shoulders. "Then I'm coming with you."

"What? No. It's too—"

"Dangerous?" She scoffed. "Don't ask me to stay here. Not after last night. And not with him."

"Him, who?"

"Your father."

Your father. He was *our* father. "What are you saying?"

She rolled her eyes. "Do you really need me to spell it out?"

No, I guess not.

Then who? Was it Hawksley? She looked so much like Margot. There wasn't any resemblance to the general. But maybe, if Margot had been having an affair for years…

That would mean she wasn't my sister. At least not by blood.

Shades. I couldn't even fathom this. How long had she known? Was she certain?

"Mae, I…I don't know what to say."

"There's nothing to say. It doesn't really matter." Mae lifted a shoulder. "No one will ever admit it. But I don't want to stay here, trapped in the migration chambers with them. With all of them. If you're leaving, I'm going, too."

Later. We'd have to talk about it later.

And she was right about one thing.

It didn't really matter.

"This changes nothing. You're my sister. You're always my sister." I walked to her, pulled her into a tight hug.

It took less than a heartbeat for her to hug me back.

Then I let her go, clasped her hand, and dragged her with me to confront the Gold King.

"Where's Ransom?" I marched up the dais and stood before Father's throne, ignoring both Captain Brix and General Hawksley.

Father's jaw clenched. "Leave us."

Brix bowed and obeyed. Hawksley lingered for a heartbeat, then did the same.

"You, too, Mae," Father said.

She huffed but followed Brix.

"Answer my question." I crossed my arms over my chest, meeting his glare.

"He's been arrested and detained."

So the maid's gossip was true. "Release him. Now."

Father leaned an arm on his throne. "He will be released after an investigation. I received a report that your tarkin attacked a guard yesterday in the gardens who was then brutally injured by your husband. I can't ask that guard because he's dead. Murdered last night, also in the gardens. Along with numerous other guards in my employ."

"You're right. That guard is dead." I tugged down my scarf so he could see the cut. "He held a knife to my throat. So I put it through his."

Father looked away from my neck. "I've also received reports from my informants that the Guardian killed General Banner. That's a crime I cannot overlook."

"*I* killed Banner. When he attacked me to get revenge on Ransom."

"You killed the most skilled soldier in Quentis?" He scoffed. "I'm not a fool, Odessa."

"It's the truth. Believe it or not. I don't care." I held out my hands, wrists bare and awaiting his manacles. "You'd better call the guards to shackle me in irons and take me to a cell, too."

Father's mouth flattened. "As he is a prince, I will not deliver the same justice as I would anyone else. But he will be exiled from Quentis. Until those arrangements can be made, he'll be held at the barracks. And once he is banished, you will remain."

"No, I will not." I turned away, retreating down the dais's steps.

Yet another pointless conversation with my father.

"Odessa," Father barked. "Do not fight me on this. You will do as I say. It's for your own good."

I paused, slowly turning back. "Was it you who sent the

guards? The one at the stables, whipping that horse. The man at the fountain yesterday, trying to steal *my* tarkin. Was it your idea to provoke Ransom so this was the outcome? What about the men last night who nearly killed Mae? The men who could have raped us?"

The color drained from his face like I'd slapped him.

So the men last night hadn't been his doing. But Father had been after the Guardian from the start. These were all feeble excuses to send Ransom back to Turah.

I was nearly across the throne room when he called my name again.

"Odessa." He stood in the center of the room, his throne empty over his shoulder. "Trust me."

"No. Never again."

The barracks in Roslo were located at the city's farthest edge, tucked against the same stone wall that stretched past the castle. The white building was short and narrow with a brown roof and teal door.

From the outside, it looked barely large enough to house five men, let alone five hundred. But the exterior was simply a facade for the underground network of rooms cut into the rock.

These were the city's original migration chambers before more had been added beneath the castle.

The rooms were cramped. Beyond the entrance, there were no windows or natural light. It was no wonder most legionnaires chose to live with their families. The only difference between the dormitory rooms and jail cells were doors instead of iron bars.

The guard stationed at the entrance to the cells was five zillahs richer as he gave me a lantern and waved me down the narrow corridor. He didn't ask which person I was here to visit.

Every cell was empty save the last.

Ransom sat at the far corner, back pressed against a rough stone wall. His knuckles were stained with dried blood and dirt. His silver eyes glowed like the twin moons. His entire body trembled, not from the cold but a simmering rage.

Two of the bars to his cell were caved outward like they'd been kicked hard enough to bend.

How long had he been here? How many men had it taken to put him in this cell?

"There you are."

"There's my queen."

I gripped a bar. "I'll get you out of here."

"If I told you to leave, would you listen?"

I set my lantern on the hard stone floor, then took a seat beside it.

Ransom closed his eyes, dragging a hand over his face. "Of all the women in the realm…"

"This one will always find you. Here, or in the shades."

He swallowed hard, his throat bobbing. The collar of his shirt was open like it had been torn. Dark-green veins snaked along his collarbones. When he opened his eyes, they were full of regret. "Go, Dess."

"No, Ranse." I reached through the bars, holding out my hand. He didn't move, so I snapped my fingers. "I'm waiting."

The corner of his mouth turned up as he scooted across the small space to lean against the bars. Then his hand enveloped mine as he brought it to his lips. He dropped his forehead to our clasped hands, his skin feverishly hot. "I'm sorry."

"I love you."

"Don't forget."

I sighed. "Why don't you say it back?"

"I do." He reached through the bars to twist a curl around his little finger. "A thousand times a day."

He tugged me close, leaning in to kiss the corner of my mouth. He ran the length of his nose against mine. He traced the line of my collarbone, his finger dipping into the hollow of my throat.

A thousand times a day.

Knowing Ransom, this was his way of protecting me. He was still so sure the Lyssa would be his end. That he was saving me pain by preparing me for the inevitable.

He'd still given up hope.

Maybe someday, when we had a cure, when the infection was gone, he'd say those words out loud.

Not that I needed them. Not anymore.

I gave the bars my weight, crossing my legs to get comfortable. Well, as comfortable as I could get on a stone floor. If Ransom was here tonight, then so was I. Except as soon as I relaxed, a sharp sting ran the length of my arm, wrist to elbow, and the zing was so intense my entire body jerked.

"Ouch," I hissed.

Ransom was on his feet in a blink, his hands balled into fists as he stared down the dark hallway. His jaw clenched as every muscle in his body went taut.

"What?" I followed his gaze, squinting into the shadows.

The sensation of spiders crawling along my skin came a moment before the swish of blue robes.

Brother Skore walked into my lantern's light and stared down at me from his towering frame.

Ransom slammed a hand against a bar. "Stay away from her."

I stared up at him, holding the priest's dark-green eyes. Maybe he was a traitor. Maybe he'd manipulated me in those waterfall caves. Maybe I would regret this decision someday.

Or maybe not.

"Help him. Please. There's an infection in his blood."

I had a feeling he already knew that.

Brother Skore lifted a hand, his grooved, clawlike nails pointed on each finger. He closed those endless eyes.

And began siphoning the Lyssa from Ransom's blood.

57

CASPIA

Four Voster walk across a cold marble floor, their burgundy robes swishing over bare feet.

Andreas faces them, hands clasped behind his back, seemingly relaxed except for the hidden dagger clutched in his fist.

Through the wide balcony doors, a wind sweeps into the large, echoey room.

Sunlight streams through windows tinted with blues and greens and yellows.

A cry rings out from a room far above.

Four priests lift their eyes to the ceiling. Then they scatter to hunt.

Two move on silent feet to the doors.

One fixes his gaze on Andreas.

And the other stalks toward me, the pain of his magic driving through my chest like a blade.

Andreas shouts for the guards to stop them. He throws his dagger toward a priest, but an invisible wind bats the weapon away, its blade clattering as it skids across the floor.

We cannot fight them.

We cannot win.

Not as we are.

...

I stood on the balcony, staring across Roslo to the sea. It had been hours since I awoke from the vision, but it had stayed with me, refusing to loosen its grip.

I'd seen that room before. I'd seen those Voster priests.

Did they already know about the orbit? Now that we'd

removed it from that pool, had their magic lessened? Or would we have to find a way to destroy it first?

Maybe that vision was what awaited us after we found them all.

"Caspia," Andreas called from inside.

I didn't reply, knowing he'd find me. He always knew where to look. The man had a tether to my heart.

"There you are." He came up behind me, arms instantly wrapping around my shoulders.

"Is it done?"

"It's done."

I exhaled, the tension leaving my body in a whoosh. For the first time in suns, I could breathe. The pressure in my chest vanished.

"Can you feel anything?" he asked.

"Nothing."

The orbit was now hidden in a locked chamber in his family's vault. Far enough away I couldn't feel its magic.

Maybe it was wishful thinking, but I'd felt different since waking up after the Evon. I couldn't see quite as far as I'd been able to five suns ago. Sounds and noises weren't quite as loud.

I'd cut my finger this morning on purpose to see how quickly I healed.

Fast. But not as fast.

At least, I hoped.

Was it possible that we'd already altered the state of the continent by taking that orbit out of the ravine? If it was in an iron box, no longer touching water, sealed in a vaulted tunnel, had we lessened its magic?

Andreas reached into his pants pocket and took out a ring of keys. He peeled them apart, holding up a simple brass key that caught the light. "For now, this stays with me. Until I can find a place to keep it safe. Only you and I will ever know what's locked away."

I nodded. "The soldiers?"

"Before we left, I told them we were searching for a historical relic. They all believe that's what we pulled from that pool. Each received a sizeable bonus for accompanying us. And I've given the same to the families of those who died."

"And Seth Hay's family?"

"Will never have to travel the ravine again."

"Good." I pressed a hand to my heart, still aching for the kind merchant's death.

Seth's body, and those of the other fallen soldiers, had been taken out of the chasm so they could be returned to their loved ones and mourned properly. Half of the people who'd stayed with the horses and supplies at the bottom of the Evon had been killed by the chiropti.

I had no memory of leaving the Evon Ravine.

After I'd lost consciousness, Andreas had carried me and the orbit to the horses. He'd let the others collect the dead bodies as he rode us out of the ravine.

He reached the top by dusk with the others not far behind. He caught up with the soldiers who'd suffered from vertigo and explained that I'd suffered the same and passed out.

It was the orbit's magic and the onslaught of pain that had shut down my body. And while Andreas had been worried about separating us, he'd taken the chance.

The orbit had traveled back to Roslo with the blond soldier, a man named Taven. While Taven traveled ahead with the orbit and a few others, Andreas rode with me in that awful carriage. Not that I remembered traveling back to the city, either.

I'd woken up in my own bed, four suns after the ravine.

"We need to talk about the other orbits," he said. "We're not going after them. At least, you're not."

"I expected you to say that."

"And I'm expecting you to try to convince me otherwise. Be warned, I've had five days to prepare my argument."

"No argument."

He stilled for a heartbeat, then let me go to spin me around. "Really?"

"I had a vision last night. About the Voster. They came for us."

"Fuck." His jaw clenched. "When?"

"I don't know. Maybe not until we find them all. But if taking that orbit altered their magic, in any way, we should lie low."

His expression turned serious as he stared out over the city. "There's no way they could know it was us. Unless Hain revealed who you are."

"No, he wouldn't." Not when he was working against the brotherhood. "You're sure the soldiers won't speak a word of it?"

"None of them saw what I pulled from that pool. They were too far back, and it was too dark. I wrapped it in my cloak before I carried you out of there."

"And Taven?"

"He's loyal. But I'll still find a way to tie him to us."

"With gold? Or secrets?"

"Both."

I didn't like the idea of blackmailing Taven, but if our lives depended on it, so be it.

"We can't give up," I whispered. "We only have until the migration."

Andreas rested his chin on my head. "We won't have time. We could traipse all across Calandra, do nothing but search for the orbits, and still fail. We need help."

"But I'm the only Starling."

"That doesn't mean you have to do this alone. Now that we know what we're looking for, we'll find a way."

I leaned against his chest, breathing in the scents of wood and soap and spice, listening to his heart. "It feels impossible."

"Have faith, my heart."

"Emery used to say that. Whenever I'd get discouraged, she'd tell me to stand tall. To have faith in the Divine's grace." I closed my eyes, breathing through the twist in my chest. "I miss my sister. I miss Xandra. For her, we have to find the others and destroy them."

"We will prevail."

I hoped he was right.

Part of me wished we'd never left that cabin in Genesis. Maybe, once this was all over, we'd go back.

"What do we do now?" I asked.

"We keep our heads down. Quietly, slowly, we enlist help. It's time we told Faxon everything. I'll bring Taven into the fold. And we'll do what we can from Roslo to identify where the other orbits might be."

"Eventually, we'll have to seek them out."

"Yes. But I see no point in bringing them here until we know how to destroy them."

"And how will we figure that out?"

He gave a dry laugh. "Not a godsdamn clue."

"Have faith." I repeated his words. "We will prevail."

Maybe if we kept the faith, if we believed in each other and this fight against evil, the Divine would gift us the help we needed to succeed.

Andreas and I held on to each other as the sound of waves crashed in the distance.

"Who do I believe in now?" he whispered. "I've spent my whole life praying to gods who do not exist."

His voice was heartache. I hadn't realized until this moment how much this truth would cost him. Andreas wasn't just discovering a long-lost tale. This was reshaping the entire foundation of his history and religion.

"Believe in the Divine."

"I don't know your god," he murmured.

"I promised you once, in that cabin in Genesis, that when

I came to Quentis I'd teach you about the Divine's grace. I guess it's time for me to make good on that vow."

He searched my gaze, taking my face in his hands. "Until then, I'll believe in us."

"Us."

In a love that would carry me through eternity. A love that would bring us together again.

"Us," he repeated, sliding his hands down to my rounded belly.

The baby kicked at his hand like she was saying hello to her father.

The smile that lit up Andreas's face was breathtaking.

Us. Only us.

Until the Divine called me home.

58

ODESSA

Ransom sagged against the jail cell's bars, exhausted and weak. The dark veins that had been creeping toward his throat were gone now that the Lyssa had been siphoned.

Brother Skore had left moments ago without a word.

I reached through the bars, easing down the collar of his shirt, expecting to still find them over his heart. But they were gone. Entirely.

His chest was nothing but smooth, firm skin over hard muscle.

I doubted this was the cure we desperately needed, but it was enough. It was a reprieve from the pain and rage. This would give us time.

"He's more powerful than the High Priest," Ransom murmured. "I'm not sure if I should be grateful or terrified."

"Both." I inched closer to hug his arm and thread our fingers together.

The scorching, unnatural heat from his skin was gone. His eyes were a swirl of brown and green and gray that blended to a muted hazel. It wasn't the vibrant green I loved so much, but anything was better than silver.

"You should go," he said. "Get some rest."

"Not yet." If Ransom was going to stay in this cell until we left Quentis, then I'd stay here, too. "My father plans to exile you from Quentis. Maybe if we expedite that exile, we could all set sail in the morning. I haven't heard any news of other crux scouts. It gives me hope that we'll make it home before the migration."

"Dess?" he whispered, his voice so groggy he sounded seconds from sleep.

"Yeah."

"I need to tell you something. About the crux scout." His hesitation was enough for me to know he wasn't going to deliver good news.

"What is it? Did it kill someone else? Tillia?"

"No. She's fine." He shook his head. "I don't think the migration is coming yet."

I sat up straighter. "What? Why?"

He twisted to face me, both of his arms snaking through the bars. "The crux in Ellder was…different."

"Different, how?" It had been as deadly and horrifying as the portraits and murals in the art gallery. It had been exactly as the stories depicted, a monster that came and killed without mercy.

"After she died, her body—it changed." He swallowed hard. "It shifted into the body of a woman."

"I don't understand." I pressed the back of my hand to his forehead to make sure the fever hadn't returned.

He took my wrist, gently tugging it away. "I know how this sounds. Had I not seen it with my own eyes, I wouldn't believe it, either."

I replayed every conversation we'd had about that night in Ellder. Every time he'd called the crux *she*. This was why.

"It became a woman? So it was a shapeshifter?" Beings I'd only ever heard about in children's tales.

"Yes. And I don't believe she was a scout."

"Why do you say that?"

"Her hair." He twined a curl of mine around his pinkie. "It was the same as yours."

My hand lifted, touching a strand by my ear. "What are you saying?"

"I don't know, Dess. I don't know what to think. The reason I haven't told you is because I can't make sense of it. But there hasn't been another scout. I rode across Calandra, and there wasn't so much as a whisper. And it's too early for the migration. This woman, this shifter, I believe she came on her own. Or maybe she was always here."

The realm seemed to drop away, the sensation of falling so powerful my stomach pitched. "I don't... What does this mean? Shapeshifters. That's...impossible, right? And why would she come to Ellder?"

"Maybe she was looking for something."

Not something. *Someone.*

"Me. You think she might have been looking for me?" I hated to even speak those words, but it fit with our other theories. That monsters were drawn to me. "She came to kill me."

"Or me," he said.

No, this wasn't about him. He couldn't feel Voster magic. He hadn't been hunted by monsters at every turn.

"Oh gods." I slapped a hand over my mouth as tears filled my eyes. "If the crux came to Ellder because of me, then I'm the reason your mother died."

"No." He took my face in his hands, pulling it close so my forehead pressed against the bars. "The crux killed her. Not you. Don't take this on yourself."

"But, Ranse—"

"No, Odessa. This is not because of you."

I wanted so badly to believe him. "Why didn't you tell me?"

The skeleton forest had been ten—no, eleven days ago. All those times when I'd felt like he wasn't telling me something. This was it.

"Because I knew you'd take Ellder on yourself."

He wasn't wrong. So many lives lost. So many people slaughtered.

The image of Luella's body being cleaved in two was so crisp in my memory, even when I squeezed my eyes shut, I couldn't block it out.

"Why have I never heard of this before? If the crux are shapeshifters, it should be common knowledge." There'd been hundreds of the monsters killed in past migrations, their carcasses burned to ash. If those corpses were human, it was this continent's best-kept secret.

"They can't all be shifters. She just took their form."

My head was spinning. "What color were her eyes?"

"I didn't look."

"And her body?"

"I ordered it to be burned. I didn't want rumors spreading. Her blood was green. It...it looked like mine. Those in Ellder who saw her will keep it quiet."

Turans and their secrets.

If Thora were here now, she'd throw that right in his face.

"Does your father know? Is that why he hasn't sent word of the scout and alerted other kingdoms to prepare for the migration?"

"No." Ransom's jaw clenched. "He rode to Allesaria. He never saw the body."

So Ramsey had willingly forsaken the other kingdoms. He'd gone into hiding in his capital and left the rest of Calandra to suffer. *Bastard.*

"I don't know what to think about all of this, Ranse."

"Maybe I can help." A voice carried from the hall.

I turned, squinting in the dim light as the guard I'd bribed earlier ambled closer. "You?"

He shifted his weight foot to foot, then moved to the side, waving forward a woman wearing a bejeweled navy gown. Her hands were clasped behind her back. Her crown's jewels caught the lantern's flickering light.

"Margot?"

"This is no place for a princess, Odessa." She clicked her tongue, then looked at the guard. "Bring a fresh lantern."

"Yes, Majesty." He scurried off and returned a moment later with a lantern. He set it down beside the cell, then bowed to Margot.

"Leave us," she ordered.

The guard didn't need to be told twice.

Her posture relaxed as his footsteps retreated, and she stepped closer, inspecting Ransom's dirty cell. "I'm sorry."

"Can you get him out of here?"

"No. Your father kept the key himself." She gave me a sad smile, then brought forward a book that had been hidden behind her back.

The cover was so dark a purple it was nearly black.

Margot crouched before me, her gaze roving over my hair and face. She reached for my neck, not to touch the cut on my throat, but to tug free the necklace I wore each and every day.

"I hoped you'd never find this necklace," she said, taking the pendant in her palm. "But it called to you. She told me you'd find it one day."

"Who?"

She let the pendant rest gently over my heart, then looked to the book. "I want you to know that I always tried to protect you. From your hair to your dresses. I only meant to keep you safe. To keep my vow."

There were tears in her eyes when she lifted her chin. "Read this together. Your father will be on the balcony in the throne room when you're finished."

"What is it?" I asked, taking the book from her outstretched hand.

She cupped my face, tracing my cheekbone with her thumb. "Your dynasty."

59

CASPIA

Emery and Aunt Oleana stand side by side in the castle mews, looking out over Showe.

"I forbid it, Emery," Oleana says. "Your place is here with your daughter. Graciella has spent her life without you."

"She had you."

"I'm not her mother. Caspia and Xandra made their choices. As you made yours. The time has come for you to take your place in the Starling dynasty."

Emery stares into the distance as a breeze tickles the ends of her wild red curls. It's longer than it was when she left. Thinner.

She's older. Tired. Grieving. She wears a simple cream dress that leaves her arms bare. Her skin is covered in scars.

"Do you think I wanted to be taken captive by the Beesans, Aunt Oleana?" she asks, her voice lifeless. "Do you think I intended to spend Graciella's life in a rotting hole in Beesa, my blood stolen by their alchemists for experiments? Do you think I wanted to watch the love of my life be chained and tortured? To live at the mercy of those bastards who used my child against me until she finally broke?"

Emery swallows hard, dropping her gaze to the floor. She presses a hand to her empty womb. A tear falls from her eye, landing next to her bare toes. "They took my child. They ripped her from my arms and used her to keep me captive. Just like they used Max. We were only meant to be gone for a short time. To sail to Azzon for a lune and return home after tempers had cooled. I never meant for any of this to happen."

Oleana's chin quivers as she stares into the distance. "For what they did to you, they will pay. I vow it. But you leaving here to chase after your sister solves nothing."

"I cannot abandon them. Caspia and Xandra left to avenge me. If there is even a chance they're alive after all this time, I cannot forsake them. I cannot live knowing I didn't try."

"They are gone. It's been twenty-four summers. Let them go." Oleana's nostrils flare, but tears fill her eyes. Tears of a woman realizing no matter how hard she tries, she cannot save Emery's life. "Caspia's vision was of your death."

"You don't believe in Caspia's visions."

Oleana turns away from the city. "I do now."

Emery waits until she is gone. Then she stands tall, eyes fixed on the horizon.

Fixed on a land she cannot see.

A land that will be her doom.

...

My lady's maid stood behind me at the vanity, working a plait into my hair. Her fingers stilled. Again. When I glanced up, her gaze was not on my hair but in the mirror, staring at Andreas in its reflection. *Again.*

He sat in the rocking chair with our daughter in his arms. An adoring smile pulled at his lips as he traced the line of her delicate nose. His teal coat was unbuttoned and the white shirt beneath open to reveal a sliver of taut skin and the hollow beneath his throat. The scar from the lionwick attack was raised but no longer pink.

His golden hair was neatly combed, his jaw clean-shaven. His caramel eyes caught the light streaming through the open windows, making the amber starbursts glow.

I couldn't blame the maid for staring.

My husband had never looked more beautiful.

"Margot," I murmured.

Her blue eyes snapped to mine in the mirror, and her cheeks flushed. "Sorry, Majesty."

I pulled in my lips to hide a smile as she returned to the braid.

Margot was one of many people in this castle in love with the king, myself included.

Andreas's crown was sitting on the table beside the rocking chair. He was still adjusting to wearing it every sun.

During the final lune of my pregnancy, Andreas's mother had been taking a stroll through the castle's gardens when she collapsed. She died before the healers could be summoned. They believed her heart had given out.

It happened on the anniversary of Arick's death.

Malynn's passing to Gloree shocked the kingdom and devastated the Cross family. Andreas's father withered in only weeks and, in his grief, decided it was time to pass the crown to his heir.

Andreas took his vows three suns after the baby was born. He swore oaths and assumed the role of king. He signed treaties in his blood that were bound by Voster magic by the brotherhood's appointed emissary, a priest named Brother Dime.

I skipped that part of the ceremony, choosing to stay hidden away in this suite. The baby's rooms were my favorite part of the castle these suns.

As queen, I made a few short, select appearances at the ceremonies and celebrations. But I kept them to a minimum, wanting as little attention as possible, especially if there were Voster in the castle.

When Brother Dime finally left, Andreas and I had both breathed a huge sigh of relief that he'd been none the wiser to the orbit locked away deep within the king's vaults beneath the castle.

But it meant our quest to find the other orbits was indefinitely delayed. The treaties Andreas had signed as king would limit his freedom and actions. He'd effectively been chained by their rules.

I hoped that eventually the orbits could all be destroyed. That the Six would be put to an end and magic in Calandra erased. I hoped my visions were wrong and I'd get to see that future. Not all of them came true.

Except we still didn't know how to destroy the orbits. So for now, that worry had been cast aside. We were enjoying these quiet suns with our daughter.

Beside Andreas's crown was a carved wooden rattle—a gift from Faxon and Kos.

Tomorrow, I was taking her to the library. It was time to take her out of this suite and introduce her to my friends.

She was only three lunes old, but I had no doubt that my tiny, precious Quentin princess would win hearts around the castle. Though the heart she'd stolen first was mine. Andreas's was a close second.

I'd almost convinced myself we were having a boy because of the vision I'd had of Andreas with his blond son. But when the midwife announced the baby was a girl, it wasn't really a surprise.

The Starling only had daughters.

So I didn't think about the vision of Andreas with a son. I didn't let myself fret over what that meant. I was ignoring the sinking feeling in my stomach because if I thought about the visions too much, I couldn't breathe.

So I didn't think about the future I saw in my dreams. I blocked out the visions and prayed every morning that by the grace of the Divine, our fates would change.

If they didn't, well...

I was grateful for the chance to learn the truth, even if it wasn't gentle.

I'd been gifted a chance to see Emery in her final suns. To learn why she'd come to Calandra—for me.

I wished, so much, that I could send a message to Nelfinex. That I could tell her to stay. To listen to Aunt Oleana. To forget finding Xandra and me.

She wouldn't. Emery would come here and meet her end by the silver-eyed warrior.

If only I'd known back when I was in the palace in Showe that the vision of her death was of the future. Maybe it would all be different.

Even so, I'd never regret coming to Calandra. Not when it meant Andreas and our daughter.

Not when it meant answers to so many questions.

In another vision I'd had weeks ago, a vision of the past, I'd watched my mother fly to Calandra. Her death, like my sister's, had been a mercy. A monster slain to save countless others.

The silver-eyed warrior would kill Emery. A Voster priest who didn't walk on the earth but floated above it had killed our mother.

At least through that vision, I'd had the chance to see my mother's face, just once, even if it had been in death.

She looked like me. We had the same wild, red curls.

My daughter would look like me, too.

The visions I'd had of my beautiful girl were a painful, glorious gift.

Margot's fingers fumbled with a lock of hair, and on her gasp, the entire plait came apart. Her eyes closed, defeat weighing on her shoulders.

My hair was difficult at best, and braiding it was always easier if it was wet. But the curls were dry, and today, Margot was losing the battle.

"Don't worry about the braid. Let's tie it back," I said.

"Are you certain, Majesty? I can try again. It's easier if I have your comb. I'll run to your suite and fetch it."

"It's all right." I offered a smile at her through the mirror.

She returned it, but only for a heartbeat before she quickly averted her eyes. Ever since the baby's delivery, she'd struggled to meet my gaze.

Maybe in time she'd be able to look at me again, but I couldn't fault her for being afraid.

It wasn't every sun you helped a midwife deliver a child from a woman with green blood.

We'd kept my pregnancy a secret from the masses, mostly because of Hain's warning to hide my truths. I'd disguised my belly in thick cloaks and billowing gowns. And when there had been no more hiding it, I'd sequestered myself to Andreas's and my suite.

Nathalia, the woman I'd met the sun I wandered the streets of Roslo in my bare feet, carrying ruined slippers, had been my midwife. We'd moved her into the castle to help with the birth.

Then we'd hired her to become the nursemaid. Hali was as smitten with my daughter as Margot was my husband.

To her credit, Margot hadn't asked to be reassigned or run to the papermen to spill my secret. She'd stayed on as my lady's maid—though I suspected it was more for the chance to be near Andreas than it was for me.

That, and if she did tell people I had green blood, Andreas would probably kill her. Instead, she was being paid a hefty sum to assist me and keep her mouth shut.

Margot took hold of a piece of my hair and, once again, let her gaze flicker to Andreas. She didn't just fancy him. She was in love with him, wasn't she?

That should probably bother me more, but I had nothing to worry about.

Andreas's heart belonged to me.

It was mine and mine alone.

Still, I'd had enough of her ogling my husband. I held out my hand, palm up. "I'll do it, Margot. That will be all."

She flushed deeper, knowing she'd been caught. Again. She bobbed a bow, and a lock of her hair came loose from its own twist as she hastened from the room.

A lock of silky blond hair, the same shade as the little boy from my vision.

It wasn't the first time I'd noticed. And it wasn't the first time I'd shoved it out of my mind.

I dragged my fingers through my curls, gripping the strands too hard, until the wave of heartache subsided. Then I turned away from the mirror to face my family.

A *thrum* echoed my heartbeat, its vibration spreading through my veins with my pulse.

It had returned only hours after the baby was born.

She'd been my reprieve.

A Starling carrying a child could not shift without losing the baby. So the thrum had paused but not stopped. And since its return, it had been as persistent as ever, like it had been lying in wait for moons.

Not yet.

I rubbed at my sternum, ignoring the thrum, just like I did the visions. Then I stood, walking to my husband in the rocking chair.

Andreas looked up from our daughter and gave me a smile so bright it outshone the sun. "I've decided on a nickname."

"Have you?" I threaded my fingers into his soft hair, memorizing the feel of it against my skin.

He looked to our daughter. "Dess. Let's call her Dess."

Dess. Short for Odessa.

Named after my mother.

Another thrum bloomed in my heart, like a drum, reminding me that I was nearly out of time.

"Dess. I like it," I whispered as fresh tears sprang to my eyes.

I walked to the open windows, wiping the tears before Andreas could see.

Why wouldn't it stop? Why couldn't it leave me alone? Why couldn't I keep this life I'd found?

"What is it?" The chair gave a slight creak as Andreas stood, coming to stand behind me. With one arm, he held Odessa as the other wrapped around my shoulders.

I leaned into his embrace, soaking in his warmth. "Nothing."

"Caspia."

I loved that he knew me so well. It was impossible to lie to my husband. "I have a feeling that—"

"Majesty." A steward burst into the room, his face red and sweaty like he'd taken the stairs to the fourth floor three at a time. He dropped to an efficient bow.

"Yes?" Andreas handed me Odessa, settling her into the cradle of my arms.

She began to fuss, like she could sense the mounting tension as we waited for the steward to explain.

"I'm sorry to disturb you, sire," the steward said as he stood, his panic filling the room. "It's urgent. There are four Voster in the throne room, Majesty. They demand to speak with you both. Immediately."

Andreas's gaze whipped to mine.

The world dropped out from beneath my feet.

"Leave us," he ordered the steward.

The man was gone as quickly as he'd come.

I couldn't breathe. This wasn't happening. This couldn't be happening.

Please.

Not yet.

"Fuck." Andreas pulled me into his chest, his heart racing beneath my ear. "It might be nothing. This could be a visit to discuss politics."

No, they weren't here for pleasantries with a king.

I held Odessa closer, squeezing my eyes shut.

Another thrum pulsed in my chest.

"Stay here. I'll deal with them." Andreas kissed my hair and let me go, rushing to grab his crown and put it on.

"Wait." I grabbed his arm as he passed, pulling him back. Then I stood on my toes and pressed my mouth to his.

I kissed him like the world wasn't about to end. Like my

heart wasn't shattering in my chest. I kissed him for all the kisses I was going to miss.

I kissed him like this wasn't the last.

When I finally pulled away, I couldn't hide the tears that streamed down my face.

"It's going to be all right." He framed my face with his hands, his fingers sliding into my hair. "Breathe. We'll be okay."

"I love you."

"I love you, my heart." He caught my tears with his thumbs, searching my eyes. His narrowed, like he could read my thoughts. Like he could peer into my mind and see the vision I hadn't shared.

Four Voster. Dead. Killed by a crux.

A Starling.

"Caspia, what—"

"Trust me?"

He hesitated. "Always."

I was counting on it.

"Go." I stepped back, looking to the open door.

Andreas let out a frustrated sigh, then marched from the suite, straightening his crown.

Only when the thud of his boots faded did I hurry for the door.

The guard stationed outside bowed when I entered the hall. "Majesty."

"Find Margot. Now."

"Yes, Majesty." He bowed again, then went in search of my lady's maid as I closed the door and raced into the dressing room.

With one hand, I unfastened the necklace around my throat. Then I went to the farthest corner, tugging free the board against the wall to reveal the small compartment I'd had built beneath the floor.

Not even Andreas knew it existed.

I'd hired a tradesman in secret when we were preparing this room for Odessa. I'd paid him two pouches of gold to create this compartment and vow never to tell a soul.

I lifted out the journal I'd stowed inside, setting it on my lap. A journal I'd started writing lunes ago in a library's alcove. A journal I'd added to just this morning with my vision of Emery and Aunt Oleana.

With it on my lap, I dropped the necklace into the compartment before fitting the board closed.

The moment it was in place, another wave of tears flooded. I gritted my teeth, breathing through the pain as I held my daughter.

"Someday, you'll find that necklace, Dess," I whispered. "The elfalter will call to you. And you'll have a piece of me to wear over your heart."

She let out a quiet whimper, her eyes wide as she stared up at me.

"I love you." I kissed her forehead, savoring the feel of her weight in my arms. The smell of her skin. The sound of her gentle breaths. "Be brave, my daughter. Be fearless. Be kind. Be the light. I love you, Odessa. I love you more than my own life. By the grace of the Divine, I will see you again. In this life or the next."

A sob ripped from my throat as I kissed her again.

It wasn't fair.

We needed more time.

"Majesty." Margot appeared in the doorway of the dressing room. "Are you all right?"

I stood, wiping tears from my eyes before I kissed Odessa's soft cheek. Again and again. I kissed her for all the summers to come.

"Take her," I ordered. "Please."

Margot gave me a sideways glance before she reached for the baby.

Except I couldn't let her go. "You have to *take* her."

The color drained from Margot's face, but she obeyed, pulling Odessa from my arms.

They felt empty.

I bent and picked up the journal, clutching it instead. "Protect her, Margot. Swear it."

"Majesty, I don't know what has happened, but—"

"Swear it to me." I swallowed a sob and held her blue gaze. "Please. Vow it. Press your fingers to your forehead and vow it."

Margot looked to Odessa, then back to me. She touched her forehead. "I vow it."

"Thank you." The air rushed from my lungs as I cried. "Someday, give her this journal. It is a book about who she is. Who we both are. You will know when the time is right."

She nodded, taking it as I handed it over.

"You love him. Andreas."

Margot dropped her gaze to the floor. "I'm sorry, Majesty."

"Do not let him wither." A sob escaped as my heart seemed to break into smaller and smaller pieces. "He will need someone who loves him."

Her face lifted, the color draining. "Majesty, what are you saying? You're scaring me."

I gave her a sad smile. Then I looked to my daughter. To her red hair and golden eyes.

"By the grace of the Divine." I touched my fingers to my forehead, then to hers. "I love you."

With one last kiss to her cheek, I swept out of the dressing room and suite. I wiped the tears from my eyes as I hurried down the hall to the stairs. And by the time I made it to the main floor, the thrum was so strong it was hard to breathe.

So was the pain.

The pain of a body being turned inside out. Every step was excruciating, but I kept my chin held high as I walked to the throne room's side entrance, waving a hand for the guard to let me inside.

He was young, a newer recruit. He bowed as he pulled open the door.

"Do not go inside. No matter what you hear."

He blinked rapidly, but I moved past him. That was the only warning he'd get. Hopefully he'd listen.

As the door closed behind me, it felt as if I was stepping into the past. Into a scene that had played out in my mind so vividly, I knew every moment.

I knew the cold of the floor on my bare feet. I knew the breeze that wafted in from the balcony that overlooked the city. I knew the gold dagger, its hilt inlaid with emeralds and sapphires and rubies, that Andreas kept behind his back.

And the Voster.

The pain spiked, and I slowed, a moan coming from my throat. The sound drew Andreas's attention.

He faced me, eyes wide as they flickered over my shoulder to the door. A silent command to leave.

I kept walking, my hands fisted as the pain grew so sharp I nearly dropped to my knees.

"Brothers, I would ask for a moment alone with my wife." Andreas took a step toward me, but one of the Voster held up his gnarled hand.

With a twirl of his finger, he shot a blast of air at Andreas that pushed him backward three steps.

Another priest sent that blast of air my direction, forcing me to stop.

I leaned into the wind, eyes narrowing as I glared.

"This will be your end," I warned.

They shared a look as the wind died and the throne room went eerily silent.

Quiet enough to hear the echo of a baby crying on the fourth floor, her wail drifting from the suite's open window to the balcony below.

It happened exactly as I'd foreseen.

The four Voster lifted their eyes to the ceiling. Then they

scattered, two moving for the doors to go in search of my daughter.

One stalked toward me, the pain of his magic driving through my chest like a blade. But it was nothing compared to the pain in my heart. The pain of what I was about to become.

The fourth Voster fixed his gaze on Andreas.

"Stop them," Andreas shouted at the guards as he threw his dagger toward the priest stalking my way.

The blade sailed through the air, but with a flick of the Voster's wrist, it was blown away and to the floor.

We couldn't fight them.

We couldn't win.

Not as we were.

They would slaughter Andreas and Odessa. They would not allow a Starling descendant or her child to survive. Not when we could take their magic.

They would kill us.

Unless we killed them first.

I looked to Andreas. "I love you."

His eyes were wild as he drew his sword.

"Straight through my heart, my love. Do not hesitate."

"Caspia, no," Andreas roared, but it was too late.

The shift ripped through every part of my body, working its way from the inside out. Tearing and clawing, the thrum became a new heartbeat. The pulse of a monster demanding to be set free.

I closed my eyes and gave up the fight.

Flesh turned to feathers. Arms stretched to wings. Toes became talons.

Golden eyes shifted to black.

The ritus was complete.

I was Starling.

The monster I became let out a scream.

And then there was nothing but death.

60

CASPIA

Fight it.

"Please, Caspia." Andreas's voice was a dull murmur against the fire raging in my veins.

The monster thirsted for death. For his blood to be part of the growing pools on the marble floor. For it to color my tongue.

Fight it.

A scream ripped from my throat, shaking the walls.

He dropped his sword. "I love you."

Fight it.

I battled against the pain. Against the bloodlust. But with every heartbeat, the monster ripped away more control.

A baby's cry carried through a window in the castle above. The sound pierced through the madness, and for one heartbreaking moment, I was in control.

I was Starling.

This body was mine to command.

I forced *my* wings to *my* will.

The monster raged.

But held her bloodlust in check.

Not for long. But long enough.

I fought for his life. And hers.

Until Andreas picked up that sword. Until he did what had to be done.

Until the Divine called me home.

61

ANDREAS

"Majesty." Taven crouched in front of me, his voice barely a murmur above the screams still ringing in my ears.

Caspia's scream.

My scream.

"She's cold, Taven. I need a blanket."

Caspia's naked body was covered in my coat, but it wasn't warm enough. Her skin was ice, her lips blue.

"Majesty, she's gone. It's been two days. Let's get you off this floor."

"No, I just need a blanket. Bring me a blanket." I held Caspia tighter to my chest, curling my body around hers to keep her warm.

"Majesty, if you'll let me help—"

"Bring me a fucking blanket, Hawksley," I snapped. "My wife is cold."

Taven stared at me for a long moment, his eyes full of a pity I didn't deserve. When he stood and walked away, his boots left bloody footprints behind. Blood so dark a green it was nearly black.

My fault. I did this.

I closed my eyes and rocked Caspia back and forth, burying my nose in her hair.

It smelled wrong. The sweet citrus I loved so much was gone. Now her hair smelled like death.

I breathed it in anyway.

*

A woman's gasp filled the throne room.

A baby's whimper made me sit up straight.

Nathalia carried Odessa in her arms as she walked beside Taven.

He didn't have a blanket.

"What are you doing?" My eyes blew wide as they came to stand beside a pool of dried blood. "Get the baby out of here."

Odessa would never remember this, but I didn't want her here all the same.

"Majesty, it's time." Taven dropped to a crouch as the nursemaid took a knee, angling Dess so I could take in her precious face.

She had Caspia's eyes. Her nose. Her chin. Her hair.

Dess looked so much like Caspia it cracked my heart.

And now her mother was gone. Because of me.

"I'm sorry." I lifted a hand, reaching for my daughter's smooth, clean cheek. Except my fingers were covered in dark blood.

Her mother's blood.

My fault.

I jerked my hand back. "Keep her away from me, Hali."

"She needs her father, Majesty."

"No. It's for her own good." I closed my eyes. "Please, take her away."

"Yes, my king." Hali nodded and stood, her footsteps soft as they retreated to the doors.

"Andreas." Taven used my name for the first time. "Let her go."

I collapsed forward, a sob escaping as I crushed Caspia's lifeless body to mine. "Never."

62

ODESSA

Father stood on the balcony of the throne room, staring up at the twin moons.

He'd taken off his coat and draped it over the railing. His shirt was unfastened at the collar, revealing a faint scar beneath his throat. He took one look at the journal clutched to my chest and hung his head. But he didn't seem surprised. "Did Margot have it?"

"Yes."

"She swore to me she didn't, but whatever vow she made to your mother was stronger than any promise she made to me." He tilted his face back to the sky. "Whenever your mother had visions that woke her from sleep, she'd slip out of bed and stand on a balcony. She said she liked knowing that somewhere across the Marixmore, her family was staring at the same two moons."

I took the empty space beside him, staring out over Roslo. My cheeks were still damp from too many tears cried over the story of my mother's life.

She'd written everything in this journal. Her life. Her visions.

Even the vision of her death.

There shouldn't be any more tears, not after all I'd cried in the jail beside Ransom after reading my mother's journal. But a new wave filled my eyes as my throat burned. "You killed her."

"Yes," he whispered. "And have hated myself for it every day since."

"Why didn't you tell me any of this?" A sob broke free as the tears spilled down my face. "You should have told me who she was. What she was."

Starling.

A princess. A warrior. A shapeshifter from Nelfinex. A land I hadn't known existed until I read this book.

"I'm sorry." His voice wobbled. "I only wanted to protect you."

"Protect me? Or yourself." I wiped furiously at my face, hating that I couldn't stop crying.

"Both."

"You sent me to Turah with the High Priest."

"I had no choice." He dragged a hand through his hair. "If there had been any other way, I would have kept you here. But I feared if I refused, the High Priest would be suspicious."

"You could have at least told *me* the truth."

"So they could use it against you? It was better that you knew nothing. Then you wouldn't have to lie."

My ignorance was just another part of his plan. "And now? Will you ever trust me? Will you ever tell me the truth?"

Father looked to the twin moons, the light catching every line of heartbreak, every bit of sorrow. "I've always trusted you, Dess. That's what's so terrifying about telling you the truth. I trust that you are your mother in every way. I trust that you will take up her fight as your own. I trust that you will sacrifice your life if it means saving the realm. And I cannot lose you, too."

The man I'd thought was unbreakable cracked before my eyes. His face crumpled as he folded forward, his own tears falling, splashing on his boots. He reached for me, so quickly it caught me off guard.

I fell into his chest as he pulled me into a fierce hug, the same kind of hugs I gave Mae and Arthy and Evie.

"Forgive me, Odessa." He let me go, sniffling as he took my face in his hands. "You are more and more like her every day. There are times when I look at you and she's staring back. The night you came home to Quentis from Turah, there was a moment when I thought she'd returned. I didn't mean… Forgive me."

Maybe I should have told him no. Maybe I should have pushed away.

But when I stared into his eyes, all I saw was heartache staring back.

"You should have told me," I whispered.

"Probably." A tear slid down his cheek. "She would be furious with me. And so very proud of you."

I sniffled, falling into his chest. "It's not fair."

"No, it's not."

We held each other until the tears were finally spent. Then as he let me go and leaned his forearms on the balcony's rail, I moved in beside him.

"Where do we start?" I asked.

"The beginning, I suppose. At a small hunting cabin in Genesis."

By midnight, the winter chill had driven us inside the throne room. By dawn, we'd been sitting, side by side, on the dais's stairs for hours, staring across the marble floor as we spoke. The same marble floor where he'd held her body, cradling it to his chest after he drove his sword through her heart.

I hadn't asked him about the day of her death, but he'd told me anyway. Like the rest of his story, it was a perfect mirror of Mother's journal. And Father had filled in the missing gaps.

"She killed the Voster who came that day," he said. "The

moment she feared you were in danger, she told me not to hesitate. Then she shifted. It happened in a blink. The priests were dead. This floor was coated in blood. And when she turned to me, I dropped my sword. I couldn't do it."

"But you did?"

"She never would have forgiven herself. If she'd killed me, killed any others, it would have destroyed her. Better I live with that on my conscience than her." His voice was thick and heavy with regret. But a numbness seemed to have settled over us both. "I wouldn't let anyone take her from me. When she died, she shifted back. I held her on this floor for two days. It was Hali who finally broke through. She brought you to me, and I let your mother go so Hawksley could take her body from me."

"General Hawksley?"

"He has been with me for a long, long time. Mostly helping the Kennin search for the orbits."

"But now he's your general?"

"When Banner left, with the migration coming, I needed someone I could trust. Hawksley will never betray our secrets."

"For you? Or Margot?"

Father frowned, like the secret of Margot and Hawksley's relationship was one he hadn't intended to share. "For us both."

"What did you do with the Voster that Mother killed?"

"I burned their bodies in this very room, making sure every bit of ash was taken to the sea. I destroyed any evidence that they had been here. Every guard who saw them enter is either dead or paid to keep quiet. Nevertheless, the Kennin feared the High Priest would retaliate, so they offered one of their priests to take the fall. His name was Hain."

A name I knew from my mother's book. "So the Voster have no idea what really happened."

"No. If they did, neither of us would be alive." Father

tapped the journal on my lap. "What's in here must remain a secret. I believe they have their suspicions about me, but they can't come after a king without proof. And Brother Dime acting as emissary while being loyal to the Kennin has given us some protection."

"What do the Kennin really want?"

"To return to Kenn. But they are bound to Calandra by blood oaths made at a time when their magic was new. The only way to break those bonds is to eliminate the magic in our realm. To destroy the orbits."

"Do you think it's really possible?"

"I have to believe her death was not in vain. If we destroy the remains of the Six, I believe the magic in our lands will vanish. The Voster will do everything in their power to stop that from happening. We are fortunate they have yet to understand the moves we've made against them. But that fortune will not last."

This was the reason Brother Dime had warned me of Ransom's loyalty to the High Priest.

"You know I was with Brother Skore. He took me to Orson Canyon. Did he bring you the orbit?"

"Yes. And when I found out he took you to that canyon, I told him that if he ever put you in that kind of danger again, I'd cut his head from his shoulders."

"You sound like Ransom," I muttered.

"We both have the same goal, Dess. Your survival. I might not trust your husband, but I do appreciate his loyalty to you."

"That loyalty goes both ways. I won't keep any of this a secret from him."

Father studied me for a moment, then nodded.

"You drew all over the map in your study," I said. "Do you know where the other four orbits are hidden?"

"Not for certain. Skore has spent decades searching with Hawksley. We've narrowed it down to a handful of locations in Laine, Genesis, and Turah. But the magic in them only calls to a Starling. They're somehow veiled from the Voster."

"Then you were always going to need my help."

He shook his head. "I had hope I could find them on my own. I was willing to try."

"Well, now you don't need to. Like it or not, I'm going after them. If there's a way to stop the crux and the Voster, we have to try."

"You sound like her," he said, eyes still fixed on the floor. "She was unwavering. Fearless. She was the strongest person I've ever known."

Then we'd finish this for her. To honor her memory. "How do we destroy them?"

"I don't know. Neither do the priests."

Well, fuck.

"The magic has corrupted the very glass of the orbits. They're unbreakable. Fireproof," he said. "I've a mind to send them on a ship to the middle of the ocean, but if the magic in them has bled to Calandra's waters, I don't think I want to know what will happen if it taints the Marixmore."

"There has to be a way." If this magic had a beginning, then there was an end.

"There is." He gave me a sure nod. "We just haven't discovered it yet."

"Are they together? The orbits?" I asked.

"No. I feared it would be too hard to hide them from the Voster if they were together. That maybe the magic from one would feed off the other. One is in the vaults. The other is beneath the crypts below the infirmary."

Locked far enough away that I couldn't feel their magic. Hopefully the Voster couldn't, either.

"What is in Allesaria?"

"Brother Dime can't break his oaths, and neither can Skore, but from what they have been able to imply, I think the Turans built their capital to protect the Voster's sanctuary. Which in turn could be built upon an orbit."

No wonder he'd been so set on getting there before the migration. "So the High Priest has an orbit. He's not just going to let it go."

"I'm not sure he *does* have it. Not if they're veiled. Though he likely knows it's close. If the Voster built that sanctuary hundreds of years ago, after they came from Kenn and their magic was new, they likely didn't know. They may simply have a deeper connection to magic because they were near an orbit. And the mountains gave them somewhere safe to hide during the migrations."

Well, if the High Priest hadn't known then, he certainly did now. Even if he didn't know the exact location, he'd protect that area with the full force of the Voster brotherhood.

I closed my eyes, rubbing at my temples.

So Skore had taken me to Orson Canyon as a test to see if I could find an unguarded orbit. Not the most pleasant experience, but tame compared to my parents' descent into the Evon. But finding both of those would be a hundred times easier than infiltrating Allesaria.

"This is impossible."

"Have faith, Dess." Father put his hand on my forearm and stilled, feeling the leather beneath the fabric of my shirt.

"It's Ransom's cuff. Turan tradition. He gave it to me." A half-truth. Maybe someday I'd give him this map. But not yet. Not until the trust between us went deeper than a single night. "I think the High Priest suspects Mother was Starling. I guess I should have kept dyeing my hair."

The High Priest's suspicion was likely the reason Dime had taken me from Ellder. He'd stolen me away before the High Priest could do it himself.

"It's not your fault. It's mine." He sighed. "I never should have brought the Turans here."

"Then I never would have met Ransom."

Father studied me for a long moment. "You truly love him?"

"He is my life."

If the realm ended tomorrow, I would have no regrets in loving Ransom.

That my mother's quest to rid Calandra of magic had brought us together was as bitter as it was sweet.

"My spies told me about the Guardian's gifts before he ever came to Quentis. Your mother had the same. If she cut her finger, it would heal almost instantly. She could see at night as if it were day. She moved as fast as the wind. And her eyes…"

"Gold, like mine?"

"Not always. They would shift depending on her moods. Gold most of the time. Silver when she was angry. And sometimes, they were a green so beautiful I couldn't look away."

"You thought Ransom was Starling?"

"I thought the Guardian was not from our realm. I feared what he might become. And I knew he had to be the silver-eyed warrior from your mother's vision."

"So you asked me to kill a legendary warrior. Me?"

He shrugged. "It was worth a try. I saw the way he looked at you. It wouldn't be the first time a man was killed because he dropped his guard for a woman."

"Then you underestimated him."

"No. The only person I've underestimated is you. For that, I am deeply sorry."

This was what I'd wanted for so long. His confidence. His trust. So why did it feel hollow? Why did it feel like it paled in comparison to the courage I'd found in myself?

"I stumbled upon a journal in Turah. It's in her handwriting." The same elegant script as the book I'd read tonight. I fished out the necklace from beneath my shirt, letting the metal catch the light. "And it has this same winged emblem on it."

Father touched the pendant, his eyes softening like he was lost in a memory. "Another gift from Margot?"

"No. I found it hidden in my closet."

He hummed.

"There are stories in the journal I found that are coming true. Were those her visions?"

"Probably aboard the *Cirrina* while she sailed here. I didn't know they were visions at the time. She told me she was just writing down stories." He dabbed at his eyes. "I made her that journal when we were in Genesis. Or I should say I took a journal I already had and tooled the cover to match her necklace. She didn't know how to write in Calandran yet, so she did it in the old language."

"How did it end up in Turah?"

"Someone must have found it in the cabin. I thought she took it, but she must have left it behind. And I left in a hurry so I wouldn't lose her."

So that book that had somehow found me in Turah had been from them both.

"I wish I had just kept her in Genesis. Forgotten all about Quentis and duty and titles." His eyes went unfocused again. "Shades, she was mad at me when she found out that I was a prince and heir to the crown. She was livid at the betrothal my mother had arranged behind my back. Mostly, she was furious, rightly so, that she'd had to read about it all in Chapman Leek's paper. I was already in love with her at that point. I think I loved her from the day I pulled her out of that river in Genesis. But if not, that would have been the moment I fell for her. She didn't care about titles and wealth. She wanted me for me. No one ever loved me the way she did."

"Not even Margot?"

"No."

"Did you ever love Margot?" I asked.

"She is a good woman. But no."

"Yet you married her."

"A wedding to a servant gave the public enough fodder about their new queen that most quickly forgot about your mother."

And to most, Father probably looked like a man who'd already been sleeping with that servant, especially considering Margot had been Mother's lady's maid.

"Are Mae and Arthy your children?"

"As far as the royal records are concerned, yes, but the last woman to share my bed was your mother."

The truth was rarely gentle.

Whether we shared a father or not, Arthy and Mae would always be my brother and sister. But it still felt like I'd lost something. Tears pricked the corners of my eyes as I dabbed them away.

"I never wanted you entangled in this." Father gave me a sad smile. "She would be proud of the woman you have become. Like I am."

Father took the journal from my hands, opening it to the first page. He traced a finger over Mother's words like he could still feel her on the page. Then he carefully closed the book and handed it to me.

He shifted to dig into his pocket and pull out ten rings, all made from the same reddish-orange metal as my necklace.

Elfalter.

Father gave me the rings.

And the key to Ransom's cell.

63

ODESSA

Ransom was curled around me, his body keeping me warm beneath the thin bedsheet. His chest was to my back, his leg entwined between mine. And his arm was draped across my ribs, pinning me in place as he slept.

I lifted his wrist, slowly easing it away so I could slip free. But as I tried to tug my leg out from beneath his bulky thigh, his hold cinched tight and he hauled me back.

My third escape attempt. Thwarted.

"You can't keep me in this bed forever."

He buried his nose in my hair and inhaled. "I can try."

"Rest. I'll be back soon." I twisted to kiss his nose, then wiggled free. This time, he let me go.

Another morning, he would have fought harder to keep me in bed, but his eyes stayed closed as he hugged my pillow.

The siphoning and a sleepless night in the jail cell had drained him so completely that he was already asleep by the time I was dressed. With my satchel over my shoulder, I eased out of the room.

The suite was quiet and still. Cathlin, Zavier, and Evie were all still in their beds. So I tiptoed out the door and made my way to the infirmary just as the light of dawn kissed the castle's golden spires.

Alore answered on my second knock. Her hair was piled on top of her head, secured by two wooden sticks. She wore a pair of tangerine glasses and a matching frock. "Highness. Is everything all right?"

"Here." I handed her the small glass vial I'd filled with my spit on the walk downstairs. "Test this with the elixir instead."

Two familiar figures loomed in the castle's foyer, their heads bent together in quiet conversation.

One was dressed in black, the other in armor that shone nearly as brightly as her white hair.

Thora wore her signature scowl, while Jodhi sported an arrogant smirk that widened when he heard me approach.

"You're back?"

"Miss me, doll?" Jodhi grinned.

"Actually, yes." I missed feeling like there was someone else in this castle, besides Ransom and Mae, who would take my side in a fight. Granted, these two would tell me I had to pay for it, but I had a feeling both were more loyal to people than they showed.

"What are you doing here?" I asked.

"Your father called us back," Thora said, her voice flat. "He made us an offer we couldn't refuse."

"When?"

"Five days ago."

Five days? That would have been long before our conversation last night.

"What was his offer?"

"That we'll have our chance to be rid of Salem. In turn, we just have to keep you alive." She frowned like she'd been manipulated into this agreement. "Do me a favor, Sparrow. Try not to die today. I'm not in the mood to play bodyguard at the moment. I'm going to find a bed and take a nap."

I waited until they walked away to smile.

The library was every bit as intimidating and magnificent as I remembered from my youth.

The atrium smelled of lilies, cedar, and old books. If wisdom had a smell, it was this library.

Margot had always arranged for lessons to be in our private rooms, rather than in the library with the students taught by the library's scholars.

At the time, I'd thought she didn't want Mae or me to mingle with the other children, even if they were noble born. That she'd deemed our education more important and therefore separate.

Now I wondered if all the seclusion in my childhood was really just another part of her keeping me safe. Keeping the little girl with golden eyes hidden away.

It was strange to see a person I'd known my entire life in a different light.

I couldn't remember the last time I'd walked through the library's gilded double doors. Maybe when I was four or five. I weaved past tables and chairs in the atrium, making my way toward a tall, empty bibliosoph's desk. The head librarian was nowhere to be seen.

As I reached the counter, an old man with a beard that fell to his belly emerged from behind a towering bookshelf, carrying a stack of tomes.

He took one look at me, and the books tumbled from his arms. "Caspia?"

"Oh, um, no. I'm..." Hearing her name was such a shock that I momentarily forgot my own. "Odessa. I'm Odessa. Her daughter."

No one spoke my mother's name. Either because Father forbade it or because she'd been forgotten.

But hearing it nearly brought me to tears.

A man with silky black hair and smooth, olive skin rounded the same corner and stopped short when he saw the mess of books on the floor. "Father, what happ—"

He noticed me, and his jaw dropped. But unlike the older man, who was still gaping with watery eyes, the younger man recovered quickly. He blinked twice, and then a handsome smile lit up his face. "Welcome, Highness. Please excuse my father. He believes in ghosts."

The old man scoffed and shot his son a glare. "She just startled me. It's not my fault they look exactly alike. I haven't seen her since she was this tall." He held out a hand, measuring it to his waist.

"My name is Kos." The younger man bowed. "This is my father, Faxon."

Two people so important to my mother that she'd filled page after page with stories of them in her journal. If we'd met before, I didn't remember. But today, I knew them both through her words. Through the love she'd left behind with ink and paper.

I wished she were here to make this introduction. I wished she were here to see her friends.

I wished I had come to the library a long time ago.

More tears flooded my eyes, and I wiped them away. "Sorry."

"No apologies," Kos said. "What brings you to the library?"

I took a calming breath and patted my satchel. "I was given a journal of my mother's. She wrote about how much she loved this library and how she had a special place to read. A carrel. I was hoping I could see it for myself."

Kos and Faxon shared a smile. Then the older man waved me forward. "Right this way, Highness."

"Odessa," I corrected. "Or you can call me Dess."

The carrel was cramped but clean. The air had a slight stale smell, like the tiny room was rarely used.

After he waved me inside, Faxon insisted I sit behind the desk while Kos went off to retrieve a book he wanted me to see.

And so as we waited, I let my hands skim the desk's smooth surface, imagining my mother bent over a journal, writing her own history and the story of Nelfinex so that someday, I would come to understand my dynasty.

My satchel was beside me, the flap open and the books spilling out.

"Here we go." Kos swept into the carrel and handed me a green leather journal.

"Where did you find that?" Faxon gasped. "She told me to hide it."

"Third floor. Tucked behind a series on fundamental arithmetic principles."

Faxon frowned and smoothed the length of his beard. "You know, I hid that book so well I forgot where I put it."

Kos chuckled. "Then it's a good thing I enjoy arithmetic."

I flipped open the cover and found a note tucked inside.

"She brought that to me after you were born," Faxon said. "Told me to add it to the journal I'd stashed away. That was before I forgot where I hid the book."

"May I?" I asked, taking out the note.

Kos nodded. "Of course."

Dear Kos,

My sweetling boy. (Though when you find this book, you won't be a boy.) Please do me three favors. Give your fathers my love. Take a piece for yourself. And when my girl comes to see you someday, give her this book.

Caspia

"How she knew I'd find it, I have no idea," Kos said. "But

I'm glad I did so I can give it to you." He touched Faxon's shoulder. "We'll leave you to your reading."

"Thank you." I didn't look up as they slipped out of the carrel, instead turning the page of the book.

...

A boy sits on a floor, surrounded by scattered books. He has silky black hair and eyes so dark they shine blue. He picks up a book and tosses it into the air. But the book doesn't fall. It floats, like it's hooked to an invisible string as it lifts higher and higher in the air.

...

Visions. This was another book of her visions, just like the journal I'd carried with me across Calandra. Each entry was written in the old language in her familiar script. Each was a story that I hoped would eventually come to mean something.

But if not, each was a piece of her I would cherish.

I was reading the fourth page when a shadow fell over my desk.

Brother Skore swept into the carrel, taking the spare chair.

I couldn't feel his magic. Not a sting or prickle.

"Is it difficult, suppressing your power?"

"Yes."

"You don't need to. I can manage it."

"You will have the chance to manage much when it comes to magic. Today, take the respite."

I nodded, closing the green journal to take the black book with the winged emblem from my satchel. "This was my mother's. She left it in a cabin in Genesis. How did it come to find its way to me in Turah?"

"Destiny."

Luella had told me she'd found this book hidden away at the apothecary's shop. Maybe the person who stole it from my father's cabin in Genesis had owned that apothecary. Maybe this book had changed hands a dozen times before it fell into mine.

Destiny? "It sounds more like magic."

"If you've read all of those books and still don't believe in magic, then you've missed the point, girl."

Then I guess it was a good thing I believed in magic. "My mother had visions and wrote them in these books. Some were for her. But others were for me. Brother Dime told me it meant I was going in the right direction."

"Yes. And here you are, with the last of what she left for you." He pointed to the green journal Kos had found hidden in the library.

"Did you ever know her?"

"Yes. Though she knew me as Brother Nold when I still wore red."

Was she part of the reason he'd joined the Kennin? Someday, maybe he'd tell me the story of why he'd left the brotherhood.

"Where will these visions take me? And please don't answer with some vague, grandiose, one-word statement, like 'Destiny.' I've had about as much *destiny* as I can stomach."

Skore's mouth turned up in a faint smile. "I do not know what you'll find in that book. But if I had to wager a guess, you are correct in your understanding. Her visions were both of her future and of yours. Some have come true. Some might never. She was blessed by the Divine, and by that grace, those stories will lead you to the other orbits."

"Finding them won't do any good if we can't destroy them."

"No. But it is a start. Have faith, Sparrow. Hope is not lost." He made no move to leave, like he could sense I had more to say.

"Why do I feel your magic? Why does it hurt when I touch you?"

"You are Starling. Magic is poison to your bloodline."

"Then why doesn't the magic impact me like it did my mother? My blood is red. I can't see in the dark or move at twice the speed of normal people."

Skore steepled his fingers beneath his pointed chin. "You were born on this continent. Your father is Calandran. The magic in this land has been a part of you since your conception. The ancient texts say that the original Starling left when they became trapped in their shifted forms. When the monsters they became took control. I believe you are more like your distant Starling ancestors than you are your mother or relatives from Nelfinex."

"And if I shift?"

"Let us pray that you do not."

My stomach knotted. "When I was a girl, I was poisoned with fenek tusk powder. It should have killed me but didn't. And everywhere I go, it seems that monsters follow. That they're drawn to me."

"The Starling have always had a special bond with beasts."

It was a confirmation I didn't really want to hear, but it was not unexpected. "Ransom's gifts are similar to my mother's."

"Similar." He nodded. "But not the same."

"Will the Lyssa ever cause him to shift?" I didn't have the strength to do what my father had done. I wouldn't have the courage to kill Ransom if he became a monster.

"No. He is not Starling."

So the Lyssa would kill him instead.

Not an option.

"Why is King Ramsey burning books in Turah? Was he looking for this?" I touched the black journal.

"It's unlikely he knows any of those exist. Neither does the High Priest. But Ramsey is likely doing the High Priest's bidding. There might be something else he's trying to hide. It wouldn't be the first time the High Priest has obscured our history."

The history from before the Voster's time. The history of magic.

Maybe the High Priest and Ramsey were trying to hide the truth of Lyssa, too.

"Mother came here with a cousin. Xandra. She shifted into a bariwolf and never shifted back. Ransom was bitten by a bariwolf. I think it was Xandra."

Luella believed that Lyssa was created from the combination of her elixir and a monster's saliva. But Ransom hadn't been bitten by just any monster. This was the reason Alore's experiments with Faze's saliva hadn't reproduced Lyssa.

He'd been bitten by a Starling. By Xandra. And with the elixir, together, they'd created Lyssa. The magic in Calandra that had trapped Xandra as a monster, that had driven my mother to bloodlust, was the same magic taking its toll on Ransom.

The High Priest had told Ransom there was no cure for Lyssa. Was that a lie? Or was ridding Calandra of magic the cure? A cure that meant eliminating the priests' power and the demise of the brotherhood.

The Voster would sacrifice Ransom to save themselves.

"I tasked my father's head healer with trying to find a cure for Lyssa. Is it possible, even if the magic remains?"

"It's unlikely."

Damn. I was hoping for a *yes.*

"This infection is different than the Starling. It spreads through the blood, but it is not a bloodline," Skore said. "Yet they are linked. Magic fuels Lyssa while it poisons the Starling."

"So even if we destroy the orbits, it might not cure Lyssa?"

Skore hesitated. "I cannot say for certain."

I had to believe it was possible to save Ransom. That where there was poison, there was a cure. Magic or not, I wasn't giving up. I wasn't losing him. While Alore worked on her part, I'd do mine by destroying the orbits.

If only I had a godsdamn clue of where to start. "How do you destroy a god?"

"There is only one god."

"You're asking me to turn my back on everything I've been taught to believe."

"No, I'm asking you to believe your mother."

That, I could do. I stared at the books on the desk. "You told me to find a warrior. You meant her."

"No, girl." Skore stood. "I meant you."

64

ODESSA

Balanced on the edge of a sheer cliff, I stood at the mercy of this realm. The winds thrashed and pulled and pushed, threatening to topple me into the sea. A storm brewed in the distance, the clouds mirroring the chaos in my heart.

Forty feet below, waves crashed against rock, the water's spray white as it broke against stone. Oh, how I wanted to jump. To feel the freedom of falling. To let go of the burdens for just one godsforsaken moment.

A gust lifted me to my toes.

Strong arms wrapped around my shoulders, anchoring me to the earth. To him.

"You found me." I rested my head against Ransom's chest, my curls whipping around us both.

"I always will." His thumb stroked the elfalter rings on my fingers as the silver circlet across his brow shone in the afternoon light.

"The Mavins are back. My father hired them."

"Good. We'll need their help."

"Can we do this?"

"We can try. Together."

I closed my eyes, lacing my fingers with his. "Together."

Ransom bent as I lifted my chin. His mouth brushed across mine, and with a kiss, the realm seemed to calm. The waves below stopped their crashing. The storm on the horizon wasn't quite so fierce.

And when he broke away, I let myself dive into the green of his eyes.

"I love you, Odessa Wolfe." He spoke the words I'd been desperate to hear for months.

But I didn't need them. Not really. "Yes, you do. Don't forget."

"Never. Let's go in before it rains." He took my hand, pulling me away from the cliff's edge.

Something tugged me right back.

A tingling sensation crept up my arms. My blood stirred, and something inside me pulled so hard I stopped.

I stilled, looking over my shoulder.

A *thrum* pulsed through my chest, like my heart was beating too hard. The vibration spread from my heart to my hands. It was there one moment, gone the next.

But it would return. If the visions in Mother's green journal came true, the thrum would return.

"Dess? Is something wrong?"

I stared into Ransom's eyes, as green as the Turan wilds, and told my husband what I feared would be the first of many lies. A lie that broke my heart. "No. It's nothing."

...

A silver-eyed warrior falls to his knees as the ground trembles. Dark-green blood drips from his fingertips. A deafening scream pierces the air. The beat of massive wings blows the hair from his face.

He stares at the monster and sets down his blade.

And before the warrior meets his end, he whispers...

"My queen."

Author's Note

Thelvi'ank yelvi'u felvi-or relvi'eed-elfing thelvi'is belvi'uk.

My husband and I met when we were going to college at Montana State University. Our first year dating, he was living in a room at his fraternity called The Cave with one of his good friends. Whenever I visited, they loved to torment me with "Elk Talk." It's basically the cowboy equivalent of Pig Latin. It took me months to convince them to teach me the mechanics.

Now, twenty-plus years later, "Elk" became the foundation for the fictional *old language* with some brilliant enhancements from my editor, Rebecca Heyman.

The rules are fairly simple.

Add "elvi" after the first consonant of the first syllable in a word, then tack on the rest of that syllable, spelled phonetically. For example, *you* becomes *yelvi'u*.

If a word begins with a vowel, use "elvi" before the rest of the word.

If the word begins with a consonant digraph (th, sh, wh, etc.), then "elvi" goes after the first two letters.

For words with multiple syllables, use the same rules above but add "elf" instead. Each syllable is separated by a dash. *Starling* becomes *Stelvi'r-lelfing*.

Thelvi'ank yelvi'u felvi'or relvi'eed-elfing thelvi'is belvi'uk translates to...

Thank you for reading this book.

This story has been such an incredible journey. I'm so grateful you're taking it with me.

Acknowledgments

Thank you for reading *Rites of the Starling*! Writing this book was a whirlwind, and I'm so very grateful that you've followed these characters into the next chapter.

Many, many thanks to Liz Pelletier and the team at Red Tower Books for the opportunity to tell this story. To Becca, Melanie, Heather, Meredith, Stacy, Erin, Cai, Victoria, Hannah, Curtis, Britt, Bree, ETS, LJ, Juho, Lindsey, Molly, Rebecca, Stella, and so many others, thank you!

To my incredible agent, Georgana Grinstead, thank you from the bottom of my heart. You are my constant source of sunshine and stoicism. Thank you for chasing my dreams like they are your own.

To Logan Chisholm, there are not enough thank-yous for all you do each and every day. I am so grateful that once upon a time you opened a box of Clifton Forge books. I feel incredibly blessed to have you in my corner.

A massive thanks to my incredible editor, Elizabeth Nover, for your insight and advice to make each book its best. I'm not sure what I did to get so lucky in finding you, but I'm eternally thankful.

To Vicki Valente and Judy Zweifel, thank you for always being willing to jump into a project. Your input and attention to detail are truly remarkable.

Thanks to Hannah Lindsey and Rebecca Heyman for helping polish this story to a shine.

To Nicole Resciniti, thank you for the constant support and encouragement. Thank you for always being my steady champion.

To Samantha Brentmoor, Jason Clarke, Megan Wicks, and the entire team at Tantor Audio and Recorded Books, thank you for bringing these characters to life!

Thank you, Kaitlyn, for being the best friend I could ask for and always being up for an impromptu plotting call. Thank you, Karla, for a thousand texts of encouragement and for diving into the first draft of this book. Thanks to Rachel, Marni, Monica, and Valentine for being the best support squad. Thanks to my wonderful friends and family who support me every step of the way. And to Bill, Will, and Nash, you are my whole world. Thanks for making my real life so special and letting me get lost in these fictional ones from time to time.